HEART
COLLECTOR

JACQUES VANDROUX
HEART COLLECTOR

TRANSLATED BY WENDELINE A. HARDENBERG

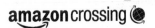

Text copyright © 2013 Jacques Vandroux
Translation copyright © 2014 Wendeline A. Hardenberg

Previously published as *Au Coeur du Solstice* by the author through the Kindle Direct Publishing platform in France in 2013. Translated from the French by Wendeline A. Hardenberg.

Published by AmazonCrossing, Seattle

www.apub.com

Amazon, the Amazon logo, and AmazonCrossing are trademarks of Amazon.com, Inc., or its affiliates.

ISBN-13: 9781477826829
ISBN-10: 1477826823

Cover design by Edward Bettison, LTD

Library of Congress Control Number: 2014911233

Printed in the United States of America

To my wife

Foreword

Although it takes place in real locations and venues, this book is a work of fiction. Character names and events came from the imagination of the author. The only intention in depicting real places is to lend the fiction an air of authenticity. Therefore, any resemblance or similarity to names, people, or facts currently or formerly in existence, particularly with regard to the characters who hold real positions, is pure coincidence and under no circumstances renders the author liable.

The historic sites and museums described in this book actually exist, and the author strongly encourages you to visit them should you one day find yourself in Grenoble.

Chapter 1: The Present

The young woman had a graceful walk. Her white dress swayed with the rhythm of her steps, and the sun drenching the city lent her a luminous aura. She paused at the edge of the sidewalk, waiting for the traffic light to change. The young man hesitated for a moment. What was happening to him? He enjoyed looking at a pretty girl when he saw one on the street, but those were no more than glances, moments that vanished as quickly as they came. Never before had he followed someone!

Yet now it had been more than fifteen minutes since he had seen her on the Isère riverfront. Moved by an impulse he couldn't explain, he had veered from his own path to follow in her footsteps. He had always kept a reasonable distance between himself and the young woman, and she hadn't noticed anything. In late afternoon, the streets were full of gawking *badauds* making the most of the first intense heat of summer.

The light turned red, and the woman resumed her moderate pace. Julien continued on, not knowing where he would end up. Because really, what was his intention? He concentrated on the details of the silhouette moving ahead of him. She was tall, with slightly curly brown hair that bounced atop her shoulders. Her loose white dress fell airily to just above her knees. Julien could see the outlines of her body beneath the clothing. He'd never been very good at guessing ages, but he observed that she had young-looking features that nevertheless showed an air of maturity. It was that sense of maturity that had attracted him.

She had just ducked under the portico of the Notre-Dame de Grenoble Cathedral and entered the building. Julien stopped and sat down on a stone bench nearby, trying to gather his thoughts. Why was he following this girl? Why was he gripped by such an overwhelming desire to follow her into the church? It was almost frightening.

Fine. Let's think about this logically, however little logic may apply to the situation. This girl is pretty, but not sexy enough to trail for a mile. She doesn't look like anybody I know, and yet I feel like she's calling to me like she needs me. It's completely ridiculous. In fact, I'm ridiculous.

Despite feeling ridiculous, Julien continued to monitor the cathedral portico. At that time of day, it was the only way in, and therefore the only way out. Julien decided to wait a few more minutes. He thought back to her face. Though he'd caught only a glimpse, it was her face that had struck him. Both sweet and serious—very serious. It radiated serenity, but also an indescribable need for protection.

Julien scoffed at himself again. *Psychoanalysis for dummies! You poor sap, you're pathetic.* He glanced at his watch. It was seven in the evening. What if she was just attending mass? Almost in spite of himself, he stood up and entered the church.

The cool interior contrasted with the summer heat outside. He shivered. Speakers hidden among the pillars created a background of Gregorian chants, inviting calm and meditation. He looked around slowly to take in the scene. Few people were there at that hour, and no mass was being conducted. He couldn't see her. She was doubt-less in one of the side chapels or in the adjoining Saint-Hugues

Church. He walked slowly, reverentially, discreetly inspecting the chapels while regularly glancing at the exit.

The church gave off a scent of burned-out candles and centuries-old stone. He'd always loved old churches, with their protective arches, mysteriously timeless and at the center of things.

Five minutes later, he'd made his way all the way around the cathedral. She had to be in the adjacent church then, which could be accessed via a side door. He exited the Gothic cathedral to enter, one yard farther, the little neighboring church. No one! He came back out immediately. Noticing that an old woman was staring at him insistently, he left the church and found himself once more in the open square outside, blinded by the June sun. He returned to his observation post. Perhaps she had escaped his notice in the church, but he was absolutely certain that she hadn't come out. He was intrigued. He didn't know when the church closed, but if he stayed long enough, he couldn't miss her.

"You okay, dude?" Julien felt a hand on his shoulder. "Everything all right? You haven't moved in ten minutes, just staring into space."

"I'm fine, thank you, just a little tired."

"Well, when you're tired, dude, you gotta lie down. By the way, d'you happen to have a li'l spare change for the guy who woke you up?"

Julien looked at the man who had accosted him. He recognized him as a bum he'd passed under the portico earlier and had an idea.

"I've got a whole bill if you answer my question."

"Ah, I'm not the police, dude," the man said, but lured by the prospect of easy money, he asked, "Whaddya wanna know?"

"Since you've been here, have you seen a young woman come out? Pretty, tall, wearing a white dress?"

The bum burst out laughing. "If it's about your heart or her ass, I can answer you. But let's see the dough first."

Julien took a twenty-euro bill out of his wallet and handed it over. The bum whistled as though he hadn't been expecting that much.

"Well, aren't you feeling generous! For that much you can have two questions. But to answer your first one, no. I saw a couple old ladies, but they were all bent over, and if they were ever pretty, it was back when they built Notre-Dame in the first place." Pleased with his joke, he burst into laughter punctuated by coughing. "But I can also tell you, for the same price, that I've been here for over two hours and I didn't see your fair maiden."

"You've got to be kidding, she just went in around seven o'clock!"

"In your dreams, dude, in your dreams. Look, I gotta go. I gotta take advantage of my new wealth."

The bum departed via a little street across from the square, leaving Julien in a daze. The man must have been drunk or looking elsewhere. Still, he seemed quite sure of himself. Julien had watched the mysterious woman go in, though, and he was certain of it. Besides, even if he had been daydreaming, he'd still kept an eye on the door, though he was less certain of that.

The whole thing confused him, and he was wasting his time. He decided, however, to take one last look around the church.

The cathedral was now nearly deserted. The old woman who had noticed him a few minutes earlier was still there. Maybe she could help him after all. He approached her slowly. "Good evening, madame, I'm looking for a friend and was wondering if maybe you could help me?"

She eyed him mistrustfully and replied, "And what does that have to do with me?"

He responded even more gently. "I arranged to meet her here half an hour ago, but I can't find her."

The parishioner stared at him for a long while. He remained impassive. After many long seconds, she seemed to relax.

"And what does your friend look like?"

"Very pretty, dark haired, and she was going to wear a white dress today."

"Sorry, young man, but I've been right here since midafternoon and I haven't seen such a beauty." A slight smile lit her dour face when she uttered that last phrase.

Julien was stunned. Before she could leave, he asked, "Is there another door she could have used to enter or exit?"

"No, only the portico is open to the faithful."

"Thank you."

"Don't look so down in the mouth. Women are often unpredictable at your age . . . and at mine, too, for that matter," she added, her eyes twinkling.

He smiled at her. "You're probably right. Have a good evening."

He returned to the open air and decided to take a walk through the city to clear his head. Why did this episode leave him with such a strange feeling?

Chapter 2: Ready for Action

The man's hand groped at the wall, catching on the rough plaster. He swore and stuck his fingertips in his mouth to ease the mild sting. Then, after a few seconds of feeling around, he found the light switch.

He pressed it, and bright light flooded the room. He blinked for a few moments as his eyes adjusted, then approached the table in the center of the room. With a lover's touch, he caressed the woman slowly. He stepped back to encompass her with his gaze. The dark black tabletop complemented the stainless steel support, reflecting the neon light particularly well.

He had not chosen machinery that would allow her to orient herself. A simple table was sufficient for his purposes. But he had taken much care in selecting the lamp, which was cleverly mounted on an articulated arm. He was quite proud of this high-end equipment; he'd had to engage in a great deal of subterfuge to order it and have it delivered without attracting attention.

He moved to the sideboard on which several closed pouches lay. He opened them and pulled out several implements, laying them side by side with maniacal precision. He had been so successful in his profession because he left nothing to chance—when the task at hand required all of an individual's concentration, even the smallest discrepancy could lead to disaster. And he had known only a single failure in over thirty years. He admired his work and then, satisfied, headed toward a large metal cabinet set against one wall. He opened the door. Three green smocks, impeccably ironed, dangled from hangers. He took one of them, put it on, and looked at himself in a small mirror resting on one of the shelves. Everything was perfect. He was ready.

He left the room and headed down the dark hallway. He came to a heavy security door. Taking a key from his pocket, he inserted it carefully into the lock. His healing process had begun.

Chapter 3: Police Intervention

"This is Dispatch. Calling all units located in Sector Three. Break-in in progress at the Banque des Alpes, on Boulevard Agutte Sembat."

"Unit Seventeen to Dispatch. This is Captain Barka. We're on Rue Lesdiguières. We'll be on the scene in two minutes. Make sure to send backup as soon as possible."

"Roger, Captain."

Captain Nadia Barka hung up the radio, grabbed her siren, and stuck it to the roof.

"We'll put some pressure on them as soon as we arrive on the scene. Lieutenant Fortin, it's time to prove your driving skills are as good as you've always claimed they are."

"Buckle up, Captain."

The tires screeched on the asphalt, and the police car was off like a shot, filling the quiet street with a sudden roar and the scent of burning rubber in the air. Captain Barka settled back in her seat, then checked her service weapon one last time. She was particularly wary of the new class of burglar, who carried military-caliber weapons but didn't really know how to use them. Still, they didn't hesitate to use their weapons when cornered, and the police were among the first targets. She reached into the backseat and grabbed a bulletproof vest. She pulled it on and adjusted the fit.

Lieutenant Étienne Fortin took a right turn and entered Boulevard Agutte Sembat. Captain Barka put her hand on his forearm.

"The bank is just past Place Victor Hugo. Stop here and put on your vest. Then step on it, and I'll turn on the siren. That should psych 'em out."

"You don't think we should wait for backup?"

"We can let them finish their work and escort them home if you want."

"That's not what I meant!" he replied as he tugged on his bulletproof vest.

The radio crackled. Captain Barka answered, listened for a few seconds, then hung up.

"Drancey will be there in a few seconds. Let's move!"

The vehicle charged ahead, the siren's strong, shrill notes penetrating the Grenoble night. Within a few seconds, Captain Barka had scanned the scene and identified the perps. A car used as a battering ram had smashed through the bank's front entrance, and three men were in the midst of plundering the ATMs. Another high-powered car was waiting fifty yards farther on, with the driver behind the wheel.

The siren had the desired effect. The burglars stopped, hypnotized by the vehicle headed toward them. Two hundred yards behind, another police car was barreling down at breakneck speed. The three men fled the bank. It was clear they were unsure what to do.

"Careful, Étienne, we've got amateurs here." Captain Barka grabbed the radio. "Drancey, we're going to box in the black BMW. Go past it fifty yards and stop. FYI, they don't seem to be in control of the situation."

Lieutenant Étienne Fortin realized what his superior was angling for. It was risky, but it would be a total surprise. The crooks would never expect such audacity.

The three masked men were running toward their vehicle, but they stopped short when the police car passed them, then blockaded the BMW in a perfectly executed maneuver. They looked panicked when they saw the second car stop behind them. Things weren't supposed to go like this.

Captain Barka leaped out of the car, weapon in hand. "Police! You are under arrest. Lie down on the ground."

Lieutenant Rodolphe Drancey and his partner got out of the second car, holding the burglars at gunpoint. One of the crooks pulled a pump-action shotgun out from under his jacket. Without thinking, he fired at the first police car. The sound of the exploding windshield mingled with his scream. The bullet from Captain Barka's Sig Sauer had just shattered his knee.

"The next one goes down your throat!" screamed Drancey as he crouched behind his vehicle.

With only a glance at their accomplice, who was rolling around on the ground in pain, the two other burglars turned back toward their car. The driver, pinned against the trunk, had been overpowered by Fortin. The crooks' escape was cut off. This wasn't how the job had been sold to them. They were just supposed to get as much cash as possible and then go live it up on the coast with their buddies and some girls.

"You have three seconds to put down your weapons. Three, two . . ."

They could tell by the cop's voice that this was no idle threat, and they didn't want to die. They put up their hands in a clear sign of submission. Two of the police officers approached the crooks, keeping their weapons trained on them. In the light of the streetlamps, sweat trickling down their backs, the crooks realized that the one who had fired at them was a woman. They shrugged—they weren't punk kids to be impressed so easily. But what they saw in Captain Barka's eyes paralyzed them.

"Fuck, large caliber," the second cop said, relieving them of two handguns. "Where would they get these?"

"For the moment, that's not on the agenda," said Captain Barka. "Cuff 'em. The judge will have all the time in the world to ask that question."

Then she lowered her gaze to the man on the ground. A pool of blood was starting to form around his shredded knee. She picked up the shotgun, then stroked the wounded man's temple with the barrel. He howled. She spoke to him with mock pleasantness.

"Before playing with this kind of toy, you have to think about the risks you're running. And tonight, you learned what they are. So, you either need to play nicely at home or learn how to use it. If you had shot me, it wouldn't be your kneecap spread all over the sidewalk, but your brains. The police have a very strong sense of solidarity."

She leaned over the man on the ground and pulled back his hood and realized he couldn't be more than twenty years old. What a waste! She lifted the gun away from his face.

"Rodolphe, call an ambulance. He's starting to go into shock."

Then she turned back to the two men in handcuffs. She got within inches of their faces and stared them down for a long while. Her icy glare shook them to the bottom of their souls. She pulled back and then tapped her temple with her index finger.

"You're in there now, forever. So make sure you never have to deal with me again. Never again!"

"Yes, madame," replied the two perps, who had lost all their composure.

"Captain. You say, 'Yes, Captain.'"

"Yes, Captain."

Lieutenant Drancey, who had been working with Captain Barka for several years now, couldn't help but be impressed with his superior. He knew she wasn't joking.

Chapter 4: The Woman in the Baptistery

The flash illuminated the stone walls one last time, then allowed the premises to return to their natural gloom. Silence fell, utterly. The photographer gathered his equipment and withdrew without a word.

The body sprawled, lifeless, staring at the ceiling with a look of astonishment.

Captain Barka crouched down beside the body and closed the eyes. She felt a cold shiver run down her back. Dressed in only cotton slacks and a light jacket, she didn't know whether the temperature of the room or the scene before her was to blame. Though this was far from her first cadaver, on this particular morning, the body seemed out of place. Yes, *out of place* was the phrase—this girl should never have been here. In spite of the scene before her, Captain Barka's mind drifted back three years, but she strongly willed it to return to the present.

She looked at the girl again—quite young and beautiful. The girl appeared to be in a deep sleep, one she would never wake up from. Captain Barka stood at the sound of footsteps.

"So, Captain, what do we have here?"

She turned to see Commissioner Alain Mazure, a big shot from the Grenoble judicial police.

"I was in the neighborhood when the call came," he explained. "What are your initial findings?"

"Tough to say, Commissioner. Just looking at the body, there's no apparent wound, but the ME will know more once he examines it."

Captain Barka paused when two paramedics arrived to take away the corpse. Overawed by the solemnity of the crypt, they took particular care in sliding the dead woman into a plastic body bag.

"How sad that such a pretty girl should find herself in there," blurted the older paramedic as he held the stretcher.

"D'you know where we are?" asked the younger one. "I don't feel like we're in Grenoble anymore."

Captain Barka answered him. "You're in the city's old baptistery. You've just jumped close to sixteen hundred years into the past."

"Never heard of it."

"Quite possible, really. It was rediscovered about twenty years ago during the subway construction. It had vanished from the records for almost ten centuries."

The older man interjected, "I appreciate the fact that you're improving yourself, Antoine, but we have to get going. Say thank you to the young lady and help me wheel this body out. We're sending her to the morgue at MUMC for you, mademoiselle."

"Captain. Not mademoiselle."

"Captain if you prefer, mademoiselle."

The young woman smiled wanly as the two men left with the lifeless body.

"So, Captain, I knew you had many talents, but tour guide is a new one. What happened here?"

Captain Barka turned toward Commissioner Mazure. Short and slender, he was not impressive at first glance, but his energy and instinctive understanding of human nature earned him the respect of his teams and everyone who crossed his path.

"The body was discovered this morning around seven o'clock by one of the museum employees doing his morning rounds. He notified the police immediately. Berroyer was on duty and responded first. He called in the forensic team as soon as he arrived on the premises and contacted me. The initial findings have revealed nothing. No one touched the victim."

"No marks on the ground?"

"No, not a trace, which isn't surprising, since we're talking about rock. The museum curator came by, and he didn't notice anything special. He was shaken, though, so we'll have to interview him a second time."

"So, no evidence this was a murder?"

"For the moment, no. But I don't see what could have gone through that poor girl's head to make her come here to end her life and, in particular, how she could have gotten in. We'll know more when the autopsy results come back."

"Is Blavet on it?"

"No doubt."

"Well, if there's something to find, he'll find it. What's the next step?"

"The curator just arrived. He's waiting to answer our questions, Commissioner."

"Take the case, Captain Barka. Let's go chat with this curator."

The commissioner headed back upstairs with the young woman and two other officers who were still on the scene. The sun was now high in the sky. In the lobby of the Old Diocese Museum, some of the staff were waiting, both frightened and curious. The commissioner sent them gently on their way and regarded the man heading toward them: a good fifty years or so old but still youthful, with crew cut hair and a neat suit. He looked like a fashion plate. His face, however, was ashen, marked by the events that had just taken place in his museum.

"The curator, Monsieur Boisregard," whispered Captain Barka to the commissioner.

"We'd like to talk to you for a few minutes, Monsieur Boisregard. I'm Commissioner Mazure," he said, introducing himself.

"I assure you I'll do everything in my power to help the justice system figure out what could have happened. If you'd care to follow me, it will be quieter in my office."

The curator brought the two officers into the administrative area with him. Once in Boisregard's office, they seated themselves in comfortable chairs.

"A corpse in the museum, and in the baptistery of all places. My God, what a horror! And who is that poor girl? How did she get in here? And . . ."

Commissioner Mazure held up a hand to stop him. "If you'll allow it, we'll be the ones to ask the questions, or rather Captain Barka will."

"Monsieur Boisregard, explain to us how the surveillance in the baptistery works."

"The museum is open from nine a.m. to six p.m. during the week. After the museum closes, we check to make sure no visitors are left."

"What staff do you have available?"

"There are eight people during the day and two security guards at night who make regular rounds."

"What's the timetable?"

"The first check is during the evening around eight o'clock, another around midnight, and a final one at about seven o'clock in the morning. That's when Marcel Jugal discovered the young woman's body."

"Then the body was dumped between midnight and seven a.m."

"Yes, that's correct."

"How does one access the baptistery?"

"There are two staircases that lead from the lobby to the entrance of the baptistery."

"And how many access points for the lobby?"

"The main door we came through and another internal route via one of the Old Diocese buildings."

"In your opinion, which way would the body have been brought in?"

The man chewed his manicured nails, gripped by strong emotions. "That's part of the mystery. Both doors are wired to an alarm, and nothing was detected. So theoretically, no one came in."

"Except we found the body. Could the alarms be defective?"

"Impossible. They were just overhauled, and the security system was improved after an intrusion we suffered six months ago now."

"Could a member of your staff have disconnected it?"

The curator shot out of his chair, affronted by the insult he'd just received.

"Also impossible! I have every confidence in my colleagues. I've known them for years, and I'll answer for them. Do you really believe the Old Diocese would welcome scoundrels?"

"The Church, holy as it may be, has welcomed more than one . . ." murmured Captain Barka.

Seeing that the curator was close to apoplectic, the commissioner motioned to his colleague. Captain Barka ended the interview. "Thank you for your cooperation, Monsieur Boisregard. We'll get back to you when we have more information. I'm sure you'll prove a valuable resource. I'd like to request that you keep the baptistery closed for today. There could be teams who have yet to gather evidence, and I don't want the premises to be disturbed. In addition, we're going to check your security system."

"At your service, madame. I doubt I'll sleep much until you find out why that poor young woman was here. Do you think it could happen again?"

"Unlikely. Still, I'll put two men on guard duty tonight at the museum entrance. You can indicate the most appropriate positions."

Chapter 5: A Summer Night's Dream

The day dragged on. Once again, the young man's gaze left his screen, drifting toward the slopes of the Chartreuse Mountains, rippling in the June heat. Never in Grenoble's memory had it been so hot at this time of year. Thankfully, the offices were air-conditioned to keep the powerful computers from overheating

"Julien, I remind you that we need to release a new version of the software by the end of the week. I have nothing against you admiring the mountains, but I'm not thrilled about spending the next four nights here."

Julien turned to face the colleague who had spoken to him. He shrugged. If somebody was going to have to spend his nights here during crunch time, it would be him and not the guy with the running commentary.

"I'm going to refuel at the café. If anybody wants to come with, the round is on me," Julien said. No one responded to his appeal—everyone in the room was glued to their computers, some busy finishing their software projects, others discreetly surfing the web. "Sorry I woke you up, guys!"

"Wait, I'll go with you."

Julien turned to find a smiling petite brunette crossing the quiet room to join him. They ran down two flights of stairs and emerged directly onto the street. A small bar, conveniently located barely ten yards away from the main entrance, replaced the automatic coffee machine installed in the company's lobby. They took a seat at the back, hoping it would be cooler there.

"What'll it be, folks?" called the waiter without leaving the counter.

"Two espressos, please."

"Two hot espressos, two!"

While the barista prepared the coffees, Julien looked around the bar. He'd been working for three years now at Megatech, a software implementation company for the accounting departments of small and medium enterprises. Nothing particularly remarkable had happened to him in the last three years, even though his days had been quite busy: job, evenings with friends, hikes in the mountains, a breakup, some occasional flirting . . .

"Ah, Julien," Sophie said, interrupting his thoughts. "If you brought me here just to sink into your inner world, you should tell me. I may as well go back to the zombies; at least there I won't be expecting anyone to talk to me. I'll already know where I stand."

He smiled. He loved Sophie's wit and energy. "You're right, my dear, but I'm still preoccupied with something, probably insignificant, that's bothering me more than I thought it would."

"You're going to have to be more specific, because I'm not following."

"Really, it's stupid, and you're gonna give me a hard time."

"Come on, stop making me beg." She added, smiling, "I love being the gal pal handsome guys confide in."

Julien looked at Sophie. He'd only recently gotten to know the young woman, who was rather guarded about her private life. They had started at Megatech on the same day. He'd never developed very strong friendships with his coworkers. But by chance he and Sophie had found themselves on the same one-week trek around Mont-Blanc, and he'd discovered a lively, funny girl. He was convinced he could trust her.

"Okay, I'll tell you, but promise me you'll keep it to yourself."

"I promise, Juju."

"Okay, but if you could stop calling me Juju . . ."

"So what's the scoop?"

Julien told her about his adventure the previous day. The girl he saw on the street, the incomprehensible urge to follow her, his wait in front of the cathedral, and the mysterious woman's disappearance in the church.

"That's just the beginning," he continued. "I went home and realized that it had affected me more than I thought. I dreamed about it last night."

"So do you think she liked you?" interrupted Sophie.

"You joker! Let me get to the end of my dream. At first I thought someone was trying to shake me awake. So then I opened my eyes. There's a girl in a room, she's looking at me, but everything's pretty blurry. Then all of a sudden, there's a loud noise, or a strong gust of wind, or I don't know what—a kind of biblical cloud comes over me. You know the type . . ."

"I have yet to experience it, but I'll do my best to put myself in your shoes."

"Basically, her face appears to me quite clearly, and I recognize her: the woman at the cathedral. But her features, which were calm in the afternoon, are full of distress now. A shadow comes up behind her, threatening. She tries to yell something, screaming and fighting, and then I woke up for real."

Sophie looked at him silently as she stirred sugar into her coffee. "Well, I can understand why that affected you."

"It's not over. I looked at my alarm clock, and it was around three o'clock in the morning. I managed to get back to sleep, and I had the same dream. Again, the sensation of being called in my sleep. Then I see the room again, and there's the girl again. But this time, she's panicked. She's crying, but no sound comes out. The shadow's there, denser, like it's solidified, bending over her. Then I wake up. The first time, I was already shaken, but the second time, you better believe I was flipping out."

"It's disconcerting, to say the least. Guilt for having followed that pretty girl in the street?"

"Geez, you're going strong today! Fine, tell me what it means, O great psychologist?"

Sophie looked at her watch. "The psychologist says if we don't want to get lynched, we should think about getting back to our projects posthaste. Then again, if you ask me out tonight, I'll be ready to give you my diagnosis."

Julien smiled. "Eight o'clock, Place du Tribunal, in front of the Café de la Table Ronde. I'll let you pick the restaurant."

"Oh, no, if you do the asking, you have to choose the location for our feast. That's the deal!"

"You're right, my dear, I am beneath contempt. Here, for your trouble, I'll let you pay for the coffee."

Sophie stood up and left three euros on the table. "Very well, monseigneur! Let's go now, or else Denis will have a nervous breakdown."

Chapter 6: The Autopsy

Nadia Barka greeted Doctor Blavet's arrival with relief. She'd witnessed a number of horrors in her career, and it took a lot to rattle her. But she'd never been able to stand the ambiance at the Institute of Forensic Medicine. She'd had to participate in autopsies several times, but seeing a corpse cut open surgically, weighed piece by piece, analyzed, and then sewn up before being returned to its loved ones always left her with an impression of the individual's final downfall. She found it depressing.

She understood perfectly well the importance of the procedure and knew that it was, after a fashion, the final act requested of the victim to unmask her killer, a sort of posthumous vengeance, but it always did something to her.

Doctor Blavet broke into a huge smile when he saw her. Around sixty years old, he was one of the best forensic pathologists in France. His good humor and nearly constant smile made him far from a Frankenstein, which a jealous colleague had tried to nickname him.

"Hello, Nadia, how's it going?"

She always insisted that, apart from her close colleagues, her official title be used and a professional tone be observed, just like for her male colleagues. But she made an exception for Henri Blavet. He had always regarded her with benevolence devoid of condescension. He also appreciated her unwavering determination and effectiveness in a male-dominated profession. He'd supported her when, several years earlier, Commissioner Carpot (who had since been transferred to the Paris region) had tried to get her to take the blame for a failure that absolutely wasn't her fault. What doesn't kill you makes you stronger.

"To be quite frank, Doctor," she said, "not terribly well. It still gets me when I see a murdered woman."

"Yes, I know, since Laure Déramaux's killing."

Silence settled between the two of them. Captain Barka clenched her fists and forced herself to breathe slowly. The doctor spoke again. "I'm afraid we've once again stumbled onto a complicated case."

The police officer flinched, as though from an electric shock. "But she didn't have any apparent wounds."

"No *apparent* wounds, you are correct, but when I undressed her, that assumption went out the window. Come, let's go sit in my office."

They walked down a long hallway with venerable white walls that hadn't been repainted for quite some time. Undoubtedly a result of the hospitals' budgets melting like snow in the sun! The room was small but well furnished. Two comfortable chairs faced the doctor's desk. Captain Barka sat down, nervously crossing her legs. Action and danger had never scared her, and she'd captured more than one criminal who was amused to be up against a woman. Well—amused to start with! But over the last three years, she sometimes felt boiling within her a hatred that terrified her. Ever since she'd had to investigate the death of Laure Déramaux, a young woman, twenty-three years old, found slain in a Vercors forest.

She found herself faced with a glass of fruit juice, which the doctor had just proffered. She smiled at him, pulled herself together, and regained her professionalism.

"I'm listening, Doctor Blavet."

"Good, I'll send you my official report tomorrow, but I can already give you the main outline. The victim is a Caucasian woman, in good health, between twenty-five and thirty years old, likely closer to thirty. As you've noted, there was no trace of a blow or wound on the body when you found it in the baptistery."

"Yes, she had a surprised look before I finally closed her eyes. You'll be able to see it in the photos taken by the forensic team."

"When my assistants undressed her and laid her on the autopsy table, I immediately noticed a large wound on her side. Difficult to miss. The body had been cut open and then sewn up again, undoubtedly during the crime."

The policewoman said nothing more, anxious to hear the rest of the story. But she forced herself not to show it.

"The fellow who killed her has a serious problem. When I continued with the autopsy, I saw that her heart was no longer in her rib cage."

Nadia let him go on.

"He made an incision just under eight inches long at the abdomen, spread open the two sides, then utilized a very sharp instrument to reach the heart. He barely nicked a few other organs on the way, proof of undeniable skill. This was clearly not the first time the murderer was engaging this type of activity."

"Do you think he's a doctor?"

"A doctor, or a veterinarian, or perhaps someone who very closely studied an anatomy textbook and practiced extensively on animals."

A question burned on Captain Barka's lips. She asked it. "Was she alive when he did that? Did she suffer?"

"No, she was dead. The blood remained in the organs. If she had been alive, she would have lost all her blood."

"And why did she look so surprised?"

"I ordered some blood work. There were traces of a powerful soporific that we haven't had time to analyze yet. You'll have the results tomorrow."

"Was she raped?"

"No, no evidence of sexual assault or seminal fluid. This isn't one of those rape murders."

The doctor had finished his summary. His shoulders slumped imperceptibly. "I'm describing this to you as though I'm reading a scientific report, but despite all my years doing this work, I'm not impervious to this sort of situation. And whoever did it is one hell of a scumbag."

His perpetual smile no longer graced his lips. His face had gone hard as stone. "I will do everything I can to help you catch him. Because the killer is a sick man, albeit a methodical one. If he's acting on impulses, he's managing to control them, and nothing says he won't do it again. Well, I'll leave it to your psychologist."

Captain Barka stood up. Her decision was clear, irrevocable. It would be war between her and the killer. She wouldn't let such a dangerous creature escape a second time.

Chapter 7: *Adieu*, Magali!

The sun was setting behind the Vercors Mountains. It still shone brightly, but the air was starting to cool. Barely. The man closed the shutters. The summer solstice was approaching, and he dreaded nightfall—*that* night, years or centuries before, which had wounded him in a way he'd never recovered from.

But now at last he'd discovered how to rid himself of the nightmare that pursued him relentlessly. Oh, how powerful he'd felt the previous night! Powerful and temporarily delivered from the sickness that had been devouring him for so long, always at the same time of year, before that cursed summer solstice! Now when the fever took him, and he felt the darkness, the pain, seep into him, he knew how to make it fade away. He opened his clenched fist and blew sharply on the palm of his hand, pleased. *Adieu*, Magali!

He knew his torture would come to an end, he was sure of it. The one who had initiated him could not be mistaken.

For years, he had tried all sorts of drugs and treatments. But those only knocked him out, rendering him unable to react and quashing the energy that had carried him through his whole career. It was always there, lurking in the shadows, ready to seize him as soon as that fatal date arrived! It then disappeared and returned, year after year, tirelessly, leaving him no respite, growing stronger. He suffered so much he felt like he was going to die, but he could not entertain the thought of death, which he knew would have offered him the reprieve he longed for. He was incapable of committing suicide.

Finally, he'd found it! He'd found it, without ever engaging those incompetents who call themselves psychiatrists and claim the right to treat the souls of their fellow men. He'd found a way to definitively lift the curse and rediscover peace.

It was only a matter of days, he knew it.

He smiled lovingly at the mass of reddish flesh enclosed in the jar he'd just taken out of the refrigerator. He would allow himself a fresh morsel of this lifesaving heart later in the evening.

Chapter 8: A Cozy Restaurant

Julien had stopped dreaming about the mysterious woman at the cathedral, but he couldn't manage to shake the profound malaise the nightmare had given him. He had to move on. He looked at his watch. It was almost eight o'clock.

The Place Saint-André—or Place du Tribunal, as the locals called it in honor of the old sixteenth-century courthouse bordering it—was packed. Every student in Grenoble seemed to be there that evening, either to celebrate the end of exams or to keep their spirits up while taking them. Julien smiled inwardly. He had frequented these bars only a decade or so ago. He looked at each, knew them all. They were part of his routine back then. He'd even had a fling with an Austrian student, a waitress in her spare time. It all seemed both very recent and increasingly distant. *Fine, I'm getting older*, he said to himself with an amused inner pout.

The atmosphere was relaxed, the temperature was growing pleasant, and a sudden levity came over him. Life was beautiful, open before him. He wasn't about to ruin such a promising evening because of a stranger he'd only glimpsed the day before.

He moved closer to the Café de la Table Ronde, which prided itself on being the oldest café in Grenoble and the second oldest café in France, after Le Procope in Paris. Ah, yes, the eternal rivalry between Paris and the provinces. Julien, having lived in both cities, had decided not to weigh in when discussions on this highly controversial topic came up.

He looked around as he waited for Sophie. She was generally punctual. Indeed, he spotted her at a distance waving to him as she came out of the Jardin de Ville. He was happy to see her.

The Sophie he consorted with on the job was a sportswoman extraordinaire. Always dressed in jeans or capris and addicted to polar fleece, she clearly spent more time at Au Vieux Campeur than at Zara or Esprit. During their trek around Mont-Blanc, she'd led the group with prowess, verve, and good humor that had impressed him.

But the Sophie he saw coming toward him had nothing in common with the one he knew, at least as far as clothes went. Wearing a little summer dress that suited her perfectly, highlighting the shapes she typically contrived to keep hidden, she walked with surprising ease on a pair of stilettos. She even wore subtle makeup, which made her appear otherworldly.

He was still gaping when she kissed him on the cheek.

"So, Julien, cat got your tongue? You look like you've seen a ghost."

He recovered. "You're just magnificent!" He was rather pleased to see her blush slightly under her usual tan.

"Nice of you to say so, thanks. Since you're taking me to some awesome restaurant, I had to match the decor. So where are we going? Kebabs or Chinese?"

"If only I'd known! So sorry, but I picked something else."

"What?"

"A nice little place right nearby—intimate, warm, good food, and friendly service."

"You memorized their website? I trust you completely. Take me." She grabbed his arm and asked, "Which way?"

"Toward the cathedral."

She saw him flinch and immediately understood what had just crossed his mind.

"Don't worry," she said, smiling at him. "I'm not going to evaporate, at least not before dinner's over."

Julien had reserved a table in a corner of the tiny room, which was already mostly full. Aged walls and exposed beams blended well with the more modern design of the tables. The two friends settled in and ordered two margaritas while they studied the menu.

"All right, the restaurant is worthy of the effort I put in for you!" Sophie admitted to her companion.

"I would have had to choose a restaurant that was truly beyond my current budget to be worthy of you."

Sophie smiled. "I was sure you were better at compliments than at reading a National Land Survey map. Much better, even!"

They reminisced about their vacation and the one-mile detour the group had had to take when a storm came dangerously close to them.

"I think that story is going to haunt me my whole life. And it's your fault, too!" she said.

"And why is that?"

"Trusting the map to a guy who grew up in Paris—that's risky business!"

"I'd like to point out that I was doing my studies there while you were doing yours here."

"Yes, but darling, you used to gambol with cows and dahus in your native mountains."

"Fine, you win, it was partly my responsibility. And to celebrate that, I'm going to have seared scallops on a bed of fresh spinach.

I've just discovered you need to win the Goncourt Prize for French Literature to open a restaurant."

"Same for me, with a small glass of Sancerre. Will you drink a little tonight?"

"A little? Why a little? We can start right in by ordering a bottle!"

Chapter 9: Initial Briefing

Commissioner Mazure stood in front of the board. Eight people, seated behind the tables arranged in a circle around the room, were waiting for him to speak. He lifted a cup of hot coffee to his lips, grimaced at the invariably poor quality of the beverage supplied by the administration's distributor, and dove in.

"Captain Barka distributed the file on the baptistery crime to you two hours ago. I have no doubt you read it through, but I'm going to ask her to give us a quick summary of the situation. Nadia, your turn."

Captain Barka stood up, ran a hand over her hair to smooth it, and got right to it. "Yesterday morning, at seven o'clock, the body of a still-unidentified woman was found in Grenoble's Old Diocese Museum, in the baptistery in the basement, underneath the cathedral square. The body was laid out directly on the paving stones, without any apparent wounds. Doctor Blavet conducted the autopsy as soon as possible. And that's when things took a different turn. The murderer removed the victim's heart, then sewed her back up before redressing her. According to the doctor, the killer did not do this while she was alive. He killed her first, perhaps by poisoning. The time of death was estimated to be three or four o'clock in the morning, which is to say three or four hours before the corpse was discovered by the security guard."

A hand went up. Captain Barka ceded the floor to Lieutenant Étienne Fortin, a burly fellow whose hair was never combed, who often worked in tandem with her, and whose tenacity for the work she appreciated.

"Do we have any idea how the body came to be in the baptistery? Was the crime committed at the scene?"

"No. The crime was committed elsewhere. The forensic team found nothing at the scene. Not a drop of blood. As for how the body got into the museum, that remains a mystery for the moment. There are only two entrances to the site. According to Boisregard, the curator, those doors are wired to an alarm and anyone moving through them would have been detected."

"His staff must be able to deactivate them, though?"

"He swears to high heaven that his people are above all suspicion. But our specialists went to study his security system. According to them, there was evidence that the system had been overridden, but don't ask me anything else for the moment. The investigation is ongoing."

A middle-aged man raised his hand next. She called on Jérôme Garancher, squad archivist for more than twenty years. "Who's going to handle the press? I've already seen two or three reporters outside the station."

"I'll take care of it," announced Commissioner Mazure. "We somehow managed to suppress the news yesterday, but given the number of people on the scene at the museum, it was bound to leak. So early this morning, I called our contact at the *Dauphiné Libéré* to release the first round of information. Obviously I made absolutely no mention of how the victim had been mutilated. But still, we should expect an onslaught of reporters. The warden's chief of staff has already been contacted by the twenty-four-hour news networks. I will be with the prosecutor when he addresses the reporters. A press conference is scheduled for noon. As usual, not a word on your end."

Another hand went up. Mazure called on Lieutenant Rodolphe Drancey, a man in his middle years dressed in a leather jacket, who made it a point of honor to keep his scalp perfectly shaved ever since one of his colleagues told him he looked a little bit like Bruce Willis. Nasty during interrogations or police raids, Drancey loved this role that gave him an authority he didn't possess at home.

"Rodolphe?"

"Any leads on the identity of the victim?"

Nadia Barka answered. "Not for the moment. She doesn't appear in our files, which isn't at all surprising. We made the rounds of hospitals in the area as well as the police stations in Grenoble and Isère, but no missing persons report was filed. We can assume she was single, otherwise her family would have shown up. We've sent her picture to the newspapers and television stations. That means we should get ready to handle dozens or even hundreds of ridiculous calls to try to ferret out the good intel."

A mocking voice rang out across the room. "And when will you bring us the second victim? That's your specialty, isn't it?"

"If you have nothing to say but bullshit, Rivera, you can go back to sleeping in your corner!" retorted Captain Barka.

Captain Stéphane Rivera, a former senior investigator who was frustrated in his career, had a gift for getting on her nerves. Approaching retirement, he had been sidelined by his superiors and colleagues alike, who could no longer stand his constant mockery, particularly with regard to women. He had committed a grievous error that had cost two people their lives ten years earlier. He could have been forgiven for the error, but he'd tried to falsify the facts. The deception had been uncovered, and he'd kept his job only because of well-placed supporters. Nevertheless, his advancement had been stopped cold. Because his superior at the time was a woman, he'd become the archetype of the misanthropic misogynist.

A stern-faced woman, hair pulled back and wearing a gray suit, answered him. "I am not aware of this specialty of Captain Barka's that you mentioned, but I know she possesses qualities you do not have, Captain Rivera. Now, if your contribution is finished, I would like to speak." Isabelle Tavernier, a psychiatrist, regularly got involved in the course of investigations to help flesh out the profile of certain offenders or murderers. Stéphane Rivera shrugged but didn't respond to her.

"We currently have little information, and I will have to spend some time with Dr. Henri Blavet. These conclusions are therefore quite preliminary, but here are the hypotheses I can put forward. The man—or woman, because anything is possible—who committed this murder is someone who is particularly methodical. No evidence, a corpse that came from nowhere, but a process of killing or mutilation that follows a very clear logic for its perpetrator. He presents his work to us, like a question we must find an answer for. Does he wish to taunt us, or is it part of a ritual whose significance only he knows? We cannot tell at present. Based on the photos that were taken, it does not appear that the position the body was left in has any importance. The corpse was laid directly on the ground, faceup, and nothing suggests any staging. Why leave it in a locked sacred space rather than abandon it in the woods? That's what we have to figure out. And that's what makes me fear that our killer's process is only beginning. The victim's identity could potentially help us. I'll finish up a preliminary report that will be available to the entire team in less than an hour."

A murmur swept around the room when the psychiatrist ended her speech. A serial killer, with opaque motives to say the least, and ritual murders. Summer was going to be hot in Grenoble, and not just because cars would be set on fire in certain neighborhoods.

Mazure broke the wall of silence that had settled on the gathering. "Ladies and gentlemen, it is our responsibility to find this criminal as quickly as possible and prevent any more murders, in case we're dealing with a potential serial killer. I'm meeting with the warden and will ask him for maximum resources to solve this case as soon as possible. The killer must have left clues—ask questions, dig out files, find out if similar murders have already taken place in France or Europe in the last twenty years. You know your jobs, and I don't need to teach them to you. Captain Barka is in charge of organizing and monitoring the investigation. Starting today, there will be a briefing here every morning at ten o'clock. You are potentially on call twenty-four hours a day, and nobody better piss me off with any noise about comp time or planned vacations. They're being postponed."

None of the participants said a word. The deadly risk one or more women were running without knowing it, a risk that was perhaps living right next door to them, fully justified the overtime.

Captain Barka distributed tasks to the participants, then the team dispersed.

Chapter 10: The Shock

7:00 a.m. Julien dropped his backpack next to his desk. He had to finish an important software user's guide by the end of the week—in other words, that very evening. His work from the previous day led him to think that what he had at first taken for a challenge would ultimately be doable.

The team usually arrived much later, but the imminence of the deadline had gotten them all out of bed this morning. An unusual excitement prevailed in the office.

Julien saw Sophie just arriving.

"A little coffee so we can get to work in top form?" she asked.

"Okay, but quickly, because I still have some work to do to finish my document."

They sat on the terrace of their usual café. Upon seeing them arrive, the waiter immediately made and delivered two espressos. Julien leaned over to a neighboring table and snagged a copy of the *Daubé*, which was the local nickname for the regional daily paper *Dauphiné Libéré*.

"Hey, let's look at the weather. It wouldn't hurt to go looking for a little mountain freshness this weekend," he said. He unfolded the paper and froze.

"Earth to Julien," said Sophie. "Did you see a ghost?"

Julien lowered the paper and looked at his friend. "You have no idea."

The pallor of his face surprised her. He handed her the paper without saying another word.

Sophie scanned it. "A murder in the Grenoble baptistery—that's unusual, to say the least. This is what put you in such a state?"

"Partly. Look at the picture."

She looked it over and scanned the caption. "It's a call for witnesses. Don't tell me you know her . . ."

"It's her!"

"Her who?"

"Her, the one I followed the day before yesterday and told you about yesterday morning!"

Sophie put down the paper and looked at Julien. He looked upset. His hands were shaking, but he wasn't trying to stop them.

"This is madness," he said. "I'm living a nightmare."

"Wait a minute before freaking out. First of all, are you certain it's her?"

"Certain, no, but she looks so much like her that it can't be a coincidence."

"And why not? Are there psychics in your family?"

"Not that I know of."

She thought about what her friend had just said. He was truly upset. The nightmare thing had rattled him, and maybe he was projecting his dream image onto this photo. Or maybe not. She read the article over again and took down the telephone number underneath the missing persons report. "You have to call the police. It's the best thing to do."

"But wait, they're going to think I'm a crazy person."

"I don't think so. You might have key information for their investigation."

39

"But it's madness!"

"A woman is dead, Julien," she said, raising her voice to pull him out of his stupor.

The customers seated at neighboring tables turned to look at her. She lowered her voice. "You have to go there as soon as possible. We'll take just an hour, and then we'll come back and finish our work."

"We? You'd be willing to come with me?"

"Of course!"

"Thank you. Can you give me the number? I'll call right now."

Half an hour later, Julien and Sophie were shown into a large room by a police officer. Their phone call had immediately piqued interest, and their contact person had asked them to give their testimony as soon as possible. They were led to a small meeting room where a sporty-looking woman was waiting for them. Julien was surprised by her haggard appearance. A man in uniform seated behind a desk prepared to take notes on what Julien was going to tell them.

"Hello, I'm Captain Barka, the officer in charge of the preliminary investigation into this murder. Would you like coffee? It's disgusting, but drinkable if you add two or three sugars."

"With pleasure," replied Julien. "With lots of sugars. I think I need it."

"And you?" she asked Sophie.

"I'll be fine, thank you."

"May I ask who you are and why you've accompanied Monsieur Lombard?"

"I'm Sophie Dupas. I'm here to testify that Monsieur Lombard spoke to me about the murder victim before the news appeared in the paper."

"Regardless, I don't see any problem. Doctor Tavernier, who is in our offices this morning, has asked to join us. She should be here within five minutes at the most. She's our behavioral analyst, what the Americans call a *profiler*. And your testimony is the first potentially serious lead we have."

Captain Barka went out into the hallway to look for Isabelle Tavernier. She came back two minutes later, accompanied by a severe-looking woman who introduced herself and sat down on one of the chairs at a round table.

"Please proceed, Monsieur Lombard," Captain Barka said. "Tell us everything you remember, even what you think are just details."

Julien spent fifteen minutes telling his story, then relating the dreams that had plagued him, without anyone saying a word. When he'd finished, the captain opened a file deposited in front of her and took out three photos.

"Do you recognize this woman?"

"Yes."

"Are you one hundred percent sure?"

"You know, when you run across somebody just once and only dream about her the following night, it might seem difficult to be so certain, but as far as I'm concerned, that's the same woman."

"Another question. You told us she had on a white dress. Can you confirm that?"

"Absolutely. It was dazzlingly white, even. No doubt that's what caught my eye first."

"And in your dream, do you remember how she was dressed?"

"The same dress, but without that luminous aspect."

She once more pushed a photo toward him. He'd seen only the victim's face in the previous photo, but now he had a complete picture of the woman, stretched out on a rough floor. She was dressed in a pale blue skirt and red T-shirt.

"In this photo, she isn't or is no longer wearing a white dress. Does what she's wearing mean anything to you?"

"Absolutely not," replied Julien.

The psychiatrist broke her silence. "Let's go back to the chronology of facts. You say you followed her, without understanding why. I imagine you must have thought back on it. Do you see any reason at all, even if it might seem trivial at first?"

"Will that help you in your investigation, or does it make me a potential suspect?" asked the young man with a touch of doubt in his voice.

Captain Barka intervened. "Theoretically, the entire population of the region is suspect. But Doctor Tavernier's questions are not covert charges, I assure you. You're our first witness, and your account is mysterious, to say the least. We're trying to understand along with you just where it might lead us."

"All right. Thinking back on it, I got the impression that it was her aura that had attracted me. How do I put this? She didn't specifically look at me, but thinking back, it felt like an inner voice told me to follow her, that she had something to show me. I know that sounds stupid, but that's how it felt."

"It's not stupid," commented the psychiatrist. "The capacity for communication between individuals often goes beyond simple gestures or speech. Do you have an idea of what she wanted to tell you?"

"No, and that's probably why I followed her—to understand."

The man sitting at the computer took down their conversation, the clicking of the keyboard punctuating the silence that had just fallen.

The psychiatrist tapped the table with her pen. Julien saw a shadow of annoyance pass over Sophie's face. She was generally patient, but there were two or three things that profoundly irritated her, and this was one of them. He was inwardly amused by it.

Tavernier spoke to him again. "Are you certain you didn't dream that scene in the street? Are you certain this woman existed?"

Julien was taken aback by the question. "Can you clarify the meaning of your question?"

"Do you think this woman was real?"

"I didn't just invent what I told you, if that's what you're implying!"

"No, that's not what I'm implying," she said, softening her tone. "And I'm sure you're telling the truth."

"So I'm supposed to have followed a ghost only I could see?"

"I don't know, not everything can be explained right away. You've never known a woman who looked like her?"

"No, why?"

"You could have transferred her face onto an anonymous passerby."

"And recognized the photo of the dead woman! No, that face really wasn't familiar."

"Think carefully, Monsieur Lombard. Replay the whole scene calmly at home, and perhaps you'll uncover new clues. Maybe this woman wanted to give you a message? Maybe she didn't run across you by accident?"

"I don't know what to say. I already thought about it, but if it might lead somewhere, I'll think on it some more."

Captain Barka ended the interview. "Thank you, Monsieur Lombard. Your testimony is valuable. I'm going to ask you to leave us your telephone number so that we can contact you if we need additional information. I'll also give you mine. If something comes back to you, even if it seems like just a small detail, don't hesitate to call me."

Chapter 11: Relaxation

"That's it, all done!" Julien stretched, yawned, saved his file, and sent it via e-mail to the program manager. "Bodes well for a nice warm weekend," he said, looking out the window at the blue sky just beginning to darken. He turned around and realized only three of them were left in the room. Sophie, a computer scientist named Michel, and himself.

"To celebrate, I'll buy you a pizza on the riverfront," Julien said. "We can walk there in ten minutes, and it'll give us time to stretch our legs."

"I can't," said Michel. "I'm leaving right away for a weekend of windsurfing at Cap d'Agde. And I'm already late. *Ciao*. It's the wind, the beach, and the girls for me."

He ran out of the office.

"Okay, a little pizza, Sophie?"

"We're inseparable at the moment. I have something else to suggest."

"Couscous?"

"No, a session at my club's gym. It'll do us so much good after today's excitement."

Julien grumbled. He wasn't a fan of exercise or weight train- ing, but the desire to be with Sophie surpassed the desire to eat a Neapolitan pizza, washed down with a little beer, on the terrace of one of the many pizzerias on the Isère riverfront.

"Okay, it can't hurt. But give me five minutes to run and get some shorts and a pair of sneakers. I could do exercises in bare feet and boxers, but it might raise some eyebrows."

"Indeed, be careful. About fifteen of us girls go there, and you'll be the only guy. My trophy for the day, in a way."

"Now you've convinced me. I'm hurrying!"

Liquid was probably the best word for him. Julien, covered in sweat, was stretched out on the gym floor, no longer able to feel his abdominal muscles or his glutes. Or rather, he felt them too much! An alert-looking woman with short hair came toward him.

"So, Julien, you can't hack it in front of these women?" she asked with a smile.

"You've convinced me, Aimée, I really have to come back and train."

"Very good, there'll be a man among us. There's only one more session before summer vacation, but we're counting on you in the fall."

"Certainly. That'll give me two months to muscle up. I don't know if it'll be enough."

He got up, put away his mat, downed his bottle of mineral water, and left the room. Sophie was waiting for him at the exit.

"So, not bad, eh?" she asked.

"Cut it out—this is nuts! And I stay pretty active!"

"Yes, but if you want to keep your pretty little ass for another few years, you have to keep working on it."

Julien looked at her and whispered in her ear. "That's the nicest thing you've ever said to me."

She burst out laughing. "Does the offer for pizza still stand?"

"Of course, but I definitely need a shower first."

"Me too, we'll meet outside the locker rooms."

The weather was divinely pleasant. A light breeze chased away the day's sultriness, and a slight coolness rose up from the Isère flowing at their feet. Remarkably, the riverfront in the Saint-Laurent neighborhood, on the Isère's right bank, was closed to motor vehicles. The restaurant owners had taken the opportunity to set up tables on the little street, still quite busy in spite of the late hour. Their conversation had been very lively. They'd avoided the topic of the baptistery murder, which had dominated their thoughts.

Julien enjoyed being with Sophie. He had appreciated her as a companion for outings at first, but then realized that he'd been thinking about her a little more every day. Last night's dinner at the restaurant had been revealing—he loved being with her. She was energetic, beautiful, and knew how to be seductive when she decided someone was worth the trouble. But it frightened him, too. He wasn't stupid and knew he was starting to fall in love. And that he did not want. It had hurt too much when Sylvie left.

"What are you thinking about, my handsome athlete?"

"You!" He realized that he'd answered without paying attention and blushed, hoping she wouldn't notice.

"An admirable subject for daydreaming. I almost want to leave you be."

"What if instead we took a walk on the slopes of the Bastille fort? Aimée destroyed my abs and glutes, but I still have energy in my legs. If you still have time, of course."

"I have time tonight. And that seems to me an excellent way to use it. You can tell me scary stories on the way."

"You've chosen well. That's my specialty."

They left the table and headed at a leisurely pace toward the Chartreuse foothills.

Chapter 12: Magali

The man's eyes were fixed on the calendar. In one week, it would be June 21: the thirtieth anniversary. He lay down on his bed, and the images streamed through his brain once more, the years replaying with incredible sharpness.

Magali was there before him. Magali, the light of his life, his Holy Grail, the apple of his eye. She was the heart of his passion, his mission. He wanted to protect her against the dangers of the world he knew so well, keep her free of all external impurity. A wave of tenderness washed over him as he thought about the woman facing him. She was gentle and beautiful; he took care of her. But today, Magali had a suitcase beside her. A small suitcase, a pathetic sign of her obstinacy. Why? Why was Magali so stubborn lately? Hadn't he explained to her every day about the dangers of the world outside? Did she no longer understand that without him, the depravity of others would seize and soil her? Where was this sudden ingratitude coming from? The last time, she even accused him of having been violent with her.

The accusation had doubly grieved him. First, hearing reproach from the mouth of his wife when he was so devoted to her that he'd built his life around her! Then, wasn't force a means of returning people to their senses when they'd lost their minds? To put her back on the right path and quell passions he dared not imagine in her, he'd given her the treatment he'd prepared, to defuse any chance of rebellion.

Magali, the woman he loved and revered, had become docile once more. When he'd sensed that her foolish ambitions for autonomy had disappeared, he had lowered the dosage of the remedy he imposed on her. All had become calm again, restful, reassuring—just how he liked it.

And today, there she was again, before him. Her face was impassive, but that little suitcase was a sign of rebellion he could not accept. She had just endured a terrible blow to her stomach, leaving her doubled over in pain. Would she never understand? He would explain it all to her again, using everything in his power to make her understand, for her own good, of course!

The man jerked his head violently and sat down. He looked around him. The room was in shadow. He was on a large bed, set against a wall papered in faded pastel. A large table sat opposite him; a wardrobe, practically empty, stood on one side of the wall. He couldn't bear this time of year anymore. The light, the heat, the world's rising sap—everything was an assault.

After the twenty-first had passed, it would all be better. But he had to hold on until then. The previous year, he'd nearly gone mad, but this year, he'd found the solution. He already felt calmer just thinking about it. He stood up and left the room. He went down a long hallway, then descended a staircase. He reached the ground floor, felt the cool tiles under his feet, and crossed the foyer. He entered a large kitchen and headed for the refrigerator, which emitted a quiet purr. That was the only sound in a house he had dedicated to silence, a house that had become his ultimate peace, his refuge.

The man opened the door and reached for the lifesaving jar. He was shocked when he saw it. He realized that almost nothing remained of the heart that gave him back his energy and prevented him from being sucked into the past. He had abused it without noticing. He had consumed it much more rapidly than he'd planned. No matter, he would go out again in search of this indispensable redemptive substance.

Chapter 13: Monica

The tension had risen a notch since the last meeting. Commissioner Mazure looked at his staff. He knew they were working tirelessly, but Paris was demanding results. Rumors were beginning to circulate on the Internet about the removal of the victim's heart. Television news had picked up on that immediately, and the baptistery victim was increasingly of interest to the public—and the authorities. They had even asked him to invent clues if he had to, to show that the investigation was moving forward. Actually, they hadn't asked him straight-out like that, but he knew how to read between the lines.

He headed for the espresso machine as the last to arrive settled in. He had just purchased it at his own expense so that the team could finally enjoy a decent cup of coffee. At first he'd purchased the coffee capsules without telling them and witnessed firsthand just how addicted to caffeine his team was. In the absence of the pay increase they'd been hoping for, he could at least provide them with a way to enjoy a few minutes of gustatory pleasure.

Étienne Fortin came in almost at a run, his hair sticking up wildly, dressed in a pair of his famous sweatpants and brandishing a large paper bag. Out of breath, he said, "Sorry, I had a mishap this morning. My car let me down. A Peugeot 205 that just celebrated its twentieth birthday. Since I didn't have time to eat, I bought two dozen croissants."

A murmur of thanks rippled around the room. Fortin distributed the pastries and sat down at his table. "Now that everyone is here and properly fed," Mazure said, "we're going to let Captain Barka give us an update on the search. Nadia, all yours."

Nadia Barka jumped right in. "We've made little progress in three days. It's as if this murder never took place. I met with Doctor Blavet again along with Isabelle Tavernier. We're now just about convinced that the killer worked or works in the medical field. It took a steady hand and excellent knowledge of human anatomy to do what he did. We've initiated investigation in this direction. We've also been back to see the curator of the Old Diocese Museum. He gave us nothing new. He was horrified when we told him that his alarm system had been tampered with."

"Do you think the murderer could be one of the museum employees?" asked Captain Rivera.

Captain Barka looked at him. There was no trace of his usual scorn in the tone of his question. She remembered that Mazure had called him into his office after the last meeting. That seemed to have calmed him down.

"Rationally, no. The risk of discovery would be immense. But we're continuing to investigate the staff. Furthermore, we have an appointment this afternoon with Father Bernard de Valjoney, one of the people in charge of the Diocese of Grenoble. I want to find out whether it's possible to hang this murder on some religious ritual. We've sent him certain parts of the file, and he's stated, with the consent of his superiors, that he's willing to help us. That will perhaps allow us to gather a few clues."

Captain Barka's phone rang. Commissioner Mazure frowned. He didn't like his meetings to be interrupted, but his associate's look of concentration stifled the comments he was about to make.

". . . Okay! Send me the details immediately via e-mail. Goodbye." Then, addressing the group, she said, "They've identified the victim." Nadia read aloud directly from the e-mail she'd just received. "The victim's name is Monica Revasti. She's originally from Turin, and her parents saw the picture of their daughter early this morning on an Italian television station. One of our people will go question them as soon as we're done with this meeting."

She looked in the direction of Rivera. His family had left Calabria to come to France when he was twelve years old. He spoke fluent Italian.

"Stéphane, I think you are the most qualified to conduct this interrogation."

"All right. We're only two and a half hours from Turin."

"We'll have a briefing before your departure to prepare you for the meeting." She went back to reading. "Monica Revasti was twenty-nine years old and worked as the manager of a travel agency in Turin. She had gone to Grenoble for a very specific medical examination that MUMC, Michallon University Medical Center, has advanced techniques and specialists for. Her examination took place over two days. She came on Wednesday and had another appointment the next day. She never showed up."

"We finally have something solid," announced Fortin with satisfaction.

"We'll go to the hospital right after the meeting. Now Étienne and Jérôme are going to report on their research."

Jérôme Garancher looked at his colleague, who let him know with his eyes that Garancher would do the talking. The archivist liked to talk, and he didn't often have the opportunity to speak in front of such an attentive audience.

"Ladies and gentlemen, we've worked hard with Étienne and Charles to look into other crimes that could be linked to the one we're investigating. We conducted our work over a period of twenty years, starting with the Rhône-Alpes region, expanding to all of France and, since this morning, Europe. Étienne did a quick Internet search for the United States, but there are so many sickos over there that you have to wonder why the country isn't completely depopulated."

Pleased with his touch of humor, he looked at his audience. Two or three of his colleagues forced themselves to conjure up a smile so as not to disappoint him. Even if Jérôme Garancher was pompous, he was still appreciated by those who worked alongside him.

"Unfortunately the results did not reflect the energy we put in. You cannot imagine the number of murders that have taken place in Grenoble and the surrounding area: knives, acid, poison, even piano wire. We've set aside homicides by firearm. We also took another look at the massacre of the members of the Order of the Solar Temple in the Vercors Mountains. But at the moment we've found nothing that resembles the crime we're currently confronting. We kept up with two or three leads, but nothing very substantial so far. We've also contacted our colleagues in Paris. The media coverage of the case is so interesting that we didn't have to insist that they consider our request."

"And so?" Nadia asked.

"So nothing," replied Garancher, somewhat crestfallen. "Twisted bastards in spades, but none who cut their victims up surgically and sew them up after. We'll keep looking, but we're really going to need further evidence."

"It's your job to act before further evidence is provided by a second corpse!" said Mazure impatiently. Then he began again. "Have you pursued doctors? Maybe they can guide us?"

"We've started work on that lead," Fortin went on. "Doctor Blavet is a valuable help, because it's difficult to find a more closed environment. We've brought in two investigators who used to work in the hospital field to speed up the progress. But we have days of work ahead of us."

"Take the necessary time. In any case, we have very few leads to sink our teeth into at the moment."

Chapter 14: Father de Valjoney

Accompanied by Rodolphe Drancey, Nadia Barka walked through streets overwhelmed with sunlight. The previous high temperature records had been smashed.

They had decided to go on foot to the Diocesan Residence, where Father de Valjoney would be meeting with them. They passed by the art museum, which Nadia gazed at longingly. She loved wandering through the galleries, sitting in front of a painting and admiring it. She could spend hours in front of a single work of art and still discover details that astonished her. She went there as often as the opportunity presented itself—it also allowed her to forget, for the space of a visit, her daily cares and the horrors she regularly confronted.

Drancey glanced toward the museum as well and noticed her pensive air. "I'd like to be able to go there, too."

She looked at him in amazement. Drancey was unbeatable in his knowledge of cars, soccer, and firearms, but art?

"Well, yeah, they have AC throughout the building!" And he broke into a hearty laugh.

She shrugged and smiled. "As appalling as ever, you poor bastard! Your wife still has some work to do."

"More than you know. Hélène dragged me here last Sunday, and that's how I know it's air-conditioned. But spending an hour looking at the works of Gaston Chaissac gave me a headache. They looked like my grandnephew's drawings from before he started kindergarten."

"She certainly didn't pick the easiest starting place for tackling art. But keep at it, Rodolphe, and ask her for seventeenth-century Spaniards instead. There's a magnificent Zurbarán triptych."

"Listen, Nadia, I think you're great, but after Chaissac, the next Spaniards I'll go see are the ones from Real Madrid."

Nadia thought it best not to insist. They crossed the Place Lavalette, went down a few steps, and found themselves in front of the imposing Diocesan Residence of Grenoble.

They pushed open the wooden door and stepped into a pleasantly cool atrium. They climbed the stairs and headed for a desk behind which a young woman waited. Her severe attire contrasted with her cheerful face, which was framed by a cascade of red hair.

"Well, the Church is getting younger! I feel my childhood faith stirring," murmured Lieutenant Drancey.

Nadia elbowed him discreetly to shut him up. "Hello, we have an appointment with Bernard de Valjoney."

"Hello. He told me you would be coming. Give me two minutes. I'll go get him, and he'll welcome you himself." She set off down a long hallway, under Rodolphe's intense gaze.

"What would Hélène say?" whispered Nadia.

"Nothing, we're among priests."

"Fine," said Nadia. "You let me do the talking during the interview. I don't feel like having you antagonize our contact. We don't know who we're dealing with yet."

The young woman was already returning, accompanied by a tall man of ecclesiastical stoutness, though he was far from equaling the monks in the *images d'Épinal* or in the ads for monastic cheeses. The clergyman came toward them and offered a vigorous handshake.

"Welcome to the Diocese. I'm Father Bernard de Valjoney, at your service."

The policeman shook the father's hand, more impressed than he wanted to show. He'd expected, for no reason at all, a short, weedy man with a sly look. He realized in a split second that from now on he should beware of his prejudices. Lost in thought, he noticed that his colleague and the priest had started to move off down the corridor, chatting like two old friends. He accompanied them into a vast room, lit by the sun streaming in through a large window looking out onto a patio. In spite of the size of the room, the ambiance was cozy. The clergyman didn't sit down at his table, but invited them instead to settle on a sofa in one corner of the room. He pulled up an armchair and sat facing them. He let them speak.

"We thank you for the time you're devoting to us. We're at an impasse on this murder, and we're looking for any clue that could help us move forward. Did you have time to examine the file we sent to you this morning?"

"Yes, I studied it, and I reflected on it. Needless to say, the murder and the place where the corpse was discovered have badly shaken the Christian community. I'll let you ask your questions."

"Thank you. First of all, do you have any knowledge of similar murders in the Diocese of Grenoble in the last few decades?"

"No, this is the first time a body has been found murdered in such a building during the last forty years of the Diocese of Grenoble-Vienne. The last case goes back to 1970. A man slit his wife's throat on the altar of a church near Saint-Marcellin. The man had escaped from a psychiatric ward and was convinced that his wife had fornicated with the devil. So he'd sacrificed her. The poor woman had had a number of lovers in her life, but the devil surely wasn't one of them! The killer has been dead for more than ten years. He'd acted on an insane impulse and not as coldly as the criminal we seek."

"Do you think the crime could be linked to a satanic ritual?"

"Do you believe in Satan?" the priest asked the disconcerted young woman.

"Those are fables for children, zealots, and clergy!" Drancey interjected rudely.

Nadia stared at him in dismay. He was insulting the man who had welcomed them. But Father de Valjoney gave him a long look and a smile that took the policeman aback.

"We don't know each other, but you have a great quality: conviction. The devil has indeed been used to frighten children, entire populations, and even certain clergymen, it's true. However, it is not merely a legend. I won't go into details, but there does exist something you could call devil, demons, or forces of evil. My aim is not to convince you of this, and I will ask you to believe me just for the space of a few minutes. We have an exorcist here. A large number of the brothers or sisters who come to see him are in fact redirected to psychologists or psychiatrists we work with. In some rare instances, we must contend with cases of possession, which are expressed with the utmost physical violence. And the words these possessed persons say do not come from them, for they speak of things they do not know when they are in a conscious state. All of which is to say, monsieur, that there are groups of devotees to Satan who are prepared to make terrible sacrifices to serve him."

A shiver traveled up Lieutenant Drancey's back. This priest was certainly convincing. Drancey decided to leave his religious, or rather agnostic, beliefs to one side and listen to the clergyman's testimony.

"I studied your photos with care. Moreover, the very morning of the crime, I went to the scene as soon as the police reopened it. I didn't find anything that suggested human sacrifice dedicated to some hellish deity. First of all, no trace of blood was found around the body. The victims' blood, most often animals', is used either to draw kabbalistic symbols or to cover the body or face, a symbol of both death for the man and life for the demon. Next, no evidence was apparent on the ground. In general, there is a whole ceremony, wherein esoteric shapes are mapped onto very precise places. The position of the body was also very unremarkable. The murderer didn't try to put her in the shape of a cross, or worse, shatter her limbs to shatter the cross, the symbol of Christ's power."

"And the type of murder?" asked Nadia. "The heart removed from the body?"

"That is indeed the most troubling point. Sometimes certain animals' hearts are torn out. The famous Mayan or Aztec priests sacrificed their victims that way and offered their hearts to the gods. But here, the extraction was clean, according to the coroner's report, the heart wasn't found, and above all the victim was sewn up again. Furthermore, the murder itself didn't take place in the baptistery."

"What's your conclusion, then?" asked the policeman.

"The killer is a sick man who doubtless had a very precise reason for bringing the corpse here. But for me, the crime, as horrible as it is, is not satanic in origin. You have to find something else."

"You don't have any detail that could help us?" he asked.

"Soon I must meet with Pierre-Marie de Morot, a peerless historian who knows the cathedral's history throughout the centuries. If you'll permit me to divulge part of the file to him, we will try to understand what connection there may be between the murder and the location—if there is one."

Back out in the heat of the city, the two police officers looked at each other, disappointed by their interview's conclusions. They'd silently hoped the priest would give them a lead. But they were sinking further into mystery and ambiguity.

Chapter 15: Second Vision

Sophie admired the city spread out before them. Fatigue weighed down their legs, but they'd had a wonderful day. They had left early to take advantage of the morning cool, agreeing to meet at six thirty in the morning in front of her apartment. Carrying a substantial supply of water and salads prepared the day before, all four of them—Sophie, Julien, and two friends—had started off to tackle the slopes of Chartreuse.

Grenoble had the advantage of close proximity to the mountains. In less than an hour of walking, the group could find themselves on a hiking trail leading into what felt like the wilderness. They came to the Bastille, that famous Grenoble fortification that had kept watch over the city for years, then four hours after their departure, reached the Place Lavalette. Even though Place Lavalette was strategically located on a rocky outcrop nearly twelve hundred yards in the air and overlooked Grenoble, it had never been used to defend the city—it had, however, become a famous hiking destination.

They had walked along the ridge, passed through the village of Sappey, and then picnicked in an alpine meadow in the shade of a beech tree, benefiting from the relative coolness of the mountains.

The group then had walked back down the mountain the same way they'd hiked up. They sat on the terrace of the Bastille's scenic restaurant, joining the horde of city dwellers who'd climbed the slopes for this legendary Sunday outing.

Sophie observed the hikers. Some were soaked with sweat, having braved the heat to run up the mountain. Others, sporting heels or even stilettos, had unquestionably taken the cable car linking the city center to the Bastille.

"Here, some nice cold beer for the adventurers!" François called to Julien. François had just changed T-shirts under the indignant stare of a senior at the neighboring table. The man was quickly calmed by his wife, who understood that youth enjoys such liberties.

"One second," said Julien, who had collapsed into a chair. "Sophie, between Friday's aerobics and today's hike, I'm beat."

"When you go find the waiter, get a beer for me, too," Sophie told François, who looked at her in surprise.

"Okay, I'm going on a mission. What about you, Céline? What do you want to drink?"

Red with exhaustion and the heat, Céline thought for a few seconds. "A Perrier for me, please, with a slice of lemon and no ice."

"I'm off," said François. "If I don't come back in ten minutes, send backup."

A second round followed the first. They'd been lucky enough to snag a waiter passing by their table at exactly the right moment.

Céline, Julien's childhood friend, had met Sophie and François for the first time that day, but already she felt at ease with them. François and his jokes had animated the group; Sophie, a seasoned mountaineer, had kept an eye on everyone, offering encouragement and sound advice. As for Julien, he had been in his element keeping everybody happy. Céline had rarely felt as relaxed as she did at that moment, even if she did dread the time when they'd have to get up and finish the descent to Sophie's apartment, where they'd left their belongings that morning. As if on purpose, Sophie signaled for their departure.

They rose stiffly from their seats. Hisses of pain, held back until now, escaped from all their mouths. After the first step, the aches seemed more endurable. The group went back out to the open walkway and began the descent, amid the Sunday hikers.

"That was an excellent hike," Céline told them. "Thank you so much for inviting me."

"It was a pleasure," replied François. "Julien painted us such a flattering picture of you that we couldn't refuse."

"And?" asked Céline hesitantly.

"He was right, of course!" added François with a big smile.

They'd gone down a good part of the trail when Julien stopped short. François narrowly avoided running into him.

"What's up with you?" François asked.

Julien's gaze was fixed on a group of about fifteen people heading down two switchbacks below. He pointed them out.

"Can you explain what we're supposed to be looking at?" asked Céline.

"Down there, the girl . . ." said Julien.

"There's a dozen of them. And you already have two that are at least cute," commented François.

Julien didn't grin at his friend's joke, as if he hadn't even heard it. "The girl in the white sundress!"

Sophie's senses immediately went on high alert. She peered at the group disappearing around the bend in the trail with heightened focus. She hadn't seen the girl in the white dress her friend was talking about, but she'd caught only a glimpse of the hikers.

"What was she like?" Sophie asked.

"Brunette, with curly, shoulder-length hair, a white sundress, sandals, also white. But that's all I saw. I have to have it clear in my mind." He took off his backpack, shoved it into François's arms, and ran off down the trail.

"Where are you going?" cried Sophie.

"I have to know!" he answered without turning around, running away.

Julien had rushed off without thinking about what he'd do once he caught up to the young woman. He wouldn't have especially noticed her if she hadn't looked so pointedly at him. She was at a distance, but he was sure that was her. She'd stopped walking, turned her head, and looked at him for several seconds. It was much too long to be random. And he'd felt the same sensation when he'd followed the Grenoble baptistery victim. A sort of inner summons.

So now he had to know. He had to know if he was going crazy, if these encounters were coincidences, or if something or someone wanted to send him a message. The third possibility struck him as delusional, but he couldn't discount anything anymore.

He ran for a good minute, and he could catch up to her by the next curve, one of the last before reaching the Isère riverfront. As he went around the last bend, he finally saw the group fifty yards ahead of him. They were all going into the Church of Saint-Laurent, which had been deconsecrated and transformed into an archaeological museum. While excavating, the archaeologists had brought to light older and older layers, at last uncovering a Carolingian crypt and a necropolis from the Gallo-Roman period.

Julien slowed down and caught his breath. *Apparently I'm a regular at churches and museums*, he said to himself as he hurried under the church portico. The shade gave him an immediate sensation of well-being, but he didn't stop to enjoy it. He was looking for the young woman in the white dress.

One part of the group had just gone into the church, and she wasn't with the people lined up at the ticket window. He rummaged through his pockets—his wallet was still in his backpack.

"Entry to the museum is free, monsieur," said an employee sitting behind the counter. "I just need to know your postal code."

Julien walked quickly toward the window. "38000."

"Here you are, monsieur, and enjoy your visit. I rarely see anyone in such a hurry to visit our beautiful museum," she added with a little laugh.

"Thank you."

Julien nearly snatched the ticket and rushed to the church entrance. He climbed a few stairs and reached a platform, and was struck for a moment by the sight before him. There was no longer a floor under the nave but instead a maze of half-ruined or reconstructed walls, proof that this place was a thousand years old. He quickly realized that no woman in a white dress was among the visitors. And she wouldn't have had time to go farther inside unless she'd run, which would have made no sense.

He left the museum, disoriented. The last visitors were collecting their audio guides. He headed toward an imposing-looking woman he'd noticed when he'd come back out.

"Do you have a woman wearing a white dress in your group?"

The woman looked at him, first surprised, then with a disapproving frown. He realized how cavalier and brusque his question sounded. He tried again. "Please excuse me for how abruptly I addressed you just now. I was supposed to meet a friend to visit the museum, and I got here late. Since she told me she was going to participate in a guided tour, I thought maybe she'd joined you."

The woman brightened when she heard this much more polite request from the man in front of her. Julien used his most distressed expression to try to elicit a quick response.

"No, monsieur, I haven't seen a young woman in a dress. Perhaps she grew tired of waiting for you."

Julien couldn't tell whether she was sorry or there was a touch of wickedness in her reply, but he didn't care. He left the museum. He headed back to the trail, jogged the last hundred or so yards, and came out on the Rue Saint-Laurent, at the foot of the mountain.

He pulled himself together. He'd been mistaken in thinking that she was with the group visiting the museum. She must have continued on into the city while he'd wasted his time looking in the church.

Lost in thought, he jumped when he heard François's voice.

"So, did you find her?"

He noticed his friends waiting for him nearby. They were looking at him questioningly. He walked up to them.

"No, I missed her. She didn't go to the museum. She must have continued on down, and now she's probably somewhere in the city."

"We should be able to find her," said Sophie. "Assuming she's in Grenoble, she has to take either the Rue Saint-Laurent or the Quai Xavier-Jouvin, where she'll then have to take the bridge over the Isère. She's at most two or three minutes ahead of us. By running in those directions, we might be able to spot her."

"Run?" asked Céline. "I'm worn out! Is it okay if I stay here with the bags? That way you'll be able to move faster."

"Good idea," Julien affirmed. "I'll take the Rue Saint-Laurent, François and Sophie can check the other two ways. We'll call each other in five minutes. If nobody's found her by then, I think she's definitely gone."

After five minutes, their phones all rang. Fifteen minutes later, they rejoined Céline, empty-handed. They looked at Julien apologetically. Sophie briefly explained their friend's hitherto inexplicable reasons for the pursuit. He hadn't wanted to talk about it during their hike, but Sophie judged it necessary to bring them up to speed. They sat down on a bench, speechless. Julien broke the silence.

"I might be crazy. What do they call people who hear voices and have hallucinations? Schizophrenics, right?"

"Tell us instead about what you saw," said Céline, cutting him off. "Sophie went quickly through what happened to you this week."

"She did the right thing. I saw this woman, also in white, and I felt, how do I put this . . . *called*. She was far away, but I was convinced I would recognize her if I saw her again."

"And you think she could be one of the killer's next victims?" asked François.

"Well, shit, I don't know! I'm not an expert in the sixth sense!" shouted Julien, losing his temper. "I supposedly have the gift of seeing unknown victims of an unknown killer? That's so freaking stupid!" He let several seconds go by, but no one interrupted his train of thought.

"Sorry, that had nothing to do with you, and you even helped me out. But this thing is putting me on edge. Imagine for one second that, in some way I won't even try to understand, this girl is the second victim of the maniac stalking the city. What should I do?"

"I suggest we go home. Then, we all sit down and make a decision. Walking will likely do us good and put our heads on straight."

By mutual agreement, they got up from their bench and went to Sophie's place on the Rue Montorge. They were no longer thinking about the day's aches and pains and secretly wondered what was causing their friend's hallucinations. They had every confidence in him, but this precognition business was hardly believable.

Chapter 16: The Lead

Nadia ended the call on her cell phone. She put it back in her pants pocket and grabbed her office phone.

"Give me Commissioner Mazure. This is Captain Barka. It's urgent. This is in connection with Operation Open Heart."

Whoever had named the battle plan hadn't demonstrated extreme creativity.

"He's on the line, Captain. I'm transferring you."

"Thanks. Hello, Commissioner, this is Captain Barka."

"Good evening, Nadia. I imagine you have something new if you're calling me on this line."

"Yes, I just received a rather strange telephone call, to say the least. The man who had come to see us on Friday, Julien Lombard, called me. He told me he saw a woman, under conditions identical to those of his encounter with Monica Revasti."

"Where did he see her?"

"On the trail that leads down from the Bastille and ends up at the Church of Saint-Laurent."

"Okay, and then?"

"He didn't manage to catch her. He was with friends who helped him look for her, but she, well, truly disappeared."

"And did his friends also see this woman?"

"No, he's the only one who noticed her."

Mazure was silent, reflecting on what his colleague had just told him. "What impression did you get of him on the phone?"

"Sincere. He himself was frightened by what he was telling me. But he wanted me to share it, even if it meant sounding deranged."

"Have you continued your investigations into him?"

"Yes, and they haven't found anything abnormal in what they've been able to collect. No psychiatric trouble, no history of cult membership, normal social life, friends. Nothing that makes him a pathological liar."

"And what do you intend to do?"

"I want to give it a shot. The woman he's talking about vanished near the archaeological museum, which happens to be an old church. It's the structural similarities with the first murder that make me want to dig deeper—a museum, an ancient religious building."

"He could have made this story up."

"He could have, of course, but why? Besides, we have no serious leads. So I risk nothing in going for it. I'm going to take Lieutenants Fortin and Drancey with me. That should be enough."

"What do you plan to do, exactly?"

"Hide out around the church overnight. There's only one entrance. I wanted to keep you informed."

"Go ahead, if you feel something. You have the instincts." And then he suddenly added, "What about the lead on the Italian victim?"

"Rivera got ahold of me this afternoon. Nothing came of it. He spent a long time talking with Monica's parents. They described her as a girl without a story who had traveled to Grenoble for medical tests."

"It was the first time she'd been to Grenoble?"

"No, she'd done an internship with a travel agency two or three years ago. The Italian police launched an inquiry to validate what the parents told us and make sure the girl didn't have a secret life. But we don't really believe she did."

"So the victim would have been chosen at random?"

"At random, or according to criteria we don't know about."

Mazure had a sudden thought. "This Lombard who sees the victims, did he describe the woman he followed today?"

"Not in detail, Commissioner. The call was brief."

"Call him back, or go see him and question him about it. Also, before you go on stakeout tonight, leave an officer on guard in front of his house. We can clear him completely that way; I don't think he's connected to this crime, but no point in taking risks. And be careful. If you're right, you could find yourself face-to-face with a particularly dangerous individual."

"Thank you, Commissioner. But this wouldn't be the first time. And I'm really counting on this lead to move us forward. You see what we're reduced to!"

Chapter 17: The Abduction

At the end of her rope, the woman started screaming. Someone would hear her eventually, then find her. She cried out again, close to tearing her vocal cords. She banged with all her strength on the raw wood of her prison door. The exposed splinters lacerated the skin of her palms, but that was the least of her worries.

Would someone come let her out, for the love of God! But God seemed absent for the moment. Exhausted, she stopped, slid down the wall, and, head in her hands, began to sob. She let herself go for a while, gradually becoming aware of her terrifying situation. That same morning she'd been filled with joy for her future marriage. Denis had just officially asked her to join her life with his. He always used rather overblown turns of phrase, but she loved it and never made fun of him. They'd spent the night picking the date and location and drafting a guest list.

And then suddenly, she'd found herself plunged into this nightmare. All the events from the early afternoon came back to her, like a bad film playing on an endless loop.

She had just had an x-ray at South Hospital, in Échirolles. She'd taken a stupid fall just after lunch while coming down the stairway of her building and had felt a sharp pain. Denis had taken her directly to the emergency room, but she'd discouraged him from staying with her. The wait was almost two hours, and he had a tennis tournament. The doctor had reassured her—she hadn't broken anything, it was just a big bruise to take care of. "You can easily go home and enjoy the rest of the day," the doctor had said. Enjoy the day! If only she'd known.

In the lobby, she'd tried to call a taxi to go back to the city center. She was supposed to meet her mother and had just realized she was running late. She'd gotten irritated on the phone, then left the lobby in a rush.

That's when she'd met him. He'd seemed so normal. One thing had surprised her, though—he had been wearing sunglasses with very dark lenses inside a building. But since he'd offered to drop her off somewhere if she wanted, she'd considered his proposal and not his hidden eyes. He had to be a good fifty years old but carried it well, still in good shape and rather seductive. But at that moment, she lived only for Denis's declaration, and this man's seductive potential did nothing for her. He had taken off his white coat, and from that she'd deduced he was a doctor and that he'd just finished his shift. She remembered the time, because it was the same time she was supposed to meet her mother, who needed to give her some papers before leaving for the airport.

"Where shall I drop you?" he'd asked.

"I'm meeting someone at Place Grenette in . . . four minutes," she'd said, looking at her watch.

"We may not get there in four minutes, but doubtless more quickly than if you have to wait for the bus. I have to go by Place Victor-Hugo, so I'll be able to drop you off nearby."

Camille had sighed contentedly as she'd followed her rescuer. She'd made a quick phone call to her mother to ask her to hang on for five to ten minutes. They'd stopped in front of a blue Mercedes. She'd gotten in and settled into the comfortable leather seat. He'd started the engine and turned on the air-conditioning to chase away the interior's stifling heat. He had been shivering—strange to shiver in such heat. Now she understood, but at the time it hadn't alarmed her.

They'd left the hospital parking lot and then headed for the highway that skirted Grenoble to the south. The city center was due north. She had been surprised and let him know.

"Don't worry," he'd replied, "there are fewer red lights this way, and you'll be on time for your appointment."

She'd glanced at the car's speedometer. He had been going eighty miles an hour instead of fifty, but she didn't have a sense of his speed. She'd looked at the driver and had grown uneasy. The man's face had been covered in sweat, yet she'd noticed that his hair remained impeccable. A blond wig, he was wearing a wig! She'd cleared her throat.

"I can be a little late. Don't you think you're going kind of fast?"

He hadn't answered her. They were already within sight of the Catane Bridge. *The man was going to exit the highway and head back to the city center.* That thought had reassured her. But he hadn't slowed down as he'd approached the exit and continued on the same road, even faster, zigzagging between the cars. Camille had felt fear overtake her and raised her voice.

"Stop! Stop and let me out!"

The man had looked at her, but she hadn't been able to make out his eyes behind the sunglasses. Panicked, she'd taken out her phone. She'd try to call for help. Quick as a flash, the man snatched her phone and slid it into his jacket pocket. Beside herself, Camille had thrown herself on him to recover her property. The man had struck her violently on the chin, leaving her half stunned. In a state of semiconsciousness, she'd seen him exit the highway. They'd stopped on a road along the Isère. That was it, then, she'd stumbled onto a rapist. She'd mustered all her willpower. She wouldn't let him do it. She'd decided to continue pretending to be unconscious, and she'd jump on him when he tried to assault her.

The man had gotten out of his seat. He was probably going around the car to the passenger side. He'd locked the doors, walked away from the Mercedes, and approached another car parked under a bush. She'd barely opened her eyes to spy, but hadn't recognized the model. He'd opened the trunk, rummaged around for something, and come back toward her. This was it, he was drawing close to her again. She'd wait until the right moment to strike: once, but violently. She'd taken kickboxing classes in college.

The door had opened, and she'd waited to be pulled out of the car. But instead she'd felt a sudden sting in her arm. She'd felt herself sink into unconsciousness.

The coolness of the wall brought her back to reality. The pale light provided by a tiny basement window had disappeared. Night had long since fallen. Her concept of time was fading, as was her sense of the facts. Her kidnapper had of course taken all of her personal belongings, starting with her cell phone. But she still had her clothes. He hadn't raped her. That thought suddenly sent a cold shiver down her spine. Why, then, had the stranger abducted her? What was he planning? Dark images came to mind. The first was that of a young Austrian girl locked up in a secret basement room for eight years. If that was the case, maybe she could escape. Maybe she'd stumbled onto a cult and would be the victim of who knew what kind of ceremony. Or maybe . . . maybe what? She didn't know what the future held for her. Slumping, Camille cowered in a corner, hugged her knees, and sobbed silently.

Chapter 18: More Details

Nadia dialed the number once again and got voice mail. She didn't leave a message and hung up. Julien Lombard had turned off his phone. She'd rung his doorbell with Rodolphe Drancey and Étienne Fortin, but no one had answered. The apartment seemed to be empty. She'd assigned an officer to the door of the building to notify them in case the man came back.

She'd then obtained Sophie Dupas's number. Perhaps he was with her? But Julien's friend had assured Nadia that she hadn't seen him since the end of their afternoon hike.

Nadia certainly didn't think he was guilty, but she still would have loved to have him under supervision that night. She couldn't neglect anything.

The group headed for the Church of Saint-Laurent to lay the groundwork for their nighttime operation. "Satisfaction" suddenly blared, as if the Rolling Stones had started playing behind them. Rodolphe Drancey took his iPhone out of his jacket and picked up.

"It's for you, Nadia."

"Thanks, Rod. Next time, put your ringer on vibrate. We're on a stakeout, so a little discretion wouldn't be a bad thing."

She took the phone her embarrassed colleague held out to her. "Captain Barka here." She listened to the caller and felt her excitement mount. "When was the disappearance reported? . . . 7:30 p.m.? Call Garancher for me and tell him to be in the briefing room in fifteen minutes . . . He's already there? Perfect! I'll be joining him shortly."

She hung up and returned the cell phone to Drancey. "Someone has just reported a disappearance this afternoon. A young woman, twenty-eight years old."

"Do you know who?"

"Camille Saint-Forge."

"The lawyer's daughter?"

"The one and the same. Not the sort to run away, according to her mother. I'll let you pick the hideout. I'm going to make a quick visit to headquarters to see if I can get some intel. I'll come back as soon as possible. Étienne, hand me the car keys, please."

Captain Barka pulled up to the police station fifteen minutes later. She double-parked the car in front of the main entrance and tossed the keys to the officer on guard. "Thanks for parking it a little better for me."

Without waiting for a response, she hurried into the lobby, speed walked through the hallways, and entered the room serving as headquarters.

Five people were already present: Jérôme Garancher, another squad lieutenant, Maître Saint-Forge, and a woman with a face ravaged by worry, who must have been Saint-Forge's wife. She knew the lawyer's face well, having run into him numerous times at the courthouse. They introduced the fifth person to her as Denis de Tardieu, Camille Saint-Forge's fiancé. Nadia sat down.

"I'm Captain Barka, in charge of the investigation into the crime at the baptistery. I know this introduction is rather abrupt. Even if there's only a tiny chance that your daughter's disappearance is connected to this case, we want to get involved as quickly as possible. Tell me what happened this afternoon."

The woman, who was dressed in a designer suit, dissolved into tears. Her husband took her gently by the shoulders. Nadia was surprised to see this beacon of justice with the thundering courtroom voice be so tender. Madame Saint-Forge took a handkerchief out of her Louis Vuitton handbag, dabbed at her eyes, and described yet again her phone calls with her daughter.

"I was supposed to meet Camille this afternoon at five thirty. We'd arranged to have tea at an outdoor mall near the Place Grenette. I was supposed to give her some papers . . . And she never arrived."

"When did you see or hear her for the last time?"

"She had a stupid fall and hurt her ankle badly. So Denis took her to South Hospital in the early afternoon to get x-rays."

"And you left her there alone?" asked Nadia.

The young man who was with them, face marked by guilt, spoke. "It's all my fault!"

"Why is that?"

"I never should've left her alone. There were a lot of people waiting, and I had a tennis match at my club at four o'clock. She told me to go. She was supposed to take a taxi back to Grenoble, but I shouldn't have listened to her."

"It had nothing to do with you," the lawyer cut in. "When Camille decides something, nothing can stop her."

Madame Saint-Forge continued. "Camille called me around four o'clock, telling me it would be her turn soon. Then she called me a little before 5:30 to reassure me and tell me that her injury wasn't serious. But she was very annoyed, because we had arranged to meet, and she couldn't find a taxi."

"We'd planned to spend a week relaxing in the Canary Islands, and we were supposed to leave by six o'clock at the latest," explained Maître Saint-Forge. "My daughter found a good quality apartment that she wanted to rent over by Meylan, but she needed a cosign from us. I'd prepared the papers."

"And then?" asked Captain Barka.

"She called me back two or three minutes later to tell me a doctor who was leaving the hospital had offered to take her to the city center."

"Try to remember exactly what she said to you. The words are important."

The woman took a few seconds to dive back into her conversation from that afternoon.

"The call was very brief. She told me she'd be there within fifteen minutes and that she'd have time to hug me before we left on vacation."

"That's all?"

"Yes."

"And then?"

"After fifteen minutes, I called her back. The phone rang, but she didn't answer. I left her a message, telling myself she must be running to the coffee shop, and she hadn't bothered to pick up. Five minutes later, I called again. But that time, I went directly to voice mail. The phone had been shut off."

"When did you decide to notify the police?"

"First I called Denis. It wasn't easy to get ahold of him, because he was in the middle of a match. As soon as he found out Camille had disappeared, he went charging over to South Hospital. One of the receptionists remembered seeing the young woman leaving with a blond man."

"I asked to send a team to the scene as soon as they gave us the news," Garancher cut in. "We should also have a copy of the surveillance tapes of the hospital parking lot any minute now."

"Go see where they are, Jérôme, and gather the initial evidence as quickly as possible," said Nadia.

"They left over an hour ago. It shouldn't be too long now."

The lawyer broke in. "You're worrying me, Captain. Do you think the risk is as great as all that?"

"I'm going to speak frankly, Maître. Like all people who read the paper and own a television set, you are no doubt aware of the crime that was committed near the cathedral. What we haven't revealed to the press—and I will ask all three of you to keep the information to yourselves—is that the victim's heart was removed by the murderer."

Camille's mother shrieked, then started to whimper. "No, not my daughter, not my little girl."

"I'm not saying that your daughter is in the hands of the killer, madame, but I want to leave no stone unturned. Do you have a picture of Camille with you?"

Denis de Tardieu took out his wallet and removed a small photograph, which he handed to the police officers. "We took it yesterday in a photo booth, just before I proposed."

Nadia grabbed it and looked it over quickly. A rather pretty girl, a little haughty looking but not excessively arrogant. She handed the photo to the officer next to her.

"Make a copy and give the original back to the gentleman. I think he's fond of it."

Jérôme Garancher came into the room, followed by a woman with a vigorous, almost masculine appearance and a certain charm. Captain Barka gave her the floor.

"I've just come back from the hospital. I left Roger and Alberto there. They're still questioning the staff."

She addressed herself to the missing woman's parents. "Your daughter left with a blond man, between fifty and sixty years old, not bad looking according to two nurse's aides who saw them. Does your daughter know a man who might answer to this brief description?"

"Absolutely not, or at least she never mentioned him to me. He just happened to be there at the right moment, or that's what Camille thought."

Marie Bauchard continued her report. "According to our witnesses, he's not a doctor at South Hospital. He was waiting there for two or three hours, going back and forth between the lobby and the parking lot or the adjacent hallways. One of the nurses on duty asked him what he was looking for, and he replied that he was waiting for an acquaintance who was supposed to get out today. The nurse told herself he must be from another clinic and went back to her rounds."

"She didn't show more curiosity than that?" the lawyer interjected sharply.

"From what we understood, monsieur, the emergency room doesn't lack for work, especially on a Sunday. I'll continue. They then went out to the parking lot, and a patient taking a walk saw them getting into a blue Mercedes."

"How can he be sure?" asked Nadia.

"He'd noticed Camille Saint-Forge. 'A pretty little package' is what he told us."

"So we should be able to find her thanks to the car."

"I'm getting there. The surveillance images just confirmed what the patient told us. I'll show them to you so that you can formally identify your daughter," she added, addressing the parents. "But the radiologist, whom we managed to reach, already confirmed to us that your daughter was indeed wearing the same red outfit as on the tape."

"Yes, that's what she'd put on before leaving," confirmed Camille's future husband.

"We immediately made inquiries about the car. It belongs to a surgeon who was operating at the time of the disappearance. He became aware of the theft when he tried to leave around nine o'clock. The keys and his registration card had vanished from his jacket pocket."

"But how would the kidnapper have gotten access to them?"

"The staff told us that anyone who knew where the locker room was and had a lot of nerve and something to force a basic lock with could do it," explained Marie.

"Marie, when did you gather this information?" asked Nadia.

"Just before coming here to see you."

"Good, we'll look into the car. It's eleven o'clock and the abduction took place at five thirty. It's no use putting up roadblocks—he could already be in Paris if he'd wanted to flee with Camille. Highly possible since the kidnapper is unlikely to have left the *département* if he's the one we're thinking of. Even so, we're going to ask them to patrol the region. Inform all the squads out on the beat. Call Commissioner Mazure, too, so that he can request support from the *gendarmerie*. And you, Marie, go join Roger and Alberto at South Hospital to learn more. You've already done great work. Keep it up."

"Okay, Captain, I'm off again."

Marie Bauchard left the office while Garancher set up the parking lot video surveillance film. The quality was mediocre, but Monsieur and Madame Saint-Forge recognized their daughter without hesitation.

"That's definitely her!" exclaimed the excited mother.

"Can you zoom in on the bastard's face?" asked the lawyer.

Garancher did so. The film quality prevented them from distinguishing his features accurately.

"Given the mane he's got and the age the witnesses gave, I'd be tempted to say he's wearing a wig," noted Garancher.

"Make me a few enlargements and give them to all the teams out there. I'm going to call Commissioner Mazure so that he can distribute these photos to the press and media. They won't need any coaxing to print them in their papers or broadcast them on a loop. Do you give me permission to include the picture of your daughter, Camille?"

"Of course. Use the photo Denis just gave you," agreed Saint-Forge.

Captain Barka stood up, signaling the interview was over—at least as far as she was concerned.

"Rest assured the search for your daughter is our priority. We'll keep you posted on how the investigation is going. For your part, the second you have anything new, even if it's just a detail that's come back to you, call us."

She nodded to the missing woman's parents and fiancé, who left the room. Then she addressed Garancher. "Find me a dozen pictures of girls who look more or less like Camille Saint-Forge. Print them for me photo booth style, like the missing woman's. And bring me all of it within the next fifteen minutes!"

"Fifteen minutes?"

"Yes, with all the material at your team's disposal, that should be more than enough time."

"And how is that going to help you?"

"It'll tell me if I'm being lied to or not."

Chapter 19: No Doubt

Julien paced the streets of Grenoble, partially deserted at this late hour. He'd just spent several hours with Céline. They'd eaten a quickly prepared salad and discussed the past few years they'd spent apart, their loves, and obviously the hallucinations he'd suffered the last few days. Very tactfully, Céline had advised him to see a doctor. He still felt a chill thinking about it. Of all illnesses, psychiatric ones scared him the most. *Maybe because I've always been in good health*, he said to himself.

He stood on the porch of his building. As he entered the building's access code on the keypad, a shape emerged from the shadows and grasped his arm.

"Are you Julien Lombard?"

He tried to escape the stranger's grip, but the man held him firmly. His attacker put a hand in his pocket and took out a wallet. He opened it and showed him a tricolor card.

"Police, follow me, please."

Julien regained his composure and replied with confidence, "If you tell me who you are, what you want with me, and that you'll let me go afterward, I'll come with you without resistance. Did Captain Barka send you?"

The policeman hesitated for a second, then nodded. "Yes, that's right. I'm Lieutenant Campet. We've been looking for you for several hours, but you were unreachable and unfindable."

"Maybe, but there's no law against turning off a phone and going to dinner with friends, is there? Fine, where do we have to go?"

"I'm escorting you to the Rue Saint-Laurent. Captain Barka is waiting there for you. Come on, my car is parked a little farther down the street."

Saint-Laurent! His phone call had been taken seriously, then. He climbed into the unmarked car, a black Clio three door. When the policeman turned the ignition and took off, Julien thought to himself that the engine must not be standard. He instinctively checked that his seat belt was buckled and took advantage of the short ride by telling himself he would never again have the opportunity to see the Grenoble streets go by so quickly.

Even so, he was relieved to get out of the car. Nadia Barka was waiting for them at the corner of the Rue Saint-Laurent and the Rue Sappey. A man was walking away from her, limping and screaming insults.

"Did you have a problem, Captain?"

"Oh, no, but the jerk proved a bit too insistent with his advances. Sometimes I'm calm and then other times, not so much." Then, turning toward Julien Lombard, she said, "Sorry to have intruded on your evening, but I need you. Follow me. We'll go sit in the car."

For a moment, Julien felt dread at the thought of being subjected to Lieutenant Campet's driving again, and he was relieved when he saw the policewoman take an envelope—not a set of keys—out of her bomber jacket, then pull a dozen ID photos from it. She turned on the dome light and showed the photos to him. He understood immediately.

"A woman disappeared this afternoon, and you want to know if I can identify her—correct?"

"Aren't you perceptive! That's right. Take your time, and tell me if one of these people is the person you saw or thought you saw this afternoon."

Julien was about to find out if he'd been dreaming earlier. To the depths of his soul, he hoped he wouldn't recognize any of them. That would be much more reassuring. He sat back to take full advantage of the dim car light.

He reviewed them slowly. He paused at the fifth one and paled. He had absolutely no doubt—the woman in the photo had the same intensity in her expression and the same happiness emanating from her. This made him heartsick.

When Nadia saw the mood change on the face of the man sitting next to her, she was convinced that he'd immediately recognized her. He handed the photo back to the policewoman.

"That's her."

"Indeed. You are astonishing, Monsieur Lombard. Either you're a psychic or you're bound up with the kidnapper."

Julien couldn't stand this accusation leveled at him in the middle of the night and reacted forcefully. "I'm doing all I can to help you find the killer, even if it makes me look like a crackpot, and that's all you've got? Insults? The next time I encounter the paranormal like this, I'll keep it between me and my psychiatrist, and you can sort out your own damn clues."

Nadia gently laid a hand on his arm. "I don't believe the second hypothesis I just stated, but know that the question has to be asked, even if we can eliminate it quickly. The woman in the photo is named Camille Saint-Forge."

"I don't think I've met her before."

"She's twenty-eight years old and an associate at an architectural firm."

"No, really I haven't. When did she disappear?"

"We know the precise time of her abduction and even have images collected from a closed-circuit internal surveillance camera. She was taken at 5:26 from the parking lot at South Hospital."

Julien considered this for a bit. "Five thirty. That matches the time I saw her, because it was definitely her. Then she disappeared. But if you have pictures that prove she was in the parking lot, who did I see, or what did I see?"

Nadia Barka was quiet, pondering the answers now available to them. She was convinced that Julien Lombard wasn't lying. She had almost fifteen years of experience with the police and had always demonstrated astute judgment. Campet was waiting outside the car and lighting his third cigarette.

Julien was stunned. He broke the silence. "Number one, I am neither crazy nor schizophrenic, which is somewhat reassuring to me. I was already envisioning myself at the psychiatric hospital in Saint-Egrève. Number two, I did in fact see these women gesturing to me, whereas you have proof that the second one was several miles away. Who is sending me these visions, provided they really are visions? And why me? And finally, why did I see her on the slopes of Chartreuse when she was abducted at another location? Does it mean her body will be brought here?"

"With respect to the last point, that's what we want to check. You'd seen the previous victim, Monica Revasti, go into the cathedral, and we found her in the baptistery, which is practically adjacent."

"So her name was Monica. But I'd seen her calling me during the night."

"The night isn't over yet, Monsieur Lombard."

"Stop, that's terrifying. To know that a woman could call to me when she's being killed and not be able to do anything!"

"For a reason none of us knows right now, you've been chosen. By whom? Why? It's a mystery. But if she will be killed, that's what will happen. So if you have that nightmare, look at everything carefully. It might be a message sent to help us find this killer who's running rampant at the moment."

"I don't have a choice anyway, do I?"

"I'm not the one who put you in this situation, Monsieur Lombard, but someone who wants to help us did. So, play your role. Maybe you'll be able to save lives—I hope!"

"You're right. But you can't keep me from stressing over this situation."

She stared directly into his eyes. He was impressed by the depth of her gaze and the struggles he read there. This woman had doubtless lived through situations much more serious and traumatic than the one he was involved in. He had confidence in her. He sensed she'd stand by him even though his story could be used against him.

"I'm going to ask Lieutenant Campet to escort you back."

"No, it's fine. In less than twenty minutes I'll be home, and it'll give me time to think."

"And avoid Dany Campet's Formula One driving?" she added with a smile.

"Now that I think about it . . ." Julien got out of the car. "If anything happens tonight, I'll call you."

"I'm counting on it. My hope is to recover Camille Saint-Forge alive, but if that doesn't happen, I want to make sure the shithead can't hurt anybody else."

The young man headed down the Rue Saint-Laurent, his mind spinning. Nadia waved to Lieutenant Campet. "Dany, you follow him discreetly and keep watch outside his building all night."

An annoyed look passed over the policeman's face but was quickly chased away by his sense of duty. Besides, he loved working with Captain Barka.

"It seems to me you trust him, Captain."

"I do. But if anything happens tonight, I want you to be able to swear that he really was at his domicile."

She got out of the car to rejoin her two colleagues on their surveillance mission around the church. It was her first time facing an investigation that bordered on the paranormal. She'd already dealt with pathological liars who tried to pass their offenses or crimes off as heavenly interventions—or devilish ones, for that matter. But Julien Lombard wasn't a pathological liar, she'd just had proof.

Chapter 20: Escape

Camille had long since given up calling for help. She'd realized that if her kidnapper had left the basement window open, it was because there was no hope she would be found there. But why had she followed him? If only she'd gotten that goddamn taxi, she'd be home by now, cuddled up in Denis's arms dreaming of marriage. How far away he seemed at the moment, far away and even unreal! Had she really lived anywhere but here? Her initial rage had turned into despair, and she'd cried every tear in her body. Her kidnapper had hardly spoken to her since she'd followed him into the Mercedes. This silence and the waiting were unbearable. Had he abducted her at random? Yes, he must have, because her visit to the hospital that afternoon had been totally unexpected. But why her? His plan was well orchestrated because he had two vehicles and he'd prepared an anesthetic. Where was she? Probably in the Grenoble area. Outside light had been filtering through the slit in the wall for a good hour or two, but she no longer had any sense of time.

The sound of a key in the lock made her scream. Her breathing accelerated, and she tried to reason with herself. She, who had always prided herself in controlling her feelings in public, tried to summon the Camille Saint-Forge who had an imposing presence in business meetings and social gatherings. But that Camille was too far away, inaccessible. Nevertheless, she forced herself to control her tremors.

The powerful flashlight he was holding blinded her. She couldn't make out her kidnapper's features. He took her by the arm and yanked her out of the corner she was cowering in. She felt her shoulder dislocate and screamed. The man took no notice and pushed her ahead of him. They ended up in a hallway made of exposed concrete. They were probably in the basement of a house in some isolated place. Five yards farther on, a door stood ajar. The stranger pushed her violently. Camille caught her foot on a step as she was thrown into the room. She lost her balance and fell heavily, landing on her dislocated shoulder. The pain spiraled through her body, insisting she stay focused.

She looked around the room while the man was busy closing the door. Its center was occupied by a table, over which stood a multifaceted lamp. The lamp was turned on. Next to the table, a cart with tools that shone under the harsh light of the bulbs. *An operating room, this guy has made himself an operating room and I'm . . . his guinea pig.*

Her kidnapper was coming back toward her now. He'd put on a surgical gown. She was right. She concentrated on a single objective: get out of this room. She temporarily closed her brain off from the panic that was taking her over. She was lying on her back, eyes half closed. The man leaned over. Camille judged the distance—she'd get only one chance. She extended her leg violently, her foot rebounding off her attacker's inner thigh and kicking his crotch. He crumpled with a low moan. Camille hoped she had neutralized him long enough to escape, but she didn't have time to check. She scrambled upright, grimacing. Her fall had left her quite sore, but she didn't have time to think about that.

The young woman opened the operating room door and found a power switch in the hallway. She headed to the left; there was bound to be a stairway leading up—it had to be there, it couldn't be otherwise. The staircase was there, a flight of steps to freedom. She mounted them as quickly as her strength allowed and came out into a large foyer. The house seemed deserted, and all the shutters were closed. A single round window let in the tentative glow of the moon. She moved through the shadows. Quick, the front door! She spotted it on the other side of the foyer and ran to it. The outside world was just a few feet away. Then she'd easily flee into the night and find help. She leaned on the handle and pushed forcefully. But nothing happened. Nothing. The door stayed closed. Panic swept over her, and she redoubled her efforts. She looked for a lock, a key, something. *Open up, you fucking door!* The sound of the handle she was rattling like a maniac echoed in the eerie silence of the room.

Camille stopped, despondent, then listened intently. Noises were coming from the stairway leading to the basement, hoarse groans. No! He'd recovered and was coming to get her. She held her head in her hands. What could she do? A window! She had to get a shutter open.

A halo of light cast by her attacker's flashlight as he climbed the last steps grew more and more distinct. Fear paralyzed her. She had to run, but where? Her eyes darted around the darkened room. Across from her was a wide staircase leading up. She hadn't seen it before. A glimmer of hope! She pulled herself together and, without trying to be quiet, crossed the hall just as the killer finished climbing the stairs. She passed right through the beam of his flashlight. He let out a roar. She would have cried, but now was not the time. Luck had to be with her, she had to find a way out, she had to jump out the window. She was athletic and flexible. He wouldn't follow her.

She slipped on the stairs as she ran and twisted the same ankle she had hurt that morning, but the pain intensified her survival instinct. She got up immediately and headed for the first room she saw. She could hear the man's ragged breathing behind her. He wasn't running. That would give her the precious seconds she needed.

Camille entered the room. An odor of dust and mildew assaulted her. The furniture was draped in coverings from a bygone era. A mausoleum. But she didn't waste time itemizing the decor. She dragged a chair with her good arm and wedged it under the door handle, preventing the door from opening for a few extra moments. Next to the door, a light switch. She flipped it, but no bulb illuminated. She was in darkness. She forced herself to breathe calmly. She could get out of this, she had to. She didn't have the luxury of giving in to a nervous breakdown now. Her eyes adjusted to the dark, and she noticed a slightly lighter surface on one of the walls—the window. She'd found it! She rushed over, electrified by the noise she'd just heard. He was savagely twisting the door handle.

Find the window lock, open the window, push aside the shutter, jump. Her brain was focused on these four movements that would save her life. The man banged violently on the door—the chair had to hold. She grew agitated. It was impossible to find the window lock at night . . . and the door was starting to give way under the staggering blows of her attacker. In despair, she threw a punch at the window. The glass shattered on impact. Camille instantly felt the heat of her blood begin to run down her arm, but now she could reach the shutter latch.

At the same moment, she heard a crash behind her. The door was open, and the man was there, five feet away. He'd left his flashlight in the hall, and she could only see his silhouette. She'd run out of time. No more time to get through the broken window, to open the shutter, to jump and flee. A sudden stillness chilled the room. She could barely make him out, but she knew he was studying her, like a beast studies its prey before devouring it.

With the power of despair, she flung herself through the window, breaking it completely. Perhaps the shutter would give way under the weight of her body, but she heard only a small squeak—it barely moved. She turned around. The man was there, just behind her, scalpel in hand.

Her drive abandoned her, and she crumpled. In an instant, all her dreams paraded before her—her marriage, her two children, her architecture career. Then, the film stopped, and night descended. She heard more than saw the man lean toward her. He took her by the arm, she stood up, following without resistance. Maybe he was taking her home? She'd see her mother again, who surely would have made chocolate pudding for her, since she loved it so much. She descended the main staircase to the foyer. The nice man was taking her home. She was eager to get there and see her teddy bear again. She was going to tell him everything.

Chapter 21: Nightmare

Julien had just turned off his computer. He'd been randomly surfing websites. He was afraid to go to sleep, afraid to be carried away by a nightmare again, afraid to see a woman murdered—the same woman whose identity he now knew.

There was no indication something would happen that night. He tried to hold on to that idea, but there were too many troubling signs for him to take it seriously. He was bathed in sweat. The heat, fueled by the fear that oppressed him, was making him almost ill. He'd considered calling Sophie or Céline, but he'd felt ridiculous and hung up his phone twice. He regretted it now. A cool shower would do him good, a bath, even . . . he could relax in it. He started to run water in the bathtub and lit a candle, which he set on the edge. He went to turn off the lamp in his bedroom. The moonlight guided his return to the bathroom. He turned off the tap, got undressed, and slid into the tub. The water's coolness salved him; he instantly felt his muscles unclench.

Fatigue came down on him hard. He'd been challenged by the Chartreuse hike, the chase into the museum, Captain Barka's rather forceful meeting, and the fear that had seized him when he'd recognized the young woman in the series of photos the policewoman showed him: Camille Saint-Forge. *A pretty name*, he thought to himself. He repeated it, then dozed off, lulled by the music it evoked within him: Camille Saint-Forge, Camille Saint-Forge, Camille . . .

A sudden current of air woke him. The water had grown cold, and the sense of well-being flooding him earlier now had faded away. The candle flame flickered, then twisted in on itself and suddenly went out. Julien shivered and remembered having left the bedroom window open. He didn't feel like leaving the comfortable refuge of his bath, but he was cold now. He stood up, feeling the water slide down his body. The air was icy. He grabbed a robe and wrapped it around himself. None of this was normal, not normal at all. Fear seized him again—no, not that! His legs started to give way. He had just enough energy to leave the bathroom before collapsing into bed. An iron fist gripped his chest. He sank into unconsciousness.

Julien came to. He had the strange sensation of being in thick fog. He didn't understand where he was. He felt a presence at his side. He turned around briskly, but he was alone. The place was dark and cold. In the distance, way in the distance, a light pierced the darkness of a room. Julien went closer to it—a voice was calling him! He looked around, saw he was in a cellar. But what was he doing here? And how had he gotten here? He'd figure it out later— the voice was still calling. He moved cautiously down a long, narrow hallway. Diffuse and muffled sounds reached his ears, overlaid by the voice talking to him, but he couldn't understand what it was saying. It was a woman's voice, he was sure of that, but his brain couldn't discern words.

The luminous halo suddenly widened. Julien pressed up against the wall. They mustn't see him, they mustn't! He wasn't welcome, he could feel it. But no one paid any attention to him. He watched the scene with renewed focus: the image was getting clearer. A man, dressed in blue, was bent over a table. He looked like a surgeon. A surgeon at the end of a hallway, but that didn't make sense. He was concentrating on his work. The lamp casting the light was positioned just above the man, whose back was all Julien could see.

Julien stopped and crouched down. He had to understand where he was, what he was doing here in the middle of the night. But everything seemed so unreal, unreal and uncanny. The woman's voice was making him more and more uneasy. She was afraid, he was sure of it. Now a masculine voice, aggressive, covered hers up. He had to know. He got up and continued to approach. He'd reached the room, the door of which was wide open. Should he enter? All his senses told him to flee, but the voice begged him, and it was stronger than his will, mesmerizing. His ears buzzed, and suddenly he saw the woman who had drawn him here. Her face appeared to him in a flash. Yes, he knew her, he'd already seen her recently. She gazed at him like a blind person—eyes staring into space, in endless distress. Her eyes were a desperate call for help, but she'd already left this world.

Suddenly, a scream jolted him from his stupor. Camille, this was Camille he had in front of him! Camille who, all at once, writhed in pain, her face ravaged by unspeakable suffering. Tears shone in her absent eyes, her mouth trembled in rhythm with her death throes. Then everything stopped cold. Julien fell to his knees. No more noise, no more murmurs, the silence of the tomb. He heard only the sound of the blood flowing through his veins, laying waste to his exhausted mind, like a torrent jumping its banks . . . until that laugh. That laugh froze him.

He looked up. The man in blue had just turned around. His forearms were glistening, glistening with the blood of his victim. He slowly lifted his arms while laughing dementedly. In his right hand, he was holding the still-beating heart of Camille Saint-Forge.

With a bright smile, he brought it to his mouth and tore off a piece with his teeth.

Julien screamed, thrashed, and regained consciousness in his bed. His heart was racing, and he was hyperventilating. Soaked in sweat, he sat on the edge of his bed and forced himself to breathe calmly. No doubt—what he'd feared had just come to pass. He'd witnessed the death of Camille Saint-Forge, more like her execution. And he'd been able to do nothing. But who had plunged him into this nightmare? He'd sensed a presence beside him for a moment, but he'd been too preoccupied by what he was seeing to pay attention to it.

His heart rate had slowed down now, and he recovered his train of thought. First thing he had to do: call Captain Barka. If his assumptions were right, the killer would soon dispose of his victim near the archaeological museum.

He turned on his bedroom light, naively hoping to chase away his demons of the night. Where had he put his phone when he got home? He found it in the pocket of his jeans and looked at the time. Three o'clock. He dialed Nadia Barka's cell phone number immediately.

Chapter 22: The Stakeout

Nadia rejoined her two colleagues. They looked at her questioningly. She shook her head. "I just got a call from Lombard. According to him, Camille Saint-Forge was just killed ten minutes ago. At least that's when he woke up from his nightmare. He claims to have formally recognized her."

"Do you think we can trust him?"

"We've already been over this twenty times. Either we assume he's a pathological liar or he has unexplained visions. We have proof he didn't lie to us. So, we're going to drop it for the moment."

"Was he able to identify the killer?" asked Étienne Fortin.

"He was totally stressed out when he called me, but he glimpsed several features. His story was still incoherent. We'll debrief him tomorrow."

"So if the killer is working with the same modus operandi as last time, we might be able to apprehend him tonight," Fortin finished.

"It's a possibility I'm counting on. I'm going to contact Commissioner Mazure for additional manpower. We can't blow this chance."

"What should we do in the meantime?"

"The killer could be here within minutes if he lives in Grenoble. We're going to do like we planned. You two position yourselves at the trailhead, and I'm going to be in the fortifications, two switchbacks higher. That way we'll have the entrance to the church in sight, whether he comes from the bottom or the top. We'll stay in radio contact, the usual frequency. Get in place. I'll call you with the results of my discussion with Mazure."

Nadia hung up, incandescent with rage. It had been impossible for her to obtain the reinforcements she needed. The commissioner's response had blown her away: "The minister of the interior is coming tomorrow to monitor the progress of the investigation, and I need every man to prepare for his security." But what risk was the minister running? Would the crazed killer jump him in the middle of the street? If his arrival meant nothing but depriving the investigation of its manpower, then he could very well stay at the Place Beauvau in Paris, safe inside his ministry! What had affected her the most was the doubt she sensed in Mazure about the merits of her night maneuver. However, she'd proved to him over the years that she was a cop he could trust. Unless the Déramaux case caused ghosts of the past to resurface. She dismissed her dark thoughts. She was convinced Julien Lombard was telling the truth—her feminine intuition, which had served her well more than once, wasn't leading her astray. She grabbed her radio.

"Leader to team, do you copy?"

She found this code rather ridiculous, but Rodolphe Drancey had insisted they use it among themselves. His *Top Gun* side? She'd made him very happy by agreeing.

"Team here, yes, we copy."

"We'll have to sort this shit out ourselves."

"Don't worry, Captain. If he comes, we'll nail him. I promise you."

"I'm counting on it. We'll check in with each other every fifteen minutes or if there's anything new to report. It's three fifteen. Next check-in at three thirty."

"Roger," concluded Lieutenant Drancey.

Church bells struck four o'clock, pacing the night's advance from a distance. Nadia's nerves were set further on edge with each passing minute. He'd come, she knew it. What she wondered was how he'd manage to leave his victim inside the museum, and especially why he'd chosen this place. Her eyes peered at the access road. The killer could come either from the top, directly from the Bastille, or from the bottom, from the street. This latter hypothesis was by far the most plausible. The full moon was their ally. Nadia leaned back between two walls and radioed her colleagues.

"Still nothing up top, what about your side?"

"A few lone pedestrians in the street, but no one suspicious for the moment."

"Keep your eyes peeled. It'll be dawn within the next hour. If he's coming, it's only a matter of minutes now."

A noise came from above her. Shouts in the distance. She listened intently. A group was descending from up by the Bastille. But what were they doing here at this hour of the night? She hid so as not to be caught. The sound grew louder. About a dozen people surged down the path. She would see them better in a few seconds, when they passed a gap in the trees. The moon illuminated them. Nadia cursed inwardly. She'd just recognized a guy, just over six feet tall, wearing a baseball cap: Nikita Bogossian, known as the Chechen. She'd frequently encountered him at the Grenoble courthouse and had even arrested him once right in the middle of a drug deal. Bogossian had been born in Sassenage, a Grenoble suburb, and the only Chechen thing about him was his nickname, which had to do with the violence he used to rule his gang. He'd gotten his start with a little hashish peddling, then had begun dealing hard drugs and likely gotten mixed up in arms trafficking. But the police had never managed to prove it. He had an excellent lawyer who always quickly got him off the hook.

The screams of his gang broadcasted that they were blind drunk. Bogossian didn't drink alcohol; he always wanted to be capable of controlling the situation. He was particularly intelligent and vicious, and Nadia would have preferred to see him elsewhere tonight.

She heard her radio vibrate and picked up.

"What's that racket up there?" asked Drancey.

"The Chechen and his gang."

"What the fuck are they doing there?"

"No idea, but with the noise they're making, I'm afraid they'll wake up the whole neighborhood."

"What assholes! They're going to wreck this for us. You can't calm them down?"

"There's a dozen of them, some probably armed. So we sit tight and hope they move on fast."

Nadia hung up. The gang had stopped in front of the church portico. A glass door protected access to the museum. She saw a flash, followed by a clear gunshot. In the next second, the sound of exploding glass and coarse alcoholic laughter.

"If you gotta puke, Marvin, you can do it in one of this fucking museum's sarcophagi!"

"Naw, I'm saving it for a cop car as soon as I see one."

The policewoman balled her hands into fists. To think assholes like this were now serving as role models for directionless young people. They started moving again. In a few seconds, they would pass within ten yards of her. Not a chance they'd spot her. In five minutes, they'd have disappeared.

"Fuck, Chechen, I gotta piss, like Niagara Falls if you know what I mean."

"I'll come with you," added one of his companions. "Between the two of us we'll repaint the building."

Nadia felt alarm as she watched them approach. Another few yards and they'd find her. She took out her radio. "I might need you guys. Stay on the lookout."

"No problem. With the noise they're making . . ."

The two men stopped short, surprised to see the policewoman's silhouette ahead of them. She'd quietly taken hold of her Sig Sauer SP 2022, loaded with 9 mm bullets. She was an elite markswoman among the French police.

"Hey, guys, there's a chick!" shouted one of the two men.

"Bitch looks good, too."

The gang surrounded her.

Nadia stared at the one who'd called her bitch and said coldly, "You take your piss and clear out."

The man was startled by her composure.

"Who does this chick think she is, bossing us around!" interjected a boy who came toward her. He was barely seventeen years old, but she could tell he wanted to prove to the others he was a tough guy, too. "All you're gonna do is shut your mouth and suck us off, bitch," he announced.

Nadia realized things were going to turn bad. He'd spoken loudly enough for her colleagues to hear his remark. Nikita Bogossian came over, stared at her, then recognized her. "Hey, boys, it's a cop. She already tried to lock me up!"

An ominous roar burst from the gang. A cop. They were going to have some fun with her, and not much of her would be left afterward. She might just regret meeting them for the rest of her life.

Nadia grabbed the one nearest to her by the wrists, put him in an armlock, and held him tight against her as she pressed her gun barrel into his ribs. "I'm telling you for the last time, clear out."

She saw three firearms slide into the hands of her adversaries.

"Come on, let our buddy go or you're getting a bullet in the gut, you little bitch."

Nadia was calm and determined. She kept her eyes on Bogossian, because he was the one she feared most among the gang. If he was armed, he hadn't taken out his piece. They all had to leave as quickly as possible. They might cause her team to miss the killer, who would turn around if he saw the skirmish.

Bogossian approached her. She pressed the barrel more firmly into the belly of her human shield.

"Hold it, guys, cut the crap. I think she's nuts."

"Oh, no," said the Chechen softly. "A cop isn't going to shoot a minor. Max and Ibra, you're gonna calm this little bitch down for me. Don't kill her. You can have what's left of her when I'm done."

She watched the two men grinning with desire encircle her. They were going to have themselves a cop and blow her away. Nadia still had a few seconds to react. Only one solution—take out the gang leader.

A bullet whistled over the gang's heads, inciting disorder.

"Drop your weapons or the next one goes down your fucking throats!"

Nadia suddenly recognized Drancey's colorful style. For once, she appreciated it. She knew she could count on the accuracy of his shots. She had a few seconds to react and take advantage of this reprieve. Their alcohol-addled brains didn't understand what was happening. Nadia threw herself at the man on her left and sent his pistol flying. In the next second, a roundhouse kick to the throat sent him down. Her second attacker raised his arm toward her. Wielding an automatic pistol, he let fly a spray of shots. Luckily, he hadn't taken the time to learn how to use it. Nadia sprang up quickly, but found herself face-to-face with Bogossian's weapon.

"You're going to cop heaven!"

No, she couldn't die like this. She threw herself to the side and heard two bangs. A burning sensation tore through her shoulder. She slid to her knees and felt a body fall on top of her. A hot liquid trickled onto her neck.

For a few moments she'd lost all sense of time, and the silence surprised her.

She crawled to get out from under the weight of the body that had just flattened her to the ground. She recognized him—Nikita Bogossian—a look of surprise forever frozen on his face. His chest had a gaping hole in it and was covered in blood. The gang members, bewildered by the death of their ringleader, had let their weapons slide to the ground.

"You all right, Captain?"

Nadia felt her shoulder. It was horribly painful. She bit her lips and replied, "Better than him."

"What should we do with the others?"

"Line them up."

Nadia watched as the men, completely sobered by the violent disappearance of their leader, obeyed like sheep. They were obviously stunned by this turn of events. For once, they weren't the ones committing the reign of terror. She knew they sensed they were at the mercy of two men and a woman who knew how to fight and weren't afraid of them.

Without a word, Captain Barka observed them in the moonlight, saying nothing, memorizing their faces and their fear. The youngest started to shake uncontrollably and let go of his bowels—there was a foul odor. She looked at him. She should have hauled them off to jail, but catching the murderer was her priority.

"War isn't a game. This time you've come out alive. But it won't happen again."

"Get lost now," Fortin instructed them.

Immediately, the group fled in silence, running as fast as they could.

"You all right, Nadia?"

"Somewhat. What time is it?"

"4:20."

"Shit, we lost twenty minutes. Let's get back down right away."

The disorganized gang was now entering the Rue Saint-Laurent. Nadia was following them with her eyes when suddenly . . . there he was, motionless, with a shape in his arms! His victim, whom he was transporting to her final resting place.

He stood there, motionless, disconcerted by the arrival of this silent horde jostling him in the middle of the night. He had to be alone, alone with this girl and his memories. Alone with this girl, facing his destiny.

He looked up and saw three shadows running toward him. His instincts told him to flee. He was their target. He didn't know what could have happened, but he was being hunted, him, the hunter. He immediately dropped his victim, turned around, and broke into a sprint.

"Catch him," screamed Nadia.

She stopped, took a knee, and in spite of the pain in her shoulder, reached for the pistol attached to her belt. Nothing! She must have forgotten to collect it. "Rodolphe, stop him!"

Drancey took out his weapon, stopped running, and fired twice. The first bullet missed its target, and the second grazed the fugitive's arm.

"Shit! Don't worry, I got this!" he shouted, now running again.

One, then two sirens pierced the night. Two police cars pulled up in front of them. Finally, they'd have the backup they'd so cruelly lacked. The tires squealed to a stop, and six men piled out of the cars. They threw themselves on Fortin and Drancey.

"Police! Put down your weapons immediately!"

"Fuck, he's getting away, fuck you!"

"Put down your weapons or we'll shoot!"

"We're on the same side," screamed Drancey while trying to get his badge out.

"Hands on the car, move it!"

Realizing that conversation was impossible for the moment, Drancey dropped his pistol, heartsick.

He and Fortin were shoved unceremoniously against the cars. Nadia ran over after recovering her Sig Sauer. When she saw the scene, she understood immediately the mission had failed. She approached the group, badge in hand, and explained calmly, "I'm Captain Barka. These two men are with me. What's going on here?"

One of the policemen came up to her and looked at her papers. "You can release them. They're ours."

Drancey exploded. "Fuck, I never stopped telling you that was the case. Where'd the guy I was chasing go?"

"Which one? There was a whole crowd."

Drancey looked at the street. It was empty now. Lights were appearing in the buildings, and a few curious onlookers leaned out their windows. "What are we going to do now?"

Captain Barka addressed the officer in charge of the intervention. "Give my colleagues two or three men. We're after the baptistery killer."

"Shit! Lefort, Sarita, and Bouvet, go." Fortin, Drancey, and the three men took off running.

"Why did you interfere?" asked Nadia.

"We got several calls reporting gunfire. What's going on?"

"Call some ambulances, we've got two cadavers on our hands."

"What happened?"

"I'll tell you on the way. Just one thing—nobody touch the woman's body before the EMTs get here. It might still hold clues for the investigation."

"Yes, Captain. And you mentioned another body?"

"A drug trafficker, an arms dealer probably."

The policeman looked at her, stunned. "Long night?"

"A little, yes."

Then he noticed in the harsh light of the streetlamp that the captain's jacket was covered in blood. "What happened to you?"

"Collateral damage, but rather painful."

Upon reaching the Bastille trailhead, she saw the body of Camille Saint-Forge stretched out on the ground. Unlike Monica Revasti's, this death had permanently marked the girl's face with suffering. Her dress was smeared with blood around her chest. Nadia touched nothing and sat down next to her.

"I'm going to wait here. You'll find the other body a hundred yards up."

The policeman left with one of his men.

Nadia looked at Camille and buried her face in her hands. The adrenaline faded, and the reality of the situation overtook her, like a tsunami of contradictory feelings. They'd been just seconds away from catching the killer. Now he was on the loose again, and maybe another woman was already in danger. The ghost of Laure Déramaux flitted before her eyes again.

Exhausted and weakened from blood loss, Captain Nadia Barka slipped into unconsciousness and slumped gently onto the sidewalk.

Chapter 23: Harassment

Dominique turned off the ignition. The car fell silent, and only the sound of the garage door automatically closing covered the driver's heavy breathing. The final clatter of the door hitting the frame reassured him. He was safe.

He opened the vehicle's door and extricated himself with difficulty. He looked at himself in an old mirror leaning against one wall of the garage. The harsh light of the naked bulb hanging from the ceiling gave him a sallow look. He didn't linger and climbed the cement stairs slowly. He entered the foyer, then went up to his bedroom.

The man looked at the broken glass littering the floor near the window. Everything came back to him. The girl who'd tried to escape, who'd tried to block his road to his salvation. The one before had been much more sensible, and he'd been nice with her. But this one, what a bitch! Right to the end she'd interfered with his plans. He'd sacrificed her without pity—she didn't deserve his mercy. But what had happened when he got to the church? No one had followed him, he was sure of that. Why had those men descended on him out of nowhere? They hadn't even looked at him. Yet when he'd seen the woman and two men chasing him and the girl, his sixth sense had screamed at him to flee. So he'd abandoned his victim without being able to finish the ritual. Too bad. The ritual wasn't necessary, but he would have liked defying Magali again.

As he ran, he'd felt a burning in his arm and hadn't understood right away that they'd opened fire on him.

Now he was tired, so very tired. In spite of everything, he had enough to last him until the solstice, or at least he hoped so. His thirtieth solstice . . . and his last. Arsène had promised him. He had to rest now.

Dominique pulled off his shirt and looked at it. Blood had run down the sleeve. The bullet aimed at him had barely grazed his skin. He threw the shirt in a corner of the room. He finally undressed and got into the shower. The scalding water running down his body washed away the impurities of the night. *Hang on until the solstice and it will all be over.* He took full advantage of this time to cleanse, then exited the bathroom naked. He was hot enough as it was. He lay down on his bed.

He looked at his alarm: six o'clock. It was time to go to bed. He closed his eyes, savoring the silence of the room. Suddenly, he tensed. He wasn't alone. No, she couldn't come back again and harass him further. He shouldn't open his eyes, he should ignore her. But the urge was stronger than he was. He looked out in the room.

She was there, in front of him, suitcase at her side. Her face was still just as emotionless. Dominique's gaze fell on Magali's rounded belly. His anger was instantly tinged with bitterness. Why hadn't she accepted the future he'd always offered her? He would have provided the child with complete protection—no one would have sullied him. He who had used and abused his fellow men knew well the dangers of the world. This son would have allowed for his redemption! He'd already prepared two rooms: one for Magali and one for the little one. He would have raised him according to his precepts and taught him everything he should know and fear. Magali had dared to make a scene when he'd spoken to her of his projects. He looked at her again. She hadn't moved. Her long brown hair seemed to float in the breeze, even though there wasn't a breath of air in the room.

Abruptly, exasperated, he addressed her. "What do you want from me, really? You've been coming to torture me for years! You probably think yourself a victim, the innocent lamb, sacrificed by the executioner?" He burst into stilted laughter.

"My poor Magali, I gave you everything! But the little girl knew better than everyone else, the little girl who knew nothing of the world felt ready to confront it and lose my son to it! What do you blame me for now? Trying to rid myself of the hatred you've brought me over the years? Because yes, it is hatred to pursue me like this every year at this time. But you're solely responsible, Magali! If you'd accepted my advice and my love, you'd still be here . . . and my son as well! What are you trying to do? Make me feel remorse? Ridiculous, ridiculous . . ."

The man, his body seemingly paralyzed, was now screaming in his room. His mouth, distorted by a sneer, warped his features. He continued. "But Arsène, who's always helped me, found the way to get rid of you . . . once and for all! And you know it!"

He looked at her and seemed to see pity pass over her eternally young features.

"Still trying to plunge me into remorse or guilt? But you're wasting your time, my poor Magali. These girls are giving me their hearts to banish you from my existence. You're the one killing them, Magali! In any case, you'll have left my life permanently in less than a week. So get out, get out before I get angry and I shut you up in the penance closet! You remember, don't you? Get out!"

He closed, then reopened his eyes. The woman had disappeared, as if she'd never been there. He relaxed. So Arsène was right! The writings of Fra Bartolomeo were effective. He'd hang on until the solstice and then would be delivered.

Chapter 24: Rude Awakening

Nadia opened her eyes. She didn't seem to be in her bedroom. She felt like she was moving through cotton wool. She concentrated with difficulty on the shape in front of her.

She was lying down. Yes, that was it, she was in a bed. She tried again, and the shape in front of her started to take on substance, then an identity. "Commissioner Mazure? What are you doing here? And where am I?"

"You're in the hospital, Nadia. You lost a lot of blood, then consciousness. You were brought here to urgent care, and a doctor removed the bullet in your shoulder."

With an intense effort at concentration, Captain Barka recalled the night's chain of events and became gloomy. "We almost had him, Commissioner, we almost had him . . . but I failed."

Mazure gently laid a hand on her forearm. The young woman was surprised by her superior officer's gesture. "Fortin and Drancey have made their report, and you have nothing to blame yourself for. How are you feeling?"

"Groggy. But after a few hours of rest, I'll be out of here and ready to continue the investigation. I'm gonna nail that bastard."

The policeman looked upset. His colleague stared into his eyes. Mazure felt transfixed by the young woman's angry glare. "No, Nadia. That won't be possible."

"But why?"

"You've been temporarily relieved from the investigation."

The news stunned the young woman. "Relieved? But why are you relieving me from the investigation?"

"I had a long talk with the surgeon who operated on you. You absolutely must recuperate. Your body wouldn't be able to sustain the same pace."

"Just give me twenty-four hours, and I'll be right as rain! I'll see this through, even if I have to sacrifice my health."

"That's exactly what I want to avoid. Besides, I got the ministry to assign ten additional investigators."

"Perfect! Let me lead them!" Her volume was increasing.

A nurse passing in the hallway came into the room. "You need to calm down," she scolded. "You've just come out of a delicate procedure."

Nadia was not in the mood to be lectured. "Leave me alone. I didn't ask anyone's permission to get shot. I don't need yours to talk with my superior officer."

The nurse looked at Commissioner Mazure, who motioned to her to let it go. She shrugged and left the room.

The policeman let Nadia talk. He perfectly understood her frustration and was convinced Nadia was ready to continue leading the investigation. He was aware of her ability to keep going as long as she had a breath of energy. But he also knew her well enough to know she wouldn't respect the limits imposed by her own body and that she could potentially suffer grave consequences. He was also afraid the similarity between this case and the Laure Déramaux case would push her over certain lines.

"So who's taking up the investigation?" asked Nadia.

"Captain Rivera."

The young woman didn't respond. No other name would have been so hard to take. Stéphane Rivera was taking over her investigation. She was too depressed by her superior's decision to express her anger.

"You'll have to give him all the documents and cooperate, obviously, when necessary."

"I know my duty, Commissioner," she replied coldly.

Mazure looked at her, immediately regretting his remark. Captain Barka was one of his best colleagues. But he thought he'd made the right decision.

"My main objective is always to put the killer out of commission. I'll cooperate one hundred percent. But I'm tired now. And as you reminded me, I have to get some rest."

"Of course, I'll let you get to it. I left my personal phone number on your bedside table. Call me if you need anything."

Nadia looked at him, bewildered. "Leave me the number for the emergency room instead. It'll be more useful to me in the next few days," she replied sarcastically.

Alain Mazure didn't react to his colleague's jab. Seeing her that way almost reassured him—he hadn't expected her to accept his decision cheerfully.

"Oh, I almost forgot. You'll have visits from Lieutenants Fortin, Drancey, and Garancher this afternoon. They're already aware of the change in leadership."

He left the room, without a glance from the young woman.

Chapter 25: The Déramaux Case

Nadia felt her courage leave her. She let the nurse who'd just returned administer antibiotics and saturate her with pain medications. She turned her head toward the clock: it was almost two in the afternoon.

She felt a lump rise in her throat. The humiliation she'd just endured wasn't going away. When she faced facts, she knew she had nothing to blame herself for. She'd taken Julien Lombard's stories seriously, even at the risk of looking gullible in the eyes of others. She'd done well.

Now they had a new corpse that would give up its secrets under the expert hands of the medical examiner; the killer had taken form, and a thorough investigation would doubtless allow them to put a name to the man. Julien Lombard would also probably be able to help them. She knew she would have been able to make progress on the investigation, especially with the backing of ten specialists. How much faster it all would have gone!

But now, she only had the right to stay in the hospital and answer questions if Rivera asked them. What a shitty situation.

Without wanting to, her mind drifted to Laure Déramaux— her only unsolved case with the police. For months, Laure's ravaged face had haunted her. She'd finally accepted the help of a psychiatrist to expel the young woman from her dreams. That's how she'd met Dr. Isabelle Tavernier.

Laure had disappeared three months prior. Responsibility for the search had fallen to Nadia. For the three months they'd scoured the city, then the *département*, to find her. Laure's father, Gilles Déramaux, was a rich industrialist from Lyon, very influential in governmental circles. He'd invested his own funds to enlarge the team already provided. But despite a colossal amount of labor, they hadn't gathered any valuable information during that time.

Then one day, a backpacker had found a corpse in the Machecoul forest. They'd barely recognized Laure's tortured body. The medical examiner had written the most terrifying report: she'd been tortured since the first day of her imprisonment. Her body looked like a playing field, with marks and scars in cleverly constructed geometry. But no one had been able to understand why. Nadia had looked at the photos until she'd memorized each wound inflicted on Laure's body.

Very detailed investigations had obviously been conducted at the crime scene. The zone had been gone over with a fine-tooth comb by the forensic team, but no leads had resulted. A total mystery!

Laure hadn't suffered any sexual offense. Her executioners had merely amused themselves with torturing her in accordance with a ritual that undoubtedly made sense to them but not to the police.

The young woman's corpse was still warm when they'd found it. But no one had noticed anything.

Gilles Déramaux had never accepted his daughter's death. He'd asked Nadia to make herself available to search for the murderer or murderers. Obsessed by this murder, the young woman had agreed. At the industrialist's request, the administration had given its permission.

For weeks she'd tried to understand, skimming through police and library databases. She'd frequented the underworld, delving into the very closed S&M scene and rubbing shoulders with Satanist circles. Working as a lone knight, she'd succeeded in infiltrating them. But after three months of work, she'd abruptly ceased her activities, to the despair of the victim's father. She'd been too personally invested, going beyond what professionalism allowed her. This investigation had gradually transformed into personal vengeance. It was when she found herself on the verge of participating in an S&M party that she'd suddenly recognized the risk she was running. She was losing all concept of firm boundaries. So she'd decided to stop. Her three months of relentless research had led her nowhere, except to the edge of what her psyche could stand.

"Is something wrong, mademoiselle?" asked the doctor upon entering the room.

"I'm tired."

Nadia hadn't been aware her face was dripping with tears. The tension of the last few days, the memory of Laure, being ousted from the investigation, it was all too much. Not even counting the misery of her personal life.

"I'm going to examine you, if that's all right." The doctor was young and seemed impressed by the policewoman. "It's the first time I've seen a gunshot wound," he explained in an attempt to justify his eagerness.

"If you're still around in three or four years, you ought to see me back here."

He called a nurse, who pulled back the dressing. "The wound is very neat and should heal up quickly. You've bled, but alongside your misfortune you were lucky that neither the bone nor the tendons were touched. You should recover fairly quickly."

"So much the better, since I'm going home this afternoon."

"Are you joking?"

"Do I look like it?"

The doctor looked at the woman. He'd rarely seen such fierce determination.

"I'll sign all the papers you want. Give me the drugs I have to take, and I'll stop being a drain on public funds right this second."

"But, as a doctor, I can't let you go in this state."

Nadia tried going for broke. "I'm on the trail of a killer, the one the press and all the TV channels are talking about. I don't want him to attack another innocent victim."

As the doctor hesitated, Nadia sat up on the edge of her bed. Her head swam, but she grabbed on to him to keep from lying down again. After a few seconds, she regained her balance.

"Could you remove this, please?" she asked the nurse, holding out the IV drip.

Sensing the young woman's determination and the young doctor's hesitation, the nurse obeyed. She added, "Your shirt and jacket are bloodstained. I'm going to get you a T-shirt. We must be about the same size."

"Thank you. If anyone comes looking for me, tell them I'm at home."

She stood up, walked carefully, and headed toward the room's closet. The doctor stared at her uncomprehendingly, fascinated by his patient's graceful, muscular body. His eyes didn't leave her long, slender legs. The nurse's voice brought him back to earth.

"Doctor, I've prepared Mademoiselle Barka's medication."

"Yes, yes, very good, give it to her."

Nadia pulled on her jeans, slipped into the sneakers she'd donned for her night mission, put on the T-shirt, took the medication, thanked the nurse, made an effort to give the doctor a grateful smile, and left the hospital room gritting her teeth.

Chapter 26: Key Witness

Monday afternoon. Julien was slumped in front of his computer. He'd seen the special broadcasts running in a loop on the twenty-four-hour news channels. The Rue Saint-Laurent, the picture of Camille Saint-Forge as he'd seen her in his dreams—or his nightmares—the Grenoble prosecutor announcing that the investigation had resumed, supported by a team of specialists sent directly from Paris. What had become of Captain Barka, then?

Since then, he'd been staring at his screen without seeing anything. He was aware of being at the heart of this case, but in a way he didn't comprehend.

Sophie sat next to him. At first, he hadn't wanted to talk to her, to protect her. Julien didn't want to further entangle her in a grisly situation completely beyond his control. But his friend's insistence had gotten the better of his resistance. And this time, she hadn't laughed at all.

Many of their colleagues had taken a vacation day after the intense week they'd spent getting their project in on time. Julien and Sophie were alone, except for a secretary whose office was situated near the entryway and a young engineer who seemed to be spending more time on Facebook than on writing lines of code.

"The situation is becoming truly worrisome, Julien. You're really sure you didn't have any psychics or people with special powers in your family?"

"Of course, Sophie, I've already told you ten times. I called my parents and asked them. I even called my grandmother, who was nicknamed the witch by some people. It scared me a little when I was a kid. She admitted to me one day that she'd given herself that reputation to keep men in the area from flocking around her—the price of her beauty. That's it. So I don't have any paranormal gene that's been officially detected."

"I have an idea, but it might seem strange to you." Sophie looked at him quite tenderly, and he was ashamed of getting carried away. She was trying to help him, and her presence did him good.

"I'm listening, and I promise you I'll consider it carefully," he said with a half smile.

"I know someone who might be able to help you."

"Who?"

"Father Bernard de Valjoney."

"Have I met him before?"

"I don't know. Not with me in any case."

Sophie donated her time. This activism had always seemed bizarre to Julien, but he respected it and even admired her to a certain extent. She knew how to devote time to others and still was able to lead a busy social life.

She continued, "Father de Valjoney is a priest of the diocese, and he has a lot of experience with this sort of thing. He doesn't like to talk about it, but I had the opportunity to see him soothe someone, let's say, in torment."

"You want to send me to an exorcist?" he asked, stunned.

"Father Bernard isn't an exorcist. He knows a lot about the human soul and his religious activities have brought him into contact with people who—how do I put this—say they've had encounters with spirits."

"He's what, then—a psychic?"

"Julien, if I'm suggesting you meet with him, it's because he's a very intelligent and insightful man who could help you. At worst, you'll waste your time."

Julien looked at his friend. When he saw her serious and worried expression, a wave of gratitude washed over him. He felt like taking her in his arms and hugging her, begging her to never leave. But the presence of his colleague and a chronic difficulty expressing his feelings prevented him.

"I promise, Sophie, I'll go see him. It's undoubtedly a good idea. I need an enlightened opinion."

The front door buzzer rang insistently. The visitor seemed to have very limited patience. After a dozen piercing tones, the secretary got up to let the person in. She'd barely touched the handle when the door banged open in response to a strong push. Julien and Sophie looked up, surprised. Three men had just entered in a rush, dispensing with the most basic courtesies. The first two, rather young, wore T-shirts, whereas the third was dressed more formally in a shirt and summer jacket. He didn't look any classier for it, though.

"We're looking for a Julien Lombard."

"And who are you?" asked Julien, eyeing him.

"Police."

"Can we see your papers?" he asked.

The question annoyed the man, who took out his badge and shoved it in Julien's face. "Will that do?" he barked aggressively.

"My request seems most legitimate to me," the young man continued. "You show up here like—"

"I asked you a question!"

"Could you repeat it?" asked Julien. He knew he was riling him, but the man was particularly unpleasant to him. He also wondered what this rather forceful raid meant. He'd clearly cooperated with the police by going to see Captain Barka.

The policeman breathed deeply. He wasn't going to lose his cool because of this jerk. A greenhorn who lived only by computers, a geek, as they said down at the station, wasn't going to get the better of Captain Stéphane Rivera's nerves.

"Are you Julien Lombard?"

"Yes."

"Then I'm going to ask you to come with us."

"May I know the reason?"

"You're a key witness in the Monica Revasti and Camille Saint-Forge murder cases. We want to hear from you."

"But I already told Captain Barka everything I know." His answer annoyed Rivera immensely.

"Captain Barka is off the case. I'm leading the investigation now. So stop being a pain. I have a murderer running around Grenoble!"

Julien realized it was pointless to negotiate anything with the policeman in front of him. "Okay, I'll come with you."

One of the policemen grabbed him roughly by the shoulder. Julien shook him off vigorously. "It's fine, I'm following you! I'm not being arrested for murder, you know!"

"Don't say anything, Julien, I'm going to call my mother. She might get to the police station before you do."

Julien looked at her in astonishment. He knew her mother was a notable lawyer, and this reassured him. Being alone with this policeman who was more like a mafioso—and impatient, to say the least—didn't give him a good feeling.

"She can't deny her favorite and only daughter anything, especially since I don't ask her often," whispered Sophie, who had understood his expression.

"And who are you?" Rivera asked Sophie.

"Your prisoner's fairy godmother. Be careful on the drive, I like him."

The cop looked at her, puzzled. He'd dealt with tough guys who wouldn't talk, young thugs who'd insulted him, dealers who'd threatened him with revenge. But he couldn't tell what these two suspects were playing at. Because he was sure this Lombard wasn't clean. And if there was something to find, it wouldn't take him too many hours to find it!

As soon as the policemen had left, leaving the secretary befuddled, Sophie rushed to her phone.

"Give me Madame Dupas, please . . . Thanks . . . Hello, Mom, I need you. Yes, you're working on a big brief, but give me three minutes to explain."

Three minutes later, Sophie ended her conversation. "You're awesome, Mom. And you won't regret getting out of there . . . Yes, I'll repay you. We can do some shopping together next Saturday. I saw a suit and a dress at Hirondelle that would look great on you! *Bisous*."

She hung up. Julien would be in good hands, and the policeman was going to regret crossing paths with her mother.

Chapter 27: The Blues

Nadia stretched out on the living room sofa in her two-room apartment. She'd always loved the atmosphere of the Quai Perrière, with all its pizzerias one right after the other. Sometimes an exotic restaurant or bar broke up the line, but directly beside it would begin another long string of pizzerias. The window opened onto the Isère, and the last rays of the setting sun brought a relaxing light into the room.

Nadia, however, was not in sync with the atmosphere of the evening. She was in a state of depression she'd rarely experienced. Her injury, the stress, the exhaustion, and above all being removed from an investigation so close to her heart had depleted her last resources.

The visitors who'd just left had finished her off: Captain Stéphane Rivera and three detectives fresh from the academy. Rivera had put on quite a show. To think she'd believed for an instant that he'd put his old grudges aside! For once, her intuition had been sorely mistaken. It hadn't been mistaken, however, about the young doctor at the hospital. She'd immediately noticed his attraction, and it wasn't completely by accident that she'd paraded around in front of him in her undies while gathering her clothes. She'd anesthetized his critical thinking. She'd even gotten one week of sick leave out of him. How inspired! She'd finally shown the order to Rivera, thus sparing herself exhausting hours at the police station.

Obviously she was quite ready to cooperate. But that discussion—if you could call the strutting of that jackass to impress the young recruits and to show his colleague who was boss now a discussion—had deeply annoyed her. The three youngsters hadn't been as impressed as Captain Rivera might have wished. Coming in that morning from Lyon, they'd read the files prepared for them and had had time to see Captain Barka's résumé, which was rather impressive. When they'd arrived at the apartment, they'd seen a woman whose sadness contrasted with her beauty, and this had troubled them. Doubtless they had subconsciously leaned in her favor.

Nadia had been amused when she noticed the gaze of one of her colleagues from Lyon slip unprofessionally toward her cleavage. Never in her career had she played on this level. She was even obsessive about keeping her femininity out of her professional activities. But that night, she was in her own home, wounded. She'd surprised herself by valuing even the most banal benefits from the young man. That revealed what she'd been reduced to! Rivera had done all he could to demonstrate to her she was out of the game, that she'd failed in her investigation and finally *he* was going to make progress. She'd understood his ploy from the outset, but she hadn't been able to keep herself from feeling vexed and despondent.

Now she was alone. Alone! The word terrified her. She didn't know whom to call, if she even felt like calling someone. She hadn't seen her father since she'd joined the police force without his permission—it had been fifteen years now. Her mother saw her in secret sometimes, and her brother, a dentist in Bordeaux, snubbed her completely. She got along well with him in her youth, but he'd become an arrogant and pretentious sort of guy.

It had been more than three years since she'd had anybody in her life. Her last boyfriend had deserted her, tired of her random appearances, and had fallen for a bitch whose family had a magnificent estate somewhere on the Côte d'Azur and a fortune she couldn't even guess at. That was indeed proof they weren't meant to be together. But could she have someone in her life with her profession? Could she have children someday? For years she'd made fun of friends who carried on about their noisy progeny, but these days she felt like looking away when she met them in the street or at other friends' houses. If she'd allowed herself to envy them, she would have burst.

It was after her breakup that she'd thrown herself wholeheartedly into the Déramaux case. She'd definitely not chosen the best therapy. But when destiny knocks, feminine intuition is nowhere to be found.

Then again, if she'd counted the number of men who'd tried to sleep with her, she'd practically be in the *Guinness Book of World Records*. She knew she was beautiful, even very beautiful, and she knew how to gain sympathy when she wanted it. Furthermore, she was a cop, which excited more than one fantasy! But she didn't want any of it. Once she'd agreed to go out with a guy, not bad-looking, a few months after her breakup. Just sex, they'd said. But she'd come out of it with a hellish sensation of nothingness, and she'd had only one desire after intercourse—to flee!

Immersed in her dark thoughts, she wavered between a glass of rum and several sleeping pills, and even considered both, but she pulled herself together and settled for her antibiotics and a powerful sedative.

She had to sleep. She'd taken a two-hour nap upon returning home, but she was worn out.

Nadia went to the bathroom and pulled back her dressing. The wound was still raw, and she regretted having left the hospital on a whim. No, she'd been right! She didn't know anymore. She knew only that she had to take care of herself. She'd taken a number of first aid courses during her career with the police. So she gathered up the products her nurse had given her. She disinfected the wound, remade the dressing, then left the bathroom and turned out the light behind her.

The living room was now in shadow. Nadia opened the window, letting the still-warm air in. She drank a large glass of water and stretched out on the sofa again. The sounds of the street, the conversations of passersby and diners sitting at terrace tables, the clinking of glasses, and even the smell of pizza wafting up from the restaurants soothed her.

Then she told herself the story of the little donkey in the mountains. It was the story her father used to tell her when, as a little girl, she was afraid of a storm or the night. Her eyes grew misty when she thought about it. Despite everything she'd sworn to herself, she hadn't been able to drive her father out of her mind. And she was convinced he couldn't drive her out of his. Lost in her childhood memories, Nadia finally fell asleep.

Chapter 28: New Team

The sun was shining that Tuesday morning, and the day promised to be sweltering again. One room at the Grenoble police station had been specially arranged to accommodate briefings for Operation Open Heart. Commissioner Mazure surveyed the thirty men and women settling into the chairs set up for the occasion, satisfied. At his side, Stéphane Rivera flaunted his finally acknowledged importance. He was having his revenge. He was going to take the opportunity to give everyone who had talked down to him a taste of their own medicine.

The hubbub quieted little by little, and silence fell. Mazure began to speak. "The minister is following this case very closely and wants quick results. Reinforcements have been allocated to the investigation, and I'd like to welcome them. I'll also take this opportunity to officially announce that Captain Rivera has been tapped to coordinate police efforts."

The majority of the policemen had already been informed, but some couldn't hide their astonishment. Mazure explained.

"Captain Barka is on rest. She was seriously injured by a gunshot. She would put her health in danger if she continued to fulfill her role. And I have every confidence in Captain Rivera as he follows in her footsteps."

Étienne Fortin sighed inwardly. The arrival of the reinforcements was excellent and would allow them to enhance the effectiveness of their search, but whose idea was it to turn control over to Rivera? He knew Rivera had been a good cop, if not honest, before the incident that had precipitated his fall from grace. But the bitterness obviously clouded his judgment. Fortin concentrated on the briefing. He had to suppress his feelings while at work, but he couldn't stop thinking about Nadia. She should have been in Rivera's place, without a shadow of a doubt. He'd go see her during the day as soon as he could get free. The arrival of all these new forces should open up his schedule.

Chapter 29: Arsène

Arsène pushed away the files spread across his desk. He got up and headed toward a small safe hidden behind a painting. Nothing very original about it except that there was only one key and he was its keeper. He'd asked his staff not to disturb him, and he knew his secretary, a devotee to his cause, would respect that order no matter what the cost.

He took the key out of his pocket, slid it into the lock, and entered the opening combination by using four dials arranged on the front of the safe. He'd had the safe installed when he'd taken office. He gingerly removed what appeared to be an ancient book from it, not very thick, which he placed on his desk. His masterpiece! The testament of Fra Bartolomeo.

He had before him the source of his power and his fortune. A brilliant idea that had germinated when, years earlier, he'd met that eccentric old millionaire. Actually, more psychologically disturbed than eccentric, but also more billionaire than millionaire!

Arsène recalled the encounter. He'd just spent seven years working toward his diploma. After his studies were over, he'd felt a visceral need to enjoy life. On a whim he'd gone to a seaside resort in the South of France. He was young, and his savings had melted away after two months of dates and partying.

Shortly before the end of his stay he'd met that man on the terrace of a bar. What was his name again? Oh, yes, Régis Duclerc. Duclerc had been standing alone, watching the sea and his Campari Orange. Eventually he'd approached Arsène's table and offered him a glass. Since Arsène had been admiring the sea for long enough, and time was starting to drag, he'd accepted.

Duclerc had introduced himself right away. Starting off as an assistant in a jewelry shop, he'd become one of the most influential gem cutters in the country. His career, and especially the fortune he'd amassed, had aroused Arsène's curiosity. For fun, Arsène had decided to impersonate an archaeologist. Duclerc had reacted predictably with the overblown enthusiasm of an eager admirer: *You must have extraordinary adventures! What a life! What do you think of Tutankhamen's curse?* and on and on.

With his boundless imagination, Arsène had had no trouble telling adventure stories worthy of Indiana Jones. He slipped in secrets that gave the jeweler the impression of entering a world of insiders.

That day he'd decided to introduce himself as a specialist in the Aztec world. He had only a sketchy familiarity with the subject. But he said he'd done a thesis on the influence of Mayan culture in Aztec society. The Toltec peoples, the Chichimeca or Totonac, held no secrets for him. To say that Régis Duclerc had been fascinated was an understatement. He drank in Arsène's words. At dinnertime, Duclerc had invited him to a restaurant by the water, highly rated by Michelin, and he'd accepted, famished and curious to see where this story would take him.

And that's when Arsène had first given life to the character of Fra Bartolomeo. Fra Bartolomeo was a Genoese monk, excommunicated for fornication and murder, who had lived with Cortés among the Aztecs to escape the law and a death sentence. Arsène had expounded upon the terrible tortures reserved for sinners and homosexuals at that time. *Always provide details that could be reused to impress and awe.*

He thought his conversation partner's rational mind would soon reject his invented character. But the diamond dealer was so impassioned and charmed by the tale that he didn't doubt the veracity of Arsène's statements for a second.

Thus Arsène had begun, in strictest secrecy and in the company of a fifteen-year-old cognac, to reveal to Duclerc the first fragments of the lost manuscript of Fra Bartolomeo. He'd taken on a conspiratorial air that he himself found laughable, but Duclerc was enchanted. Arsène left him waiting expectantly for the rest of the story, arranging to meet the day after next. He wanted to let a day go by to better gauge how hooked the jeweler was.

They saw each other again two days later. Arsène had kept Régis Duclerc waiting for more than an hour, and he could see the intense excitement in his eyes. Arsène wondered how a man who had made a fortune in the diamond world, which he imagined to be anything but unsophisticated, could swallow his story like this. He obviously needed to escape, to get away for a moment from the monotony of sixty years struggling and laboring to get rich.

An idea had taken root within Arsène the previous day, and he wanted to see just how far he could push it. He first solemnly asked the jeweler to keep the conversation that followed strictly to himself, no matter what happened with their relationship. He was going to tell him about an ambitious project that could revolutionize their limited knowledge as rational Europeans. Duclerc swore on everything he held dear.

Although they were alone at their table, Arsène preferred to walk on the beach, empty at that hour of the morning. From his historian friends, he'd heard that the tomb of Fra Bartolomeo was about to be discovered in the Guatemalan jungle. By purest chance, a Swiss team had found the ruins of a little chapel they'd dated to the middle of the sixteenth century. Fra Bartolomeo had last been seen in that area, and priests were few in number. It wasn't the funerary chapel of one of Cortés's conquistador companions, because its decoration wasn't that of a Spanish noble. And a soldier would have seen his bones rot in the ground. Only a clergyman could have been interred in that way. At that time, it was quite possible that Fra Bartolomeo had a few disciples who would have cared for him and buried him with his work, *The Book of the Sun*. To this day, the original had never been found. Only a few fragments had survived.

Arsène explained that he had waited for their meeting that morning before revealing this key information. He'd wanted to be sure he could trust him completely. Then he'd looked at Duclerc. If he took the bait, Arsène would have him in the palm of his hand. The diamond dealer hadn't just taken the bait—he'd *swallowed* it. He was wriggling in his chair.

"Let me join you in this adventure!" Duclerc implored him.

"What do you mean?"

"I'm much too old to be running off into the jungle, but you should go join this team in Guatemala right away. Do you think they'd accept you?"

"Yes, I know the leader of the mission, and my knowledge would undoubtedly be valuable to them. But I don't have the means to get there."

"That's what I was getting at. I'll finance your expedition and everything you need. In exchange, I'll ask only one thing of you—you tell me every detail of your adventure, and share the contents of *The Book of the Sun* with me, if you find it."

He looked at the diamond dealer. The old man was dead serious. Arsène was quiet for a while, letting Duclerc sit with his impatience. Arsène pretended to ponder, and then said, "Monsieur Duclerc, your offer is very generous, and I appreciate it. But you can't imagine the expense of such an enterprise. Especially since, even if we do find the tomb of Fra Bartolomeo, there's no proof that he's really buried there, and even less proof that his book is with him . . . and what condition would it be in, anyway?"

"It's to your credit that you've revealed your concerns to me, but my mind is made up. Even in my most successful business dealings I've never felt this kind of excitement. I have money, monsieur, a lot of money, and I'm prepared to support you financially to meet this challenge. No point in talking about this any longer. We're both men of action. Let's go to my hotel to discuss the terms of this enterprise."

Seated at his desk, Arsène caressed the document's leather binding. The memory of the three months he'd spent back then delighted him all over again—living in luxury hotels in Acapulco, enjoying life, and writing Fra Bartolomeo's testamentary manuscript, *The Book of the Sun*, whenever the creative urge inspired him. Régis Duclerc had been more than generous.

Arsène had seduced several dozen men and women since then. He'd chosen them from all social classes, and the generosity of a few rich initiates had allowed him to live in comfort. His cult had been a success.

He paged through the manuscript, scanning it with his eyes, even though he'd known it by heart for years. What he'd considered a game at the beginning had become his raison d'être. He'd plunged back into the study of Aztec religion. His objective view as a historian, provided a historian can have an objective view of the elements he studies, had little by little transmuted into the subjective view of this vanished culture. He'd developed a growing interest in the legend of Huitzilopochtli, god of war and the sun.

Arsène had immersed himself in his creation, retaining just enough clarity and perspective to promote, with all the necessary discretion, the cult of his new religion. He'd pulled off a masterstroke. He stood up and returned the work to the safe with mock reverence.

Chapter 30: Worries

Commissioner Mazure entered Étienne Fortin's tiny office. The lieutenant was immersed in the report for the investigation conducted that day at South Hospital. He turned when he sensed the silent presence of his superior behind him.

"Take a chair, Commissioner."

"That's all right, I'll stand. Anything new on the abduction of the Saint-Forge girl?"

"Nothing! All the nursing staff have been interrogated. The files of patients who were treated Sunday afternoon have been scoured. Most of the patients have been contacted, some of us went to question them at home, and nothing. I've never seen so much energy spent on a case. And it's as if the murderer were invisible. Some people remember having seen a blond middle-aged individual, but they didn't notice anything other than that."

"And the medical staff? They weren't surprised to see this individual roaming around?"

"They're on constant overload. One of the nurses asked him who he was looking for or waiting for. He gave her an evasive answer. She wanted to know more, but she had to tend to an emergency in the recovery room. When she came back, the man had moved on and she thought no more about it."

"What do the surveillance cameras say?"

"He arrived on foot in the parking lot around three p.m. and left around five thirty driving a car. With his sunglasses and wig, he's almost impossible to identify."

"Why do you say he had a wig?"

"Julien Lombard, the man who saw the murders in a dream, caught a glimpse of him during his last nightmare. He can't describe him precisely, but he confirmed that he wasn't blond."

"Do you believe his story?" asked Mazure.

"Yes. We had some doubts in the beginning, but the accuracy of the facts is too uncanny to be a coincidence or the delusion of a pathological liar. Nadia is convinced, and so are we."

"We?"

"Rodolphe Drancey and me."

"And what does Rivera think of it?"

Fortin sighed and looked at Alain Mazure with dismay. "For Rivera, Lombard is just Captain Barka's creature. You know how much he *loves* Nadia. Besides, he's convinced that Lombard is, in one way or another, connected to the killer. As if he would ever admit he might be mistaken! Rivera can be a real ass when he puts his mind to it!"

"And where did that lead?"

"He went to find him at his workplace, raid style. But right after they got here, Lombard had secured a lawyer, ready to defend him."

"Who?"

"Madeleine Dupas."

A large smile lit up Mazure's face for the first time that day. "I imagine he didn't stay here long."

"That's right," confirmed Fortin. "I saw Rivera pass by a little later, enraged. But if you want more details, go see Garancher. He looks so innocent, but he gets gossip from everywhere. He's the one who got the wig story. Rivera doesn't trust me—I'm too close to Nadia for him."

"She's the one I wanted to talk to you about. I haven't heard from her since she left the hospital yesterday. What could have come over her?"

"Having any second thoughts, Commissioner?"

"Yes, but from there to not answering her phone or intercom?"

"You went to see her?"

"She hasn't liked me much since I stuck her on forced rest. But I still tried to see her at home. She didn't answer her intercom. I didn't want to insist, but I'm a bit concerned."

Étienne Fortin looked disgruntled. "She didn't open up? Even for you?"

"Even for me. But our last words were heated. I'm worried. She's very strong and has an unusual ability to take a punch, but I still remember the state she was in after her investigation into the death of Laure Déramaux."

"I remember, too. But she resurfaced pretty quickly."

"Exactly. I don't have a doctorate in psychology, but I'm convinced what just happened is causing a relapse—with the guilt of not having caught the killer yet and the frustration of no longer being able to work on the case."

"Commissioner, I have to participate in the review of the research that was done on all doctors in the area with Garancher. It's four o'clock, but I should be able to go visit Nadia around eight."

Chapter 31: Meeting with the Priest

7:00 p.m. Place de Lavalette. Julien stood in front of the door to the Diocesan Residence. In the end, it took a command from Sophie before he had decided to see Father de Valjoney. He pushed at the door. Locked. He looked at the schedule of reception hours. It closed at six. A sort of cowardly relief came over him—he'd come back tomorrow. He was getting ready to leave when the door swung open. A tall man, solidly built and wearing a clerical collar, was exiting the building. Without thinking, Julien went up to him and asked, "Please excuse me, but are you Father Bernard de Valjoney?"

The man looked at him in surprise. "Yes, that's me. What can I do for you?"

There it was. Now Julien had to jump in. "My name is Julien Lombard. I'm a friend of Sophie Dupas. She advised me to meet with you."

The priest listened with interest. He'd known Sophie forever. He'd baptized her when he was still a young priest. He knew she'd sent the young man to him for a good reason.

"Give me two minutes. I have an appointment, but I'm going to push it back."

"I don't want to bother you . . ."

"Leave it to me," he said, speed-dialing a number on his smart-phone. "Pierre-Marie, this is Father Bernard. I'll be a little bit late for our meeting . . . Yes, start without me, and save me a little of your wife's delicious chocolate mousse . . . Thanks, see you later."

He hung up. "Now we have some time to talk. Let's go to my office."

They entered the building, its coolness relaxing Julien. He fol-lowed the priest through the hallways of the vast architectural com-plex and accompanied him into a large office. Father de Valjoney invited him to sit on the leather sofa and went to get a bottle of sparkling water from a refrigerator, which was built into a large library overflowing with books. After they were settled, he asked, "First off, tell me how Sophie's doing."

"Well. I'm impressed with her energy, which is a great support for me right now."

Bernard de Valjoney gave him a long look. "She is indeed an invaluable young woman. Why did she send you to me?"

Julien took a deep breath. Either the priest would take him for a madman in spite of all Sophie had told him, or he might have the beginnings of an answer. In any case, it was too late to turn back now.

"Like everyone else, you've heard about the murder of two young women in Grenoble?"

The priest immediately paid closer attention. "Yes, especially since the first victim was found in the old baptistery."

"Good. In a nutshell, I had a vision of each of those two murders."

He waited for the clergyman to interrupt him, but the priest gestured for him to continue. He told his story for fifteen minutes, without Father de Valjoney saying a word. When he'd finished, he was dripping with sweat but felt a great burden had been lifted from his shoulders.

"May I ask you a few questions?" inquired the priest.

"Of course."

"What are the names of the police officers you encountered?"

"The first person I met was Captain Nadia Barka—at the police station and, the night of the second murder, in the Quartier Saint-Laurent. The one who interrogated me today is Captain Rivera. Captain Barka was very understanding, but I was relieved when Sophie's mother saved me from the clutches of Captain Rivera."

"Ah, so you've met Madeleine Dupas. It would be difficult to find better hands to be in."

Julien Lombard looked questioningly at the priest. "What do you think of my story?"

Bernard de Valjoney took his time before answering. "As a priest, I've met a number of the faithful, and not-so-faithful, who have come to me with all sorts of stories, from the most trivial to the most complex, even unbelievable. Yours is clearly one of the strangest I've ever heard."

"So you don't believe me, do you?"

"Did I say that in the slightest? Let me finish. You can't deny that your story goes beyond conventional understanding. But it's coherent and in line with what I know of this case. I myself met with Captain Barka. Besides, if Sophie sent you to me, it's because she thought you told her the truth."

"So you believe me?"

"Yes, as strange as your visions may be, I believe you are telling me truthfully what you experienced. Furthermore, the facts speak for themselves."

"How do you explain these visions? Who's sending them to me? Why me?"

"I have no idea."

"So you can't do anything for me? What if the killer is getting ready to strike again?"

"I didn't say I couldn't do anything for you. The Church, you see, is very cautious about everything that involves . . . how shall I put this . . . communication with the spirit world. Its precepts are clear—man's salvation is through Christ and the Gospels, and there is no need to talk to spirits in order to get answers."

"I get that, but Bernadette Soubirous had visions of the Virgin at Lourdes, and the Church recognized that as fact."

Father de Valjoney smiled. "Naturally, but one must exercise judgment, a lot of judgment. One name for the devil is Lucifer, the light bringer. If from time to time God manifests his divine power in men in order to edify them, how many men have run to their doom by delving, more or less consciously, into occultism?"

"What does that have to do with me?"

"What do *you* think?"

"First of all, it's terrifying. In fact, it was especially terrifying the second time, when I realized that Camille Saint-Forge might die. Even worse when I saw her get killed. At the time, I didn't understand why someone was inflicting that on me. But then, once the fear passed, I thought back on the facts, on what I saw, and I tried to make sense of it all."

"And what were your conclusions?"

"I think that someone, or something, I don't know, is trying to warn us . . . that I'm just a channel. The police almost arrested the killer at Saint-Laurent, if I rightly understood what Rivera told me. Besides, when I was . . . how do I say this . . . at the scene of Camille's crime, I felt a presence near me."

"What type of presence?"

"A reassuring one, one that encouraged me to move forward. I didn't realize it at the time, but the reason I made it down the hallway to the room where the murderer was sacrificing his victim was because I felt protected."

"And why do you think you were a witness to this murder?"

"That's what I've wondered. Thanks to the vision at the Saint-Laurent museum, I was able to tip off the police about the place where the body would be dumped. I also clearly recognized Camille Saint-Forge's face, which could have helped find her. When she was murdered, I couldn't do anything, but I saw . . . the murderer's face."

"You didn't tell me that just now."

"First I wanted to know if you would believe me. Sorry."

"It doesn't matter. Did you tell the police?"

"Yes. But it didn't appear to me quite clearly enough for me to describe it to them accurately."

"Let's go back to your dream. So you're telling me that someone, whoever it may be, is using you to inform us about the killer's intentions."

"Yes. And the sense of security that I felt makes me think that it's—I don't know—a good spirit."

"Perhaps, but don't be fooled by it. To be effective, the devil must be seductive."

"So what do you think of this whole thing, Father? Can you help me?"

The priest didn't answer right away. He was deep in thought. Julien respected his meditation.

"Personally, I won't be able to give you much help. But I'm going to seek guidance from a few people. Leave me your contact information, and I'll call you tomorrow morning."

"Thank you. What do you plan to do?"

"It's too soon to tell. But tomorrow, before noon, you'll hear from me."

Chapter 32: Four Seasons Pizza

Étienne Fortin had parked in the Grenoble museum lot. Finding a spot around there, at that time in the evening, required a sharp eye, catlike reflexes, and lots of luck.

He'd walked along the Isère in the direction of Nadia's apartment. Those few minutes of walking had done him good and changed his mind. The day had been hard, and Rivera's presence hadn't made it any easier. They had to find something to feed the press and the minister's need for rapid results, which set the whole investigation team's teeth on edge.

He'd stopped to buy two pizzas before going up. He was hungry and knew that Nadia had a weakness for Four Seasons pizza. He was one of the rare colleagues who had been to her apartment. She was very secretive about her private life, but the long hours they'd spent together on stakeouts had fostered a little closeness. In truth, he'd confided more than Nadia. All he'd managed to find out from her was that she didn't have a man in her life.

Étienne pushed open the door to Nadia's building, which was sandwiched in between two Italian restaurants. Because the common areas in the building had no windows, they were completely dark. He flipped the switch, revealing a stairwell that had seen better days. He climbed three flights before arriving in front of his colleague's door. He rang twice. No one answered. He waited thirty seconds, then pushed the button again. He thought he heard a muffled sound inside. He decided to call out. "Nadia, it's Étienne!" Nothing moved. "Nadia, it's Étienne! I have two pizzas, and one's a Four Seasons with oregano."

He waited. Suddenly, he heard the sound of a key turning in the lock. The door opened slowly, and a tired voice said, "Come in."

Étienne entered the shadowy room. Heavy curtains were pulled across the open windows. He looked at his colleague. He'd known her for seven years, but he'd never seen her in this condition. Her face was streaked with tears, and she wasn't trying to hide her distress. She closed the door, took the pizza boxes from him, and carried them into the kitchen. She was wearing only a rumpled sleeveless T-shirt and denim short shorts that she'd thrown on just before coming to the door. She slowly came back out of the kitchen and gestured toward the sofa.

"Sit down."

He obeyed.

"What do you want?" she asked in a tone he found surprisingly curt.

He decided not to take offense. She hadn't asked him for anything, and he was disturbing her solitude. But he didn't regret being there, no matter what the outcome was.

"How are you?" Étienne asked.

She spread her hands evasively. "What do you think?"

"Not looking good . . . but maybe after a Four Seasons? They should still be warm."

"Maybe you're right. I'll go get them."

Nadia came back from the kitchen with the two pizzas and a bottle of chili oil (one of the rare culinary preparations she still took time to do herself), put them on her living room coffee table, and waited.

"I asked him to slice them for us," Étienne told her.

"Okay. I think I'm hungry."

They ate in silence. Étienne would have liked a lively discussion, but he recognized his colleague wasn't ready to talk yet. They didn't leave a single crumb in the boxes. Nadia looked at him, then seemed to reconnect to the world around her. "I was hungry."

She finally came out of her stupor. "I didn't offer you anything to drink. I'm going to see what's left in my fridge."

She reappeared with a bottle of Coke, a bottle of water, and a six-pack of cold beer.

"I'll have a glass of water and a beer, please."

She left the bottle and the six-pack on the table, put the soda back in the fridge, then returned with two glasses, which she placed in front of them. Étienne decided to initiate the discussion.

"Was it the Four Seasons that got you to open up for me?"

She gave a weary, enigmatic smile. "Maybe. I didn't feel like seeing anybody. I imagine your culinary argument was worth all the sermons in the world."

"We're worried about you."

"Who cares about me?"

"Rodolphe, Jérôme, Marie, and lots of others. And me!"

"That's nice of you. It's true I'm having a hard time right now, but it'll pass. It's always passed," she added, almost imperceptibly lowering her head.

When Étienne saw her so demoralized, he felt his heart break. Captain Nadia Barka, always at the heart of the action, always the first to comfort a colleague who needed it, an officer who was relied on by her higher-ups and her colleagues, now needed his help. He remembered her unfailing support during the Barciglia case. He had to say something, even if she sent him packing.

"Nadia, we're all disappointed not to have you in charge of this case anymore."

"It's not that, Étienne," she cut him off. "Far from that! Let's just say it's the straw that broke the camel's back."

He fell silent, guessing she needed to talk, to purge everything that had been spinning around in her head for two days.

"My life is pathetic. And only at thirty-six years old do I finally have the courage to realize it. What have I gained by putting more than fifteen years of service into law enforcement? Look at the state I'm in! My head in a muddle, nightmares one right after the other almost continuously, the jealousy of half my colleagues, the hatred of a chunk of the population, two bullets in my skin and a knife wound, and, especially, a disastrous personal life. No one to talk with about little everyday things in the evening, no one to reassure me when things aren't going well, no one to ask how they are when I come home! That, Étienne, is what I've come to . . . And when you finally open your eyes, and you let all the walls you built to protect yourself fall, it hurts—a lot."

Étienne didn't reply. Nadia's words had just made him think about himself. Was his life really any more enviable? No doubt, because he wasn't living his colleague's nightmares, but the loneliness she spoke of frightened him. He wasn't seeing the years pass as quickly as the young woman was, telling himself that he'd always have time to start a family. But his private life was as hopeless as his friend's. Because he was pretty handsome, he'd always managed to go out on dates now and again. But he was starting to wonder when he'd find someone to build a life with.

They looked at each other silently, immersed in their gloomy thoughts. Nadia was sitting on the sofa, legs tucked underneath her. Étienne had a sudden flash of insight: what if the person he was waiting for was right in front of him? No, that was absurd. First of all, never date someone from the office. And then, why Nadia? He'd always had a weakness for her, but it was an imaginary world, a sweet dream. He'd never imagined trying something serious. Or maybe he'd never dared imagine it?

He looked at her large dark eyes, framed by a squarish cut of black hair. A mouth that could threaten as easily as it could enchant. Her exhausted face exposed a fragility that touched him. As for her body, it was perfect, sculpted by constant workouts, but that wasn't what Étienne was looking at. He felt himself gently carried away by a wave that took him far from the shore of reality.

"You okay, Étienne?"

He was startled by Nadia's eyes examining him. The darkness in the room hid his confusion, but even so, he must not have been very discreet. "Yes, just fine, thanks. What about you, how's your wound?" he said, seeing the bandage visible underneath the young woman's T-shirt.

"I have to redo my dressing. I was just about to start when you buzzed."

"Let me help you. You know I was a nurse for a few years."

"Do I know? Given the number of times you came to our rescue, I'd have to have Alzheimer's not to remember! Okay, take care of me, it'll do me good, and it'll probably be better than what I've been able to cobble together the past two days."

They proceeded to the bathroom. It was huge and tiled in warm ocher. A shower stall with a massage showerhead occupied one corner; another stall, enclosed by a glass door, faced them.

"What's that?" asked Étienne curiously.

"A sauna. I gave it to myself two years ago, but I've hardly had the opportunity to use it. Here, I'll turn it on. It'll do us good. Let me take a shower first."

Étienne left the bathroom, more confused than he could say. He hadn't imagined finding himself in this situation when, less than an hour earlier, he was on the landing outside the apartment wondering if his colleague was going to let him in.

Nadia came out of the bathroom, dripping, wrapped in a towel.

"Your turn. In the time it'll take you to shower, the sauna will be at the right temperature."

He came closer to her and looked at her shoulder. "First let me see how it's healing."

She undid her towel and nonchalantly dropped it to her waist. Étienne concentrated on the wound. Shit, he felt like a teenager on a first date. God only knew if he'd ever get a second one.

His professionalism regained the upper hand, and he saw that the injury was healing nicely. The wound was clean. The skin was puckered around it but would return to normal soon enough. "Everything looks good. I'll redo your dressing after the sauna. But don't turn it up too hot."

"Okay, Doc."

A puff of heat escaped into the bathroom when Nadia opened the sauna door. They stepped into the small space and sat on the wooden bench. Étienne had brought a bottle of ice water and two glasses. They had towels around their waists. He appreciated the heat enveloping him and drawing the fatigue and stress of the last few days out of his body.

Nadia's face had recovered its suppleness and, eyes half closed, she abandoned herself to the relaxation overtaking her bit by bit. Why didn't she use this sauna more often? Undoubtedly because she didn't feel like coming face-to-face with her loneliness. But that evening, things were different. She nearly hadn't let Étienne in, and it really was the reference to Four Seasons pizza that had been the trigger. Now, she didn't regret it in the slightest. She really needed the company.

They got out twenty minutes later and, after a cold shower, sat on the living room sofa. Étienne took the bottle of soda from the fridge with him. Nadia went to find him a T-shirt that was too big for her, a souvenir from the Berlin Marathon. Then Étienne redid her dressing, his nursing expertise coming back to him. They drank the cold soda slowly.

"That feels good. Thank you for coming over."

"If we're not there to comfort each other during the rough patches, who will be?"

"It's still very nice." She seemed to hesitate, then asked him, "Are you authorized to discuss what's going on with Operation Open Heart?"

Étienne was surprised. "Of course. They took you off the case, not off the *force*! But . . . I'm surprised you want to discuss it."

"No matter how far down in the dumps I've been, I couldn't stop the little wheels in my head from turning. Can you sum up for me what's happened over the past two days?"

Étienne brought her up to speed on the case and the ongoing investigations. When he'd finished, Nadia said, "So, for the Chechen's death, no big headlines in the papers."

"They're talking about it, but the murder of Camille Saint-Forge has drawn media attention. Besides, the bullet you took in the shoulder is irrefutable proof of self-defense. His lawyer will probably get involved, but he shouldn't have much to latch on to. And Bogossian was more feared than loved by his gang."

"I'm surprised I haven't been summoned yet for that case."

"It's Mazure's responsibility. He saw you at the hospital, he has my testimony and Rodolphe's. I think he wanted to let you rest as long as possible."

"I appreciate the gesture. But there's a question I haven't asked you yet. Who dropped Bogossian?"

"I did."

She gave him a long look. "Thank you: I owe you my life. A pizza and my life."

"No . . . the pizza I gave to you willingly. And I'm enjoying your life tonight. I can also assure you that the Chechen's ghost has yet to come haunt me at night."

"Let's go back to what you told me. You've launched inquiries to identify the killer's car, but nothing concrete has been found, correct?"

"Correct."

"Have you looked into the guys from the Chechen's gang?"

"I recognized one of them in the internal files, but it's impossible to identify the others."

"I've identified five of them, the ones I'd caught two years ago in a drug trafficking case. I'm going to write down their names. They've all got files, and you can gather the addresses by tomorrow morning. There's a good chance they saw something."

She got up and went over to her desk. She picked up a pen, noted down the names on a piece of paper, and handed the list to him. "If you want peace with Rivera, tell him you busted your butt all night with the files and recognized them."

"Thanks for the alibi, Captain."

"I thought of something else, too, and I have to admit it disturbed me."

"Go on."

"I wondered if there might be a connection between the Déramaux case and today's."

"I'm listening."

"It's just a theory, but in between naps these past two days, I surfed the Internet. And I stumbled across a site on Aztec tribes. The Aztecs tore out their victims' hearts to give glory to their gods. But when I looked more closely, I saw that mutilation was also practiced in certain tribes under Aztec rule. I wondered if there could be a connection between the two. Laure wasn't tortured randomly, but according to a very structured ritual. She was tended to after each ritual they inflicted on her."

"Nadia, are you sure you want to go back there?"

"Yes. You have to resume investigating all the disappearances that have taken place over the last ten years. If a hiker hadn't found her, Laure's body would have disappeared without anyone ever knowing what happened. Can you open it up again?"

"Okay, I'll look into it," replied Étienne, impressed by his colleague's transformation.

Then Nadia turned inward, daydreaming. It seemed to him she was drifting away again. The room was now completely dark—night had descended over the city. Street sounds drifted in through the open window, and a Neapolitan hit song from the pizza place below, a mandolin tune, dissolved into the night air.

Étienne looked at his friend. It was nice here, but he had to let her rest. He'd experienced a moment of deep intimacy, but he wasn't dealing with just anyone. He mustn't rush her. He cared too much.

"I'm going to let you rest. You must need some sleep. Thank you for this evening, Nadia."

She looked at him in surprise. "You want to leave already? We've talked about practically nothing but work."

"What do you want to talk about?"

"Why not you? We've worked together for years, and I don't know much about what you're like, your life."

"Do you think it's interesting?"

"I don't know yet, but I really, really want to find out."

"Fine, but to be fair, you have to tell me about yours."

She paused for a moment. "Okay. You know this will probably be the first time."

"I'm well aware of how lucky I am."

Nadia got up and slid a disc into her CD player. The music of Cesaria Evora wafted into the air, offering up its sweet Cape Verdean chords.

The bells of Saint-André chimed one o'clock. They were sprawled on the sofa, leaning against each other, and they had little by little confided far more than they'd intended.

Étienne forced himself back to reality. He knew he was on a slippery slope. That evening, he hadn't seen Nadia as an ace cop anymore, but as a seductive woman, mysterious and fragile, whom he felt like conquering and protecting at the same time. But he knew he was putting himself in danger—danger of falling madly in love with a woman who appreciated him, of that he was certain. Nadia likely even considered him a friend, which was a wonderful gift. But she surely wasn't hooked like he was now. He'd fallen in love. He'd waited thirty-five years for it to happen. And he didn't want to suffer, because he knew he would suffer terribly if it went wrong. He had only one solution—run away.

"I'm gonna head out, Nadia. I don't want to impose on you."

She stared at him intensely. Despite the darkness, he felt her gaze penetrating the deepest part of him.

"Stay and make love to me."

His heart raced. Her gaze became insistent and melted his already weakened will.

She brought her mouth close to his and kissed him. The heat of her lips thrilled him, reducing his last arguments to cinders. Never again would he have a moment like this. He'd have time to think about the consequences later.

Chapter 33: Julien's Testimony

"So you don't even want to go get a coffee?"

"Sorry, Sophie, but I'm drained. At night, I wonder what nightmare I'm going to have, and during the day, I flip out as soon as I see a girl wearing so much as a white T-shirt!"

"Well, that's one more guy who isn't ready for marriage!"

Julien smiled at his friend's joke. He was grateful to her for trying to pull him out of his bleak thoughts.

"Okay, fine, I'll go with you. It will give us a break. I think I'm even going to take a few days of vacation—given how productive I am at work right now, it'll be to the office's benefit. Give me five minutes, I'm going to see Patrick about my leave."

When he came out of the company manager's office, he motioned to Sophie, and they met in the stairwell.

"So?" she asked.

"No problem, he understood. I'm on leave until the beginning of next week. To celebrate that, I'll buy the coffee."

"Yeah, I should take advantage! Such an opportunity rarely comes around twice!"

They sat in their usual corner.

"Father de Valjoney still hasn't called you back?"

"It's only ten o'clock. I don't know what he's up to. You don't have any idea?"

"You're the one who spent time with him," commented Sophie. "He didn't call me afterward for a morality check or to find out if you were of sound mind."

"That's absolutely not what I meant, but I was up half the night thinking about it. He seemed like he had a solution or a lead that could help me, but he didn't want to tell me anything."

"You know very well the Lord works in mysterious ways," she said with a wink.

"Okay, fine. Let's move on to another topic."

The young man was interrupted by a vibration that quickly changed into a Lady Gaga hit. The sound grew louder until Julien managed to extract the phone from the pocket of his jeans.

"Hello?" He let a long moment go by. Sophie was surprised by his focused look.

"When would you like me to come by? . . . Okay, I'll check with Sophie about her availability, and we'll be right there." He ended the call.

"An invitation for two to Zara?" asked Sophie.

"Not this time. You remember Captain Barka, from the police station?"

"She liked you that much?"

"Stop joking around for two seconds, Sophie. She wants to meet with us to go back over the murders from the last few days. And she'd like us both to come."

Sophie grew serious. "But didn't you tell me she'd been replaced on the case by the cowboy who came for you at the office?"

"Yes, and she confirmed it. But she's still working on the murders. What do you say?"

"I think I'm going to take a vacation day, too. We can pop into the police station."

"She's not there. She asked us to come to her house."

"Well, fortunately she insisted I come with you, because with that girl, I would have been suspicious."

"Are you jealous?"

"Would that make you happy?"

"A little, but not too much."

"No, I'm not jealous by nature. But best not to betray my trust when I give it."

"And I have it?"

"I think so. Come on, enough discussion, where does she live?"

Julien looked at her, embarrassed. "I think I forgot to ask her address—or she forgot to give it to me," he added quickly. "But no problem, I'll call her back."

Julien and Sophie finished off the fruit juice Nadia Barka had given them. Sun streamed into the orderly room. They'd just talked for almost an hour and now knew details that hadn't been revealed in the papers. Julien had described precisely what he'd seen and whom he'd seen. Sophie had corroborated his statements, and Nadia had listened to them with great interest.

"Have you given the same deposition at the police station?"

"Captain Rivera took me for an idiot when I told him all that. I gave him every detail, but I'm not sure he took my testimony seriously. He's not the sort of man whose company you seek out."

"That's putting it mildly. But I'm going to ask you to go back and meet with Lieutenant Fortin. He'll be very interested to hear what you have to say, even more so because I'll give him a heads-up. Your description of the facts, and especially the killer, can really help us."

"I'll go after I leave here."

"Thank you. I'll keep at it on my side, researching the Aztec people and their customs."

"Do you think it could have a direct link to the murders?" Sophie interjected.

"Maybe! I don't have any proof, but something like a hunch."

"My father teaches history, at the Université Pierre Mendès–France. I'm not sure pre-Columbian civilizations are his specialty, but if he can't help you, he'll surely be able to direct you to one of his eminent colleagues."

"Could you get me an appointment with him?"

"Let me make a couple of calls, and if you're available, we'll go meet him. He'll be happy to see me."

Chapter 34: Raid

The sun scorched the grass, already yellowed by the heat wave. Ripples of heat shimmered over the ground, displacing from the lawn every trace of activity.

Drancey glanced at the car's thermometer: almost ninety-nine degrees. Still five more minutes to cook inside the Subaru before they could start. Each of the three men was focused on the plan. Everything could quickly spin out of control in this type of operation.

Drancey glanced at his watch—2:00 p.m. He motioned to the two police officers. They got out of the unmarked car and headed toward the buildings.

"There's the entrance to number sixteen," confirmed Drancey. "We have to take it easy, boys. We're not here to bust him for attempted murder, just to get his testimony."

"No worries, Rodolphe, the mission is clear to us," replied Pierre Galtard, a stocky man with a thick mustache.

The third team member, Rio Sissoko, simply nodded. He'd just spent three years in some rough neighborhoods around Lyon. He knew how to keep cool.

They approached the lobby. In the early afternoon, only a few people were out and about. Most were inside their apartments protecting themselves from the relentless sun. The arrival of Drancey and his team had yet to be noticed. They walked up to the mailboxes. Some had been vandalized. Luckily, they found the name of the man they were looking for.

"Eighth floor," said Drancey. "We'll take the stairs."

The building's stillness surprised Sissoko.

"We'll all strike at the same time," said Drancey. "They won't have time to sound the alarm."

That morning, Étienne Fortin had provided the names of the five suspects to target. Five teams of three policemen had been sent to get them at 2:00 p.m. in a synchronized plan.

After some inconspicuous climbing, they reached the eighth floor. They pushed away a shopping cart cluttering the hallway and inspected the doors.

"Of course, no names!" groused Galtard.

"What'd you expect?" replied Drancey. "Welcome signs on the doorknobs?"

Galtard didn't react to the sarcastic comment.

"He still lives with his mother. She's the one we'll ask for. Come on, we'll start on the left. In any case, we'll get some information."

"Maybe," Sissoko quipped doubtfully. "Let's go."

Drancey knocked on the door. He heard someone bustling around inside the apartment. Nobody opened the door. The men felt the tension building. He knocked again. A feminine voice answered.

"Who is it?"

"Police, open up!"

After a moment, the sound of a key in the lock could be heard and the door opened halfway. The men stood back slightly. A wrinkled old woman appeared silhouetted against the light.

"What do you want?"

"Are you Madame Sikorski?"

She gave the three men in front of her a long look. She pointed at the door across the hall. "Over there. Nobody's doing anything wrong over here."

Then she slammed the door behind her. The policemen looked at each other, then crossed the hallway.

"Here we go. If Sylvain Sikorski is there, the welcome may be less peaceful."

They knocked on the second door. Once again, they heard noise inside the apartment. Doors slamming, then nothing. They knocked again.

"Who's there?" screamed a masculine voice.

"Police, open up!"

A child heading up the stairs passed by the landing. He saw the three policemen and ran back down.

"That's just what we needed. We have to act quickly." Drancey hammered on the door. "Open up. We need to speak with Sylvain Sikorski. He may have been an inadvertent witness to the murder of one of the young Grenoble women found dead."

"You think he'll believe that?" asked Galtard.

"Probably not, but he should," answered Drancey. "Open up!"

No one was moving in the apartment anymore. The neighbors from other floors were starting to peek at the scene from the stairwell, as if called by an invisible signal. They stared at the police on the landing, some curious, others with aggression. Sissoko decided to speak to them.

"Maybe you can help us. Monsieur Sikorski has likely witnessed a murder. We absolutely have to talk to him."

A man of about thirty, with a shaved head, approached them, followed by three swaggering acolytes. The cops were on their turf.

"Hey, fool, you think we're pussies? What do you cops want with Sylvain?"

Drancey recognized one of the men from the Chechen's gang. He stepped away and let Sissoko do the talking. If that guy remembered Drancey, too, things would get damn complicated. The situation wasn't getting defused.

"Go on, get lost, cops, before you get on our nerves," continued the ringleader, raising his voice.

Sissoko tried again. "Nobody's getting on anybody's nerves. We're here as part of the investigation into the murder of two people. We're looking for Sylvain Sikorski as a witness. That's all."

The ringleader came closer to Sissoko, still backed by his bodyguards.

"You're a fucking stupid cop! Didn't you understand what I said? Here, we don't negotiate. You fuck off."

Drancey saw the crowd growing. About fifteen people were now watching the exchange. He boiled inside. He couldn't stand guys like this. Sissoko looked his counterpart dead in the eye.

"We're not interested in any trafficking taking place here. We just want to interview Sylvain Sikorski as a witness."

He noticed the subtle nod the ringleader gave to his neighbor on the right, a wild-eyed kid. Sissoko was instantly on high alert. The kid took a knife from his belt and jumped on the policeman. On his guard, Sissoko dodged the stab and, in two seconds, disarmed his attacker by trapping him in an armlock. He tightened it, causing a whimper to escape from the kid's mouth.

"Intimidation is useless. We just want to talk with Sylvain Sikorski."

His calm surprised the crowd, who were expecting an outbreak of violence. The ringleader hesitated for a moment, then looked at his troops.

"I think they don't understand who we are, or whose house they're in! We'll have to show 'em different. They're gonna learn about my rage. I make the law here, not three asshole cops."

He looked at the policemen, certain of his power in this building. Drancey walked confidently up to the man and seized him firmly by the right arm. Then he exploded.

"Poor bastard, cut the crap. You remember, Sunday night, when you were with the Chechen. When you tried to rape that girl, threatening to kill her. And then all of a sudden, the Chechen collapsed like a piece of shit, killed by the bullet that should have nailed him long ago. Well, we were both there! And what did he do, the big man who makes the law here? You tell your friends what the big man did? No? Well, I'll tell them. He shit his pants!"

Drancey looked at the mesmerized crowd. "He sniveled like a little kid. 'Please, don't hurt me, I have to take care of my family.' You shit yourself over it, you poor bastard. Did you tell your pals about that?"

The gang leader's face had changed color. His features were clenched, and he couldn't manage a response to Drancey's attack. The cop kept going.

"But we're not here about that today. I think my colleague explained it to you very clearly . . . unless it didn't make it through your thick skull, moron."

The man reacted to the last insult. "Slaughter them!"

An uproar answered his order. Drancey's remarks had been effective.

"He's lying!" screamed the humiliated ringleader.

The voices of the different gang members rose to a crescendo. The hoodlum, sensing he was on the verge of losing his authority, pulled a pistol out of his jacket pocket and aimed at Drancey. Galtard intervened, quick as lightning, and twisted the ringleader's arm. With a cry of pain, he dropped his weapon. The policemen looked at each other and decided to leave their weapons undrawn. They had to take advantage of the situation and avoid adding to the tension.

"Help me, fuckers! Help me!"

But no one moved.

"That's enough now!" A deep voice was heard from the stairwell. All conversation stopped immediately. "Max, you didn't keep your word."

The ringleader's face paled, frozen by that simple sentence.

"You're going to obey these nice policemen's orders. If anybody has something to tell about those murders, let him do it."

The policemen looked up. They saw, standing at the top of the stairs, a short man wearing an old-fashioned suit. He looked well over sixty and seemed totally inoffensive. He withdrew and went back downstairs, without another word.

The aggression instantly relaxed. Rio Sissoko looked questioningly at his colleagues, then released his prisoner. Drancey let go of the ringleader's arm and pointed at the door. Max, as he'd been called, rubbed his arm, then obeyed the order.

"Sylvain, it's Max. Open up, it's . . . you know who asked you to," he added, looking distrustfully at the three policemen.

"They're bluffing, Max, I know they want to nab me."

"No, Sylvain, you have my word!" Voices rose up behind him to affirm the truth of his statement.

The door opened. Sylvain was standing upright, a pistol in his hand. The policemen immediately took note of his hugely dilated pupils—he must have done a tremendous amount of coke. Sikorski looked at the men standing in the door frame. He immediately recognized Drancey, who was standing behind Max.

"Motherfucker, you lied to me! They've come to bust me!" He raised his weapon and fired two shots at Max, who crumpled. Then he turned his handgun toward Drancey. Hampered by the fleeing residents, Drancey couldn't get his Manurhin out. He threw himself on the floor. His reflexes saved his life. The bullet grazed his shoulder. A second shot echoed it, followed by a cry,

"That's it now, we're done playing!" Sissoko put his weapon back in its holster. Sikorski was on the ground, his wrist shattered by the nine-millimeter bullet. Panic had overtaken the building. Galtard was leaning over Max.

"You okay, Drancey?" asked Rio Sissoko.

"Yes, it only got my jacket."

"Good reflexes!"

Drancey and Sissoko explored the apartment. They found a terrified woman in one of the bedrooms.

"Are you Madame Sikorski?"

The woman nodded, trembling.

"You can come out, it's all over!"

"Is he . . ."

"Alive? Yes. A little banged up, but alive."

"Thank God."

They went back to the entrance. Sikorski was sitting against the wall and screaming like a madman. Galtard examined Max, stretched out on the floor.

"Not too bad by the looks of it. He took one in the belly fat and the other in the leg. For being shot at close range, he came out okay. What about the other one?"

"Wrist shattered. It'll be some time before he can write again. Call an ambulance and Dispatch."

The old man in the suit presented himself before the three police-men, interrupting the hubbub in the hallway. He was a head shorter than they were, but his severe facial features and authoritative man-ner impressed the police officers. He motioned to Galtard to put away his phone, who obeyed without really knowing why. The crowd watched the scene silently, as though they were witnessing a religious service. The old man removed his astrakhan cap to address the policemen.

"I'm very sorry about what's happened, gentlemen."

"We are, too. Double attempted homicide and two wounded—you don't see that every day," replied Drancey, who was in charge of the mission.

"I understand. There was a lot of nervousness today."

"There's been too much nervousness lately, monsieur . . ."

"Call me Monsieur Ibrahim."

"We're going to have to take Monsieur Sikorski with us. It wasn't our initial objective, but there are things that are just not done, Monsieur Ibrahim."

"I understand, I understand completely. But perhaps we could nevertheless come to an agreement?"

"An agreement? I don't quite see how, given the current situation."

"Let me suggest something to you. Will you follow me?"

The policemen looked at each other. This man, and his influ-ence on the local population, intrigued them.

"All right. But I'm at least calling an ambulance."

"Wait." Monsieur Ibrahim spoke to two men in his native lan-guage, who then ran off. "We'll have a doctor in five minutes."

They followed the man into the kitchen and sat around the table.

"Here is my suggestion, gentlemen. You've come looking for information on the murders of Monica Revasti and Camille Saint-Forge."

The policemen looked at him in surprise.

"I read the papers. Sylvain Sikorski could have given you a clue, then?"

"And the one called Max, too."

"Here's what I propose. You interview young Sylvain for five minutes. Anyway, in his current state, I doubt he'll give you much."

"You mean high on coke?"

"Among other things, unfortunately. Next, we'll regard this altercation as never taking place."

"Altercation?" repeated Drancey. "We're not using the same vocabulary. We still have your Max on the floor and an attempted murder."

"We'll take care of Max, and we'll take care of Sylvain."

"We have to rush them to the hospital!"

"I assure you they'll have all the necessary care."

"Let's pretend I believe you. And in exchange?"

"Tomorrow, at eight o'clock, someone will come down to the police station to give you all the information on the killer you could have found here. I am personally committed to engaging all the means I have at my disposal."

Drancey didn't cut in, just let him continue. The man went on with a half smile.

"To gather this type of information, I think our sphere of influence is better equipped than yours. If there's anything to know, you'll know it. You have Monsieur Ibrahim's word."

The situation seemed unreal to the policemen: this convincing, soft-spoken old man; the two injured men who had been dragged into the apartment and were now being cared for by who knew whom; and this proposition they were seriously considering despite everything that had just happened. They looked at each other. Drancey's instinct told him they had to accept.

"Tomorrow at eight o'clock, in front of the police station. I'll be there. But your messenger will have to be there, too," he said.

"Don't worry. As you might have guessed, I'm a man of my word."

"We accept. But know this, and tell your friends—it won't happen again."

"I thank you. You won't regret it. As for the two people who stepped over the line, we're going to explain to them what isn't done. I'll take care of it myself, be certain of that. I promise you the police won't ever deal with them again."

Dumbfounded by the bargain they'd just struck, the policemen left the apartment. The hallway, landing, and stairwell were all empty once more.

Chapter 35: The Specialist

6:00 p.m. Sophie parked her VW Polo in the history department lot. By this time of year, exams were long over and only a few year-round workers, PhD students, and professors still occupied the premises.

Sophie shut the door, waited until Nadia got out, and then locked the car.

"You can never be too careful in this parking lot. My father's had things stolen several times. He never locks his doors."

"That probably keeps him from having to replace the windows," replied the police officer. She grimaced and moved her shoulders. The pain was still acute, and she'd forgotten to take her pain meds. "However," she added, "I understand your precautions."

They headed for the university building.

"You might be surprised by my father's appearance," Sophie warned. "He's an eternal daydreamer who had trouble leaving childhood behind. In fact, I'm not convinced he left it completely. But that's ideal for us children, isn't it?"

"I don't know," replied Nadia. "I never got the impression my father was ever young. Anyway, it'll take my mind off things."

"Then again, he's a wealth of cultural information, and if he can help you, he will."

They entered the building and ended up at an office with a closed door. Sophie rapped sharply three times, then twice more slowly. A voice shouted to them from inside.

"Come in with your friend, my girl, I'm waiting for you."

Sophie pushed open the door. The room was in indescribable disorder: an old oak table; a blackboard on one wall, a bunch of miscellaneous posters and a map of the world on the others; a reproduction of a Miró painting behind Professor Dupas. Two armchairs and a barstool faced the desk. A rickety coatrack occupied one corner, holding up a hat and a leather jacket, and archival boxes were deposited here and there according to the owner's mood.

Nadia suppressed a smile when she saw Sophie's father, feet on the desk, in the middle of reading a historical review. Professor Dupas resembled Harrison Ford in *Indiana Jones*. She looked around for a whip and couldn't keep herself from laughing when she saw it. She stopped quickly, realizing her tactlessness. But her laughter hadn't bothered the historian, who cultivated his natural resemblance to the character. She now understood Sophie's remark.

"Antoine Dupas, at your service. My daughter told me I could help you, but I don't know any more than that."

"Thank you, Professor, I'm happy to explain."

"Call me Antoine. Where's my head? Can I get you something to drink? I have a fridge somewhere in this mess, which is indispensable to my work, by the way."

"I'll have a glass of water, thanks."

Captain Barka gave him a rundown of events and explained her reasons for seeing him. Antoine Dupas, now totally serious, hadn't missed a single word of Nadia's explanation. He took his time responding.

"I'm not a specialist in Mesoamerican civilizations."

"Mesoamerica?"

"It's the geographic area covering the territory from northern Mexico to Costa Rica. It includes all the pre-Columbian civilizations. There just happens to be a colleague here today who can advise you."

"Who is it?" asked Sophie.

"You've already met him. It's Professor Boisregard."

"The curator for the Old Diocese Museum?" asked Nadia.

"The same. You know him?"

"I met him the day after the murder of the first victim, in the baptistery."

"What a coincidence! I know he worked for a time on the Inca civilization. He may have gone a bit farther north to the Aztecs."

Sophie interrupted her father. "This is the guy who wore a tuxedo to the party you organized for your induction into the Ordre des Palmes Académiques?"

"Yes, the very same. The one you hit on shamelessly."

"Hit on Boisregard?" chuckled Nadia. "Strange notion—he's likely very nice, but not to flirt with! He also seemed completely clueless the day the murder was discovered."

"My father is always looking for the subtleties," returned Sophie. "I just took pity on this guy getting bored alone in his corner, and I went to talk with him for a few minutes. Period."

"Indeed, I might have gotten carried away," conceded Antoine Dupas. "However, it proves you're a charming woman. Likely even a bit too sexy for a cocktail party with members of the Académie! Boisregard might have gone home with sweet dreams in his head."

"I'd like to remind you, Papa, that you strongly insisted I attend. I'd also like to remind you that I am thirty-one years old, and I don't need you to tell me about my seductive potential. But we're not here to work on my upbringing in front of Nadia. Can you introduce her to Professor Boisregard?"

Antoine Dupas was up like a shot. "You're right, my girl! Let's not waste your friend Captain Barka's time. We'll go right now!"

Nadia wondered if he was going to take his hat. But the professor was too excited to think about perfecting his look. He hurried into the hallway and rushed into the office of Olivier Ménard, a specialist in the history of Grenoble from the early twentieth century. Two men were talking quietly, and Antoine Dupas's noisy arrival startled them.

"Ah, you're still here! I have two people who need Professor Boisregard's enlightenment. Ménard, will you lend him to me?"

"Do I have a choice, Indy? Go on in, Professor."

Nadia and Sophie were still in the hallway when Antoine Dupas came out with his colleague. He introduced the two women, and then said ceremoniously, "Ladies, your mentor in pre-Columbian civilization—the eminent Professor Boisregard."

Boisregard recognized the police officer. "We've already met, haven't we?"

"In your office, a week ago."

"Indeed. I remember it well now. And, Mademoiselle Dupas—it's a great pleasure to see you again. How may I help you?"

It seemed to Sophie the curator blushed slightly as he greeted her.

The police officer explained, "I'd like some answers to a few questions I've had about the Aztecs."

Boisregard looked at her, astonished, but courteously agreed.

"I can dedicate some time to you."

"Thank you so much. Where do you want us to sit?"

"You can use my office. It's quite comfortable for conversation," offered Antoine Dupas. They returned to the lair of the French Indiana Jones.

"Sophie, are you coming with me?" asked her father.

"I'd like to listen to the discussion, if Captain Barka doesn't mind."

"You can stay, Sophie."

Antoine Dupas took his hat and settled it on his head. He shot them one of his favorite hero's smirks—he knew how to play up the resemblance to Harrison Ford.

"My friend, I leave you with your new students," Dupas declared theatrically to Boisregard. "And take care of them! I'm entrusting you with the apple of my eye."

"I'm not the specialist Professor Dupas has done his utmost to portray me as," began the historian. "I have some knowledge on those cultures, but if you really want details, I'd have to do some research beforehand. I know very prominent scholars in Lyon."

"I'm sure your knowledge will be able to help me see more clearly, Professor," Nadia reassured him. She succinctly explained the case, then asked her questions.

He began his talk by outlining the pre-Columbian civilizations before the arrival of the conquistadors, then zeroed in on the subject that interested Nadia: human sacrifice.

"For the Mexicas, or the Aztecs as they've been called since the seventeenth century, human sacrifice was part of all their religious ceremonies, their lives, I could even say. It seems barbaric to us today, but you have to remember these sacrifices were totally integrated into the customs. The Aztecs, like the Mayans as well, worshipped the sun, the rain, the moon, and a whole host of gods. They thought Quetzalcoatl, the famous feathered serpent god, had created them. This god had descended to the land of the dead, had watered the bones of the ancestors with his own blood, and thus given them new life. That's why the Aztecs offered human sacrifices to their god. There were many kinds, but if we look at the case that concerns us, the sacrificial victims had their hearts torn out so that the sun could rise every morning."

"So these sacrifices were common practice?" wondered Sophie.

"As I told you, mademoiselle, very common. Another example: the second month of the Aztec calendar is called Tlacaxipehualiztli, which means the flaying of men. Hundreds of victims were slaughtered or decapitated, then flayed in honor of the god of agricultural renewal. The skulls were exposed, and the priests made themselves clothes out of the victims' skin. To complete the picture, cannibalism was also practiced among the Aztecs."

"And who were the victims?"

"Very often prisoners of war, which partly explains why the cities were in constant conflict. But also sometimes consenting members of the society. The victims were thought to have an enviable fate, to accompany the sun in its course and be reincarnated as butterflies."

"Were the sacrifices practiced only in honor of the gods?" continued Nadia.

"Basically, because any trouble was linked to angry gods—a flood, an earthquake . . ."

"How were the victims killed?"

"The priest generally tore out the living heart, with the help of an obsidian knife. The blood ran in great gushes, thus satisfying the venerated god."

"And what did the priest do with the victim's heart?" insisted Nadia.

"Most of the time, he put it on the altar so that the god could feast upon it."

"Could he eat it?"

"Rarely, but it could happen. As I told you, the Aztecs could practice cannibalism, especially with prisoners of war."

"Would it have been possible for a sacrifice to be made not for a god, but in honor of another human being?"

Professor Boisregard paused and looked at the two women worriedly. "Do you seriously think the horrible murders just perpetrated could be an act of mimicry with regard to the rites of these American peoples?"

"I have no idea, Professor, but I want to explore every lead. Even the most improbable in this case," the police officer reassured him.

The curator thought for a few seconds, then continued his discourse.

"The Mayans believed in a sort of bioenergy. Each living being possessed it—men, animals, plants, and of course gods. The Mayans thought the bioenergy of the gods had to be regenerated regularly. Thus the sacrifices offered the victims' energy to the gods, restoring the gods' full powers, and the gods could once again lavish men with their bounty. The Aztecs took much inspiration from the Mayans."

"So could you envision sacrifices being used to revitalize not a god, but an important person?"

"It happened, but only for certain kings or emperors. These kings or emperors in turn would offer some of their blood to the gods."

He asked again, "Do you really think this could be connected to the murders?"

"I don't know, Professor," confessed Nadia. "But the killer is not of sound mind. Many serial killers have patterned themselves after templates of all kinds. Given the modus operandi, nothing should be ruled out."

"Have I answered all your questions?"

"I have a last request, Professor."

Boisregard looked at his watch. "I can give you a few more minutes."

"We've talked about rather . . . expeditious sacrifices. Were there, to your knowledge, other types of offerings to the gods? I'm thinking of longer rituals, still based on blood, but for which the victim would have been kept alive for several days, or several weeks?"

The professor looked at her questioningly. "Can you be more specific, Captain?"

"The victim would be regularly bled, according to a precise ritual, to honor a divinity. But the priest doesn't tear out the heart. He uses it regularly. He bleeds her, according to a religious code, then waits for her to regain some of her strength. Then he bleeds her again. Which today would be considered a torture session."

The curator slowly shook his head side to side. "The Aztecs honored their gods, but the objective was not at all to make their victims suffer. Which is the case in what you're describing to me."

"Still, Professor, tearing out a man's heart, drowning a child, or burying a woman alive—I don't call that philanthropy toward the human race," interjected Sophie. "So why not offer the deserving god the blood *and* suffering of the victim?"

Ever the educator, Boisregard replied. "Only the blood interested the Aztecs. Not the suffering of the victim. However, I'm going to check with my friend in Lyon. He sometimes comes to Grenoble. Maybe there are cases I don't know about?"

"You've been a big help to us. We'll let you get back to your work."

All three of them stood up and left Antoine Dupas's office. They went their separate ways in the parking lot. The women headed for Sophie's car.

"Can you take me back home?" asked Nadia.

"Of course."

Then, hesitantly, Sophie asked, "Do you have something planned for dinner?"

Nadia looked at her, surprised by the offer. But then she realized it would give them some time to take stock of their conversation with the curator. And it would also prevent her from having to spend the evening alone at home.

"No, I don't have plans. Just drop me off at home first. I have to take my meds. After that, you can pick the restaurant. Just please not pizza tonight!"

Chapter 36: The Psychic

8:00 p.m. Julien Lombard had been waiting under a plane tree for a good half hour. Father de Valjoney had called him in the early afternoon and arranged this meeting without giving him any further information. A car pulled up along the sidewalk. The window rolled down, and the priest said to him, "Sorry for the delay, Julien, I had to go pick up Doctor Blanchet. Get in, please, they're expecting us."

Speechless, Julien climbed into the little Italian car. Father de Valjoney took off, tires squealing, and merged into traffic. From the backseat, a middle-aged man with a full salt-and-pepper beard amiably extended his hand.

"I'm Dr. Philippe Blanchet. I'll be ensuring the interview goes smoothly."

Julien's flabbergasted expression surprised him. He turned back to the priest. "Bernard, you didn't tell him who we're going to see?"

"No, I had to run around all afternoon."

"The first thing to do is to actually get his consent," reminded Dr. Blanchet.

"You're right, Philippe, but I'm sure he'll agree. If that's not the case, we'll turn around and go right back."

This exchange intrigued Julien. He wanted to understand what was going on. Father de Valjoney pulled him aside.

"Could you explain to me what's happening?" Julien asked.

"Well, of course, my dear Julien. I've thought a lot about our conversation yesterday. I was troubled when we parted. I went to see one of my close friends after you left, and we talked well into the night."

He gave the steering wheel a sharp jerk to avoid a motorcycle coming at them, then turned onto the highway going south.

"The decision I made wouldn't have been approved by my superiors. But I felt the experiment was necessary. So I contacted the person we're going to see, and as soon as I explained the context of my request, she agreed to meet you. That's why we're headed for Corps."

Julien knew the little village of Corps, nestled between the Notre-Dame-de-la-Salette basilica and the majestic slopes of l'Obiou. La Salette was the most famous shrine in the Dauphiné region. One hundred and fifty years earlier, the Virgin was said to have appeared on the mountainside to two young shepherds tending their flock. But Julien didn't see how that could connect to his nightmares. And why were they bringing a doctor with them?

"Excuse me, but I didn't get why we're going to Corps."

The priest concentrated on not missing the Vizille exit, then continued his explanation. "Your visions—or nightmares! There are far too many coincidences for them to be merely an exercise in autosuggestion on your part. Someone is speaking to you. So let's call this someone a spirit. As I told you, the Church urges Christians not to try to contact spirits. In many cases, the spirits can be harmful to those who speak with them. In your case, the will of the spirit speaking to you is clearly to avert the murders, and the murderer was nearly arrested between Sunday night and Monday morning."

"How do you know that?"

"The police informed me. This spirit is talking to you and wants to help you help us stop the killer."

"But why not do it in a clearer way?"

"A spirit isn't an investigator, Julien. It expresses itself with the resources at its disposal. And we're going to try to help it."

"But how?"

"We're going to meet with a psychic."

Julien had more or less foreseen this, but the priest's announcement froze him. "A psychic?"

"Yes. That's why making such a decision required careful consideration on my part. But given the gravity of the situation, and the risk of the murderer striking again, I finally organized this meeting."

Julien turned toward the doctor. His presence here was obviously not solely to satisfy a desire to take a walk around the Corps countryside at sunset. Philippe Blanchet responded to his silent question.

"You're going to meet Lucienne Roman. She's had this gift for more than fifty years, but she's eighty now. She agreed to meet with you; however, her séances are exhausting for her. I'll be there to make sure everything goes well, and I'll interrupt the conversation if she starts to faint."

Father de Valjoney added, "It's been ten years since Lucienne last played the role of medium. We hesitated a long time before contacting her. But she agreed right away, very affected by what happened to those poor girls."

"And how is this going to work?" asked Julien.

"Lucienne is what they call a trance speaker. She allows the spirit who is present to express itself using her mouth. She is just a channel and doesn't participate in the exchanges."

"So I'll be in direct contact with whoever's been communicating with me through visions for the last eight days?"

"Exactly."

Silence fell over the car. Each passenger was lost in his thoughts. Julien saw Vizille fly by, the Laffrey lakes, the old mining village of La Mure, then they headed for Gap. They followed the Route Napoléon that had taken the emperor, traveling in the opposite direction, from Golfe-Juan to Grenoble in 1815, after his departure from the island of Elba. But the speed at which Father de Valjoney was traveling the road had nothing in common with that of the Napoleonic armies.

When Julien saw the sign for the village, he felt a knot in his stomach. He could no longer escape this meeting, which he was dreading. Who was he going to encounter, or what? What if this spirit ultimately wanted to hurt him?

The car passed through the village. The priest turned onto a dirt road, the vehicle jolting in the random rhythm of the road's ruts. A plume of dust, the sign of a land already dried out by the sun and the wind, danced around the car. At the end of the road, Julien spotted a lonely little house—an old farmstead with dry stone walls, huddled between two ancient boulders that protected it from the harsh mountain climate. Four goats were grazing around the old sheepfold. They lifted their heads upon hearing the car arrive, then resumed their search for the rare tufts of grass. Father de Valjoney turned off the engine. "Here we are."

They got out of the car. The priest opened up the trunk, held out a satchel to the doctor, and then removed a worn little leather suitcase.

A tiny woman came toward them waving her hand. Skin wrinkled by the sun, her thick bun of gray hair held by a net, she moved confidently, cheerfully carrying her eighty years. She patted the neck of a goat that came out to meet her. The image of this serene woman, in harmony with the harsh environment where she'd always lived, soothed the young man.

She headed toward the priest and greeted him respectfully. She uttered some words of welcome for Julien Lombard and Doctor Blanchet before leading them to the house.

The farmstead was rustic. A main room with the kitchen in one corner, an old woodstove, and a massive table that seemed to occupy the whole house. Through a half-open door, Julien spied a little bedroom. The rooms exuded the modesty of a hard life, but they were impeccably kept. Two narrow windows let in the last light of the evening. This house had been built, centuries earlier, to protect its inhabitants from the torments of the outside world. Julien took that as a sign.

Lucienne Roman invited them to sit at the table and served them coffee, which had been warming for hours. She'd dressed for the mission. The old woman had agreed immediately to Father de Valjoney's request, but she knew the séance would exhaust her. She'd long ago lost that incredible stamina that won the admiration of all the boys in the village. But she wasn't afraid of death. She'd lived through too many trials to fear it. She didn't wish for it, but she'd confront it with serenity if it had to come. And if her life allowed her to save a young woman, then what a good trade!

She thought quickly back on all the people she'd helped during all those years and rejoiced at being useful again. She spoke to Julien, voice cracking. "Can you remind me of your name, young man?"

"Julien Lombard, madame."

"Go pull the curtains across the windows, Julien. We mustn't be disturbed."

While Julien carried out the psychic's request, Lucienne spoke to the priest. "Father, I've prepared my bedroom so that you may rest there comfortably."

"Thank you, Lucienne. I've already stored my things there."

At Julien's questioning look, Father de Valjoney explained. "I'm going to pray in Madame Roman's bedroom while she puts you in contact with the one who's sending you messages. I will call on Christ to protect you two. But I won't listen to what is said."

"Neither will I," added Doctor Blanchet. "I'll look after the health of our hostess. If I see the effort is too much for her, I'll ask her to stop the conversation."

Seeing Julien's worried look, Lucienne Roman gave him a smile. "Don't fret, my young friend. If the father decided to bring you here, it's because he thinks you'll benefit. Leave it to me, and do what I tell you, or what the person who speaks through me tells you."

Father de Valjoney added one last detail before leaving the room. "Lucienne won't have any memory of what the spirit who wants to communicate with you says. She'll be only a vessel. As for what you're going to see, or hear, or feel, that will be yours alone."

"Now, let's get to it," said the old woman.

The room was plunged into darkness that deepened from one minute to the next. Two chairs had been placed facing each other for Lucienne and Julien, and Lucienne took Julien's hands. Doctor Blanchet seated himself off to the side, ready to intervene at the first sign of weakness in the psychic.

Julien felt the women's gnarled hands grip his wrists. She seemed about to fall asleep. The young man started to shiver. He shouldn't be afraid. And he wasn't! The temperature in the room was dropping almost imperceptibly. He could barely see the face of the woman across from him anymore. Her hands now gripped his more and more strongly, and he heard her breathing accelerate. The temperature continued to fall inside the house. Then he heard the psychic murmur, "It's coming . . . it's very near . . . I feel it, so close."

Then in a stronger voice, the old woman said, "If you are of the devil, flee this house. If you are of God, take possession of me."

More silence. The woman ceased panting. The room was now pitch-black, and cold, as if life had disappeared to make room for the world of the dead. Julien felt abandoned. He was about to find himself face-to-face, alone with the great beyond. Alone with his nightmares? Lucienne was no longer there to reassure him. She was elsewhere and had ceded her place to the stranger, a stranger such as he'd never before encountered, nor even imagined. No! He had to pull himself together. Hiding in his deepest fears was unworthy of the confidence Lucienne had in him. He breathed slowly and regained control of himself. A silhouette then appeared quietly before him. He jumped. At first indistinct and diaphanous, the image gradually sharpened. The ectoplasmic vision, far from terrifying him, enveloped him in a warmth that contrasted with the icy air of the room. Instantly, he recognized the feeling he'd had in the killer's basement—that presence that had accompanied him. Yes, it was indeed the spirit who had already spoken to him several times.

"Hello, Julien."

He was astonished by the clear voice coming from the psychic's throat. A clear, young voice—a woman's voice. Hesitantly, the young man replied. "Hello . . . who . . . who are you?"

"I am the one who was sent to stop the tragedy."

The silhouette now appeared clearly in the darkness of the room. A woman looked at Julien. A young woman with a boyish haircut. It was difficult to make out her face, a gentle face with a sad smile. Julien's gaze was hypnotized by the woman's dress. A white dress, stained with blood.

"You, too?" he asked in a whisper.

"He did kill me, too. Thirty years ago. But he's been haunted by his act all these years."

The situation was unreal. The old woman, in a trance state, was speaking with a sweet and enchanting voice. She continued, "To fight his obsession, he's begun to kill. Kill to chase away his demons! I tried to warn you."

"You can't give me his name?"

"Alas, it's not possible for me. I can tell you only one thing. He will seek to kill again. I will help you, but this time, you'll be ready."

"Why me?" he asked.

The voice fell silent. Julien feared she had vanished for a moment, but the silhouette was still there.

"Because . . . because you are someone with whom I can communicate."

He didn't understand at the moment, but he would undoubtedly have the opportunity to think about it later. "Who is he?"

"He was my husband."

"Your husband killed you?"

"Yes, he was jealous. Jealous of my freedom and the child I was about to bring into the world."

"Did he kill the child, too?"

"No, the child escaped him."

Julien had recovered his composure. He felt total confidence in the woman speaking to him. "How can we stop him?"

"He killed me thirty years ago, in Grenoble. No one knew anything about it, but seek out and go find Aurélien. He'll tell you everything."

The woman's directives were hardly specific, but they were engraved on the young man's heart. He noticed that Lucienne was starting to have difficulty breathing. The doctor noticed as well.

"Be careful, Julien, he's not alone. A diabolical man is helping him with his enterprise."

"Who?"

"I cannot give you his name . . . Julien, I'm going to have to leave you now."

The doctor was holding Lucienne's hand and trying to revive her. Julien motioned at him to wait a few seconds.

"What's your name? Please tell me."

Her gentle gaze rested on him. "My name is Magali."

Although he knew no one named Magali, the name evoked something deep inside him. He whispered to her, "Good-bye, Magali."

The silhouette was disappearing. But he clearly heard her last words.

"Good-bye for now . . . my son."

Chapter 37: Julien's Mother

The priest had come out of the bedroom, leaving Doctor Blanchet to lay Lucienne on her bed. The old woman hadn't been too taxed by the experience and was starting to come to.

Julien hadn't moved from his chair. Father de Valjoney had wanted to speak to him, but the doctor had gestured to the father to give the young man some time to assimilate the discovery he'd just made. In fact, Julien wasn't thinking. He didn't want to emerge from the fog enveloping him. He didn't want to try to understand. He'd believed this woman, Magali, but the last sentence hadn't made any sense. He pulled himself together. It was stupid, stupid, but . . . he was going to celebrate his thirtieth birthday in a few days. No, it was just a coincidence. His parents were Denise and Emmanuel Lombard, and he was born in Grenoble. This Magali had lied to him! But why? Why did he sense she was protecting him? He came out of his stupor.

"When you were praying," he asked Bernard de Valjoney, "did you feel any malevolent forces or anything like that?"

"No," replied the priest. "I felt a peace I've only rarely encountered."

"Do you think the person who spoke to me could have wanted to do me harm?"

"You're the one who knows, Julien. I can only tell you my prayer was shared with her."

This affirmation plunged the young man into profound distress. He remained slumped in his chair, despondent. Then he stood up. "I have to know. Let's go back to Grenoble immediately."

"What do you have to know?"

"That woman called me 'my son.' I have to see my parents, right away."

The priest looked at the young man who was torn by contradictory feelings, facing a question as sudden as it was jarring. Bernard de Valjoney spoke briefly with the doctor. "Philippe is going to spend the night here. He'll return tomorrow morning. Let's go."

They reached Grenoble in record time. It was just midnight when the priest dropped Julien Lombard off on Rue d'Agier, in the heart of the old city. He'd barely opened his mouth during the drive, relating in a few short sentences the conversation he'd had with Magali—his *mother*?

He punched in the building's entrance code at the door and went in. His parents lived on the fourth floor. They generally went to bed late. Julien rang for a long time. The sounds of voices and bursts of laughter emanated from the apartment.

The door opened. A tall man with a grizzled beard stood there.

"Julien, I wasn't expecting you! But come in. The Margays are here. They'll be happy to see you again."

The young man entered brusquely, not saying a word to his father. In the living room, a couple in their sixties were chatting with his mother, a short, stout woman with plump cheeks and a charming smile.

"Julien! To what do we owe the pleasure, my boy?"

Withdrawn and somber, Julien eyed her. His father came to join them.

"I'm not sure it's such a pleasure. I want to talk to you, now!"

His father tried to lighten the mood, not understanding his son's attitude, usually so cordial. "Could it possibly wait until Georges and Marie-Solange have gone home?"

"If they leave now, yes."

Denise Lombard read such determination in her son's face that she stopped her husband from reacting.

Their friends had followed the whole scene. They'd known Julien most of his life and understood the situation demanded they leave.

"We're going to leave you to it. You have something to discuss in private. Denise, I'll call you tomorrow about our weekend in Chamonix."

Denise Lombard walked them to the door. When she came back, her husband and son were still facing each other. She immediately took note of the worry that had seized Emmanuel, her husband for over thirty-three years now. Julien wasn't saying anything, but staring at them as if he'd never seen them before. It was frightening. Denise Lombard broke the silence.

"What's going on, Julien?"

The young man couldn't get the words out. They spun crazily in his brain. Did he not have his biological parents in front of him? Was his mother killed? And the most terrifying question—was he the son of a perverse and sadistic killer? No, it wasn't possible. This Magali had lied to him. But why?

He walked over to the living room coffee table, which hadn't been cleared, and poured himself a glass of cognac. Then he came back toward his motionless parents.

"Tell me exactly what happened thirty years ago!"

"Nothing!" shrieked his mother a little too shrilly.

Julien looked at her despairingly. So Magali had told the truth.

"If you love me, and I know you love me, tell me what happened."

Emmanuel motioned for them to sit down. Julien sat in an armchair, facing his parents, who had settled on the sofa, pressed close together, as if preparing to confront what was coming next.

"I don't know what someone could have told you, or who for that matter. But we owe you the truth. I don't know if we can talk about truth, since there was no lie, strictly speaking. You're right about one thing. We love you, and we've loved you since you were born, since your first day of life."

Julien sensed his father was going to tell him something he didn't want to hear. The truth about Magali.

"You are legally our son, your mother's and mine. It'll be thirty years on June 21, the first day of summer."

His father sighed. "I don't know how to tell you these things!"

"Factually! As factually as possible."

Emmanuel Lombard began his tale. "Your mother was eight months pregnant. We were expecting our first child, a boy. On June 20, the child she was carrying stopped moving. At first, we weren't panicked. The next day, when she couldn't feel him moving anymore, we went to see one of our excellent doctor friends who lived next door. It was a Sunday, and that seemed simpler to us than going to the hospital. That's when he gave us the news. The child had just died."

Julien looked at his mother, who was staring into space. His father continued.

"It was midnight when we found out. We had to go to the hospital so that Denise could give birth . . . give birth to a dead infant. But for us, he'd been alive, and we wanted to bury him. So we went back to the house to get some clothes for your mother. I went to get the car, which was parked on the other side of the Jardin de Ville. While passing through the garden, I suddenly heard cries. At first I believed, because of the emotional turmoil, my senses were playing a trick on me. But the cries grew louder. I went toward a clump of bushes. And there was an infant, wrapped in white cloth, resting on the ground."

Julien listened to the story. His story! A story he'd never have imagined a few hours earlier. He didn't say anything, letting his father continue.

"I approached the child and looked around. There was no one. I was alone in the street. So I picked him up. He was naked, swaddled in a torn piece of white dress, still bloody and covered in the coating he had inside his mother. He'd just been born. You'd just been born," he added. "I called out several times, looked for anybody. But there was no one, and no response. So I looked at the child, and I felt overcome with love . . . I felt like protecting him, all his life. I went back to the house with you in my arms."

Julien felt as though he were living through a second birth, rediscovering his parents. His mother took up the rest of the account.

"When I saw your father arriving with the baby in his arms, with you, I didn't hesitate for a second—*we* didn't hesitate for a second. We went back to see our friend and told him our idea. At first he thought we were crazy, but I think we were convincing enough to change his mind. He delivered my deceased child."

"So you traded children, is that it?" asked Julien.

"Yes, that's it. We gave ourselves three weeks before filing your birth certificate. We didn't want to be child stealers. After burying our dead baby, your father brought me to the cottage in Annecy, to your grandparents' house, while they were on vacation in Réunion. I lived shut up in there, alone, with my first child."

"During that time," continued Emmanuel Lombard, "with the help of our doctor friend, I discreetly inquired about whether a newborn had been reported missing. But it was as if you'd never been born. So after three weeks, I went to get your mother. With the complicity of our friend, we filed your birth certificate. Julien Lombard, born June 21, 1983."

His parents broke off. Julien was thinking. He couldn't blame his parents. They'd saved his life.

"And you never found out what happened?" he asked.

"Never!" replied his father. "Even though my whole being told me to just be grateful, I tried to find out when you were two. But I found nothing."

"And why didn't you say anything to me?"

"What would you have wanted us to say? Your biological parents were unknown, and we raised you, loved you. We watched your first steps, your mother taught you to read, I took you to play soccer every weekend for years, we were there to console you when you weren't doing well. You would have hated us if we'd told you this story."

"Probably," conceded Julien. "But imagine how discombobulated I feel."

"I understand," replied his mother, "but can you tell us who gave you enough information to make you ask us the question? Who knew and never turned up?"

Julien told his bewildered parents about the events of the past few days.

"Of course, you'll always be my parents. But I've learned that my biological mother, Magali, was murdered, probably just after bringing me into the world. And that this killer is my father. You realize, Papa, I'm the son of a killer!"

"No, you're the son of an agricultural engineer, not necessarily the best of men, but a loving man. And you're not responsible for the actions of a man who was responsible only for your conception."

"That's easy to say, very easy to say. What if certain genes of his are in me?"

"But that doesn't make sense, Julien," his mother said gently.

"What do we know about it? Whatever it is, tomorrow morning I'll tell Magali's story to the police to get a clearer picture. And that could potentially help them quickly catch my father—that man," he said, looking at Emmanuel.

"Will you tell them about your relationship to them?" asked Denise hesitantly.

Julien looked at her with a sad smile. "That's our story, Mama. My parents are still you and will always be you. But I have to understand. One last question. Did you know an Aurélien at the time?"

"No, it doesn't ring a bell," replied his father. "Why?"

"No reason. Can I sleep in my old room?"

"What a question! It'll always be yours."

Chapter 38: Girls' Night

Sophie closed her eyes and enjoyed the breeze riffling through her hair. She inhaled the scent of the cigarette Nadia had just lit. She'd never been a real smoker, but from time to time she liked to breathe the heady, acrid fragrances of tobacco. The young woman felt cocooned, slightly drunk on the wine that had accompanied their meal. She came out of her comfortable languor and looked around. The tables had emptied, and the pedestrians seemed taken with the tranquillity of the night. All was calm. She heard the wind gently shaking the branches above her. Nadia was pensive, lost in the curls of smoke from her cigarette.

Sophie never would have imagined such an evening. When she'd invited Captain Barka to have dinner with her, she'd envisioned rapidly eating a salad in a little restaurant, then going home. But they'd started with a leisurely aperitif on the terrace of a café over by Halle Sainte-Claire. Then they'd had a second. Hunger had drawn them toward a nearby restaurant. The simple salad had transformed into a full-blown meal washed down with wine. Not the classic dinner in American TV shows or women's magazines, but a marvelously pleasant evening.

Sophie had feared that the conversation would quickly devolve into triviality. Despite their totally different careers and diametrically opposite lives, they'd chatted for hours. They'd grown familiar without even realizing it and hadn't noticed the time passing. Sophie heard the bell tower at Saint-André chime eleven o'clock. The waiter was hovering discreetly around their table, in a desperate attempt to make them understand he wanted to close his restaurant. Nadia noticed his orbit. She nodded to indicate her desire for the bill. With a wide smile, the waiter came up to the table and deposited the check he'd been holding for the last several minutes. Sophie grabbed it.

"Tonight, I'm treating you."

"Whatever for?"

"I don't know. Let's say it's because I invited you to dinner, and I'm pleased to do it."

Nadia looked at her and hesitated. "Okay, thank you. But you have to come for one last drink at my place. I don't live far from here."

The waiter seized Sophie's credit card, hastened to the counter, and just as quickly returned to the table. While the young woman punched in her PIN, Nadia took a last puff on her cigarette, stubbed it out, and stretched.

Nadia listened as her new friend told her, very humorously, about one of her hiking trips in the mountains. She didn't understand what had happened to her. Yesterday, before Étienne came to see her, she'd been in a state of agonizing depression. And tonight, she felt good, really good. She dove back into her memories. She didn't know whether she'd experienced such relaxation since she'd joined the police. When the church bells had sounded eleven o'clock, she'd felt like Cinderella listening to the clock strike midnight.

Nadia had seized the first opportunity to prolong the evening, and she was relieved to hear Sophie accept. She loved her smile, her energy, her way of looking on the bright side of things without being naive. She nearly envied Julien. She wasn't attracted to women, but her new friend's *joie de vivre* brought her out of her usual gloom.

The two young women were ensconced on the sofa, each with a glass of planter's punch in hand. The purr of Ella Fitzgerald's warm voice gave the night a particular charm. They looked at each other, then burst out laughing. Sophie composed herself.

"I didn't dare ask you this question, Nadia, but I think I can now. If you don't want to answer, I—"

Nadia cut her off. "If you'd asked me at the start of the evening, I would've made it very clear to you that it would be better to change the subject. But now I know it's not simple curiosity motivating you. Only my father, my mother, and my two brothers know why I joined the police."

From her friend's tone, Sophie understood that Nadia was about to reveal something.

"I was eighteen, and I was studying in Paris. My parents were living in Bordeaux and renting a studio apartment for me in the heart of the city, not far from the Sorbonne. I was in a preparatory class for literary studies, at Henri-IV High School. My father wanted me to be a diplomat, and I wasn't against the idea. I was preparing myself to attend the Paris Institute of Political Studies then, to follow the path that would lead me to the Ministry of Foreign Affairs. I think I was motivated enough to get there, if I do say so myself."

She paused, as if she were reliving her student days for a moment. Then she continued, "In the middle of the year, I'd met a boy who was one year ahead of me, and it was love at first sight. We saw each other whenever our schedules allowed us to. Each moment spent together was magical. One evening, at the end of the school year, he invited me to the theater. A dinner theater, actually, over by Montparnasse. Do you know it?"

"Yes, I did my engineering studies in Paris. I made the most of it by exploring the city for three years. Needless to say I didn't finish at the head of the class, but I did some great partying!"

"So we had dinner and came back on the Métro. I took it every day, like most Parisians. Except that night . . ."

Before she could continue her story, Sophie guessed what had happened. She wordlessly put an arm around Nadia's shoulder. Only Ella Fitzgerald's voice covered Nadia's grief.

"I'm sorry, really sorry. I shouldn't have asked you."

The policewoman sat up straight. "You have nothing to be sorry about, Sophie. Besides, I have to dig up this story. It's been eating at me for too many years."

"Nothing is forcing you."

"Yes, *I* am! So that night, we were waiting for the Métro. We were alone on the platform, sitting on a bench. The trains were infrequent at that hour. We were chatting quietly. In fact, we were kissing, lost in our own world. All of a sudden, we heard laughter near us. I think I'll never forget that laugh. I've also sworn to myself that someday I'll find the one who . . . produced it."

A gleam of hatred crossed Nadia's eyes at this thought, then she resumed her story.

"There were six of them, visibly sloshed. They started to bother us, and several of them were attracted to me. I'd already faced that type of situation, and I'd always gotten myself out of it pretty well. I was fearless, and it took a lot to spook me. But this time, my instincts screamed 'danger!' at me. I took my friend by the hand, and I tried to head for the exit. But the six men surrounded us, started to hit him and paw at me. So Manuel went wild—he was usually so calm. He hit the two bastards who were holding me and shouted to get help. In a split second, I understood it was the only way to get out. So I ran, scrambled up the stairs. There was no one at the ticket window. I was panicked about what could be happening to my friend. I had to leave the station, and I stumbled across a policeman after a minute of haphazard running. I explained the situation to him. He quickly understood. He called for backup and headed for the Métro station with me. That's when I saw the six men who had attacked us running away. I think I realized at that moment my life was changing radically."

Nadia paused in her story. She grabbed the pack of cigarettes resting on the table and brought one to her mouth. The glow of the lighter flame flickered in the darkness, shining in the young woman's dry eyes. Sophie was huddled against the back of the sofa, waiting for the inevitable.

"I ran down there like a madwoman. Manuel was lying still in his own blood, covered in stab wounds. I threw myself on him, and I took him in my arms. He wasn't moving anymore—he was dead. He was dead, and I hadn't been with him during his last moments. When I realized everything was over, irretrievably over, I screamed, screamed like an animal. I don't remember anymore what happened after that. All I know is my parents were in my studio apartment the next afternoon to take me back to Bordeaux. But I refused."

She looked at Sophie, calling her to witness.

"I couldn't let that act go unpunished. So I told my father I was stopping my studies, and that I was going to join the police. I wanted to prevent that from happening again. I wanted to take revenge on Manuel's killers and people like them. At first he thought it was a passing fancy, a pronouncement made in anger. But when he realized my decision was final, he knew nothing could make me change my mind. Since then, he hasn't spoken to me."

"Just because you wanted to join the police?"

"Our fathers are opposites, Sophie. Mine couldn't stand for his decisions to be contradicted. He was charming when you agreed with him, but when you didn't . . . There, now you know the source of my vocation."

Sophie looked at the woman across from her. She was an elite police officer, but such suffering and hatred lined her insides.

Nadia continued, "I have to thank you, Sophie."

Surprised, Sophie questioned her. "Why thank me? I'm grateful to you for sharing your story with me."

"Thank you for giving me the strength to trust someone."

Chapter 39: Monsieur Ibrahim

A teenager wearing a sweat suit jacket designed in Olympique de Marseille colors stepped hesitantly into the police station lobby. He glanced around warily and went up to reception. "I need to talk to M'sieur Drancey."

The officer on duty looked him over. He'd have taken the time to explain to the kid that the first thing to do when addressing someone is say *hello*, but the lieutenant had requested he be notified as soon as someone asked for him. The officer looked at his watch. It was eight o'clock, on the dot. He grabbed the telephone handset, dialed a number, and exchanged a few words with the person on the other end. The teenager watched him anxiously.

"He's coming," said the officer.

Three minutes later, Drancey arrived with two other police officers. He nodded toward the OM fan to the man on guard.

"Him?" Lieutenant Drancey asked, more affirmatively than questioning. As soon as he had confirmation, he approached the teenager. "I'm Lieutenant Drancey. You can give me the information."

"Sorry, m'sieur, I'm just s'posed to take you to someone."

"Someone?"

"Yes, I'm just here to guide you. Follow me?"

Drancey and his colleagues immediately started after him.

"Just you, m'sieur. They told me you had to be alone."

The police lieutenant's two colleagues frowned.

"It's okay," Drancey reassured them. "I'll go alone."

They left the police station. Without a word, the guide motioned at him to follow. They crossed through the little park on the other side of the street and came to the Saint-Roch cemetery. In the shade of a tree, seated on a bench, a man was waiting. He was smoking a cigarette and watching a squirrel jump from one branch to another. He was wearing an astrakhan cap. The police officer headed toward him. His companion had vanished.

"Hello, Lieutenant Drancey."

"Monsieur Ibrahim himself. The information must be important."

"I think I have something to interest you. But do sit down next to me."

Drancey was surprised by this old man's personality. He'd asked his colleagues about him, but they knew absolutely nothing.

"The car you're looking for is a Peugeot 307, gray. The man who was driving it is between fifty and sixty years old. He's rather tall and was wearing a white shirt."

"Were you able to get the car's license plate number?" asked the policeman hopefully.

"You know the conditions under which the events took place, Lieutenant. Everything happened quickly, and those who provided this information were . . . stressed, to say the least."

"Let's not get into those details, Monsieur Ibrahim. Your inform-ers would have raped and killed one of my colleagues if we hadn't stressed them . . ."

"And their behavior upsets me—be sure of that! But you're right, I will continue my story. I wanted to know if the same car had been spotted over by the Old Diocese Museum the night of the first victim's murder."

Drancey felt his heart rate quicken. Monsieur Ibrahim paused, took another cigarette out of a century-old tin box, and lit it.

"Allah was with you."

"And how did Allah manifest himself?"

"Allah manifests himself in many ways, Lieutenant. Happy is he who knows how to listen. Someone who lives in the neighborhood was coming back from a party. It was four o'clock in the morning. The Peugeot had stopped just in front of his garage door. The man, displeased, therefore took down the license plate number in order to make a complaint later, then went to park in an adjacent street. When he came back, the car had disappeared."

"But how did you get this information?"

"Thanks to Allah . . . and a few friends."

Monsieur Ibrahim took a piece of paper out of his pocket. He handed it over—the killer's license plate number was written there in a shaky hand. Drancey folded it and put it in his wallet.

"You've kept your word, and impressively so. We're even, Monsieur Ibrahim."

The policeman intended to get up, but hesitated. The old man fascinated him. He emanated a serenity and power that nearly intimidated him. His wrinkles seemed to have been formed by wisdom, and the amused gleam the lieutenant saw in the depths of the man's eyes intrigued him. Drancey knew the man had sized him up long ago.

"Who are you, Monsieur Ibrahim? Who are you to be respected to the letter and to find the information you just gave me in just one night?"

The old man hadn't stopped looking at him. He shook his head slowly. "I'm just an old man who wants to see peace around him. The two boys you left me yesterday had committed the most reprehensible acts. But rest assured the discussion I was able to have with them was much more beneficial to them than prison could have been."

"I hope so for their sake. You can also rest assured that we've disclosed nothing, but get it into their heads that it won't happen again."

"You made the right choice. Most of those who live around me are good kids. Some are more difficult to focus. But I'm working on it," he added with a tired sigh.

"So are you a sort of priest or sage?"

"God is above us all, my friend. It's up to us to take his counsel and act according to his will."

"Certainly," remarked the policeman. "I've heard more talk of God in three days than in the last ten years of my life. Anyway, tell him to watch a little more closely over the victims of the butcher who cut them up."

Rodolphe Drancey stood up and extended a hand to the old man. "Good-bye, Monsieur Ibrahim."

"As-salamu alaykum," replied the old man, bringing his hand to his heart.

Excitement dominated the meeting room. Commissioner Mazure had urgently convened all the teams. Everyone was awaiting orders. Rivera couldn't hide his joy at finally being in on the action. Drancey and his colleagues felt their adrenaline rising. They were finally going to bust this son of a bitch. Mazure took several seconds to quiet the conversations.

"Ladies and gentlemen, we've just obtained a key piece of information: the license plate number of the car the killer used. This car was spotted at both crime scenes, which leaves little doubt that it belongs to the criminal. We're in the process of verifying the address of the owner in the files. I just spoke with the magistrate. Men from Lyon police's tactical GIPN force will be here in less than two hours. We'll launch the attack as soon as possible."

A policeman suddenly entered the room.

"Commissioner, we have the name of the killer and his address."

"Who is it?"

"The man's name is Dominique Sartenas. He lives in Saint-Martin d'Uriage."

Chapter 40: The Attack

10:00 p.m. Julien Lombard walked resolutely into the police station lobby. He had to know who Magali was, and who this father was who horrified him. He'd decided to deal with his mental state later and instead concentrate on action. On finding clues to his mother's murder, which would inevitably lead him to his "father" and allow him to stop the man before he committed another murder.

He addressed the officer on duty. "I need to see Lieutenant Fortin."

"Do you have an appointment with him?" the man asked in an unfriendly tone.

"No, but I have extremely important information that would lead to the killer currently running rampant."

"Lieutenant Fortin just left for the courthouse. I'm going to contact the officer in charge of the investigation, Captain Rivera."

Julien hesitated for a moment, but the situation was serious enough for him to get over his resentment. "Perfect, I'm at his disposal."

Julien waited barely five minutes in the lobby. Captain Rivera arrived, accompanied by several men overwhelmed with excitement. He frowned when he saw the young man.

"Your lawyer isn't with you to protect you today?"

"Listen, Captain, I didn't come here to waste your time or mine."

"What do you have that's so important to tell me?"

"I have information on the killer."

Stéphane Rivera looked at him in astonishment. "I'm listening."

"I know his wife's first name—Magali. He killed her thirty years ago. You must be able to find his name with that."

"Another one of your visions?" he tossed out mockingly, looking at the men around him.

Julien breathed deeply to keep his cool. "Correct. But I can give you hard evidence."

"Don't worry about it anymore, Lombard. You have visions that got you the wife's name; *I* have investigators that got me the killer's name. Aren't the police effective? We haven't just been standing around twiddling our thumbs waiting for this information. We studied all the murder cases over a period of thirty years. And I can assure you that Magali wasn't killed on French soil thirty years ago. So if you'll excuse me, my men and I have work to do. We have a murderer to take off the streets."

Then, addressing the man at the desk, he added, "Vincent, take the gentleman's statement when you have some free time. I'll read it over later. It'll relax me. Come on, guys, the cowboys from Lyon should be here any minute."

Surly bastard, thought Julien, enraged, as he watched them move toward the exit.

The officer on duty had only moderately appreciated the role that Rivera had forced him to take on. The power had gone to Rivera's head, and the officer dared not imagine the state Rivera would be in after the criminal's arrest. He spoke to Julien, who was leaving the building.

"Monsieur, Lieutenant Fortin isn't here, but I can call one of his teammates, Lieutenant Garancher."

Julien turned back.

"He's nothing like Captain Rivera," added the policeman.

"Okay, I'd like to meet with him."

Julien sat down on one of the lobby chairs. Rivera's comments had shaken him. No murder of a Magali thirty years earlier. And he'd seemed sure of his facts! Julien struggled with himself. He shouldn't let it go. He had to understand what had happened.

Noon. The four vehicles slowly climbed up the deserted road. The house was two hundred yards away. It was isolated and hidden by large trees. A steep, narrow driveway about fifty yards long led up to it. They had little information about their target, and at the present moment had no other means of judging what kind of threat he was. Was he on his guard, did he have a firearm? They'd done a very quick survey of the neighborhood. The man lived alone in the house. No one knew him very well; he was rather solitary. But he'd never caused any trouble.

The house was far enough away from the neighboring buildings to limit the potential risk of collateral damage during the attack. Captain Garin, head of the operation for GIPN, had managed to obtain the house blueprints. He didn't know how his guys had gotten them, but he owed them big-time. Three entries—one via the garage, one via the front door facing them, and a third one located behind the building. He'd sent two men into each of the neighboring properties, accompanied by an officer from Grenoble. He wanted to use their yards to take up position behind the house.

Six men were with him. Stationed on the edge of one yard and hidden by the bushes, they blended into the surroundings. They had to be discreet to avoid being seen by the occupant, who might be on the lookout. In twenty yards, they could get a visual on the main entrance.

Garin brought his binoculars up to his eyes. It was strange. All the shutters were closed, as if no one had ever lived there. The building was large, two stories. Garin observed the windows and doors one by one—nothing moved. Only the remains of shrubs recently crushed by the wheels of a vehicle gave this area a semblance of life.

Garin brought his walkie-talkie up to his mouth. "On my signal, team one, you go in on the ground floor. Team two, you neutralize the second floor. Team three, you enter through the garage and secure the basement."

As soon as he was assured the three teams were in place, he launched the attack. Like a perfectly orchestrated dance, the men sprang into action. Within a few seconds, the doors were open. Two minutes later, the sweep was done. The occupant of the premises was nowhere to be found.

His second in command brought the men together in the living room. "We checked all the rooms, Captain. He's flown the coop. He must have left recently, since there's still a half-cooked meal in the kitchen."

"Shit. Come on, don't touch anything, and fall back. I'll notify Captain Rivera so that he can come in with the forensic team. That's it for us."

Rivera vacillated between anger and dejection.

"Are you sure he won't come back?" he asked the GIPN officer.

"He's gone, and he won't come back. In my experience, there's a ninety-nine percent chance you won't see him here again. He's on his guard and will notice that something happened. You can always leave two guys on duty during the day, just in case."

"That's what I'll do."

"As you wish . . . I'll leave you to your work. From the little we saw, the kitchen looked like your invisible man's favorite living space. I'll go back down to debrief Commissioner Mazure."

Chapter 41: Rain Man

Garancher and Lombard pushed open the café door. Nadia Barka and Étienne Fortin, ensconced at a table in the back of the bistro, waved them over hurriedly.

Julien greeted them.

"So?" Garancher asked his colleague.

"The judge was sympathetic to the Chechen story." Nadia showed her still-painful shoulder. "There won't be any difficulty proving legitimate self-defense. And what about you?" she said to Julien.

Julien told her about his adventures from the day before, ending with Stéphane Rivera's flat refusal.

"Do you know how the operation turned out?" Nadia asked her colleague.

"It's happening right now," replied Garancher.

"So we'll know in a few hours."

"Yes, but why did this Magali speak to Monsieur Lombard about a murder when we didn't find one?" said Garancher. "I was on the team that conducted the research, and I can assure you it was thorough. We looked at all of France. I now have enough to write an encyclopedia of horrors with everything I saw, but nothing on the murder of a Magali in the early eighties, I'm sure of it."

"And on that, we can trust Jérôme's memory."

Deep in thought, Julien concentrated on the officers' discussion. He declined the daily special the waiter offered them. Then suddenly he said, "There's another possibility. Magali was killed by her husband, but the murder could never be proved."

"Like, a body buried in the yard and an unexplained disappearance?"

"For example. Did you look into disappearances?"

"No, the proven murders already required a lot of effort," commented Garancher.

"And do you think you could dig around in that area?"

"I doubt Rivera wants to put any energy into it, especially if he returns with the killer in handcuffs," replied Garancher. "But . . . well, I don't know . . ."

"Are you thinking about Villard?" asked Nadia.

"Exactly, he could help us, but we'd need his address."

"He left it for me the day of his retirement shindig," Nadia explained, smiling. "I never thought I'd use it one day, but I kept it without really knowing why."

"Do you have all the retirees' phone numbers?" asked Fortin, amused.

"Practically all of them. I always took them. After all, it made them happy, and they could be useful to us today."

"And who is this Villard?" interjected Julien.

"Jean-Jacques Villard is a cop who worked in Grenoble for more than thirty years. He didn't go out in the field much, but he was a first-class archivist and analyst. With a memory like Rain Man," explained Garancher.

At Lombard's questioning look, he went further.

"Rain Man! You know, that movie with Dustin Hoffman! He plays an autistic guy with a phenomenal memory—he learns the phone book by heart just by reading it. Well, Villard is almost there. If a Magali disappeared thirty years ago, it must have gone through us at one point or another. And he'll let you know about it. All right, I'll leave you to it. I have to go back to the station, but Nadia is the best in you can get with our friend Villard. He always had the · hots for her."

"I want to clarify that he was always very courteous," noted Nadia.

"Considering his wife was keeping an eye on him, it was in his interest to behave," added Fortin. "Jérôme, I'll take your car." Then to Julien, he asked, "You have a ride?"

"My car is in front of the police station."

"Come on, we'll take you back."

1:30. Julien wondered if he might be dreaming. He was sitting in a wicker chair, a plate with two merguez sausages on his lap, and a glass of Côtes du Rhône wine in his hand.

"You see," commented Jean-Jacques Villard, "I go get some every year from a little Ardèche winegrower I discovered twenty years ago. He's famous and very reasonably priced. As for the merguez, I buy them from Maurice, a butcher around the corner. A delicacy! Not the kind where they add spices to cover up the taste of fat and cheap cuts. Oh no, he's a sausage master, my Maurice. You can almost believe he makes them exclusively to be eaten with my little glass of wine."

Seated in the shadow of an arbor at a house in Domène, Julien felt like he was living in an alternative universe. Overjoyed at the chance to see his old colleague, Jean-Jacques Villard had invited them for a barbecue. Julien had noticed Monique Villard grimace a bit when she saw her husband embrace the statuesque and charming Nadia, but Julien could tell Monique liked him. He'd understood it was in his best interest to appear charming—a relaxed atmosphere would help them steer the conversation toward the subject that interested them.

While Madame Villard cleared the plates and went to make coffee, the retired policeman became professional once more.

"I had a wonderful time with you, and it gave me great joy to see you again, Captain Barka. You are even more charming than I remember. But what's the real reason that brings you here? Might I still be of use to you?"

"I think so, Lieutenant Villard."

"Call me Jean-Jacques, now that I'm retired."

Julien once again told his story, and the hypotheses they'd just constructed at the bar. Jean-Jacques Villard cut him off in the middle of his last sentence. He looked at his two guests, then at his wife, as if to prove to her that she still lived with an important man.

"I remember that story well. The wife who disappeared is named Magali Dupré! Well, Dupré was her maiden name. She married a certain Cabrade, Dominique Cabrade."

"And what do you remember?" cut in Julien, suddenly hopeful.

"Quite a few things. But I'd very much like a little Chartreuse. Monique, can you bring us the bottle and four glasses?"

Monique Villard normally would have rebuffed him, but she sensed the drama of the situation and certainly didn't want to risk upsetting her husband. She ran to the living room and came back with the bottle and glasses.

The old policeman admired the green shine of his liqueur, gave it a long sniff, and sipped. Then he resumed speaking. "Dominique Cabrade came in one summer night in 1983. I remember it well: I'd bought my Chrysler that same afternoon. His wife hadn't come home for four days, and he had just come to report her disappearance . . . Strange."

"What do you mean by strange, Jean-Jacques?" asked Nadia.

"He seemed despondent but also—how shall I put this—convinced that he'd never see her again. Whereas usually people who report disappearances cling to all they can, even denying tangible proof."

"But not him?"

"No. He seemed affected, but fatalistic. Never seen a guy like that! His wife had disappeared on the first day of summer, and he assumed he wouldn't see her again. He signed his statement, explaining to us that he trusted us completely in the investigation. But he wasn't thinking about finding her again one day. She was gone. That was it!"

"And?" asked Nadia.

"Obviously this story seemed shady to me. I talked about it with Commissioner Diston, who immediately asked me to find out more about the players. Cabrade was a young surgeon, about thirty years old, with a promising future according to his boss."

Nadia quivered. A surgeon—a man capable of operating properly on his victims in order to extract their hearts from their chests. Villard continued.

"I carried out a quick investigation on him. He was originally from the north and had come to Grenoble to study medicine. He was well appreciated by his colleagues and seemed to have a very active life. He'd been married for a little over a year, and the witnesses I interviewed hadn't found anything about the couple to object to. I also looked into his wife."

Julien was tense as a bowstring. For the first time, he was going to hear someone talk about the mother he'd just discovered.

"Magali Dupré was twenty-five at the time of her disappearance. She was pregnant and close to giving birth. But it wasn't her husband who told me that. She had studied engineering and obtained a doctorate at the Center for Nuclear Studies in Grenoble. I easily collected information on her. Everyone seemed to love her, and she overflowed with life. But exactly one year before disappearing, she started to change, to become more distant. Six months later, she stopped working on her dissertation for medical reasons."

"How do you remember all that, Jean-Jacques?" asked Nadia, impressed by her ex-colleague's memory.

"My nickname of Rain Man is well earned," he replied, smiling. "And this story affected me. I continued to investigate, and I met her parents, Pierre and Nicole Dupré. They were teachers and adored Magali, their only daughter. They adored their daughter as much as they hated their son-in-law. They didn't understand how she could let herself be seduced by this doctor, and especially how she could marry him. They were convinced this man was behind their Magali's disappearance."

"What was Cabrade like—physically, I mean?"

"Good-looking guy. Blond, a bit like Robert Redford."

"I understand how she could've fallen for him," commented Nadia.

"Yes, but if you'd seen him when he came to the station, you wouldn't have fallen for him. Distant, almost unsettling."

"How far did you push the inquiry?"

"Not very far. We put out a few missing persons reports, asked around the neighborhood, but nothing turned up. I should say that at the time, we had a lot going on trying to break up gangs of drug traffickers and pimps."

"Did you see Cabrade again?" asked Nadia.

"I never crossed paths with Cabrade again. But for years Pierre Dupré came to see me regularly to ask if I had any news. Little by little he was convinced his daughter had been killed by her husband. I saw him again from time to time until 2005, the year his wife died."

"Do you know if he's still in the area?" asked Julien, full of hope.

"He was in a retirement home, over by Sassenage, or Fontaine. If he's still alive, I imagine he's still there."

"And Cabrade?" asked Nadia.

"That bird flew the coop. Six months after she died, he left the Grenoble hospital. He went to practice abroad. When they looked him up for further investigation, he was impossible to find. Vaporized!"

"And no one tried to find out more?" Nadia said, incredulous.

"No, unfortunately. Magali Dupré wasn't important enough, and her disappearance had been eclipsed by front-page courtroom news."

"What are your thoughts, Jean-Jacques?"

The man hesitated, then started in. "I'm not on the payroll anymore, so I can go there. I'm convinced she didn't just disappear on her own. Either she was abducted—except who would kidnap a woman about to give birth—or her husband made her disappear. That investigation was botched. In fact, aside from the inquiries I was able to make, it didn't happen."

A long silence followed the policeman's last words. Julien looked at him. His face was flooded with great sadness. Only the chirping of sun-drenched insects could be heard in the garden.

Nadia got up from her chair. "Thank you, Jean-Jacques, your testimony was very precious."

"You're welcome, Captain. But how can it help you?"

"It would seem that Cabrade has returned."

He looked at her questioningly.

"The murders over the past few days," she added.

They thanked him, leaving him dazed, and went back to Grenoble.

Chapter 42: Gruesome Discovery

"All right, goddammit, what are you finding for me in this shit show?"

Captain Stéphane Rivera was in a state of apoplectic distemper. Within a few minutes he'd gone from intense excitement to black rage. Where had that fucking killer flown off to? He'd called for reinforcements to search the house. They'd go over it with a fine-tooth comb from cellar to roof, and they'd find what it was hiding.

"Captain, come look!"

Rivera headed for the kitchen. A man, planted in front of an open refrigerator, was holding a jar.

"Are you inventorying his pantry?" asked Rivera, annoyed.

"Sort of, Captain, but look closer."

The officer forgot his bad mood for a moment and carefully examined the contents of the jar. "My God, but that's . . ."

"Yes, Captain, a heart, or what's left of it. We may have before us the remains of Camille Saint-Forge."

Rivera took the jar in his hands and looked at the piece of flesh covered in tooth marks. "We're really dealing with a sick fuck," he muttered, going pale. He returned the jar and went up to the second floor. Two men were looking carefully at a bedroom with faded curtains.

"It's the only room that was inhabited recently, Captain. The window is broken, and there's blood on the shards of glass. We have enough to analyze the DNA."

"Nothing else?"

"Yes, actually. Georges found a stack of documents on the desk. We'll have them examined, but this one caught our attention. It looks like a copy of the cover from an old manuscript."

Rivera looked at the sheet. He moved closer to the window, whose shutters had been opened and read over the page.

"*The Great Book of Fra Bartolomeo.* What the hell is this thing? We've got ourselves a weirdo. You give a copy of these pages to Saroyan as soon as we get back to Grenoble."

As he went back downstairs, Rivera started to develop a sense of the killer's personality. Or at least of the mental complexity of the man he was supposed to track. He crossed the foyer and saw Magnusson coming toward him, white as a sheet.

"What's happening now, Karl?"

"Come downstairs with me. What I want to show you defies all description."

He realized his colleague wouldn't say another word. He followed him down the narrow concrete staircase and arrived in a long hallway. On his right, a door opened onto a well-lit room. Rivera went in, took three steps, and stopped cold. It took him several seconds to recognize what was in front of him.

"That bastard set up his own operating room!"

Next to the table, a box filled with pouches containing scalpels, spreaders, and other instruments he didn't even know existed. The table was impeccably clean, and the instruments reflected the light from the faceted lamp. On the floor, brown stains.

"The blood of his victims, no doubt!" commented Magnusson.

"*Il diavolo,*" murmured Rivera in his native language. "Come on, let's get out of here and let the specialists analyze this room. We need to avoid getting prints on anything."

He went back upstairs with the other officers, more shaken than he wanted to admit. He wasn't just dealing with a murderer, but a pervert, a lunatic who took apart his victims in order to eat their hearts! He'd never been confronted with this type of criminal.

Before he realized it, his thoughts had drifted toward Nadia Barka. Barka and the Déramaux case! He'd mocked her pretty well, but at the present moment, he felt ashamed. How would he have reacted if he'd been faced with that tortured corpse unprepared? One thought led to another until he came to Lombard's testimony. Could what he had taken for a schizophrenic delusion a few hours earlier now make sense? When faced with a criminal who devours his victims, why not pay attention to a man who receives messages from the great beyond? Barka had taken him seriously, and she'd clearly been right. He'd contact Lombard as soon as he was back in Grenoble. He noticed his men watching him, waiting for instructions. He grew serious.

"Gentlemen, we're looking at a sicko, an extremely dangerous sicko. He's on the loose now, but probably not far from here. This house needs to give up its secrets—it's the forensic team's turn now. Magnusson, Vivain, and Jaouen, you'll stay with that team. Everyone else come back with me. It's 2:13 p.m. Meeting at three thirty in the briefing room."

Chapter 43: The Final Hour

Sartenas had abandoned his car in a supermarket parking lot. Then he'd taken a bus and was now wandering the city center. His eyes no longer saw anything. He walked like a zombie, unconscious of the world around him.

"Is everything all right, monsieur?" asked a voice behind him.

He turned, surprised, and met the inquisitive gaze of a municipal police officer. He responded automatically. "Everything's fine, thank you. I'm just a little tired."

The officer moved away. That scare reawakened his senses. He mustn't appear suspect. He'd already had extraordinary luck in escaping the police. It had been a matter of a few minutes. He'd gone down to the village in the car to do some shopping. As he was heading back up to his house, he'd noticed vehicles parked at the end of his street—that was peculiar. Each property had its own garage. Then he'd spotted men moving discreetly toward his house. He'd already survived an identical misadventure in Florida, so his instinct had taken over. He'd passed by his house without slowing down and then drove toward Grenoble.

How had the police managed to find him? It was a mystery, but it didn't matter. One point, however, perturbed him terribly—the heart was still at his house. He had nothing left to resist Magali's attacks until tomorrow night, the day of the solstice! He forced his way through groups of high school students, who were chatting and eating ice cream and churros, enjoying their free time between classes. Despondent, he sat down on a bench in the Place Victor-Hugo. He noticed he was the target of glances from a group of students who had gone for this bench at the same time he did. He stood up to leave it to them—he absolutely did not want to be noticed. He went up the Boulevard Agutte Sembat, walked along the Isère riverfront, then crossed the river. A few minutes later, he found a bench in a much less traveled place. He settled in. He took some time to calm down, to let his logical mind regain the upper hand.

He'd been identified. How? Likely because of his vehicle. A wanted poster with his photo would most certainly be released, which would make him a hunted man. He had to react before that happened. First question: Where to hide? A name came to mind immediately—Arsène! His friend would be able to help him out for two or three days, enough time to perfect his healing and turn things around. After he was rid of the curse Magali had cast on him, he'd be able to take control of the situation again. He'd leave Grenoble for good, and his money would allow him to remake a life abroad. He knew many countries, and not necessarily in exotic locations, where a bank account offshore was more valuable than a passport from the Republic of France.

But that was for later. Arsène absolutely had to help him. The heart was still at his house! He needed it to keep himself together until the solstice. There was only one solution—find another. He needed Arsène, his advice, his knowledge of Fra Bartolomeo's writings, and his logistical support. He'd be able to thank him financially;

he'd support his work extensively. When he thought about the heart now out of reach, he felt nervous tremors throughout his body. He was in withdrawal! He looked around him, worried. No, Magali wasn't there. She never came to him outside, he knew that. For twenty-nine years she came to torment him only at night. The very first year after her death, she'd embarked on her revenge. She would arrive the first of June and vanish on the twenty-first—always the same dates. And year after year she'd tried to break him, to push him to suicide. But he'd resisted. And thanks to Fra Bartolomeo's science and Arsène's wisdom, he'd send her straight back to the land of the dead.

Lost in his delusions, Dominique Sartenas slipped into the mind of Dominique Cabrade, thirty years earlier. Magali had disappeared. He'd made everything ready at their home so that she could give birth under the best conditions. He'd prepared the child's bedroom. He'd even spent nights developing the education he'd give his son. He'd separate him from his mother within the first hour: she was too weak and prone to falling into the snares of temptation. He was a doctor and knew men's weaknesses, starting with his own! His son would be pure—he'd be his mentor. His son would be his redemption! But his wife had circumvented his vigilance. She'd managed, by what sorcery he didn't know, to open the window shutter in her room, on the second floor. Yet he had barricaded it. Then she'd jumped, despite her condition. Then she'd left. It had been a good fifteen minutes before he noticed. They lived in a house in town, and she could be anywhere. He'd then called some of his acquaintances. They'd crisscrossed the city. Sartenas was now Cabrade, looking for his wife.

At one o'clock in the morning, the streets were almost deserted. He knew she wouldn't take refuge with the police. He'd done his work well enough—the word of a respected doctor was worth more than that of a depressive woman running away as her labor pains began. He found two men to help him. They had seen her from afar. But why had she fled? Suddenly, the truth jumped out at him—terrible! She wanted to steal his son from him. She wanted to keep him for herself, or worse, kill him so that he couldn't have him! A black fury took him over. The two men with him didn't understand what was going on, but they were willing to blindly obey his orders. He called to her, but she didn't answer. He was still ready to forgive her, but she would have to give him back his son. The boy was his! She was just the carrier. He would have to put her on the right path again, and then he'd be able to forgive her . . . maybe.

There, in the distance, appearing under the wavering halo of a lamppost, he saw a white outline moving hurriedly. He recognized the dress she had been wearing that afternoon. It was her. He started running, followed by his two assistants. She was at most two hundred yards ahead. She rushed into a side street. He lost sight of her. By the time he entered the street, she was on a bridge over the Isère. She was heading for the Saint-Laurent neighborhood. All the restaurants were closed at that hour of the night. She was running along the Isère. He'd soon reach her. No pedestrians in sight—luck was with him. He caught his wife by the shoulder and spun her around violently. He was going to teach her some manners. Her expression stupefied him. Where he'd expected to see terror, he saw serenity. The two other men caught up with them, out of breath. He unceremoniously dismissed them. They didn't need to be asked twice.

He pulled roughly on Magali's arm and walked along the Isère, sheltered from the prying eyes of any unlikely night owl. Now close to her, he realized with horror that she'd already given birth. But where? And when? It wasn't possible.

He looked at her, filled with hate, and gave her a terrible slap. She fell to the ground, without crying out, maintaining her serene gaze, which he already couldn't stand. He pulled her roughly upright and placed a hand on his wife's stomach, to confirm a fact he already knew. She was no longer carrying his heir, the flesh of his flesh. He screamed.

"Where is he? Where is my son?"

"He's not there anymore!"

"Where is he?" he cried like a madman, kneeing her in the belly. She crumpled. Tears appeared in response to the pain. He looked at her face. She still had that half smile at the corner of her lips.

"The child disappeared. He'll never become the monster you wanted to make of him! We could have raised him together, Dominique. I loved you, but what you've become repulses me. What I've endured up to now for his sake—I didn't want him to experience it, too."

Dominique Cabrade began to comprehend the meaning of his wife's words. "But you killed him? You killed my child so I couldn't give him the best of myself? You're a madwoman, a madwoman."

In a fit of rage, he punched her repeatedly. Magali curled in on herself, trying to limit the pain he inflicted with each blow.

"Where did you put his body? Where?"

"You'll never be able to find him again."

The man screamed, screamed his despair and his hate. He yanked his wife up violently and approached the riverbank. He grabbed a large stone. Magali knew her last moments had arrived.

"You have no reason left to live. You would have been the mother of my son, I'd planned a place for you. But you wanted more, in spite of everything I did to protect you from your environment. And I failed. What you've just done deserves death."

She burst out with a laugh that transformed into a heartrending groan.

"Poor Dominique. I was unhappy enough to die during these last twelve months. I tried to find reasons to love you, despite the facts, despite what my friends and family told me. I looked for reasons. But tonight, it's over, I don't have any more reasons. You can do with me what you like."

Cabrade's eyes shone with hate. So she was trying to put the blame on him! She was definitively evil. By making her disappear, he was doing the world a favor. Magali knew he was about to deal her final blow.

"I hope one day you'll realize what you've done. And that day will be terrible for you."

He screamed and struck her like a madman. When the body went limp under his blow, he looked again at the waters of the Isère. The purity of the water was much too beautiful a casket for this whore he'd considered his wife. He hid her along the wall—no one would come by at this hour. That would give him time to get his vehicle and take away the corpse. The mountain was vast enough to make a body disappear.

Covered in sweat, he reopened his eyes and looked around him. He was sitting exactly where, thirty years earlier, he'd removed from his life the one who should have given him descendants. A sign from elusive fate, no doubt. He was wrapping up a cycle of torment. He was going to dispel the curse she'd put on him once and for all. He considered this coincidence a positive sign, stood up, and headed for his mentor's home.

Chapter 44: Why Grenoble?

Rivera leaned back in his chair and put his feet up on his desk. He was spent. He defied the administrative prohibitions and lit a cigarette. He inhaled the smoke deeply, eyes half-closed. He'd just concluded an armed peace with Captain Barka. He'd decided to make the first move and call her. He was expecting a difficult conversation, but she'd been rather conciliatory. She was quite far from accepting a dinner invitation, but she wanted to move the investigation forward as quickly as possible.

Rivera was affected by what he'd seen a few hours earlier. That ghost house, the torture chamber, that young woman's heart still marked by Sartenas's teeth. He'd really acted like a giant asshole with Barka, wasted precious time and information. But he couldn't go back. All he could do now was use his colleague's aggressiveness and intuition instead of being jealous of her.

He reopened his eyes, took a last puff on his cigarette, and stubbed it out in the bottom of his empty coffee cup.

"So, Garancher, are you done with that Sartenas file, yes or shit!" he hollered into the hallway. He heard his colleague's very calm voice answer him.

"Higher decibels won't make things go faster, Captain. Let me have one more little hour, and I'll bring you the summary of our research."

Rivera sighed loudly enough for them to hear and thought back on his conversation. He'd asked Captain Barka to get back in touch with Lombard so that he could have another discussion with him, but more calmly this time. Lombard's statements took on much greater significance given their revelations in Sartenas's house. He'd see the young man at the end of the day. He went back over the medical examiner's file while waiting for Garancher to grace him with the research results. He was eager for those results, because he knew his colleague and the team he had at his disposal would get their hands, or their eyes, on everything there was to find.

He went over the report one more time. Sartenas was a real nut job, and hate mounted inside Rivera. He'd never felt that during an investigation. He'd engaged in acts of violence he'd in fact been reproached for, but never had he felt like some kind of avenging angel, like he wanted to take a guy in his own hands to make him suffer. He had to get ahold of himself. But how could he after reading these lines:

. . . The body was cut into along the abdomen, between the fourth and fifth ribs. The ribs were then separated with the help of a surgical instrument such as three-prong pliers . . . the venae cavae as well as the aorta were severed using a scalpel. The heart was removed through the rib cage . . . the color of the flesh as well as the small quantity of blood found in the victim's circulatory system prove she was alive when the act was committed . . .

Fuck! But why make the girl suffer?

Garancher came into the office at his lethargic pace. Rivera cut him off before he could start disclosing the results of his research.

"Meeting in the briefing room in five minutes. You'll tell the whole team what you've found."

Garancher felt a sense of importance when he addressed the twenty investigators and policemen gathered around him. Mazure himself had just entered the room. At a nod from the commissioner, he began.

"If we can present these results to you this evening, it's thanks to the diligence of my colleagues and the excellent cooperation put in place between judicial services and the police. Judge Hellbronner's team has demonstrated extraordinary responsiveness."

Rivera rolled his eyes. The emphatic tone his colleague used as soon as he was speaking to more than three people at a time always irritated him. But he didn't interrupt him.

"Our man's name is Dominique Sartenas. As you know, we've been able to trace him based on his vehicle identification. He was born October 3, 1952, in Neuilly sur Seine. His official address is in Fort Myers, Florida."

"What the hell was he doing in the United States?" asked Rivera, surprised by the information.

"I'm getting there, Captain. Just know that he arrived in France in the month of April. The house we searched this morning has been rented since March. We found the name of the owner—he lives in the Paris area. We managed to reach him, and he isn't at all involved in this case. The house was rented through an agency."

"And do you know what brought this sad individual to Grenoble?" asked Alain Mazure.

"No, not yet. But to answer Captain Rivera's question, we know Sartenas is a plastic surgeon."

"You mean he does cosmetic surgery."

"Among other things. He operates in a clinic on the west coast of Florida. We managed to get in touch with the clinic, and with the help of the American police, we got the testimony of two of his colleagues. That's why I asked you for an extension, Captain Rivera. The time difference, you understand?"

Rivera motioned for him to keep going.

"We can say for sure at this point that although the surgeon might command respect, the man does not."

"Explain."

"It took less than half an hour for my colleagues to learn that he officially worked part time at the clinic, and that he spent the rest of his time in Cuba."

"Cigar fan?" said Rivera ironically.

"Not really. Cuba is an island of contradictions. Although Castro's family still holds political power, the power of money is back in force. Cuba welcomes clinics that offer low-cost surgical interventions. If you go on the Internet, you'll find addresses in spades. But there are also more discreet clinics that offer more luxurious services, sometimes bordering on illegality. Sartenas is said to have worked in that type of clinic."

"Did you take into account, Garancher, that this type of statement can be driven by the speaker's jealousy, or even anti-French sentiment?" asked Mazure.

"Certainly, Commissioner. But two people, without apparent connection, gave us the same information. Besides, the research results agree with them. While investigating the real estate agency, and thanks to the support from the Ministry of Justice services, we were able to uncover in record time the origin of the money transfers that pay his rent. They come from a bank in the Rhône-Alpes region. The account was opened in March. Two colleagues popped into the bank with convincing papers and a touch of persuasion. The money the bank received comes directly from an offshore account in the Caribbean."

"Making money isn't a sin in the United States, unlike in France."

"You're right, Commissioner. But not obeying the law is. And Sartenas's activities in Cuba seem to fall into that category."

"Good, let's continue. So we're dealing with a surgeon, as Doctor Blavet predicted. He must earn a very comfortable living, no doubt in part illegally, but he wouldn't be the first. And he came back to Grenoble three months ago. But was he already plotting his murders?"

"I know nothing about that, Commissioner. But we've obtained very surprising information. Sartenas has been living in the United States for eight years. He divided his practice between Florida and Alabama. But when you go back in time, you don't find anything more on him."

"Which is to say?"

"No trace of a Dominique Sartenas. It's as if he appeared officially only eight years ago. We called city hall in Neuilly—no trace of his birth certificate."

"They could have lost it."

"They could have, but he was born in 1952, not during the upheaval of the French Revolution. No trace of him before the issuance of his identity card or his passport, eight years ago. One could imagine he managed to procure a false birth certificate and a few other falsified official documents, then created himself an identity."

"Well, you can't create a persona out of nothing!"

Garancher looked at his superior with astonishment. "You well know, Commissioner, that with money and a few well-placed accomplices, it is possible to do many things."

Mazure didn't address Lieutenant Garancher's commentary. "So we have a guy with a fake identity who comes to Grenoble for an unknown reason, slaughters two poor girls chosen who knows how, and disappears into thin air. We've made quite a bit of progress, gentlemen. I ask the question on pure principle: have you found a link between this man and the Grenoble region?"

"None for the time being, Commissioner. He could just as easily have come here by chance as lived here for thirty years. But for the moment, we know nothing. We've planned to send out a call for witnesses by this evening. Perhaps people will recognize his photo? Anyway, if he lived here, it was under another identity."

"Okay. Now go pull out all the stops when questioning the neighbors. Comb through Saint-Martin d'Uriage with his picture. Get in touch with the American authorities. Give them the killer's pedigree and tactfully ask them to check if they've had any unsolved murders of the same type in the last few years. Gather up all there is on his American life—I want to know everything on the subject. I also want to understand how he could have obtained an official existence from nothing. Make a big stink in the Grenoble medical community to find out if Sartenas, or X—whatever his real name is—ever practiced in the area. And finally, plaster his photo everywhere in Grenoble! I'm going to ask for official authorization. I want this guy to sweat bullets when he sets foot in the street . . . with or without a blond wig."

Chapter 45: Sanctuary

Sartenas looked up and verified the building's number. He'd found the apartment. He hesitated for a few seconds, but the sound of a car braking hard at a red light startled him out of his stupor. He pushed open the door and entered the foyer. Tiled in marble, decorated with floral arrangements in soothing colors, the place instilled in him a little of the serenity he'd been lacking since he'd seen his house being spied on by strangers. His nervous tension lowered a notch, but his vigilance remained total. He was mere steps from success. Then he'd disappear again, forever, into the new life he'd dreamed of for so long.

It was seven o'clock. He buzzed the intercom, crossing his fingers that the only voice capable of helping him would answer. The speaker crackled a moment.

"Who's there?" asked a voice deformed by the poor-quality audio system.

"It's Dominique."

A pause, which seemed an eternity to Sartenas, followed the utterance of his name.

Then the door buzzed open.

"Come up, it's on the fourth floor."

Sartenas pushed open the door and chose the stairs. Above all, he had to limit the number of possible encounters. When he reached the fourth floor, he immediately noticed a door ajar. He quickly crossed the hallway. The occupant opened the door completely, let him enter, then swiftly closed it behind him.

Without a word, Arsène brought Dominique to the living room. His gaze was questioning and angry.

"What's come over you? It was quite clear between us that we must never see each other here. Our meeting point is, and will always remain, the manor."

Sartenas collapsed into an armchair. He was well aware of their agreement, but the situation was too dire.

"I didn't have a choice, Arsène. A very unfortunate setback! You alone can cure me."

Arsène observed him keenly. He'd never seen Dominique Sartenas so disturbed. In the end, it was probably better to have him close at hand than to know he was on the loose, capable of any rash action.

"Take off your jacket while I go find something to drink. You will tell me everything."

A glow of relief lit up Sartenas's face. Now he was going to pull through, he knew it. Arsène would find the means to chase away Magali for good. Sartenas began his tale as soon as his friend came back with two glasses and a bottle of fruit juice.

Twenty minutes later, Arsène was annoyed, very annoyed. The risk they faced now had significantly increased. The man in front of him usually demonstrated uncommon composure, but he was, at times, very unstable psychologically. The disappearance of his son, which Sartenas had considered the ultimate betrayal, and the subsequent murder of his wife, had sent the man into a sort of parallel world.

He'd invented encounters with Magali, which had grown stronger year after year and undermined him. Magali, a sort of female Don Giovanni, appeared to remind him of his crime but also of her betrayal. Arsène had to make some quick decisions. He grabbed his cell phone, went out to the balcony, and made his first call.

Chapter 46: Pierre Dupré

Julien Lombard pushed open the door and headed for the reception desk. A woman buried in papers looked up at him questioningly.

"I'd like to see Monsieur Pierre Dupré," he announced.

Nadia Barka came up from behind and quietly took out her badge. "We're working on a murder case . . . Monsieur Dupré may have information that will help us make progress."

The receptionist was taken aback. She looked at each of them in turn. "Is this a bad joke?"

"Absolutely not. My ID is quite legitimate, and my request is quite serious."

"But Pierre Dupré is gravely ill and hasn't left the establishment for more than six months, aside from a few stints in intensive care."

"It's actually his memory we'd like to call on. And time is running out," Captain Barka explained.

The nurse looked at them. They didn't seem like they were playing a joke on her. "I have to ask for permission from the director. Can you give me a few minutes?"

"We'll wait for you here."

Five minutes later, she came back, accompanied by a short, energetic woman.

"Hello, I'm Aline Bergson, director of this establishment. My colleague told me you would like to have a visit with Monsieur Dupré."

Captain Barka once again explained the reason for their presence.

"And who is this gentleman with you? One of the family?"

"I'm Julien Lombard. I'm a family member."

"I must warn you. First of all, Monsieur Dupré is in the final stages of terminal cancer. He's on morphine, and he won't live much longer. He's extremely weak. Even so, he hasn't had a visit in more than three months. Whoever you are, I think it will do him good to talk with someone. You can't imagine his loneliness! But I will ask you to leave him alone if you see he's no longer capable of continuing the conversation."

"Thank you, Madame Bergson."

"I will tell you that I'm not respecting the rules of the establishment by authorizing you to interview him. Police officers trump everything! But it will lift his mood, and he'll hardly have the opportunity anymore, unfortunately."

She looked at a treetop outside the window. "He was a charming man. But we all must die. Hélène, please escort these people to Monsieur Dupré's room."

The director bid good-bye to the two visitors, then left them in the care of the nurse. They passed through freshly painted hallways. The large bay windows let in bright light. She knocked on the door to number seventeen and entered quietly. "Monsieur Dupré, I have a visit for you."

Without making a sound, Nadia and Julien walked into the room. Positioned against the wall, a hospital bed took up most of the space. A man, who must have been tall but was now just a frail outline, turned his eyes toward them. An IV drip injected a color-less liquid into his arm, drop by drop, as if trying to replace the life that was leaving him. His extremely pale face reflected his physical weakness.

"Call me as soon as you need me, Monsieur Dupré. I'll leave you with your visitors."

The nurse left the room and closed the door behind her. Julien felt a strong emotion as he gazed upon this old man whose life was abandoning him. Even Nadia seemed troubled by the scene.

"I don't know who you are, but I imagine I must be useful to you in one way or another."

They were surprised by the clear voice speaking to them. Nadia decided to go first.

"Indeed, Monsieur Dupré. I'm Captain Nadia Barka of the Grenoble police. You can be a very big help to us. I'm going to get right to the point. I'm investigating the deaths of Monica Revasti and Camille Saint-Forge. Perhaps these names mean nothing to you, but they're two young women who were just killed this week in Grenoble."

"I didn't know the names, but I heard about them. All the staff and residents were very shocked. And me, too, for that matter. But I don't see how I can help you."

"I'm getting there, Monsieur Dupré."

"Can you call me Pierre? It might seem stupid to you, but no one has called me by my first name in months."

"Okay, Pierre. We've identified the killer. His name is Dominique Sartenas."

"Sorry, but I don't know that man."

"I know, and what I'm going to tell you will no doubt surprise you. We think that long ago, he was called Dominique Cabrade."

Pierre Dupré stared at her, then looked at Julien. He closed his eyes, not saying a word or moving. The two visitors exchanged a worried glance. Julien was about to call a nurse when he spoke again.

"So he's not dead. My nightmare will never end, then. Who sent you to me?"

Julien answered him.

"What I'm going to tell you will seem outrageous, Pierre. But I beg you to believe me."

Pierre Dupré's attention sharpened as Julien spoke. Emotion rose in him, like the lava of an ancient volcano finally able to vent its boiling energy. His face regained its color, but he said nothing, drinking in the young man's words. When Julien had finished, tears ran silently down the old man's face.

"And Magali had a son? But what became of him?"

"She didn't tell me, Pierre, but he's alive somewhere."

The old man repeated, "Her son is alive, her son is alive . . . my grandson." He fell silent. They respected his silence. Then Pierre Dupré told them, "Ask me all your questions."

"You knew Dominique Cabrade. In your opinion, would he be capable of such murders?"

"I don't know if I'll be objective. In fact, I know I won't be. I hate that man. He took my daughter from me, my grandson, my happiness and that of my wife, Nicole. He stole everything from me. He was a manipulator. I sensed it from the beginning, and my wife even more acutely. We tried to warn Magali, but she didn't want to listen. He fascinated her. Cabrade was a brilliant surgeon, very at ease in society, always at the center of discussion and attention. He pushed her forward, showing her a world we hadn't been able to give her. But I felt viscerally that wasn't the real Cabrade, that it was a performance.

"When Magali announced to us she was going to be married, Nicole and I were sick over it. But it was her choice. A few months after her marriage, she started to change—we were becoming strangers to her. And she stopped coming to see us. Each time we called her, we got Cabrade, who proclaimed that it was now up to him to watch over her.

"Four months before she disappeared, she came to the house. I remember the date, February 20. It was Nicole's birthday. She seemed to have lost her mind; her statements were incoherent. We brought her to her old bedroom, and Nicole took care of her. I called a doctor. In the meantime, Cabrade arrived with a man I didn't know. This was not the worldly, ever-smooth Cabrade. No, this was a madman facing me. He wanted to take Magali back. I told him she wasn't there. But at that moment, Nicole came downstairs beaming, telling me she was doing better . . . and that she was expecting a child. I'll always remember her face, so happy when she gave me that news. Cabrade pushed violently to get past me. I didn't let him and punched him twice, which put him on the ground. But his sidekick threw himself at me. He was used to fighting and overpowered me. Cabrade got up, fought off my wife, and left with Magali, who was crying and didn't put up a struggle."

His breathing had become labored. He rested for a few seconds and feverishly resumed the course of his memories.

"I couldn't do anything more to keep him from taking her. When he left, I called the police. Since Cabrade was Magali's husband, they didn't even intervene. So I called two pals and took my car to go get her. At their apartment, nothing. They'd moved two weeks ago. I went back to the police station. They took my complaint . . . and that's it."

"I imagine you did everything to find your daughter!" interjected Nadia.

"Naturally. I followed Cabrade to find out where he was living. I went to harass him as soon as my work gave me the opportunity. But one day, he told me my daughter would have big problems if I continued to harass him, and I was afraid for her. I believed he was crazy. That's followed me for thirty years now. Why didn't I keep looking for her?"

He retreated into his remorse, then said to them, "So, yes, I believe Cabrade is capable of anything, including killing two innocent women. My daughter certainly was one!"

The man was now beset by extreme restlessness. The events he'd just relived so intensely seemed to reignite the last spark of life remaining in him.

"May I ask you another question?" asked Julien.

"Go on, my boy."

"Did Magali know an Aurélien?"

A smile flitted across the old man's withered lips, soon chased away by a wave of bitterness.

"Of course, Aurélien Costel. I don't know where she met him, but he came over to the house quite often. He was a fan of auto racing, like me. He had a gift for making her laugh. Nicole and I were convinced they were going to get married. Imagine the shock when I discovered Cabrade's existence. She went from a boy who was good as gold to that worldly scoundrel. But I think Aurélien was always there for her, even when she decided to get married. He got along marvelously with my wife, and he burst into tears at the house when we told him the news about the marriage. But he retained his friendship with her."

"Do you know what's become of him?"

"Yes, he's the only one who continued to come see me here every now and then. He's managed a restaurant in Grenoble for about ten years—La Pomme d'Amour."

A nurse entered the room with a meal on a tray. She put it down precipitously and went over to the sick man. She took his pulse.

"You're going to have to leave Monsieur Dupré. He's terribly agitated. I'm going to call the doctor . . ."

The old man grabbed her by the wrist.

"You know my life is coming to an end, Simone. But these two people are giving me something precious that will help me die with dignity. Can you leave us together for another ten minutes?" Pierre Dupré's imploring look got the better of her.

"Ten minutes, Monsieur Dupré, no more."

"Ten minutes, Simone. I'm grateful to you."

The nurse left the room. The man nodded to Julien. "Come here and sit close to me."

Surprised by the intimacy, Julien took a chair and pulled it up next to the bed.

"Look at me."

Nadia quietly left the room.

"Give me your hand."

Julien extended his hands to Pierre Dupré's. They were fragile, but full of renewed vigor. The silence that fell between them brought them closer. Julien felt emotion gripping him. In spite of himself, a tear rolled down his cheek. The old man also let himself sink into intense feelings of happiness.

"You have your mother's eyes. The same eyes so full of life. I can never thank heaven enough for having brought you here."

Julien took him in his arms. The words remained lodged in his throat.

"You've given me back my life, even if there isn't much left of it. This is the greatest joy of my life . . . almost as great as the day Magali was born."

The two men stayed together for several long minutes.

The door opened, and the nurse came in with a doctor. They froze, taken aback by the scene before them. Only a few words disrupted the silence.

"Julien, my grandson . . ."

Julien stood up. The old man, gazing at the sunlight playing atop the foliage on the other side of the window, wasn't moving anymore. The smile that illuminated his emaciated face gave him a happiness he'd believed had faded away long ago.

Quietly, Julien left the room.

Chapter 47: The Manor

Arsène looked around. The foyer was empty. He motioned to Sartenas to follow him. He pushed open the door leading directly into the communal garage and walked quickly toward his car, a black BMW X6. He unlocked the doors, and Sartenas slipped into the front seat. The tinted windows assured them of the discretion they needed. Arsène had quickly decided to put his guest up at the manor, an old family property that had been passed to him through his father's unmarried sister. He'd put it in the name of an old devoted cousin, but only he used it. He'd done substantial work there over the last few years. The initial curiosity had gradually died down, and he could take advantage of the tranquillity necessary for his activities.

Sartenas's agitation had increased since he'd set foot in Arsène's home. He was in a state of withdrawal, and Arsène knew it. He'd persuaded his passenger that eating young women's hearts until the solstice would deliver him from his nightmares. Sartenas had quickly accepted his theory, unconsciously clinging to the smallest hope of being liberated from his phobia. And there was a good chance it would work. The persuasive force of Fra Bartolomeo's writings would doubtless put an end to the vengeful image of Magali that he'd created for himself.

They left the highway that led to Valence, entering the valley that would take them to the Vercors plateau.

Fra Bartolomeo: a genius invention that had given him the power he'd dreamed of. The power to control men's fates—and the power to increase his wealth. He'd discreetly enriched himself and become a puppet master.

He glanced at his neighbor, who was absorbed in the landscape. This sudden sluggishness that followed his agitation demanded a rapid intervention on Arsène's part. He'd take care of it as soon as they arrived at the manor.

His mind went back to Fra Bartolomeo. The character he'd created one summer night for a rich idler in search of a passion had taken shape over the years. A defrocked monk who had gone to Mexico to escape the Inquisition, Fra Bartolomeo had learned, during his long stay, to interpret the knowledge of souls with the help of the great Aztec priests who had survived the massacre ordered by Cortés. Arsène had gradually expanded his work. He'd fleshed out his creation with historical details, improving the consistency of his story. And eight years earlier, he'd written the final version of *The Book of the Sun—Il Libro del Sole*. He'd produced one satisfactory copy that could pass for an ancient book if you didn't look at it too closely.

He'd begun to frequent amateur archaeological circles throughout France. He'd identified a certain number of members, to whom he'd revealed, bit by bit, the existence of *The Book of the Sun*. He'd chosen them carefully—influential, gullible, and full of themselves, personalities disinclined to self-examination. He'd been careful and made sure at each stage that his victims would completely believe his pronouncements. As soon as he sensed one of his disciples was starting to doubt, he separated from him, with an adroitness that had allowed him to prevent the birth of any suspicion. The backsliders recovered . . . or not. Once, he'd had to put in place a much more expeditious method than he would have liked. Twelve people were currently part of the brotherhood he'd created. At first he'd been hesitant to give it a name, but upon the insistence of certain members, he'd relented. He'd chosen a very simple title: "The Order of Bartolomeo." He was the master, the one who knew how to interpret the words of the inspired monk. The members were now totally devoted to him. He had the intelligence not to abuse it and presented to his disciples a humble facade that delighted them to no end. Because sharing secrets from the fine collection of history, being part of an elite group—what pleasure! What a feeling of superiority over the ignorant masses around you!

Arsène had never promised them anything nor asked for anything. They'd been lucky to be chosen to share in unique knowledge. What a wonderful motivator vanity is! And how effective! Little by little, this knowledge had acted like a drug. Arsène had prepared his set pieces in considerable detail. And the success had been beyond his most optimistic hopes. Magistrates, bankers, politicians were eating out of his hand . . . without realizing it, which was the key to his success. He had become powerful and rich. The money Sartenas had promised him would allow him to undertake great projects.

The car passed through the village of Lans-en-Vercors and entered the Vercors plateau. The light was slowly starting to fail. The road was rarely taken at this hour of the evening. The inhabitants who went to work in Grenoble every day were already at home, busy cutting the grass in their yards or preparing the barbecues for dinner.

Upon arriving in Villard-de-Lans, Arsène left the major road, then took a labyrinth of little byways that led them to the manor's doorstep. The name "manor" was very pompous for this large bourgeois building, but he was proud of it. It had become the center of his parallel universe.

Sartenas was inert in his seat. He didn't take his eyes off the residence, as if he were scanning the facade for the answer to an unfathomable question. He suddenly turned toward the driver, a flash of panic in his eyes. "It can't start again, Arsène, it can't start again!"

"It won't start again, Dominique, trust me."

"But how can you say that!" he screamed suddenly. "You're the one who taught me. Eat a piece of the heart at each sunset, said the Fra!"

The historian laid his hand gently on Sartenas's forearm. The surgeon jerked it away as if he'd just received an electric shock.

"Don't try to confuse me. I've been waiting for this moment for thirty years! Don't get in my way. Let me go. I'll go to Villard, and I'll find the heart I'm missing."

Arsène took his arm more firmly. He didn't let go when Sartenas tried to escape his grip, and forced him to look him in the eye. He retained his calm tone, but now he spoke to him like a child.

"Listen carefully to me, Dominique. Have I abandoned you recently? You asked me for help, and I helped you. I revealed to you the mysteries of Fra Bartolomeo. Do you know how many of you know them? No, you don't. Just a few privileged people."

At the sound of his mentor's voice, Sartenas calmed down as quickly as he'd flared up.

"To you I revealed mysteries the dead themselves want to keep at the bottom of their tombs. And you don't trust me more than that?"

Sartenas lowered his head, sheepish and contrite.

"My apologies, Arsène. I don't know what came over me. But I'm so afraid of Magali, so afraid she'll make me live this hell I don't deserve. She's a . . . witch. Keep helping me, save me. You'll find me even more generous than you think."

Arsène fell silent, scenting an even greater profit than he could have imagined.

"Half of what I've accumulated over the last twenty years will be for you," Sartenas said. He seemed to hesitate. Then, with a flash in his eyes, he announced, "Fifteen million dollars!"

Sartenas looked with devoted confidence at the stone disc placed on an altar before him. The flames of two candles flickered at the whim of a quiet fan.

Arsène observed his guest. He'd regained his usual self-control and now seemed peaceful. Sartenas's panicky crisis had worried him. Not for the doctor's health, but for the sum of money in play. The fifteen million dollars mentioned at the end of their brief exchange in the car had awakened all his curiosity. So Sartenas hadn't told him everything about his years on the run.

He admired once more the crypt he'd created in the basement of a little building close to the house. He'd had it worked on by several teams sent specially from the north of France to avoid arousing suspicion. He'd even called on a Turkish company for the finishing touches. An agreement had been reached; the work wasn't declared, it disappeared from the workers' memories, and a large gratuity provided before they'd returned to their country had definitively chased away the last potential memories. Coordinating all that had been much simpler than he'd envisioned at the beginning of his project.

Two rooms on two subterranean levels—these rooms had never existed on the initial plans. The first company had worked on the foundations of a personal movie theater and gymnasium. The second had transformed the layout of the rooms. And the last had created the crypt and the council chamber.

The crypt, or "Sun Chamber"—here is where he had read Fra Bartolomeo's book, and where he had feigned the ensuing revelation. He'd designed it small. Only a few people could fit. There was a reason for that. He truly wanted his disciples, and he smiled in thinking about that word, to have the impression of being hand-picked initiates. He had no desire to dominate the world or create some new order. There were enough crazies on earth, and he despised cults like the Mandaroms in Castellane or the Church of Scientology. He just wanted to make money and satisfy his urges when he felt like it. To live happily, live hidden! This sense of power intoxicated him, but he'd always been careful not to let it get out of hand. Always leave initiates with the feeling they control their fate, always be at their service through service to Fra Bartolomeo, only rarely call on them. And he'd been surprised, in the beginning, by the pride they had in putting themselves at *his* disposal.

He returned to the present moment and put down on the altar the book he was holding in his hand. No sartorial decorum or kabbalistic signs of membership. He had cultivated people around him who would have fled from that type of ceremony favored by the mentally disturbed. Here, they were among people of good society, who were sharing a secret. The glory they got out of it? A knowledge others didn't have. A glory it was useless to talk about. The notion of a privileged elite would disappear that way. No, the pleasure of knowing yourself to be superior to others was quite sufficient! A vanity it was useless to share.

That was Arsène's pride. And the money had come on its own. Never had he asked for a single cent from his victims. To financially motivate his disciples, he would speak, during one-on-one conversations, of complementary research in America, the restoration of this or that piece, even unscrupulous Mexican officials. And unfailingly the proposition came: *Let me participate in this adventure.* And always the same sequence: two or three discussions before being talked into accepting the money. And the donor's pride in being the one who would help promote knowledge, which of course the donor would hear about first. Never a meeting with more than five people at a time, and always the same ones. At first, for reasons of security—even if he was vigilant, he was not immune to a traitor. If he had to make somebody disappear, it was better not to have too many people asking questions. And always confidentiality—the group knew there was another group, but less informed than they were, of course. Vanity! What beautiful projects you can accomplish when you know who you're working with!

It was with one of those groups that he'd conducted his experiment on the young Laure Déramaux. He'd transformed respectable citizens into bloodthirsty wolves. He himself had felt an inglorious pleasure during those three months of confinement and experiments. They met every week, and it was with a sort of joy that they'd finally put her to death. She'd been found shortly after they'd left her on the mountain. He'd followed the investigation with interest. But not once had the investigators approached him. The gods he was celebrating were with him!

Chapter 48: The Cabrade Lead

Nadia Barka slammed her car door. The sound echoed, then faded away across the museum parking garage. A Bach cantata distilled into parking garage Muzak drowned out the silence. She had dropped Julien Lombard off outside Sophie Dupas's apartment building, then gone back to the police station. Then she'd had dinner with Drancey, Fortin, and Garancher. Her three colleagues had decided not to leave her alone with her disappointment at being taken off the investigation. It was almost touching!

Now she was going back home. She glanced at her wristwatch: 11:46 p.m. Time to take a shower, change her dressing, and swallow a handful of sedatives and anti-inflammatories. She was exhausted, but she didn't regret her day's activities. Even if she was no longer in charge of the inquiry, she was at its heart. And putting away Sartenas, or Cabrade, whatever his name was, now surpassed all resentment she could have felt. She'd even managed to talk to Rivera, which had seemed impossible to her two days prior. She'd been surprised by her colleague's about-face. What she'd initially considered a tactic for obtaining information from her now seemed to be a true change in behavior. In any case, she would have provided the information.

However, the fact that he now considered her a major contributor pleased her.

Nadia had left the parking lot and walked down the Quai Jongkind. She took the bridge that crossed over the Isère. Two rather drunk men called out to her. She didn't answer them, continuing on her way. She had no desire to be inconvenienced tonight. They followed her, making propositions she still chose to ignore. Then they got tired and went back to a bar, drawn by the light, like alcoholic moths.

Nadia had enjoyed her dinner last night with Sophie Dupas. She'd experienced few girls-only dinners in her life. She'd joined the police very young, and it wasn't the most feminine professional environment. The young woman had a good head on her shoulders and was very good company. Never had Nadia trusted a stranger so quickly. When Sophie had left the apartment, she'd felt wistful. What if life were like that, instead of constantly fighting against the world's crap and those who make it! But she knew this vigilante mission was rooted in her—no matter what she did to move away from it, she would come back. So it was useless to tilt at windmills. She just hoped to find her Sancho Panza and had an affectionate thought for Étienne.

Half past midnight: the room was half full despite the late hour. Julien Lombard's revelations had energized them. Mazure was piloting the launch of the investigation with Rivera. Six officers accompanied them, excited by the idea of getting closer to the killer.

"Shit, it should have been Barka who brought us this lead, with Lombard, too!" ranted Rivera.

"You believe his story now?" asked Mazure.

"Yes. When I discovered the nut job's house, his testimony took a totally different turn. Okay, boys, where do you stand?"

"We've just gathered quite a bit of information, and I'm in the process of printing a photo of Cabrade. You'll have it in a minute. I'll bring you what I've collected for the moment."

Rivera laid out a dozen sheets of paper on the conference table. He flipped through them quickly.

"Dominique Cabrade, born October 3, 1952. Pignol, check Sartenas's birth date!" he barked at one of his colleagues. Then he went on: "Studied medicine in Grenoble, specialized in reconstructive surgery. Fuck, two guys who do cosmetic surgery, if that isn't a coincidence . . ." He looked through the other pages and continued. "Married Magali Dupré in 1981, who disappeared in June 1983. He leaves the Grenoble hospital six months later for an unknown destination. The rest, boys, is it coming?"

A policeman came up to him holding out a photo. "Here's his picture from thirty years ago."

Rivera looked briefly at the photo and exclaimed, "But that's not at all the same guy as Sartenas!" He dug around in another file and put the snapshots side by side.

"What is this shit? They couldn't even be distant cousins!"

Mazure looked at him and put a hand on his shoulder. "Remind me what these gentlemen's specialty is?"

"Cosmetic surgery." He hesitated for a few seconds. "I'm such an ass! He can very easily redo his own face. I'm getting tired. Pignol, do you have Sartenas's birth date?"

"Yes, Captain. It's October 3, 1952."

"Well, we've stumbled upon a romantic. It matches perfectly! Pignol, go find me the names of the cosmetic surgeons in Grenoble. Wake them up in the middle of the night if you have to, but find me one you can bring these photos to. I want to know if it's possible to reconstruct Sartenas's face from Cabrade's. I have barely any doubt, but I want to be sure."

"Very good, Captain, but I'll have to get their personal telephone numbers and . . ."

"You have carte blanche. Call all the emergency numbers you need!" barked Rivera.

He got up and headed for the espresso machine. He made himself a double and came back to sit at his desk.

"A team will have to go dig around in the hospital archives. I want to know everything about this guy. Garancher, call Doctor Blavet, and ask him to come with you on a tour of the Grenoble services—there must be people who were in contact with him. We have to know everything about this guy's personality to understand why he suddenly started killing women. I want the first tangible results tomorrow before ten o'clock. If you need Paris, or if you encounter any resistance, I think Commissioner Mazure will know how to support you outside our jurisdiction."

Mazure nodded.

"We have to have results. I'm also going to appeal to Paris central services to go all out on Cabrade. The more we know about the killer, the more chances we'll have to corner him. Gentlemen, I'm asking you to give everything you've got tonight. I know the day was long, but we have a madman on the loose who might kill again in the coming hours."

Chapter 49: Genetics

Julien checked his alarm: four o'clock in the morning. He turned over again in the bed, unable to sleep, extremely disturbed by the events of the last few hours. He'd been sustained by excitement and action since the terrible revelation about his real mother. The discussion with his parents, the meeting with his grandfather, and finally the long interview he'd had with the policemen had kept him from thinking too much. But now he just gave in to the worry, and the awareness of his biological father's personality was ravaging him.

Sophie had invited him to spend the night at her place. He would have been overjoyed under normal circumstances. But these circumstances were far from normal. They'd quickly eaten a salad she'd made, and he'd told her everything. And the further he got into his story, the more he realized the enormity of the situation. Sophie had tried to raise his spirits, but he'd rebuffed her. He wanted only one thing: to shut himself up in a cave far away, very far away, where no one could find him, and where he couldn't hurt anyone.

He felt the young woman's hand on his shoulder, vainly trying to bring him a little comfort. He stood up, went toward the living room, and sat down on one of the armchairs facing the coffee table where an open bottle of fruit juice still sat. She followed him and curled up on the sofa.

"Julien, don't put yourself in this state. You haven't changed overnight!"

"Actually, everything has changed in me. In barely more than a day, I've discovered an ectoplasmic mother and a killer father. That's not nothing!"

"But it's not a hundred percent certain."

"You're right, not a hundred percent. Just ninety-nine percent. You're being nice, Sophie, but you're always the first to look at the facts head-on. Magali tells me she's my biological mother, my parents follow on by telling me they found me in a park, and Magali's father calls me his grandson without me giving him a single clue. We're at least bordering on certainty, don't you think?"

"Okay, there's a good chance there's some truth to it. But the fact that Cabrade might be your biological father doesn't make you a monster. We've known you for three years, and you've always had a cheerful demeanor, you've always been charming, and you're considerate of others. What makes you think things will change?"

"Genetics! I must have the genes of that sicko in my blood. And one day, it all could surface. And I don't want anybody near me who could be adversely affected. I want to protect you, too—especially you."

Sophie raised her voice. "Now, Julien, it's time to come back to earth. What is this Z movie you're making for us? If the children of Nazis who participated in the Holocaust were destined to act like their parents, Europe never would have been reconstructed. In thirty years, you've never had a deviant behavior, and now bam, all at once, you're suddenly becoming a public menace? I completely understand you're in shock, Julien! But you have nothing to do with Cabrade. He lived his life, and you're living yours. Besides, he doesn't even know you exist."

257

"No need to lecture me, Sophie. What would you say if you'd just learned your Indiana Jones father had slaughtered children in your basement while you were playing quietly in the yard?"

"But, Julien, that has nothing to do with it. You—"

"It's okay, Sophie. I think I should appreciate you taking care of me like this, but it's tiring me out. I'm going to let you sleep peacefully."

He took his pants off a chair, put them on, and without a word, headed for the door.

"But where are you going in this condition?" Sophie said, alarmed.

"I don't know, somewhere where I won't drag you down with my stories. A place where I'll be able to sit and take stock."

"But we can keep doing it together. I'm ready to sacrifice my upcoming nights to you if you need them."

"Considering my progenitor, I don't know if the word 'sacrifice' is the best choice. I'll let you know." He pushed open the door and disappeared into the darkness of the stairwell.

"Let me help you, you stubborn mule! I love you!"

The man's steps didn't pause, fading away a little more with each floor.

"I love you," she repeated for herself in a whisper.

She closed the door again. She felt exhausted. Why? She was also at the heart of this drama, which was affecting her much more than she'd imagined it would at the start. She'd recently realized Julien was the man she'd like to spend the rest of her life with. Never had she felt such an attraction to someone. A legend from who-knows-what country says that, somewhere on earth, there's a person who is made for you. She'd found him, she was sure of it, even if the statistics didn't support that legend. She'd started at Megatech the same day as Julien. She hadn't particularly noticed him at first—one colleague among many, not disagreeable, but nothing more. Then there had been their hike around Mont-Blanc. And there she had discovered him! Simple, funny, and above all available. It all snapped into place during an evening when the group had knocked themselves out cooking merguez sausages over the few twigs they'd managed to gather. A collective laughing fit had initiated the connection. She'd gradually moved closer to him, and these last few days had been wonderful. Until he'd come back from Corps, destroyed by the news he'd just learned. She knew he wasn't like Cabrade: she sensed it in her bones and in her soul. Julien was a fundamentally good guy. But how to convince him of it? She had to save him . . . and save their future, even if he'd just behaved like a lout. These were extenuating circumstances.

Chapter 50: Witnesses

7:30 a.m. Business was already in full swing in the hallways of the Michallon University Medical Center. Jérôme Garancher had been in front of one of the establishment's administrative unit computers for more than half an hour. He'd gone through the archives from 1975 to 1983 and gathered precious information.

One of the hospital administrators, reticent at first, had ended up cooperating fully. A list of a few names, hastily scribbled in ballpoint pen on a sheet of paper torn from a notebook, was sitting next to the keyboard. The policeman, consumed with the lines scrolling on the screen, eyes red with fatigue, jumped when he heard the loud voice.

"So, Garancher, is the treasure hunting good?"

He turned around and recognized the medical examiner, who seemed fresh as a daisy. Fortin was standing at his side. Garancher was relieved to see Fortin—he was exhausted and dreamed only of having a little rest. His colleague's presence was going to allow him to get a few hours of sleep. Reassured by this idea, he got up to greet them.

"Hello, Doctor. Hello, Étienne. Yes, it's been rather good, thanks to Monsieur Palmain's assistance. Without his help, I would have spent hours lost in these files."

"You were lucky to run into André. He's been here for forty years. His career must be as long as the life of this hospital."

"You couldn't be more right, Doctor. I started work on MUMC's inauguration day, in 1974. I've seen doctors come through! I'm far from remembering everyone, but when Monsieur Garancher spoke to me of Dominique Cabrade, I immediately placed the character."

His three listeners waited for more. Even Garancher forgot, for the space of a few minutes, his desire for rest.

"I didn't know him personally, but he was—how shall I put this—one of the rising stars of the establishment. A talented plastic surgeon. He was barely thirty years old, and he was already taking the lead on difficult cases—large burns, complex pathologies. I crossed paths with him a few times. At the time, there was still some conviviality in our hospital."

"What did he look like?"

"I think if I'd been a woman, I'd have fallen for him," commented Palmain with a melancholy smile.

Fortin looked at the plump and pleasant little man and wondered, just for an instant, if he'd fallen for him anyway, even without being a woman.

"He was good-looking, with a little something of Robert Redford. He was always surrounded by young doctors his age, and the nurses fantasized about him. Then he disappeared. But Professor Delépine will tell you more."

"He's on the list," added Garancher, handing the piece of paper to Fortin.

"What do you mean by 'he disappeared'?" resumed Blavet, pulling André Palmain from his memories.

"He vanished overnight, without any warning."

"Do you know why, or how?"

"No. But I can tell you it was a shock to us all. I believe his wife had disappeared some time before. He'd been affected, but nothing foreshadowed such a decision. Many of us missed him."

A small sigh escaped the administrator's lips. He went on. "I've given you the names of the people who should be able to help you. There aren't many left, because thirty years have gone by since those events. But luck is with you, because two of his old colleagues are here this morning. As well as Madame Guyancourt, who's in charge of the gerontology nurses."

He added, hesitantly, "Monsieur Garancher told me the subject of the investigation was confidential, but, if I dare insist, has Dominique reappeared somewhere?"

Fortin looked at him. "It's possible, Monsieur Palmain. And we're trying to make sure that it really is him."

The response seemed very mysterious to Palmain. But he contented himself with it.

"We thank you for your availability and the quality of your assistance, Monsieur Palmain," concluded Jérôme Garancher. They said good-bye and left the office.

"What do you think?" asked Garancher as they headed toward a coffee dispenser.

"Strange. We go looking for a serial killer, and we stumble onto this ladies' man, and not just for the missing ladies, it looks like," replied Fortin. "Jérôme, go to bed. You look like you could be in *Night of the Living Dead*—without makeup. We'll be able to deal with Doctor Blavet. There are only three people to meet."

"Thanks for the compliment. I will indeed go get some sleep."

"You did good work."

"Thank you."

Garancher went off, with an unsteady gait, to get a few hours of lifesaving sleep. Étienne Fortin and Henri Blavet watched him go, then concentrated on the list of names.

"Do you know them, Doctor?" asked the policeman.

"I've never met the first one, Mathieu Gascon. I know him by reputation. He's a neurologist as renowned for his expertise as for his self-importance. We'll have to work him with finesse," he added with a smile. "On the other hand, I know Professor Delépine well, even though he is retired. He's a reputable surgeon. If you want the truth, he's the exact opposite of Gascon. A few years back, he was still going to spend three weeks of his vacation in African countries operating for free on gravely ill patients. It would be a pleasure to see him again."

"And Hélène Guyancourt?"

"I don't know her. I'm going to call them to make appointments for this morning."

Fortin closed the door to Professor Gascon's office and walked for a few seconds down the hallway before being able to express what was in his heart.

"What an ass! Who does he think he is? Did you see that medicine-outraged-by-the-dirty-work-of-the-police drama he acted out for us? I'm going to ask Mazure if we can call him into the station, maybe he'll stink less."

Doctor Blavet put a hand on his arm to calm him down. Fortin took a few more steps before stopping. Blavet looked serene, as if he hadn't participated in the conversation. "I'm probably more used to such people than you are. They're rather contemptuous, but it's partially a way of protecting themselves from the suffering they see every day."

"Because we don't see violence and suffering? It soaks into us every day, gradually draining us of our energy and, for some of us, our will to live. Do I act like other people are less than shit when I talk to them?"

"Don't tell me you've been faced only with people who speak to you with respect."

"Absolutely not, Doctor, but I didn't expect it of them. A doctor is supposed to heal the body as well as the soul. I wonder how this guy's patients react."

"You won't change people, Étienne."

Fortin looked at him. Henri Blavet was confronted with death on a daily basis but always maintained his good humor. That wasn't logical either.

"You're right, Doctor, I got carried away. Let's get back to what we learned, which is to say not much. Cabrade had magic fingers, an extraordinary career ahead of him, and he disappeared one day. But we don't know any more than that."

"Professor Delépine will see us in fifteen minutes. He'll be much more cooperative. Let's head for his office."

Étienne Fortin followed Henri Blavet through the maze of hallways without trying to orient himself. The smell of pharmaceutical products turned his stomach. He'd often had to frequent hospitals in the course of his career, primarily to meet with witnesses or suspects in criminal cases, but he couldn't manage to get used to it. He'd seen his mother die there in less than a month when he'd been only about ten years old; something of that remained.

They encountered a good-natured man with messy hair, a bushy beard, and wearing a smock two sizes too big for him. The man spoke to them joyously. "Henri, such a pleasure to see you again! How long has it been?"

"Hello, Professor, the pleasure is mutual."

The man turned toward the policeman and extended a hand. "I'm Robert Delépine."

"Lieutenant Étienne Fortin. Thank you for seeing us so quickly, Professor."

"Don't mention it. And I must confess the prospect of chatting with Henri again helped me push back a meeting to see you sooner," he added mischievously.

They followed the surgeon into a quiet room. So the man Fortin had taken for a tramp lost in the hallways was the famous doctor. Despite his already advanced age, he continued in his work. The policeman suddenly felt sympathy for him, especially after the miserable meeting with Gascon. After several minutes of conversation between the two doctors, which was punctuated with the names of colleagues they'd lost track of and shared memories of illustrious moments, Robert Delépine grew serious again.

"Explain it to me, Lieutenant. Why are you interested in Dominique Cabrade thirty years after he left us?"

"He's probably mixed up in a criminal case. We think he could be the man who killed two young women these last few days."

Professor Delépine let out a long whistle. Then he sat up straight. "I won't ask you what brought you to these conclusions. I think if you reveal them to me, it's because you must have good reasons to suspect Cabrade. Ask me your questions, and I'll do my best to enlighten you."

"As Doctor Blavet told you, your name was given to us by André Palmain. He didn't tell us any more than that. Could you tell us what your connection with Dominique Cabrade was?"

"Of course! I don't remember all the young doctors I've seen go by in more than forty years of practicing medicine. But Cabrade was rather remarkable. I got to know him in 1976—I remember it because I met him for the first time just after Guy Drut won the one hundred ten–meter hurdles in the Montreal Olympics, one of the only French gold medals. Everyone has his landmarks," he mused, making fun of himself. "Cabrade was one of the youngest doctors. He'd been brilliant on all his exams and entered my service."

"How was he?"

"Astonishing. He was already particularly handsome. He'd enchanted nearly all the women on my team by the end of the first few days."

"Did he use it?"

"No more or less than the others. But he loved to seduce. Rather quickly, he was at the center of a group of young doctors who almost worshipped him."

"What were the reasons for such admiration?"

"His talent for surgery, at the beginning. Within the first few months, he'd successfully completed very complicated procedures. Everything goes very fast in that world, and despite the jealousies, he managed to forge a reputation for himself that no one tried to tarnish. His way of acknowledging those who surrounded him, as well—he didn't look down on others. He'd quickly realized how to get himself appreciated. He started to change toward the end, to become conceited. But his court was already in place, part of his glory reflected in those who accompanied him."

"And what did *you* think?"

"As a doctor, he had a gift. He was working with extraordinary precision and sensed things. I remember a very delicate operation on which he assisted me. At one moment, I had doubts about being able to perform a procedure. He asked me to let him take over. I was going to refuse his request, but I saw him so focused on the patient. In his eyes was something that said 'I will succeed.' Never have I let such a young doctor take responsibility for a procedure, but I said yes, without thinking. And he impressed me. When he finished, he thanked me for the confidence I'd shown in him."

"And did you have the opportunity to know the man in his private life?"

"I understand your question, in view of the suspicion about him. In general, I'm not interested in the young doctors' private lives. Each one already has more than enough to deal with. But Cabrade fascinated me, and I must confess I observed him much more closely than the others. After a while, I had the impression that he'd built himself a character. I sensed in him a sort of flaw, without being able to explain it. Everything was too smooth—he operated like a prodigy, he was regularly praised to the heavens, he regularly went out with the most beautiful girls, he even took the time to participate in society parties. One day, in 1980, there was a complaint. A corpse had disappeared—a John Doe who was found in the Isère and brought to the morgue. I wouldn't have paid it any more attention if it hadn't been found four days later half buried in the woods. It was quickly identified, because it had a very large birthmark in the groin area. I was called as soon as it came back to the morgue. And what I saw took my breath away!"

"What did you see, Professor?" asked Fortin, in anticipation of what was to come.

"The corpse had been emptied with . . . surgical precision. All the internal organs had been removed, but cleanly, as if they'd been precut. The skin of the face had also been cut, leaving the muscles and tendons exposed."

"Was there a legal investigation?"

"No, because there was no murder. The man who had suffered these outrages was already dead. But I made my own internal inquiries. For me, only an experienced surgeon who had access to the morgue could have carried out that dead man's desecration. I summoned four people, including Cabrade. When I had him in my office, at first he remained very calm. I'd called them all as witnesses, not as suspects. When I grew insistent, the polish cracked. He made incoherent statements on the power of the doctor over the patient, on the superior knowledge he held, on the right of life and death he would be able to assume if he wished. His statements were staggering. When he regained his normal state of consciousness, and he realized what he'd said, he burst out laughing. It lasted fewer than two minutes, but I remember it like it was yesterday. And he went back to being the excellent Cabrade everyone knew."

"What did you do?"

"I let him leave. I had no proof he perpetrated that act, even if I had the inward conviction. Then he distanced himself from me."

"Did you talk about it with anyone around you?"

"I spoke about it with one of my colleagues, who chalked it up to fatigue. I still pursued my investigation by looking into his studies. It was the first time I had spied like that on a doctor, but his statements had put me very ill at ease. And I discovered that he'd been caught doing forbidden experiments on a cadaver when he was in his third year. It's normally grounds for expulsion, but he'd been kept because of his potential and the excuses he'd presented."

Henri Blavet interjected, "The two victims had their hearts surgically removed. So do you think he'd be capable of that?"

"Without any problem."

"Another question, Professor. Do you know why he left?"

"After that business, Cabrade separated himself quite a lot from me, and I must admit I no longer sought out his company, aside from in the operating rooms, where his competence was becoming truly remarkable. He got married the following year, I believe. Over his last months at the hospital, he'd grown gloomy. Then his wife disappeared, and he botched a procedure well within his reach—his only failure! I'd put it down to emotion, like everyone else."

"How did he react to his wife's disappearance?"

"I can give you only my sense of it, because I didn't discuss it personally with him. To me, he seemed more annoyed than worried.

But he deceived his entourage. A few months later, he departed and left behind a letter."

"Did you have access to it?"

"Yes. It wasn't addressed to me, but they showed it to me since we'd worked together. It was short. In it he said he'd been affected by his wife's disappearance and he was leaving the area to forget about that period in his life."

"Surprising, to say the least!" commented Blavet.

"Yes. He left one night, after a successful operation, just one more. He'd said 'see you tomorrow' to his colleagues, and he never came back. All the staff were shocked."

"Did you hear from him?"

"No, no one did. He must have left France. There were a lot of conversations for a few months, then life continued its course. It's been almost thirty years since I stopped hearing about him, and given what you told me, I would have preferred to keep it that way."

"May I ask you one last question, Professor?" asked the policeman.

"Please."

Fortin took a wallet out of his backpack and removed two photos. He placed them side by side on Delépine's desk while the owner looked on.

"One is a picture of Cabrade, which you must recognize, and one is a picture of someone called Sartenas. Sartenas is the man who killed the two girls; we have proof. The last victim's heart was found at his home. As a specialist, can you tell me if Sartenas's face could be Cabrade's, reconstructed?"

The doctor didn't hesitate for even a second. "It's entirely possible. There's no major alteration in the shape of the face. It would require clearer photo sets to do a thorough study, but the shapes of the faces allow me to answer affirmatively without hesitation."

"Thank you, Professor. I'm going to ask the question, even though I know the answer: Do you have any idea where Cabrade could be hiding?"

"Alas, no idea, Lieutenant. I didn't even know where he lived when he worked with me."

The two men warmly thanked the old doctor, then went back down the hall.

Chapter 51: Hélène

Half an hour later, Hélène Guyancourt joined them. The woman in her fifties who stood before them must have been beautiful. She still had a certain charm, but the years and the stress had weighed on her, and she wore a mask of deep weariness. Her handshake, however, was vigorous.

"Hello, I'm Hélène Guyancourt."

The two men introduced themselves in turn.

"Thank you for clearing your schedule so quickly, Madame Guyancourt. I imagine it's particularly busy," said Henri Blavet.

"Indeed, there's no shortage of activity. But you can't imagine the shock I felt when you said the name Cabrade. I didn't think I'd ever hear about that person again. Will it bother you if we go outside and talk while walking? It'll do me some good and let me smoke a cigarette."

They left the hospital and sought the protection of a few sickly trees that were trying to give visitors a little shade.

"So Cabrade is back?" asked the nurse.

"According to our investigation and the discussion we just had with Professor Delépine, there's a strong chance that's the case."

"But he disappeared thirty years ago. How did you find him?"

Lieutenant Fortin took the time to explain to Hélène Guyancourt the allegations against Cabrade. The woman's face sank over the course of the policeman's explanations. When he'd finished, he added, "We're looking to gather as much information as we can on him. André Palmain told us you had known him. Do you think you'll be able to offer some clues that would help us locate him, or predict his future movements?"

Hélène Guyancourt took a long drag on her cigarette, let it out, and crushed the butt with her heel. She crouched down to collect it, looked at it as if she were looking for a source of inspiration, and threw it in a transparent plastic garbage bag.

"I don't know if what I'm going to tell you will let you get your hands on him, but you're dealing with a perverse and dangerous individual."

"Anything you'll be able to tell us will be welcome."

"Of course. I'm just going to tell you a rather pathetic story. It takes place in 1980. I was twenty-three, and I was already working as a nurse at the hospital. I'd just gotten my degree, and I was discovering this world with passion. Being a nurse had always been my vocation—my Saint Bernard side, probably. I was pretty quickly brought in to work on the same team as Dominique Cabrade. And like all the girls on the team, and even in the other departments, too, I fell under his charm. A pretty face, notoriety despite his young age, and a natural capacity for seduction. I started dreaming about him, very sentimentally despite the reality of the suffering I encountered daily. I didn't miss an opportunity to get closer to him, to try and attract his attention, to exchange a sentence or two. A real flirt, you know?"

"So he was very charming?" asked the policeman.

"He turned out to be a dreadful bastard, but yes, he was terribly charming, and he was brilliant. One evening, after a long and complicated operation, he spoke to me while coming out of the operating room. He proposed going for a drink with him to recover from the procedure. I think it was several seconds before his offer made it to my brain, and I was floating already when I answered yes. He took me to a Grenoble bar in his sports car. He was charming, attentive, amusing. I was diving deep in my adolescent world. In the following week, he invited me out to a restaurant twice. I still remember what I ordered. If nothing had come of it, that could have been one of the best memories of my life."

"How did things change?"

"After the last evening at the restaurant, he asked me for the first time to come have a nightcap at his house. To be frank, I had been waiting for that since the first time he took me to the bar. So I accepted before he finished his sentence. I wasn't even in a state of pretending to resist."

"Do you remember where he lived?" asked Fortin.

"He had an apartment that looked out on the Place Victor-Hugo. It was huge, but he lived alone there. So we went up to his place. We settled in the living room—he'd strewn pillows around a coffee table. I remember he'd put on some muted jazz. And then after two or three glasses, I really started to lose control of what I was doing. It didn't bother me, since my intention was to end up in his bed."

Hélène paused for a moment. The memories were flowing through her and taking possession of her mind, like a tranquil river flooding its banks in a sudden storm. She smoothed her scrubs and looked at them again.

"I'm probably boring you with all these details. I thought I'd succeeded in erasing them from my life. And you see how they come back as if this whole story had taken place yesterday."

"We're sorry to inflict this on you. Please don't hesitate to take your time. Perhaps one of those details will actually be able to help us!"

"Well, I'll go on. He asked me to wait for a few minutes. He went into his bedroom, then called for me. I joined him, ready to give him everything. But I was surprised when I stepped through the doorway. The bedroom was painted black, and he'd lit black candles. They were on all the furniture. And he was in front of his bed—he'd put on a black tunic that came down to above his knees. I told myself it must be one of his fantasies, that it helped him get past the daily stress of his profession. And I felt like making love with him."

"And how did it unfold? If you're willing to tell us, of course," added Doctor Blavet.

"No problem. I was torn between the violence with which he took me and the pleasure I had in being with him. I won't go into the details, but he wasn't a good lover. Then again, I was addicted to him, and that was much stronger than the physical disappointment."

"Did you continue to see him?"

"Yes, I was afraid he'd drop me once he'd slept with me. He would have been able to have all the girls he wanted in his bed. But he continued to invite me out, and I continued to accept his invitations. When we were outside of his home, he was always charming and attentive. All my friends were jealous. But as soon as we crossed the threshold of his apartment, he transformed. I became an object for him. And the most incomprehensible thing was that I submitted to his games for weeks. I was afraid of losing him. I accepted his nocturnal misbehavior in exchange for the attention he gave me during the day."

"I beg you to pardon me for the question I'm going to ask you. But what sort of act did he make you submit to? Did he try to scarify you, inflict wounds on you?"

"No, let's be clear and say things as they are. Dominique Cabrade was obsessed with the practice of sodomy and used me like an object. He never wanted to take the time for a caress, and giving me pleasure wasn't his priority."

"So the night Cabrade was the opposite of the day Cabrade."

"Completely. He had a dual personality. I never knew if he had control of the night personality or not. Anyway, I was living through hell. All my being cried out to me to leave him, but a force deep inside me hooked me to him. I made excuses for him, and his attention the following mornings chased away what he'd been able to make me suffer at night."

"What finally made you decide to leave him for good?"

"One Friday night, he proposed taking me on a dream weekend, promising he'd take care of me like a queen. I knew it wouldn't happen, that he'd keep imposing his fantasies on me. But I felt like lying to myself, believing he could change. The weekend was hell! On the first night when I strongly refused to take part in one of his more perverse than usual games, he calmly went over to a satchel he'd brought, took out two pills, and forced me to take them. I lost all will. I knew I didn't like what he was doing, but I no longer had the strength to oppose him. The next morning, when I regained control of my senses, he was still sleeping. I looked at what he'd made me drink."

"Rohypnol?" interjected Doctor Blavet.

"That's right. How did you guess?" asked the nurse.

"We found some in the blood of the first victim, Monica Revasti."

"Rohypnol, that's what's now called a date rape drug?" asked Fortin.

"Yes, that's right. It's a hypnotic in the benzodiazepine family, normally used in severe insomnia cases. It didn't take long for unscrupulous individuals to hijack its use."

"He easily had access. He only had to help himself to the hospital pharmacy. And he's still hurting people . . . ," whispered Hélène Guyancourt. "Stop him, he's the devil."

Fortin looked at her. She'd just sat down on a bench they'd come across while walking and shriveled in on herself. The policeman really did get the feeling the devil had just terrified her.

"I have only one thing in mind, madame," he said, laying a hand on the nurse's shoulder, "and it's putting that bastard out of commission."

She looked at him, and a wan smile, fleeting, brightened her face.

"I'm going to tell you the end of my story. I went back home, bent on taking revenge for what he'd inflicted on me during those weeks. But when I started talking about what happened, not one person believed me. I looked like a liar, sex starved, the latest slut. And he, all honey, always had his court around him and pushed his depravity to the point of fabricating excuses like stress and fatigue. His magnanimity with regard to me was praised by the choir of well-meaning souls! I fell into depression, and if I hadn't met the man who became my husband, I think I would have ended up throwing myself into the Isère."

She concluded, "That's the great Dominique Cabrade."

"Thank you for this story, and we're truly sorry for having exhumed such moments."

"But they're still living! I hope I've managed to kill them a little in telling them to you. I never told my husband everything."

"One more question, Madame Guyancourt. Did you know any of Cabrade's friends who could help us locate him?"

"Cabrade had a multitude of acquaintances, admirers, but he connected with no one. Not once did he want to talk to me about his family or his close friends. One time, just once, I met someone he seemed to care about."

"Do you remember that person's name?"

"No, but he was as degenerate as Cabrade was. During the last week we spent together, he'd invited one of his friends one night. I won't paint you a picture of the games we engaged in. At the end, likely thinking I was asleep, they talked about their years studying medicine together. And I realized the other man had been expelled from the university before the end of his program."

This last revelation struck the two men. Étienne Fortin asked her, "Could it be his name was Aurélien?"

"I don't know if he called him by his first name. It's so long ago . . ."

"Thank you, Madame Guyancourt. I'm going to call on all the acquaintances I have in the Grenoble medical community to find that unknown man's name," promised Blavet.

"I only ask one thing of you," said the nurse. "Find Cabrade quickly. He's capable of anything, and more besides. And don't have any mercy," she finished, a gleam of hatred deep in her eyes.

Chapter 52: Flashback

Dominique Cabrade stretched and wondered where he was. Still sleepy, he looked at the cedar branch swaying in the window frame. He pushed aside the curtain and sat on the edge of his bed. He yawned, and the events of the previous day came back to him—running away, the meeting with Arsène, the arrival at the manor, the night of working on Fra Bartolomeo's manuscript, and the remarkable exegesis his friend had done.

Then he'd slept! He'd slept for more than five hours without waking up. He hadn't experienced such peaceful rest for months, years even. And that night, he would finally be rid of his nightmares. For a second time he'd kill the one who'd spoiled his life, the one who'd put an end to the brilliant career he should have had. Of course, he'd been recognized for his gifts in wielding a scalpel, precision, and achieving ever-impressive results. He'd worked for some of the wealthiest men in the world: industrialists and financiers as well as tyrants and traffickers. Some even belonged to several of those categories.

One of the practices that had allowed him to acquire his renown was what he euphemistically called facial remodeling. He could no longer count the number of old despots, crooks of diverse backgrounds, whom he'd given new faces. All these men he'd hob-nobbed with ultimately saw their luck turn. Facing the fear of get-ting caught by their pasts and former victims, they'd offered him fortunes for a new identity and a few extra years of life.

He'd always protected himself from his clients by depositing files with various lawyers. It would have been quite simple to have him killed in order to get rid of the last links to their old lives. So in boxes in New York, Rio, Moscow, Paris, London, and Rome lay the small photo albums that had kept him alive.

If he died violently, the presumed murderers' files would be sent to carefully selected newspapers. But if a file got out other-wise, he knew he'd die within twenty-four hours. Mutually assured destruction—it had worked well during the Cold War!

He'd also rejuvenated old billionaires in the clinics in Cuba—French universities would never recognize the techniques he'd used, but that was the least of his worries. He'd even lowered himself to redoing two or three pairs of breasts. The gain was great enough to sacrifice several hours of his life to these acts he despised.

His most remunerative operation was in fact the most comi-cal. About fifteen years ago he'd met a Colombian drug lord who had asked him to redo his wife's breasts. Following an outburst of temper, he'd accepted upon seeing the suitcase full of bills. The traf-ficker had loved his companion's new silhouette. During a dinner in honor of his spouse's chest, he'd taken the surgeon aside. Cabrade, after a moment of trepidation, had followed him. He couldn't refuse his host's hospitality, especially when a hundred bodyguards were watching over the property and the host in question had a diamond-studded pistol sticking out of his jacket.

Once he was certain no one could overhear the conversation, the crook opened up to him. Cabrade had had the decency not to laugh, which undoubtedly saved his life. The Colombian had just asked him to increase the size of his penis. He'd announced the sum of two million dollars, and that had spared the surgeon a long period of reflection. He'd accepted. He had practiced on a few more or less consenting patients and gone back to the drug lord when he thought he'd sufficiently mastered the technique. The Colombian had clearly explained to him the dimensions he wished to attain. Cabrade had acquiesced, knowing he was playing with his life if he didn't manage to meet the prescribed objective. But the challenge was new and pleased him. He'd ultimately departed with four million dollars, but not before spending an orgiastic week in the company of his sexually fulfilled patient and some of the region's high-class prostitutes and pretty girls.

Over the years, he'd also taken advantage of this affluent roaming life to indulge in his vices and morbid fantasies with total impunity. For the circles he traveled in, life had little value, and respect for others was a concept that elicited laughs during soirees hazy from alcohol and drugs.

Cabrade himself had also had to resort to surgery. He remembered those times, singularly less pleasant.

He'd redone the faces of the two Kissinger brothers, kingpins in the American underworld. They had diplomats' names but thugs' methods. Unfortunately for him, the Chow family gang, with whom the Kissingers were fighting for control over part of the drug trade in Southern California, had picked up the surgeon's trail. Only Cabrade could still link the Kissingers' old and new faces. The Chows just wanted a friendly meeting with the French doctor.

The surgeon had narrowly escaped two kidnapping attempts before deciding to change his own face. He'd contacted one of his most brilliant colleagues; they'd spent long hours choosing his new features. Cabrade had even done a practice run of the procedure with him. It was not without anxiety that he lay down on the operating table. But the result was up to his expectations. Getting new French papers had been child's play. With lots of money and good connections, solutions appear like magic.

He now had accounts in several offshore paradises and a fortune of more than thirty million dollars. He didn't know the exact amount. He paid his financial advisors rather dearly for that luxury.

The smell of coffee wafted up the stairs and stoked his hunger. He grabbed a pair of pants and a shirt provided by his host, pulled them on, and went down to the kitchen. The steaming coffeemaker was set on the table next to country bread with a thick crust and a pot of honey. He took up the knife, cut himself two thick slices, and covered them generously with honey. He leaned back against the chair and looked out at the garden park to its edge, marked by a dark fir tree.

The morning sun revealed the depth of the conifers' intense green. He'd always been a city dweller, and the beauties of nature left him indifferent for the most part. Even when he was operating in the African Great Lakes region, he didn't understand what motivated tourists to spend thousands of euros driving around in an all-terrain vehicle in areas that lacked everything. But that morning, he felt in harmony with himself and his surroundings. That night, he would be free. He'd be finished with those sleepless nights that incapacitated him, that tormented him and left him unable to resist the terror.

"Appetite's working, I see!" trumpeted a voice from behind him.

He turned slowly to face Arsène, who had just entered the room, face dripping with sweat.

"I took advantage of the morning cool for a little hour-long run."

"You haven't changed, my poor Arsène. Always this incomprehensible need to go tiring yourself out when you could quietly enjoy life."

"Look at me, nearly sixty years old and with the silhouette of a teenager!"

"I could have remade your teenage silhouette in a few hours with a scalpel! And you'd be spared the quarts of sweat and weeks of stiffness."

"We'll never agree on this point. Slept well?"

"Perfectly well. The explication you gave me yesterday from Fra Bartolomeo's text completely reassured me. And to think the Aztec people were despised by generations of Europeans. If they'd only known." Then, he added with veiled concern, "What about the heart?"

"Trust me, you will have, in due time, all the necessary materials."

"You've saved my life, Arsène! What luck to have found you. As promised, you'll have the money by tomorrow morning. Fifteen million dollars!"

Arsène knew his old friend well and knew he could trust him completely . . . at least for that. Cabrade stood up, emptied his cup of coffee, and headed toward the door.

"I'm going to go stretch my legs in the park."

"Take the hat and sunglasses on the table in the foyer. This isn't the time to be recognized."

"Don't you worry about me. I've escaped from secret police all over the world and Interpol for decades."

And you got yourself spotted in Grenoble yesterday, thought his host, but without saying it out loud. Even if Cabrade had always been an excellent actor, master of his behavior, Arsène knew the man had to be wary when he abandoned his man-of-the-world costume.

As soon as Cabrade had gone out, Arsène went to his office in the basement. He closed the door and concentrated. He had to organize the plans for the next twenty-four hours. If he didn't make a mistake, his fortune would be made. The staging he'd imagined for the coming night excited him terribly. A perverse impulse came over him. He, too, knew how to let go when he abandoned his good-citizen character.

Chapter 53: Time Off

Nadia had forced herself to stay in bed for part of the morning. Her shoulder was hurting her badly. She wasn't a superwoman. After having tossed and turned for hours, she'd finally taken a powerful sleeping pill and sunk into unconsciousness. Her sleep hadn't been as disturbed as she'd feared, but she'd woken up with terrible stabbing pains. She turned toward her bedside table: nine o'clock. It was time to get up and head to the hospital. She'd kept the telephone number for the doctor who'd cared for her; she'd call him directly. She knew he'd see her as soon as he had some free minutes. She really needed to be examined and had absolutely no time to waste in the emergency room.

Nadia took a quick shower, threw on a skirt and blouse, grabbed her bag and car keys, and walked to the museum parking lot. She loved her apartment's location, but she realized a major shortcoming—it was hard to find a parking space less than a five-minutes' walk away.

Her instincts hadn't failed her. She'd dialed the telephone number the doctor had given her during her previous visit. He'd welcomed her ten minutes later. If she hadn't been suffering, she would have smiled at the young man's enamored eyes. He'd cleaned her wound, which was starting to get infected, given her two shots, and finally remade her dressing with the utmost care. She'd let his timid hands wander once or twice to the nape of her neck or her arm. After all, it wasn't so unpleasant. Nadia enjoyed a few extra moments in the hospital bed.

Then she got up. The pain was starting to fade. Whatever the doctor had just injected her with was incredibly effective; he also went to get her the latest generation of anti-inflammatories from the pharmacy. She felt ready to resume the investigation. The doctor came back into the room. He was about to give her a sermon when she interrupted him with a wave of her hand.

"Doctor, you've put me back on my feet, and I'm very grateful to you for it. But the killer is roaming Grenoble. He mustn't strike again."

"But, in your condition, you can't be serious."

"Better to have a damaged shoulder than a big hole in place of a heart!"

The doctor looked at her, speechless.

"Everything's fine, Doctor, and thanks to you."

She went up to him, gave him a kiss on the cheek, and left the room. He watched her go without a word, sighed heavily, and headed back to the emergency room. They were waiting for him.

Nadia was passing by the intake desk when she heard a voice exclaim off to her right, "Nadia, what are you doing here?"

She didn't have to turn around to know who was speaking to her. "I'm getting medical treatment. That's why one goes to the hospital, right?"

She headed over to Étienne Fortin and Henri Blavet. She embraced her colleague and shook the doctor's hand.

"I don't deserve a hug, too?" asked the medical examiner with laughing eyes.

"Of course you do. But I didn't dare."

They took a few minutes to summarize the situation for her. Captain Barka had regained all her concentration and didn't miss a single bit of their account.

"Do you have any idea about the name of Cabrade's orgy companion? And who could be the one he performed his macabre dissection work with?" she asked.

"No," replied Blavet. "But I'm going to tackle the job. In a file somewhere, there must be the trail of that student who was expelled. It rarely happens. But it might take a lot of time, and we have little. For this administrative research, I'm going to ask you to contact Rivera so that he can put someone on the case, to support the hospital administration's search," he proposed to Fortin. "As for me, I'm going to try to find a few people who would have been able to witness it."

"Almost forty years later?" asked Nadia Barka.

"Yes, I wasn't there back then, but for a time I headed a fishing club at MUMC!"

"You do a bit of fishing?" marveled Fortin.

"My friend, you can't imagine how relaxing it is to find yourself alone with the sea, a lake, or even a little pond, listening to the silence while hoping some fish will get the unfortunate idea of swallowing your hook. Especially when you're tense after a long week. Basically, many MUMC employees were members of this club, and many have stayed in contact with me. I could have some information by tonight."

"Not before?" asked Nadia.

"They're all retired," the doctor pointed out to her.

"I understand that, but there's a good chance Cabrade is at this moment in search of a heart . . . and the woman around it."

Blavet grew serious again. "I know, Nadia, and I'm going to do everything I can."

"Thank you, Doctor. Julien Lombard spoke to us of an Aurélien. Could that be him?"

"We asked Hélène Guyancourt. That name didn't mean anything to her. But all that happened thirty years ago. It would, however, be surprising if it were him, after what Magali Dupré's father said. He seemed to hold him in high esteem."

"Maybe. But you know better than anyone you can't trust psychopaths. They have an art of dissimulation that's sometimes undetectable. Étienne, did Rivera send someone to question him?"

"Not yet, from what I understand. Although I haven't set foot in the station for the last few hours."

"I'd like to meet him. Can you call Rivera so he'll let me contact him?"

"You don't want to do it yourself?"

"We made peace last night, but I still shouldn't ask too much."

"Okay, I'm on it. Where are you eating lunch?"

"Probably the Pomme d'Amour, Aurélien Costel's restaurant—it's Michelin starred."

Étienne Fortin thought about the sandwich he was going to have to swallow and looked with envy at his colleague on leave. *There weren't only disadvantages to taking a bullet in the shoulder,* he thought sheepishly.

"Well, hello, expense account!"

"Don't be jealous. And I'm treating myself to this pleasure. Besides, if the restaurant is worth it, you can take me out to it one night!"

Chapter 54: The Meeting

Sophie left her father's office. She'd had a quick lunch with him at the Ikea restaurant a few minutes away from the university. She didn't particularly appreciate the store's commercial ambiance or the food offered by the cafeteria, but her father liked it. Sophie had never understood the famous historian Antoine Dupas's love for pseudo-Scandinavian cuisine, but she clearly had greater need to get her mind off things than to have herself a feast. And a good thing, too! Her father had relished the menu full of unlimited meatballs with its mystery sauce and a few cranberries to give it all some local color. After all, why not! She'd chosen a tossed salad, only to conclude that although the Swedes might be masters of steel manufacturing, they were still in the prehistory of their culinary evolution. But were the prepared meals at an international chain really representative of a people's culture? She'd quickly set aside her anthropological thoughts to listen to her father tell her about the university's latest gossip. The historian's head-in-the-clouds reputation attracted confidences. Sophie had laughed heartily and forgotten Julien's behavior for a few minutes.

She'd been devastated when Julien had left her so suddenly that morning. But all the excuses she'd found for him were fading one after the other. She perfectly understood the trauma he was experiencing. But that didn't excuse his behavior in the slightest. She'd proven to him he could rely on her.

After accompanying her father back to his office, she paused in the shade of a willow. She took a pack of cigarettes out of her pocket and lit one. It had been three years since she'd stopped smoking, but today, her resolutions were fizzling out. She breathed in the smoke and exhaled it slowly. She cared about Julien more than ever, but she would wait until he called her. Her phone vibrated in her handbag. Smiling, she crushed the cigarette against the tree trunk and quickly grabbed her cell:

"Hello!"

"Sophie Dupas?"

"Yes, that's me."

"This is Professor Boisregard. Pardon me for disturbing you, but I think I have very interesting information."

Sophie was expecting anything but a call from her father's colleague.

"Could you be more precise, Professor?"

"Of course, excuse me, mademoiselle. You must be wondering what's come over me. My call is in response to the conversation we had recently with Captain Barka and yourself. I'm trying to reach her, but I don't have her number. I just asked for your contact info from your father."

Boisregard's explanations were confused. Sophie sensed the curator wasn't in his usual state. "Stay calm, Professor, what's going on?"

"I'm sorry, Sophie, but what I've discovered disturbed me."

"I'm listening, Professor, but you have to call the police station!"

"It's too soon. I'm only spouting hypotheses, and I can't allow myself to submit them to others without further substantiation."

"But what are we talking about, Professor?"

"I've been thinking long and hard about our discussion in your father's office. You know I was very shaken by the murder of the young woman found in my museum. And I think I've found a potential connection between Aztec customs and that murder."

Sophie felt herself instantly petrified by what she'd just heard. Were they finally in possession of a serious lead that would take them to the killer?

The historian added, "And a name immediately came to mind."

"Well, go directly to the police station! If that's the case, you have a crucial element in the hunt for the killer!" screamed Sophie into her phone.

"I can't, mademoiselle! What if I'm wrong?" He hesitated for a moment, then asked almost timidly, "Or maybe you'd agree to listen to my theory? You could assess it. If you find it credible, then I'll go present it to the police."

"Well of course. When are you available?"

"Right now, mademoiselle. I think it would be easier for me to present it to you face-to-face rather than over the telephone."

"I understand perfectly. Where would you like to meet?"

Boisregard hesitated a bit before suggesting a locale. "I'm in Uriage at the moment. I'm waiting for a friend who's supposed to pick me up to go back to Grenoble. But he won't be here for an hour. I can try to find a taxi and you—"

"I have my car. I can be there in less than fifteen minutes. Just tell me where you want me to find you." Sophie hung up. Maybe this was the lead they were missing. She trembled with excitement at the idea of getting closer to the killer. She thought immediately of Julien. Should she inform him? No, she'd call him with the results of her discussion with Boisregard . . . if something interesting came of it. However, she was going to tell Nadia before leaving. She speed-dialed the number and waited, lighting a new cigarette. The phone rang into the void, trying her patience. Then she got voice mail.

"Nadia, it's Sophie. I've got a lead. Call me back on my cell as soon as you get this message."

She ran to her car, opened the door, threw her jacket on the passenger seat, and took off, tires squealing.

Chapter 55: Aurélien

1:45 p.m. Nadia watched two birds at play on the restaurant terrace's arbor. She felt good. The pain wasn't bothering her, and she'd eaten admirably well: a grilled sea bass with pureed onions and crunchy vegetables. She hadn't been able to resist a dessert, which had plunged her, at last, into a blissful state. She was now finishing her coffee. She looked at her watch: Aurélien Costel would be arriving soon. He didn't work at his restaurant during lunch. But when she'd shown her police badge, the waiter had given her the proprietor's personal phone number. He'd agreed to cooperate as soon as she'd told him the reason for her call. He just had to come back from Lyon.

She saw the two waiters greet a man coming in, then indicate the table where she was sitting. The epicurean who'd just had lunch now tried to focus on assuming the role of police officer. The transition wasn't complete, though—the three glasses of wine accompanying the meal, which were perfectly paired with the dishes served, had slightly slowed her power of concentration. She watched the man in his fifties approach at a leisurely pace. She gauged him more precisely—she was instantly persuaded she'd already met him and was instinctively put on guard. She usually had an excellent visual memory, but in this case couldn't recall the circumstances. She'd think about it later. She knew she'd eventually remember why they'd crossed paths.

Upon reaching the table, he bowed slightly in greeting. Nadia understood what Pierre Dupré had been able to sense the first time he'd met this man. Everything about him called out for friendship. But she politely kept her distance—wasn't Cabrade also adored by his peers?

"Aurélien Costel. I'm at your disposal, madame."

"Captain Barka."

"Very well, Captain, tell me exactly how I can be of use to you? When I heard you speak of Magali Dupré, I confess everything started spinning. You can be sure I'll do everything in my power to help you."

"Thank you, Monsieur Costel. Actually, I do want you to tell me about Magali . . . but especially about her husband."

Something nasty flashed briefly in the restaurant owner's eyes. His face had grown serious, closed. "Could you possibly tell me why you're interested in Dominique Cabrade?"

The police officer hesitated for a moment, then decided to lay her cards on the table. The situation was critical enough to reveal minimal information. "Yes, but what I'm going to tell you has to remain confidential."

"You have my word."

"We suspect him of the murders of Monica Revasti and Camille Saint-Forge, the two young women found dead in the last few days."

The restaurant owner didn't respond, but he sat down in the chair facing Nadia's.

"That's terrible. So he's not dead . . . I'd hoped for it, though. I'll tell you a secret, too—I myself wanted to kill him, more than thirty years ago. Maybe I should have done it . . . but that's something I probably shouldn't confess to the police," he added with a sad smile.

"You might have carried out an act of public safety. But it's always difficult to live with a murder on your conscience, even if the victim is the lowest of the low. Well, enough of the soliloquy. I'm listening, Monsieur Costel. Just give me a few seconds to turn off my cell phone and I'm all yours."

Half an hour after Nadia left the Pomme d'Amour, she was still shaken by what she'd just learned. Aurélien Costel's revelations had been astounding, but she tended to believe them. She knew now why she'd recognized him. Now she just had to check certain facts before announcing anything.

Chapter 56: Forbidden Dissection

The fourth phone call was the ticket. Henri Blavet thanked the heavens and the Lord above. He'd just landed a meeting with Jean-Paul Boucanier, the former head of sterilization in the equipment rooms at Grenoble Hospital.

His luck had turned. The first three calls were dead ends—his intended targets were either absent or unavailable. Boucanier was next on the list, but he didn't want to disturb him; after all, it wasn't as if the retiree had held an influential position at MUMC. Still, his desire for a pleasant chat with Jean-Paul overcame his hesitation, and Blavet contacted him. And how fortunate! Because as soon as he'd explained the reason for his call, Jean-Paul had given him key information. He'd actually been at the heart of this stifled story at the time.

The retiree had arranged to meet him in a bar. The doctor had gladly accepted. He'd eaten nothing since morning and felt hunger gnaw at his stomach now that it was early afternoon.

2:00 p.m. Jean-Paul Boucanier was already sitting at the counter nursing a draft beer when Henri Blavet entered the bar. The dimness of the place gave him a pleasantly relaxed feeling. Jean-Paul had already climbed off his stool and come toward him, arms outstretched and smile wide.

"Doctor, how delightful to see you again!" he boomed. "It's been a while, don't you know!"

Blavet smiled. He'd always enjoyed this man's integrity.

"Since you went into retirement, it's been . . . two or three years."

"Two or three years?" replied Boucanier, bursting out laughing. "You don't see the time passing with all your work. I've been living happily with Thérèse for seven years now."

"How is your wife?" asked the doctor, thinking back on that ever-smiling woman.

"She's fine. She's got herself a new hobby. She started playing bridge with a group of girlfriends. And to think she never wanted me to teach her to play pinochle! It seems their teacher is charming. That's probably a significant advantage when trying to learn the game. Anyway, Doctor, *I'm* not complaining. During that time, I can go trout fishing with my pals and enjoy a few glasses of chilled white wine. But you didn't come here to hear about my fishing exploits."

"Another time, with pleasure. But it's true, the investigation we're conducting is most pressing."

"Well, let's go sit in a corner. There aren't many people, but what I'm going to tell you doesn't need to be overheard."

Henri Blavet ordered a beer and a sandwich and joined his former colleague.

"When you told me about this event on the phone, I almost wasn't surprised. It happened decades ago, but I was certain, who knows why, that it would resurface one day."

"Remind me how you were mixed up in this."

"It's very simple, Doctor. At the time, I was in charge of cleaning the dissection rooms used by second- or third-year students, I don't quite remember which. They were of course cleaned after each use, and I always did the rounds in the morning to make sure everything was in order. One night, I was at the hospital for some emergency maintenance. I remember the date: April 12, 1973. Huh, that makes it forty years ago."

Boucanier went back in time. The images that came to mind were as clear as if they'd happened the day before. He resumed.

"I'd finished my work, and to leave I had to pass by the dissection rooms. As I approached the door, I thought I heard a noise. I stopped and listened. No one ever worked at three o'clock in the morning. I went up silently, and I gently pushed on the door. It was open. I was sure I'd closed it the previous evening. You know me, Doctor, I'm not frightened by much. But there, I have to say the situation sent shivers down my spine."

"What did you do, then?"

"What I had to do. See who had come to use the facilities at that hour of the night. I thought for an instant it was a schoolboy prank, but it was too quiet. So I went to the equipment room and got an iron bar that had been sitting there for months. I took a deep breath, pushed the door open hard, and screamed. What I saw rendered me speechless with surprise."

"Go on."

"The image has been burned into my memory for forty years. I regularly see it again in dreams. I've never managed to make it go away . . . Two students were looking at me scornfully."

"Two?" interrupted Blavet. "But there was only one in the story Professor Delépine told us, even if Hélène Guyancourt spoke of a second man."

"There were two of them, have no doubt on that count. They'd put on blue surgical gowns, and each one had a scalpel in hand.

My eyes immediately dropped to the table. A cadaver had been cut up into pieces, but . . . how shall I put this . . . like on a butcher's block. The pieces were neatly cut and carefully placed one next to the other. Unimaginable! When I looked at them, they burst out laughing. I didn't know what to do anymore. There were these two boys, because they couldn't have been more than twenty, apparently having crazy fun, and next to them this body presented as spare parts. Only the head and torso were still connected."

"Did they run away?"

"They didn't even try, and that was just about the most disturbing part. They knew they'd be expelled. I locked them in so that I could ask the front desk to send me a security team. The men arrived within a few minutes. When we went into the room, those two sickos had gone back to their gruesome work. Now the head was resting next to the limbs. They'd given it a terrifying smile with a stroke of the scalpel."

Boucanier was frighteningly pale. Immersed in his nightmare, he continued in a hypnotic tone.

"When the security guards approached them, they said only one sentence: 'It would have been a shame not to finish such lovely work.' They let themselves be taken without resistance. Later I learned that one of the two had been reinstated at the university. I didn't believe my ears. Sometimes, there's no justice in this world. How could they allow such an unstable man to have patients' lives in his hands? But in the end, I was just a member of the custodial staff."

"One of the two was Dominique Cabrade?"

"Indeed, the famous Cabrade who was taken back and became the hospital's star."

"But do you remember the other student's name? The one who was expelled. No one has been able to tell me."

"Of course, Doctor, you unfortunately never forget such names. The second student was Cabrade's equal in destructive madness. His name was Boisregard."

"Boisregard?"

"Yes, and I even remember his first name: Arsène."

"Arsène Boisregard . . . Do you know what became of him?"

"Absolutely not, and make no mistake, I don't want to hear about him."

Henri Blavet put his elbows on the table and buried his head in his hands and muttered to himself.

"Arsène Boisregard . . . I feel like I've heard that name recently." Then he addressed his old friend. "Jean-Paul, I think your contribution will be highly valuable. I'm going to report your story immediately. I'm certain the name Boisregard can be useful to us."

Boucanier stood up and shook the doctor's hand warmly.

"I hope you'll arrest those bastards as quickly as possible. But be careful, Doctor. Boys like that are unpredictable!"

Chapter 57: Boisregard

"Boisregard! Henri, are you absolutely sure of the name?" cried Nadia into the phone.

"Absolutely, Nadia, that's the name Boucanier gave me: Arsène Boisregard. And I can assure you there wasn't a shadow of a doubt in his statements. Apparently that name tells you something."

"The curator at the Old Diocese Museum—it's insane! That guy is anything but a killer. He'd be afraid of his own shadow," she added to herself. "What else did the guy tell you?"

"He confirmed that the bastard, and I'm quoting, 'was as deranged as Dominique Cabrade.' There you have it, I've told you everything."

"Thank you, Henri. I've crossed paths with psychopaths and freaks in my career, and more often than you'd think. But if the historian is a dissector, then the perversity of the human species is beyond my comprehension. I'll leave you to your work . . . thanks again!"

She hung up. She was sitting on a desk, eyes contemplating the peeling paint on the wall. She didn't understand what was happening. When she noticed how quiet the room had become, she snapped back to reality and returned to action mode. Fortin, Drancey, and a young policewoman were looking at her questioningly.

"Meeting in the briefing room. Notify everyone on site. We'll start in one minute."

The noises of footsteps and chairs immediately followed her order. Sixty seconds later, a dozen police officers were settled in chairs facing the podium where Captain Barka was waiting. The urgency of the meeting sent a shiver of excitement through the room. They were all hoping for a new lead; no significant evidence had been collected for several hours, despite the photo of Sartenas now decorating the streets of Grenoble and surrounding areas.

"I've just had a call from Doctor Blavet. He found the name of one of the murderer's old partners in madness. This person's name is Arsène Boisregard—if this isn't a coincidence or a homonym, then it's the curator of the museum where Monica Revasti's corpse was found."

A murmur of surprise swept through the room.

She continued. "If we're dealing with the same man, we must act quickly. He may be the one hiding Cabrade since his disappearance. Here's the plan of action."

As she uttered those words, Nadia noticed Captain Rivera had just entered the room and was staring at her pointedly. *Oh, shit!* thought the young woman. *It's his investigation, I'm on sick leave, and I'm in the middle of giving orders to his team. You've got it all wrong, girl.* She said nothing for a few moments, waiting for Rivera to intervene. He looked at the assembly, went to take his place beside her, and said, "You can continue, Nadia, you have our attention."

Nadia immediately went on. "I want four people to go to the museum. Rodolphe, you head up that team. Pick him up for me. There'll always be time to apologize later. Meanwhile, four others go to his private residence. Jérôme, find me his address, and Lieutenant Lemaistre will take charge of the operations. I also want a team digging into his past and present for me. I want to know if he has second homes where he could hide out, or hide Cabrade. And I want to know everything about his studies. At the same time we're also going to verify it's the same individual, even if I have little doubt. Jérôme, take as many people as necessary, and reconstruct Boisregard's schedule over the past forty-eight hours. You can also call Sophie Dupas: her father is a colleague of Boisregard's; they'll be able to help you. Although . . . no—let me deal with Dupas. Good, it's exactly 2:30 p.m. At 5:00 p.m. on the dot, I want you to have found me everything I've asked for. Now go, get on it!"

Thirty seconds later, the room was empty. Only Rivera had stayed, awaiting the departure of their colleagues so that he could be alone with the young woman. She decided to take the initiative.

"Sorry, Rivera, I overstepped my bounds. I imagine that annoyed you, and I confess I was surprised by your reaction."

Rivera smiled, and for the first time, Nadia didn't see the look of a hyena. "I don't know what's going on, Nadia. I feel like I was touched by grace yesterday. The Joan of Arc of the Grenoble police—surprising, don't you think?"

Nadia looked at him with genuine astonishment. She'd never known Rivera to be self-deprecating.

"On a more serious note, it was the search of Sartenas's villa that must have generated this change. I'm the one who's sorry for hounding you about the Déramaux case. When I found that girl's heart, I understood what you must have felt. I'll admit, it's a little late. You must be asking yourself, 'What's going on here, the terrible Captain Rivera fainting in front of a piece of meat in a jar?' Joking aside, I'm convinced you have the intuition to hunt down that son of a bitch."

Nadia Barka now recognized her colleague. But she'd appreciated his confession. The Italian regained his composure.

"On the other hand, don't forget I'm still leading the hunt for Sartenas."

"Don't worry, Rivera, I won't forget it. I'm just asking you to leave me Boisregard. We may have a common history."

Stéphane Rivera looked at her and continued, "Laure Déramaux?"

"A killer above all suspicion, an artist with the scalpel, a specialist in the Aztecs. Maybe I'm getting ahead of myself, but I feel it."

"Feminine intuition?"

"Call it what you like, but we have to move quickly. If Sartenas needs a new heart for a reason we don't yet know, and if he's driven by his old friend, we're in a race against the clock."

Stéphane Rivera laid a hand on her arm. "We're going to win it this time, on my word as a Calabrian."

Chapter 58: Excitement at the Museum

3:00 p.m. Drancey strode under the portico in front of the Old Diocese Museum. He pulled on his armband bearing the word "Police." The four men accompanying him pulled on theirs a second later. He paused before entering the museum.

"The guy we've come to collar is the worst kind. As soon as we see him, we neutralize him. According to Captain Barka, he'll react like an old woman, but he's a maniac with a scalpel."

The policemen looked at each other. Those who had participated in the briefing didn't really recognize the words used by their superior, but they understood the message: *Warning, viper in sight.*

"We don't have time to finesse this anymore. We have to get our hands on him as quickly as possible."

Action and fisticuffs being more Lieutenant Drancey's specialties than finesse, the roles were perfectly assigned.

The policeman pushed open the building's glass door and turned right to face the welcome desk. The middle-aged woman who gave out tickets jumped when she saw the five determined men come in. She shot a worried glance at one of her colleagues, who was replenishing pamphlets at a display on the history of the Dauphiné. Two students were examining a book on the history of the Church of Saint-André.

The policemen had the room covered in the blink of an eye. No sign of Boisregard. Garancher had printed a photo of the curator before leaving on the mission. Lieutenant Drancey took his badge out of his pocket and presented it brusquely about twenty inches from the cashier's face.

"Police. We want to see Arsène Boisregard!"

"Professor Boisregard?" the woman managed to respond, gulping. "But why?"

"I'm the one asking questions here. Do you know where he is?"

"I haven't seen him today, Officer."

"I didn't ask you if you've seen him, I only want to know where that bastard is hiding, and right now!"

The museum employee felt terror wash over her. The man arranging the historical books came up to Drancey and commented, "And who are you, monsieur, to talk like that about Professor Boisregard? You should know we all appreciate that exquisite man and . . ."

The lieutenant gripped him by the shirt and pulled him close. "Shut up. You can open your mouth only to answer my question."

Jean Renoir tapped discreetly on his mission chief's shoulder. Drancey got the message and released the man, who was starting to turn white. The cashier had come to her senses.

"His secretary should be able to answer you."

"Excellent, where is she?"

"In the administrative offices. If you want, I can show you the way."

"Well, then, now we're getting somewhere—madame . . . ?" he added with restored civility.

"Monique Renucci."

They followed their guide while her coworker went to find a flask of Chartreux liqueur hidden in a cupboard, and the two visitors left with the book under a jacket.

At the end of the hall they could see the outline of a door. The ancient floor creaked to the rhythm of their steps. The cashier stopped in front of the door.

"This is Madame Borteau's office, Monsieur Boisregard's secretary."

"Where is Boisregard's office?" asked Drancey.

"You have to pass by Madame Borteau to get to the curator."

Drancey made no comment. He realized he'd acted flippantly, but they'd rushed to the scene in under five minutes, and only the result counted.

His phone rang. He picked up and motioned to the museum employee to await his orders. The call lasted less than thirty seconds. He hung up, returned the phone to his interior jacket pocket, and addressed his men in a forceful but hushed voice.

"They worked quickly. They can confirm it is indeed the same Boisregard who studied medicine and is now curator at this museum. We'll have to be careful, boys."

Then he spoke to Monique Renucci. She'd caught snippets of the conversation, and her face revealed both confusion and agitation.

"Well, knock, please," Drancey directed.

Their guide knocked on the door.

"Come in!" replied an energetic voice.

"It's okay, you can go back to selling your tickets," Drancey said to Renucci. "And thank you for your assistance," he added, to Renoir's amusement.

Drancey went into the office. The arrival of the five men in this lofty room with exposed beams was incongruous. But the policeman didn't stop to notice those details. He did, however, decide to try a softer approach than he'd used when entering the museum. Perhaps subconsciously his strategy was dictated by the secretary's poise and trustworthy demeanor.

"Lieutenant Drancey, National Police. I want to speak with Arsène Boisregard as soon as possible."

The secretary stared in surprise at the group who had just barged into her office. Never in more than five years of working in this job had she experienced such . . . disorder, except following the discovery of that poor young girl's body.

"Monsieur Boisregard is out at the moment."

"Do you know when he'll come back?"

"He didn't come in today. Last night he left a message on my machine. He took a rare day off."

"Did he say why?"

"That's none of my business, Lieutenant!" huffed Géraldine Borteau. "The professor does what he wishes with his days."

"Indeed," commented the policeman. "He does what he wishes. Did he tell you when he would come back, and did you notice anything special about his message?"

"But why are you asking me all these questions, monsieur? Professor Boisregard is a very good person in every respect."

The cop looked at the woman across from him. She was in her late forties and had a certain charm. He appreciated her curves and wondered if Boisregard had made her his mistress, and if she was willing to protect him. Then he chased away the thoughts that had just gone through his head, silently begged forgiveness from his wife, and looked Borteau straight in the eye.

"We have a pressing need to hear the good Monsieur Boisregard's testimony."

"Yes, I imagine it has to do with the young Italian woman's murder case. But he already made a deposition, and I don't understand the urgency of your request."

Drancey decided to become an educator.

"My dear lady. You've doubtless known Boisregard for several years?"

"Five years exactly."

"And what do you know of him?"

"He's a scholar, a gentleman who is always discreet and ready to be of service."

"Very good. He's also a man who, thirty years ago, was expelled from the School of Medicine for savagely dissecting a cadaver, and was an intimate friend, at the time, of Dominique Cabrade, now known under the name Sartenas. The name Sartenas must remind you of something?"

The woman blanched and sat down on a chair.

"You . . . you're joking?"

"Look at me. Do I seem like it?"

"But it can't be the same man, it's impossible. Impossible and absurd!"

"Just like it's impossible and absurd to cut up cadavers or to extract their hearts. But enough philosophizing! Are my questions justified enough?"

Borteau was slumped over. The words had yet to completely sink in, but she knew her little world had just collapsed.

"And if it should happen we've made a mistake on Arsène Boisregard's account, he'd of course be able to prove it to us. But if I'm right . . ."

The secretary surrendered. "He seemed a bit excited on the phone. Modifying his schedule like that doesn't happen often. He's generally a man who honors his engagements and likes the routine of work."

"Have you found him changed since the discovery of Monica Revasti's body?"

"He was devastated. Such misfortune, in a museum he was responsible for, and what's more . . ."

"Did he say when he'd come back?"

"No, his message was brief. He just explained to me a personal reason was preventing him from coming to the museum today."

"Nothing that could have seemed unusual in light of what I just told you?"

"No," she said after thinking for a few minutes.

"Good. We'd like to examine his office."

Borteau hesitated for half a second. No one ever went into Professor Boisregard's office when he wasn't there, aside from a cleaning woman, once a week, and only under her surveillance. It was one of the historian's quirks. He couldn't stand the idea of someone violating the privacy of his lair when he was absent. She wasn't even allowed to go in alone. But she decided to open the desk drawer. She took out a little key, got up, and went over to a small wall cabinet. She opened it and exclaimed in surprise, "The office key isn't there anymore!"

"Excuse me?"

"There's a copy of Arsène's office keys here . . . excuse me, Professor Boisregard."

Drancey told himself he had more smarts than his colleagues gave him credit for.

"It's always there, usually. I'm the only one who knows where the little key to the cabinet is. Professor Boisregard was slow to agree to having a copy, and he wanted to be certain only he and I knew where it was hidden."

The policeman sighed. What a circus just for duplicate keys!

"Is it possible he took them before leaving yesterday, or that he came to get them during the evening?"

"Yes, it's not impossible. But why would he have done that?"

"I don't know. Okay, playtime's over."

He went up to the curator's office door. He pushed aside the curtain that covered it. The door was massive and ornately carved, but the lock was ancient and held at only one point. He turned back to one of his colleagues.

"Nicolas, can you open this for me?"

Nicolas Diozzo, a colossus at six feet six inches and two hundred and forty pounds, came up and looked at the lock.

"Yes, Lieutenant. But I don't have my tools with me. It'll take me a good twenty minutes to go get them."

"Ah, shit . . . fine, go on!"

"But given the urgency of the situation, there's a faster method, albeit less conventional," he added, gesturing to the combat boots he was wearing.

"Very good. Go to it."

Diozzo motioned to his colleagues and the secretary to move away from the door. He backed up to the opposite wall, concentrated, and launched himself at the door. The ensuing crack seemed deafening to them, totally out of place in this temple of history. The impact of the former rugby player's kick had torn out the lock. Boisregard's office awaited them.

Chapter 59: The Manuscript

"Gentlemen, gather up everything you find. We'll analyze it back at the station."

They entered Boisregard's lair, followed tentatively by Géraldine Borteau. The drawers were closed but gave up their secrets less than a minute later.

"So?" Drancey questioned.

"Nothing, Lieutenant. Basically history books."

"Take 'em. If we have to look into them, I'm sure Nadia or Rivera will find us a translator. A notebook, a diary, handwritten notes . . . ?"

"Nothing, Lieutenant, as if that guy didn't have a life. There isn't even a computer on the desk."

"Professor Boisregard has a laptop he always takes with him when he leaves at the end of the day," commented the secretary.

"Well, shit! Not only do we not know where he is, but there's nothing lying around in this fucking office."

"Lieutenant, come look!" called Renoir.

The four men and Borteau went over to the policeman. He'd lifted up a reproduction of a Rembrandt painting hanging on the wall. The front of a safe appeared before their eyes.

Drancey shot a questioning look at the secretary.

"I didn't know that safe existed! Professor Boisregard had the office renovated when he took up his post. He must have had it put in—it's his right!"

"It is indeed his right. But since you're in the business, could you explain to me what a private safe is used for in the office of a museum curator?"

The woman didn't answer him right away. She'd asked herself the same question upon discovering it behind the painting. She was torn between her loyalty to Arsène, her superior and occasional lover, and the crude, troubling facts brought to her by this policeman with a direct, uncouth manner.

"So, any idea?"

"No, I have none. There's no professional reason for this type of equipment. The valuable documents are kept and protected in the archives. Maybe he wanted to keep documents he borrowed safe, while he studied them in the calm of his office?"

"Do you believe in the theory you've just advanced?"

Borteau lowered her head. Ideas were swirling in her mind and clashing with each other, creating a chaos that would only grow.

"No. Everything you just told me bothers me greatly, even if I don't want to believe it."

"I can understand you don't want to accept it, but the bundle of facts that link him to the murderer is very tight. I assume no one knows the combination, aside from its owner?"

She shrugged her shoulders in assent.

"I want to know what's in there!" Drancey exclaimed.

One of the policemen, a lanky man with features sharp as a knife blade, came forward. He looked carefully at the safe, touched it, then turned back to Drancey.

"So, what do you say?" Drancey asked.

"It's an old one, boss. It looks sturdier than it actually is. The guy may dissect cadavers, but I can dissect his hunk of junk in less than three minutes. I don't know who recommended this model to him. In any case, he got ripped off."

"Thank you, Esteban, we'll ask him when we nab him."

The lieutenant pondered for a quarter of a second.

"All right, we're going to open this safe. Esteban, go get the tools. You have fifteen minutes!"

"We're about to gain fifteen minutes in our schedule, boss."

"*Lieutenant*, Esteban, not boss. I already told you we're not a gang of underworld thugs."

Esteban Muller, impassive, pulled the bag he was carrying off his shoulder. He set it on the wide, Empire-style desk, opened it, and took out a box of tools. He laid the box carefully on the leather blotter, then pulled a miniature drill out of the bottom of his bag.

"Do you always have your kit on you?"

"Not always. Start the clock, boss, I promise you it'll be open in three minutes, max."

Borteau watched the policeman attack the safe without turning a hair. Her passivity frightened her. Ten minutes earlier, she would have fought tooth and nail to defend her lover's privacy. But she'd broken down at once, as if the policemen's sudden arrival had brought to light an invisible rift that was already hiding within her.

"Is what you're doing actually allowed?" she asked Drancey, who had just come up to her.

The man scrutinized her insistently. He was almost moved by the secretary's lost look, by her vulnerability, which was surfacing and breaking down her defenses. He thought of his wife again and replied, "What I just ordered is totally illegal. If Boisregard wants to complain, he'll totally have the right. But I believe in my superior's intuition."

"*You* believe in intuition?"

"Don't I look like it?"

"Honestly, not really. But over the last few minutes, everything I was certain of is getting shattered. May I ask you another question?"

"Sure."

"A guy built like a tank who breaks down doors with his feet, and a safecracking specialist who goes around with his tool kit on his back. Where do you recruit your colleagues? In bars in the city's seedy areas?"

The policeman smiled in spite of himself.

"I'm going to answer you. Nicolas played rugby and is the son of a cop. A serious injury he received during a match prevented him from going pro—he joined us. As for Esteban, he worked for a safe dealer for a long time and—"

"Two minutes and thirty-seven seconds. I told you, boss—it's a piece of crap!"

The safe door was half open, revealing a cardboard folder on one of the two interior shelves.

Drancey immediately regained his concentration. "Nobody touch anything!"

He took out a pair of latex gloves from a jacket pocket and slipped them on. He delicately seized the document slumbering on the shelf, took it over to the desk, and laid it down. He called the secretary to his side. "Know anything about history?"

"If I have this job, then I know the basics. I have a master's degree with a specialty in the late Middle Ages."

"Good, we'll see if that can help us."

He undid the cord keeping the cardboard folder closed. About thirty sheets of paper appeared before their eyes.

"Do you have any idea what this could be?" Drancey asked her.

"Could you hand me a pair of gloves, Lieutenant? I'd have to look at those sheets more closely."

Jean Renoir got them for her, and the woman spent several long minutes poring over the pages covered in even handwriting, sometimes decorated with kabbalistic diagrams or pictorial representations the policemen couldn't decipher.

No longer able to stand it, Drancey inquired, "So, what was he hiding?"

"It's very strange, gentlemen. It would seem this is a copy of an ancient manuscript, written by someone called Fra Bartolomeo."

"Does that name mean anything to you?"

"Absolutely nothing, but many monks wrote during the sixteenth century."

"This thing is more than four hundred years old?"

"It's possible! The text is written in Latin, which was still the official language for writings at the time. The date appears on the second page: 1562."

"And what is this document about?"

"The title is esoteric, to say the least: *The Book of the Sun*. To be precise, I would have to read it, and it's been a long time since I worked on Latin translation. But considering the few diagrams you can see here and there, as well as some chapter headings, Fra Bartolomeo's work likely covers Aztec customs and their belief in life after death. Look, just on this page alone you can find the word *letum*, which means demise, and *nex*, which alludes to a violent death."

"Is Boisregard a specialist in that time period?"

"He has a good working knowledge, even if he doesn't rank among what I would call specialists. But how is it he's never presented this book? It must be priceless . . . I'm understanding less and less."

Drancey gently took back the document from her hands and placed it in a waterproof bag.

"Don't try to understand, and if I may give you some advice, do all you can to avoid Boisregard in the coming days. I don't think he'll forgive you for letting us discover his secret."

Chapter 60: Meeting at the Church

3:20 p.m. Julien threw his phone angrily onto the table. It bounced and fell on the floor. The bar patrons looked at him strangely. Mishandling an iPhone like that seemed to them to be an indication of mental derangement, the extent of which they didn't dare imagine.

The young man didn't even glance at them. He picked up his phone and put it back on the table, more calmly.

What an absolute *ass* he'd been that morning! What had possessed him to throw a fit with Sophie? Sure, he had excellent reasons to be disturbed, but why take it out on his friend? He'd been trying to call her back for more than an hour, and his messages were growing more and more elaborate. He'd very nearly asked for her hand in marriage over voice mail and then via text message. He smiled inwardly for a moment, telling himself he'd soon be verging on bipolar disorder.

He couldn't let a girl like Sophie slip away. Funny, intelligent . . . and so lovable. He would have fled a few months earlier, but now he felt like living with her. And all he'd managed to do was blow her off that morning and remain indifferent to her proposals. He really was an absolutely enormous ass! He'd just complicated things for himself, but he knew he'd do everything in his power to prove to her there was only one man for her: him, Julien Lombard!

He picked his phone up again and noticed the screen was cracked. Oh well, it still worked. He called Sophie for the thirteenth time. After three rings, the same message: "Hello, this is Sophie. You've just realized I'm not available, or I forgot to recharge my phone. So leave a brief message, and I'll call you back. Later."

"Sophie, it's Julien . . . again! I love you!"

He'd already made his excuses in the eight previous messages. He'd decided to go for simplicity in the next ones.

He looked around him. The afternoon sun was crushing the court-house square. The bars had lowered their blinds, and a few misters had been installed on restaurant terraces. Several lingering patrons were finishing their meals. The oppressive heat limited the number of strolling *badauds*. A shape arriving on the other side of the square via the Rue Hector-Berlioz caught his eye. He recognized her instantly: Sophie! So there was a god for idiots like him! He felt himself quiver like a teenager on his first date.

He looked for a waiter to pay for his coffee. He didn't see any-one on the terrace—the staff was probably staying in the protection of the air-conditioned room. Sophie hadn't seen him yet, but she was coming in his direction. He searched his pockets feverishly, found a five-euro bill, and put it under the saucer. It was quite a bit for a cup of coffee, but he didn't have any time to lose.

As he left the café, Sophie turned right toward the Church of Saint-André. Julien knew she was a believer; maybe she was looking for a moment of meditation. He was hurrying when a detail, more than a detail, stopped him in his tracks. Sophie was wearing a light summer dress . . . a white one! She was headed for a sacred place, and she was wearing a white dress! No, that had to be just a coincidence! Why would Sophie have . . . ?

A cold sweat immediately replaced the excitement he'd felt a tenth of a second earlier. No, it just wasn't possible! He called out to her and started running. The few passersby looked at him, surprised. Sophie didn't turn around. He was about ten yards away when she entered the church. Three seconds later, he in turn passed under the portico. He pulled off his sunglasses, adjusting rapidly to the building's dimness. A wave of panic rushed over him. He didn't see her anymore.

"Sophie, Sophie, answer me, dammit!"

His shouts bounced around the gothic vaults, then faded. He went over to the entrance and spoke to a worker who was restoring the massive door.

"Did you happen to see a young woman wearing a white dress go by just a minute ago?"

The man looked at him in surprise. Julien's desperate look likely inspired enough compassion in him to respond to this surprising question.

"No, besides you, no one has come through this door for two or three minutes."

Julien dragged himself to a bench and dropped onto it. He put his head in his hands and breathed heavily.

"It's still happening . . . and now Sophie! If only I'd stayed with her this morning!"

A lead weight settled on his shoulders. He couldn't move or think anymore and could barely breathe. He stayed motionless and sank into despair.

A hand tapped him on the arm. In an effort that seemed superhuman to him, he turned his head toward the intruder. A young child was looking at him and smiling.

"Are you sad?"

With a muffled sob, Julien nodded.

"Why are you sad?"

Without wondering about the point of this conversation, Julien answered, "I'm sad because a person I love very much has disappeared."

"When you're sad, you shouldn't sit and cry without doing anything."

The man looked at this child who was speaking to him so naturally.

"What do you do when you're sad?"

"When I'm sad, I think about my papa who disappeared, too. He's in heaven, and he talks to me."

"And what does he tell you?" asked Julien, astonished by this dialogue.

"He tells me to be strong so I can enjoy the good things in life."

"And that works?"

The boy looked at him, surprised, then burst out laughing.

"Well, yeah, it works, if not I wouldn't have told you!"

A feminine voice called to him from the nave. The child smiled once again at Julien.

"And also the one you love isn't dead, so you have to go look for her . . ."

Then he ran away toward a woman pushing a baby in a carriage. He took his mother's hand and vanished into the brightness outside.

Julien was bewildered. A six-year-old kid had just given him a life lesson. Instead of mourning, he had to do everything he could to find Sophie. Notify the police first! He stood up, then hesitated. He said a prayer for Sophie and left the church.

Chapter 61: Antoine Dupas

3:20 p.m. Professor Antoine Dupas entered Nadia Barka's office. He hung his hat on one of the hooks provided by the shiny new coat stand set in a corner of the room. He took off his Hugo Boss jacket, smoothed it distractedly, and put it on a hanger handed to him by the young woman. He'd abandoned his archaeologist outfit.

The police officer gestured him into a chair and started to talk.

"Thank you for coming to see me so quickly, Monsieur Dupas."

"The urgency in your voice required a quick response. I didn't hesitate. However, could I ask you a favor?"

"Of course," agreed Nadia, surprised.

"I came on foot from the university, and I'm on the verge of dehydration. If I could have something to drink?"

"Well, of course, I should have offered you something before." She called over an officer on duty and whispered a few words to him.

"Make yourself comfortable. We are indeed in a state of emergency. What I'm going to tell you must remain confidential. Is that clear?"

"More than clear, you can be sure. I'll be as quiet as the grave, and the Howard Carter who will try to pillage my secrets hasn't been born yet."

Nadia couldn't keep herself from smiling at Antoine Dupas's verbal emphasis. He said it without malice or pedantry.

"I'm not asking you for such a pharaonic enterprise, Professor." She was interrupted by the policeman coming back with two small bottles of cold Perrier. She handed one to the historian.

"You're saving me from an advanced state of dehydration, my dear lady."

"Let's say the title of captain is enough in the context of this room."

Nadia went over the facts while the man across from her drank his beverage. "Sartenas escaped from an operation we conducted yesterday. We found his home, over by Saint-Martin d'Uriage. We don't know if he was out when the police forces went in or if he was warned. Whichever it was, today he's at large, and we found a half-eaten human heart at his house."

Antoine Dupas nearly choked and spat out a mouthful of Perrier. He wiped his face with the back of his hand.

"I'm confused, Captain. That's terrible!"

"Terrible indeed! We now know what he's doing with these hearts. We haven't been able to locate him, despite our efforts and the wanted bulletin sent out to all the television stations. His photo is plastered around the region, all the train stations and all the airports for two hundred miles around have been warned. We've dug into his past and managed to find one of his close friends from his youth. We think he could have been helping him. Really, it's a hypothesis we've latched on to. And that's where we're counting on your assistance."

Antoine Dupas put down his small bottle, waiting for a new revelation.

"The man's name is Arsène Boisregard."

The historian looked at her with wide eyes. If there was a name he wasn't expecting, it was his colleague's.

"Arsène Boisregard? *The* Arsène Boisregard who works as the curator of the Old Diocese Museum? But that's not possible!"

"You must assume we've done our work correctly, Monsieur Dupas. I've met Boisregard, and I understand your surprise. But I can assure you fifteen years in the business have taught me to accept many hypotheses that seem incongruous at first. Tell me everything you know about him, even what might seem anecdotal to you. If it doesn't bother you, we'll record the conversation. That will give us the opportunity to listen to it again, to be certain no important detail slips by us."

"Of course, Captain. Could I ask you for another small bottle of Perrier?"

A policeman entered the office with a recording device and set it on the table. He came back a few seconds later with the historian's drink and sat down behind a laptop computer.

"I'll let you do the talking, Professor."

Antoine Dupas had utilized these moments of getting settled to organize his thoughts.

"I've known Arsène Boisregard for seven years, since he came to Grenoble. I know he worked in Paris and Bordeaux before, but he's never really opened up about his private life. Professor Boisregard is rather quiet. He listens more than he talks, which makes him an appreciated person. You know the propensity people have for telling about their lives, their little experiences, wanting to show off! So, when people meet an attentive listener, that person naturally becomes good company. Arsène has only one subject about which he is loquacious—history, of course."

"What information, even partial, can you give me on his pre-Grenoble life?"

"What appears in his CV. He studied at the Sorbonne, did a teaching degree in Babylonian civilization. I don't remember anymore the exact name of the subject, but you'll be able to find it easily. He then worked for about fifteen years in Paris, and five years in Bordeaux, where he taught. But I know hardly anything else."

"What kind of man is he, professionally? How is he judged by his peers?"

"A great man. I recently had the opportunity to participate in a meeting with the folks at city hall, at the Old Diocese Museum. He's very respected by his staff, particularly by his secretary, it seems to me. But here I'm getting into gossip and off topic."

"No, quite the contrary, go back there."

"I've known his secretary, Géraldine Borteau, for nearly twenty years. A beautiful woman, authoritarian and competent, who wreaked havoc around her."

"Be specific."

"She took more than one of her colleagues to her bed. And she kicked them out again as soon as it no longer amused her."

"So the historians' world isn't that austere!"

"No more so than any other. When Boisregard took the curator's job five years ago, we all wondered how things were going to turn out. Arsène was, and still is, unmarried. With his charm and boyish side, we were convinced he was going to get himself eaten alive. And what a surprise to see Géraldine follow him around like a lapdog a few months later! The roles had been totally reversed. The huntress had become willing prey."

"Do they live together?"

"Certainly not. Arsène wouldn't have stood for it. I think their relationship is purely . . . sexual. But I've never had any tangible proof."

"And it didn't surprise you that a woman like Géraldine Borteau, whom you describe as free and independent, would agree to play such a role for five years?"

"Me? No. But I remember talking about it with Madeleine, my wife. She'd met Géraldine several times, and she had the same reaction as you. That situation surprised her all the more because everything in Boisregard's personality gives the appearance of a retiring person. I must tell you Madeleine doesn't like Boisregard."

"Does she know him well?"

"She encountered him on occasion at little official and unofficial get-togethers."

"Let's go back to Boisregard. What do you know of his activities outside of work? Is he always such a placid character?"

"I don't know much about his private life, as I've told you. And yet, I think I'm someone who has the most contact with him. As for his character . . ."

Antoine Dupas stopped speaking. He made a visible effort at concentration, searching the depths of his memories for clues that could interest his questioner. The police officer gave him time to think.

"Look, I might have something that will interest you—well, you'll see! About three years ago, I went into a room while he was in the middle of a phone call. I know I should have made myself scarce, but I must acknowledge I'm rather curious. Arsène was arranging to meet someone at a manor, whose name I've forgotten. What surprised me, though, was his way of talking: imperious, directive. Nothing like his usual composed, retiring tone. I got the impression I was discovering a new personality."

Nadia's attention was immediately piqued. The historian continued with an embarrassed smile. "I stayed still, surprised by this aspect of Boisregard and eager to know the subject of the discussion.

He promised the person a unique experience. There was a totally unusual excitement in his voice."

"What type of experience?"

"I don't know. Boisregard turned around then, and he saw me. I tried to appear as natural as possible, but I could see that for a second or two he was furious. He then regained his calm and came to greet me as if nothing had happened. Maybe that transformation was the most frightening."

Three years. Laure Déramaux had been found dead three years ago. The clues that linked Boisregard to that case were tenuous, and any rational investigator would have laughed in her face. But she'd worked on that case for weeks, and her feminine intuition cried out to her to follow the lead. Of course, feminine intuition wasn't part of the courses at the police academy, but the resolution of a number of cases had often been made possible by something outside the books.

A woman entered the room. "I have a phone call for you, Captain. A certain Julien Lombard. He says he has to speak to you urgently."

"Give him to me right away!" She grabbed her cell phone out of her bag. Why hadn't he called her directly since she'd given him her number? Turned off! She'd forgotten to turn it back on after leaving the restaurant. The phone on her desk rang. She picked up.

"Captain Barka, I'm listening." She concentrated on his speech. "That is indeed most worrisome. Wait five minutes, I have her father in my office. Maybe he has some information?"

She put down the receiver, addressing Antoine Dupas, who'd just blanched. "Monsieur Dupas, do you know what your daughter Sophie had planned to do this afternoon?"

"What's going on?" asked the historian, suddenly stricken.

"Answer me, Monsieur Dupas."

"We had lunch together at the Ikea cafeteria. Then we parted ways around two o'clock. Then, she went back to the parking lot to get her car. I saw she had left with it, because her Polo wasn't there anymore when I left the university to meet with you, but I don't know anything more."

"Thank you. Do you know the license number on her vehicle?"

She noted it down on a Post-it and picked the receiver back up.

"Her father doesn't know what she'd planned to do this afternoon. Come meet us as soon as possible at the station!"

She hung up. Antoine Dupas grabbed her forearm and squeezed it.

"Tell me, what's happened to Sophie?"

"Nothing is certain for the moment. But according to Julien Lombard, she's been abducted by Sartenas."

The man abruptly sat up straight. "But that makes no sense. How can he say such a terrible thing?" Then, struck by the obvious, he sank back into his seat. "Julien Lombard told you?"

"Yes."

"He's my daughter's boyfriend?"

"I don't know their relationship, but I've met them together."

"Then what Sophie told me is true? This Julien has actually received signs of the abductions of the previous victims? He's not a pathological liar?"

"Unfortunately, even if the cause is inexplicable, everything points to the validity of his stories."

"Then this is a catastrophe. Sophie . . ."

The man was prostrated, felled by the terrible news. Nadia got up and shook him.

"Antoine, even if your daughter was just abducted, she's still alive! We have more information than we did during the previous cases, and her life now depends on us all. So you have to fight, not let go!"

Antoine Dupas looked at her and stood up brusquely. "You're absolutely right, Captain. We're going to find her. Just let me call Madeleine. Her presence won't be uncalled for."

Chapter 62: Search

3:40 p.m. Étienne Fortin relocked his phone and slipped it nervously into his pocket.

"We're not leaving. Backup is coming in less than five minutes with a battering ram and the appropriate papers. They'll be accompanied by two colleagues from the criminal records office."

"What happened to make you break down his door, Lieutenant?" asked Anne Pastourelle, a massive woman with lively eyes.

"The reasonable assumption of a new kidnapping!"

"So it did happen. Do they know the victim's name?"

"I met her recently. She's involved with the investigation. Her name is Sophie Dupas."

"Shit . . . we have to catch this fucker at any cost."

Fortin had finally gotten used to Anne's language, since her effectiveness went hand in hand with her colorful expressions.

"Anyway, before they get here—did you have time to finish going through all the floors?"

"Yes, Lieutenant," interjected André Marchal, an experienced policeman well accustomed to interviewing neighbors. "I can confirm the last person to have encountered the suspect is a certain Jocelyne Guillaudin. She says she came across him last night around six o'clock, after taking her dog for a walk. He was collecting his mail, and he greeted her quite civilly. No one saw him leave. Furthermore, I called headquarters to find out what type of vehicle he drives. I went to the garage to see if it was there. I didn't find it."

"He could have parked on the street."

"When you have a BMW X6 and a garage, you don't risk leaving your car outside, Lieutenant."

"That makes sense. So he could potentially have left Grenoble. Call Captain Rivera immediately to explain the situation to him and ask him to put out a bulletin on Boisregard's vehicle. It'll dovetail nicely with the search for Sartenas."

The strident wail of a siren stopped their conversation. Four men, dressed in dark coveralls, came out of a small van. Fortin waved them over.

"All right, everything's in place," he announced to his team.

"Lieutenant Jacques Gallois, GIPN. Are you Lieutenant Fortin?"

"That's me. You were very quick—all the better. I imagine you have all you need?"

"Obviously, we're equipped. They told me the suspect wasn't at home, is that correct?"

"I can only tell you we haven't heard a single sound from his place since we showed up. So I can't confirm his presence or absence."

"Understood." He turned to his men. "Possibility of encountering resistance, boys. Take the emergency response equipment." Then he spoke to Fortin again.

"We'll also need two outside witnesses for the procedure to be valid. I don't have that in my vehicle. Can you find them for me quickly?"

"We'll find 'em," replied Fortin. "Marchal, your witness, Jocelyne I-don't-remember-what, is she still at home?"

"Jocelyne Guillaudin. Without a doubt, Lieutenant, she hasn't left the building."

"Perfect, go get her for me. And then find me a second one among those you interrogated. We'll all meet on the fourth floor."

One minute later, the GIPN men were in position in front of the door to Arsène Boisregard's apartment. Fortin and his team had let them get settled. The two witnesses had been removed to the floor above, protected from the occupant's improbable resistance. The two residents, who had lived in the building for over twenty years, were living an adventure that would enable them to become important people in the neighborhood over the coming weeks.

Gallois rapped violently on the door while shouting the usual warnings. Only silence answered him.

"All right, boys, we're going in."

In less than a few seconds, the door was broken down with the help of a battering ram and four men had taken up position in the apartment, weapons poised. Thirty seconds later, they came back out to report.

"The apartment is empty, Lieutenant. You can search in complete safety."

They entered the vast sitting room, whose glass door opened onto a large balcony offering a view of the Vercors Mountains. A bedroom, an office, an ostentatiously luxurious bathroom, and a large kitchen rounded out the apartment. The eyes of the two witnesses darted everywhere. Who would have guessed austere Professor Boisregard had a bathroom with a huge Jacuzzi tub, mirrors on the ceiling, and extravagant Carrara marble that looked like it belonged in a spa?

Two new arrivals came into the room. "Emmanuel Drouksi, criminal records office," announced one of them, introducing himself to Fortin. "What are we looking for exactly?"

"Exactly, I couldn't tell you. But we want to see if there's evidence Sartenas was here, and any indication of a destination Boisregard could have headed for."

Gallois broke in. "We're leaving, Fortin. Our mission is complete."

"Thanks. Good-bye."

The GIPN men left the room, leaving the space to the investigators.

Five minutes later, Anne Pastourelle called them into the bedroom. "Come see. There's something strange here."

Fortin and Drouksi joined her.

"A closed trash bag, stuffed in the back of a closet," she said. "This isn't really the place to store it, is it?"

"Indeed," noted Drouksi. He called in one of his colleagues who had a camera. He took the bag with him and put it in the middle of the sitting room. He found a plastic tarp in his crime scene kit and unfolded it on the floor next to the bag. He kneeled down and with great dexterity, following protocol, removed the string keeping the bag shut. He opened it carefully. The policemen stopped their own search to see the result of Anne Pastourelle's find. The witnesses had also approached, giddy with excitement. With a little luck, the policeman was going to expose parts of a corpse or something like that . . .

Drouksi took out the contents of the bag one by one: a pair of beige linen pants, a shirt still stained with copious sweat marks, and an object somewhere between yellow and red.

"Can you show me that thing more closely?"

Emmanuel Drouksi picked it up and unfolded it. "Strange, it's a wig."

Fortin reacted immediately, as if struck by lightning. "Fuck, that's Sartenas's wig!"

To the astonished stares of his colleagues, he specified. "It's the wig Sartenas was wearing on the South Hospital parking lot surveillance tape, the day he abducted Camille Saint-Forge. Instead of one, we now have two psychopaths on the loose."

The news stunned the policemen.

"Keep looking. Find me any clue that will help us locate them. Take apart all the furniture if you have to. And quickly, if we want the chance of seeing Sophie Dupas alive again."

Chapter 63: Géraldine Borteau

4:15 p.m. Géraldine Borteau had taken a seat in Nadia Barka's office. The secretary had arrived five minutes earlier in the company of Rodolphe Drancey. She had urgent testimony to give, but she preferred to speak to a woman. Knowing Nadia was at the police station, Lieutenant Drancey had agreed. Nadia offered the woman a drink, but she refused and dove right in.

"I never would have imagined coming here of my own volition. But what your colleague has told me, the discoveries we made in his office, and what the search of his apartment just taught me made me change my mind."

"Lieutenant Drancey informed you about the results of the search?"

"Yes. He shouldn't have?"

"No. But if that convinced you to come talk to us, his mistake did some good. Why did you want to speak to a woman? Why not address Lieutenant Drancey directly?"

"Because what I'm going to reveal is private. I know it's stupid, since I'm going to sign my statement, which will then become public."

"I understand. Then again, do you have any objection to my recording this?"

"No, you can go ahead. It won't last for hours."

Géraldine Borteau settled into the middle of her chair. She felt ill. She was going to display her private life in front of this stranger. She was going to sully a man she had still revered two hours earlier. But did she really still revere him? She hadn't thought twice when her instincts ordered her to tell her story. She took a deep breath and looked at the policewoman, who was looking back at her patiently. She gathered up her courage and began.

"My name is Géraldine Borteau, I'm forty-five years old, I have a master's in history, and I serve as secretary for the Old Diocese Museum. I of course carry out the administrative tasks, but I also organize all the events that relate to our museum's activities. I've assisted Arsène Boisregard since he took on his duties as curator, and our collaboration has gone very well—extremely well."

So Antoine Dupas was right, thought the policewoman. She kept her talking. "I imagine it was that excellent relationship you wanted to speak to me about."

"Yes. I'll get right to the point."

"I'm listening."

"I'm single, and men like me. Until I met Arsène—that is, Professor Boisregard—I always loved the chase, helping myself to whoever I found attractive, breaking it off when my interest waned. I've always loved sex. Basically, I dominated the men I chose."

Nadia observed the historian. She was deep in her story. She derived neither glory nor embarrassment from what she was telling. She was factual.

"When Boisregard arrived, I immediately wanted him in my bed. He was a rather handsome man and reserved. In spite of everything, I sensed a mysterious side to him. When I told a few of my girlfriends about it, it made them laugh. I won't go into the patience

I had to have in order to achieve my goal. I've never expended so much energy to this day. In fact, never had a man resisted me for so long, married or not, for that matter. That resistance piqued my curiosity. It was six months before we slept together. We were at a conference in Nice. While I was getting ready to take the lead on the operation, I discovered in him another man. He metamorphosed, and in one night, I became his creature. He did with me what he wanted. I agreed to everything he asked of me, even the most demeaning. I never would have thought it possible to obey a man to that extent, and I never experienced such an orgasm."

"So in one night you plunged into sadomasochistic relations. He in the role of master, and you in that of slave?"

"That's right. I—how do I say this—revealed myself sexually within a few hours."

"And him?"

"By the next morning, he went back to being the same man. Even with me. When we made love, he was sure of himself. As soon as we left the bedroom, he was the same quiet, almost timid Boisregard everyone knew."

"And when it was just the two of you in his office?"

"He was very professional and imperturbable. It was really surprising."

"Surprising or frightening?"

"Surprising. But really, he was the master who dictated how we had to conduct our relationship . . ." Géraldine Borteau paused and looked at the police officer. "You must take me for a deranged woman or a whore, don't you?"

"No. Everyone can have the sexuality they like, as long as it doesn't endanger their partner."

"Thank you. I'll continue, since I'm not just here to tell you about my escapades. Over time, Arsène became more and more demanding, more and more violent."

"Did you rebel?"

"No, I kept asking for it, too. I didn't understand myself any longer; I just knew I always wanted more. He'd quickly started to practice bondage."

"The art of playing with rope—Kinbaku."

The historian stopped and asked the police officer, flabbergasted, "Have you had this type of experience?"

"No. But I've looked into that lifestyle."

"So what I'm telling you doesn't shock you?"

"I'm not here to be shocked or to pass judgment, Madame Borteau. But I interrupted you. Continue, please."

"These last few months, that wasn't enough for him anymore. He proposed a different type of game: scarification. It scared me at first, but I agreed, and I entered the universe of his fantasies."

"What instrument did he operate with?"

"A scalpel. And he was extremely gifted. The scars faded quickly. But during our last encounter, it was unusually brutal."

Géraldine Borteau checked that no one could see them, got up from her chair, and lifted her skirt. Her thong revealed a scar that was still very red and astonishingly deep. She dropped her skirt again.

"It was the first time the pain surpassed the pleasure I got out of it."

"Did he have the same aptitude as usual?"

"At first, yes. But I quickly noticed he wasn't worrying about me."

"Can you be more specific?"

"Our relationship was based on pain. He loved to make me undergo humiliations, to make me suffer. But he always knew how to control his acts so that I got pleasure out of it. He had a sort of instinct. That wasn't the case last week."

"How frequent were your sexual relations with Boisregard?"

"Around twice a month. At my place, or in hotels. Occasionally at his place."

"Had you already noticed such fits of violence in your partner?"

The secretary didn't hesitate long. "Once, three years ago. I thought I was going to die. I wanted to break it off, but he managed to apologize convincingly. And I was addicted."

"Do you remember the date?"

Surprised by the question, the secretary took a little time to reflect.

"It was in March."

Everything matched up. They'd found Laure Déramaux's body in March.

"Thank you for your testimony, Madame Borteau. It sheds new light on Arsène Boisregard. I'm quite afraid his real personality is that of the 'master' and not the timid curator. I imagine coming to see us wasn't easy for you."

"It's okay. I'm surprisingly relieved."

"We're going to put your deposition on paper. I'll ask you to come back to sign it at the end of the day."

"I think my day has already been disturbed enough. I'm going to wait outside, and I'll sign it immediately."

The two women stood up, and Nadia escorted the historian to the door. "Do you have a place to sleep other than your apartment? A place he doesn't know about?"

"Do you think that . . . ?"

"I don't know how he might react. I'd prefer to know you're safe."

"I have a cousin in Lyon who would probably be willing to take me in."

"Then go there tonight. Could you also leave me your phone number? We may have to contact you for the investigation."

Géraldine Borteau wrote down her contact information on a slip of paper and handed it to the police officer. Between the secretary's testimony and that of Hélène Guyancourt, which Étienne had quickly reported to her, Nadia told herself Sartenas and Boisregard really had teamed up, to the great misfortune of those who crossed their path. Nadia opened the door for Géraldine Borteau, who left the office.

Borteau passed Drancey in the hallway as she was leaving. In the space of an instant, her eyes drilled into his. Drancey turned around and watched the sway of the departing woman's hips.

"Rodolphe!"

The policeman jumped, abruptly woken from his dream. He saw Nadia smiling mockingly.

"Avoid her in the coming weeks. Your relationship and your health wouldn't stand a chance."

Chapter 64: Kill Count

4:45 p.m. The briefing room had been transformed into a hive of activity. The incessant comings and goings of the policemen who had just received instructions or were bringing the latest information created an impression of perpetual motion. Captain Stéphane Rivera discreetly stifled a yawn and stretched. The fatigue was starting to accumulate, but he knew from experience the nervous tension would allow him to continue keeping long hours. He gave his orders: all the police brigades in Isère were now on the lookout for the curator's black X6. It wasn't the most inconspicuous of vehicles, and he had high hopes sightings would be reported.

Rivera had a team of five people taking all the phone messages. Since the systematic posting of Sartenas's picture on the walls of the city and in the newspapers, they'd received more than a hundred calls. Except for the most far-fetched, such as the one who had seen Sartenas vanish in a disc of light, they'd forced themselves to check all of them out. It was a continual race. One of those witnesses seemed to corroborate the fact that Sartenas had been in Grenoble. A group of three high schoolers had seen a strange man, probably wearing a wig, whose face vaguely resembled that of the picture on display. They'd encountered him at the Place Victor-Hugo, and the look in his eyes had scared them. If only they'd contacted the police at the time.

Rivera decided to join Nadia Barka, who was in the midst of talking with the Dupas family. He sat back down, though, to look at the file that had just landed on his desk. The two words written in felt-tip pen on the cardboard sleeve had stopped him: "Boisregard/disappearances." His colleague's suspicions had little by little sunk in—what if Boisregard was directly implicated in the murder of Laure Déramaux? He grabbed the file and pulled out about fifty pages—newspaper articles, police depositions. The compiler had created a summary of his research. Good work! Rivera took the document, settled back in his chair, put his feet up on the table, and read it.

Arsène Boisregard had lived in Grenoble for the past seven years after eight years spent in Bordeaux. Prior to that he'd lived in Paris; he'd gone to the capital just after being expelled from medical school. That had happened forty years ago. Rivera already knew the historian's official CV, but he agitatedly read the rest of the note. Then he threw himself on the newspaper articles, compared the dates, carefully combed through the police reports. Fifteen minutes later, he closed the file, incredulous. He thought about it—he shouldn't let himself be guided by a feeling, a sort of interior voice. He had to base his actions on facts. But he didn't have time to piece together the facts one after the other.

"What's the reason for your meditation, Rivera?"

"Oh, it's you, Commissioner!" Rivera said, startled. "What I've just read is extremely troubling."

"Explain."

"This morning Captain Barka put forth the hypothesis that Boisregard could have taken part in the murder of the Déramaux girl."

"I know Nadia took that case very much to heart, and even though she's an excellent cop, it's not necessarily the case . . ."

"Let me finish, Commissioner. Déramaux's murder three years ago. The body is found still warm, not far from the village of Chapelle-en-Vercors. Another disappearance, also in Vercors, six years ago. A young Breton tourist. The police finally closed the case, but her parents were always convinced she had been abducted and killed. A skeleton was found three months ago, once again in Vercors. I've just made the connection with that disappearance, and I'm going to request DNA analysis."

"We can't pin every missing persons case in the Grenoble region on this guy, though."

Rivera continued his list, without taking his superior's commentary into account.

"During the eight previous years, Boisregard was teaching in Bordeaux. In May 2002, a hiker found the corpse of a twenty-year-old girl in Soulac-sur-Mer, in a bunker along the beach. The body had been lacerated with an instrument the medical examiners identified as a scalpel. A gypsy man was arrested and put in prison. But he always denied being the killer."

"I do indeed remember that story," remarked Mazure.

"And finally, in October 1998, in a forest next to Biscarosse, a hunter unearthed the corpse of a woman in her thirties whose body also bore evidence of torture by knife. There, too, a vagrant was arrested. He had worked for that woman as a gardener, then had left. The date of his departure closely matched that of the victim's murder. The file was sketchy, but so was his lawyer—he was convicted."

"But there's no proof against Boisregard."

"Absolutely none, Commissioner, absolutely none . . ."

"But it's troubling, isn't it?"

"It is indeed very troubling, especially after the deposition Géraldine Borteau just made to Captain Barka."

"Géraldine Borteau?"

"Boisregard's secretary, at the Old Diocese Museum."

"What did she say?"

"I'm going to play an excerpt from her deposition."

Rivera woke up his computer, then grabbed a USB drive sitting next to the keyboard. He plugged it in, then selected a file. He handed a pair of headphones to Mazure, who put them over his ears.

"I just learned about this fifteen minutes ago. It goes on for five minutes. I'll let you listen to the deposition."

Five minutes later, Mazure took off the headphones. "I've heard enough. We still don't have any proof, but I have enough suspicions to launch the operations. I'm contacting the prosecutor."

Commissioner Mazure left the room. He looked for a calmer place, took out his phone, and called the prosecutor. The conversation lasted for several minutes. Then Mazure hung up and went back into the room, visibly frustrated.

"So, Commissioner, what's his opinion?" asked Rivera.

"He doesn't follow. He believes the proof isn't solid enough to put out a warrant for Boisregard. 'Out of the question to throw his name to the wolves.' That's what he said to me."

"But the wig we found at his place, the text from the Italian monk, the original of which we found in his office, and the endpaper at Sartenas's? That isn't enough for the fucker?"

"No, he doesn't want to do anything official."

"Fuck, there's a life on the line!"

"I know. But nothing prevents us from sending out the gendarmes and the police on his tail. I'm covering everything!"

"Good, Commissioner."

"Ah, and still no idea where he could have gone?"

"We're pushed to the limit, Commissioner. But we have, for the moment, found no second residence in Boisregard's name, nor one belonging to close family. We're investigating vacation spots or favorite getaways, but that takes time."

"And we don't have any—"

"We're aware of that, Commissioner. The only clue we have, but it's weak, comes from a declaration by Antoine Dupas, the father of the latest missing girl. Boisregard apparently spoke of a manor once. So we're grabbing on to that, but at this point we've located two hundred thirty-seven manors within a thirty-mile radius of Grenoble. And again, the definition of the word *manor* varies from person to person. In any case, you can be sure of one thing: we're on it."

"I know, Rivera."

Chapter 65: At the Diocese

5:15 p.m. Julien Lombard hurtled down the stairs and was confronted by the intense heat, a lead weight covering the city. He had to act on his own. The discussion that had just taken place with Captain Barka and Sophie's parents had convinced him. The last information he'd collected before leaving had only expanded the fog the police were trying to see their way through: a black BMW X6 had been spotted around 2:30 p.m. in Saint-Martin d'Uriage. Two men were in the vehicle. The news had been reported at five o'clock. Captain Rivera had immediately commanded the gendarmes on the scene to look for Sophie's car. They'd found it ten minutes later, empty. Sophie had vanished.

The police had hoped that a GPS antitheft system would allow them to locate the BMW. But if Boisregard had installed such an alarm, he'd since deactivated it. Julien couldn't content himself with waiting for a miracle to put them on Sophie's trail. He was well aware that Sartenas didn't keep his prey for very long. Monica Revasti and Camille Saint-Forge had been killed during the night following their abduction. If he did nothing, Sophie would suffer the same fate.

He hurried toward the Diocesan Residence. If one person could give him information, it was his mother. Of course, that seemed stupid: *I have an informant in the great beyond.* But she'd already helped him. He had to talk to her. And to do that, he had to see Lucienne Roman again. And only Father Bernard de Valjoney could take him to her.

The two previous murders had taken place around three o'clock in the morning. If that wasn't just a coincidence, he had fewer than ten hours to save the woman he loved—and no one knew where she was. But he'd decided to put all his energy into looking for Sophie, and not to waste a single minute lamenting the situation.

He heard the sound of running behind him. He turned around.

"Julien, I'm coming with you."

Blinded by the sun, it took him two seconds before he recognized Captain Barka.

"You'll probably need my help to open doors for you."

"Captain Barka, I think I can handle this on my own. Besides..."

The woman seized him firmly by the arm. "Julien, don't be stupid. You're not going on a crusade. Even if this case touches you deeply for multiple reasons, it concerns a woman's life and taking down two criminals. I missed Sartenas once, but he won't escape me a second time."

The man thought about it, then shook his arm out of her restraint. "It seems to me I'm not the only one on a crusade, Captain. But you're right. We'll only get there by joining forces."

"You can call me Nadia. And you're right—I want those two bastards' hides. But I also want to find Sophie."

"Good. But what about the interrogations and the investigation?"

"Rivera took over. He can be difficult, but he's a good cop. In fact, he's an expert. So good—we're going to look for the priest?"

Julien spoke to the receptionist. "Hello, I absolutely must meet with Father de Valjoney."

She was typing away on her computer. "I'm sorry, Father Bernard is in a meeting until seven o'clock. Then he has an outside engagement all evening. However, I can leave him a message."

"I have to meet with him. It's a matter of life and death."

"I'm really sorry, but he's meeting with the bishop. Maybe I could help you somehow?"

Nadia intervened. She took out her police badge and handed it to the receptionist. "Captain Barka. We absolutely must meet with Father de Valjoney. I'm going to ask you to interrupt his meeting. Tell him Julien Lombard and Captain Barka need him. He'll understand why we're here."

The receptionist sighed but obeyed the police officer's orders. She left her post and headed into the building's hallways. They didn't exchange a word until the priest arrived. He thanked his colleague, greeted the two guests, and invited them to follow him into his office.

"What emergency has brought you here?"

"The killer has struck again. Another woman was abducted," replied the policewoman.

The priest sighed heavily and asked, "When did the abduction take place?"

"I had the vision two hours ago," interjected Julien.

"Do they know the identity of the victim?"

"It's Sophie Dupas," announced Nadia.

The priest grew pale at the name. The policewoman continued, "We know Sartenas's accomplice in this abduction. It's Arsène Boisregard."

"Arsène Boisregard?" He looked at the police officer and saw certainty in her face. "Who would have thought Monsieur Boisregard was mixed up in this case?"

"We've done an investigation, which quickly revealed Boisregard is a dangerous psychopath. We have only a few hours to find Sophie Dupas. But we don't know where she's hidden. Your help will be critical."

Bernard de Valjoney looked at the two of them. He was barely recovering from the news he'd just received. "I'm listening."

Julien took the lead. "The police are currently on the trail of the two men but don't have any serious leads yet. I can think of only one person who can help us . . ."

"Your mother's spirit. It must be her you're thinking of, isn't it?"

"Yes. I want to meet with Lucienne Roman to contact Magali Dupré. I'm sure she'll be able to help us."

"Unfortunately that won't be possible."

"But—"

The priest cut him off. "Lucienne Roman is currently at Mure Hospital. She had a heart attack the day after our visit. She'll probably recover, but she's very weak for the time being."

"Could we still ask her if . . ."

"If we ask her to, she'll agree. But I visited her yesterday, and I can assure you she won't be capable of getting in contact with your mother. If there were the smallest chance, I would ask her to try."

Julien was stunned. His hope was evaporating. He'd already imagined a whole scenario, but on the assumption the old woman was in good health. He went on the attack. "But there must be other people who can get in touch with my mother? I'm sure you know some!"

The priest dampened Julien Lombard's wishful thinking with a gesture.

"No, I don't know any. Understand that the session we conducted with Lucienne Roman is an exception."

"But there are clairvoyants, people who communicate with spirits!"

"Yes, they exist. But then we're getting into an area that runs from charlatanism to black magic."

"I'm willing to do anything to find Sophie!"

Julien was in a state of increasing agitation. Father de Valjoney got out of his chair and sat down next to him on the sofa.

"Julien, I've known Sophie for thirty years. I baptized her, and I have only one wish right now: to care for her. So you can be certain that I'll do all I can to help the police find her . . . alive. I'll do all I can, but not just anything. Imagine you went to see a psychic. You absolutely won't know who you'll come across. Let's even imagine this psychic puts you in contact with the great beyond, as you say. How will you know you'll be dealing with your mother and not some evil spirit who will try to lead you astray? And who knows what state you'll end up in?"

"I'm willing to try the experiment."

"You say that because it's a world you don't know."

"But Madame Roman?"

"I told you. Lucienne Roman's case is an exception. Understand that I'm going to make every effort to find Sophie, but I beg of you, believe me—you won't find your mother by going to see a random psychic, even if you do find one."

Julien Lombard was crushed. He was ready to fight when he'd started their meeting, but the priest's words had made him change his mind. He knew about the tenderness between Father de Valjoney and Sophie; he also knew he wanted to save her.

"So what do you advise us to do?" asked Barka, also disappointed by their meeting's conclusion.

The priest reflected, then seemed to hesitate. He got up from the sofa and paced around the room, searching for an idea that could end the situation's deadlock. His guests respected his period of introspection. He stopped, then spoke to them.

"I might be able to offer you our aid, but first I have to confer with my bishop."

The policewoman's curiosity was piqued. "How much time will you need for him to come back?"

"He's still in the meeting, but I'm going to permit myself to disturb him. One hour from now, I will come back to you."

"Can you tell us more about this idea?"

"Unfortunately, no. I can't get involved personally, but rest assured I'll contact you as soon as I have his response, whatever it may be. I have your cell phone number."

"Thank you. We're going to go back to the police station. Before leaving, do you think your idea will allow us to significantly speed up the search?"

"I can't prejudge anything, but it would be able to contribute. So I'd need information from you."

"You'll have it. Julien, are you coming back with me?"

As Julien Lombard stood up, the priest took him by the arm.

"I'd like to chat for a few minutes with you, if it's not inconvenient."

Julien nodded and motioned to Nadia, who left the office.

"What do you want to say to me?"

"I'm still reading disappointment in your eyes. You expected to find help for getting Sophie back quickly, with the cooperation of Lucienne Roman. Unfortunately, she can no longer offer her service. But that doesn't mean there's no solution."

"What do you mean? Each time I had a premonition about, or even saw, the disappearance of one of Cabrade's victims, she's died within hours! Do you believe he'll make an exception for the third? Surely not! So excuse me, but I don't see why I should rejoice!"

"I didn't ask you to rejoice. But if you've received the gift of communicating with your deceased mother, it's because there was a reason for it."

"I respect you, and I respect the Church. But what are you hoping for? That I acquire the gifts of a psychic during the evening? That by some miracle I encounter my mother while leaving here? 'Here you go, my darling, here's the plan for recovering Sophie. Obey the speed limit!' Don't you believe now is the time for action?"

"Isn't it a sort of miracle that you came to look here?"

Julien sat back down in the chair. He hid his head in his hands and breathed deeply. Everything was getting so confused in his mind. His mother who spoke to him, his father who was a killer and was going to sacrifice the woman he wanted to build his life with. And especially the impotence they were all subject to, while the seconds ticked by inexorably, bringing them closer to the fatal conclusion. He wanted to act, run, fight, kill if he had to. He was simultaneously in a state of intense excitement and crushed by the curse that had befallen him. He was the son of a murderer who had killed his mother and was going to kill his future wife. How could he morally get out of that discovery unscathed?

The distant voice of the priest brought him back to reality.

"First of all, Julien, you are not responsible for the actions of the one you call your father. He's at best a progenitor."

"Maybe, but don't I have half his DNA inside me?"

"Ah, the theory of crime being passed on by genes. If it were true, statistically, the earth would be filled with killers. No, Julien, everyone is responsible for his own actions in the witness of men!"

The priest was imagining the tortures of the man crumpled on the sofa and had instinctively adopted an intimate tone. His assertion had reassured the young man.

"But my mother! Why would she have spoken to me, then abandoned me when I need all her support?"

"Why do you say she's abandoned you? Listen and be patient."

"But how can I be patient when time is fleeting?"

"The evening is still long. She wants to help you save Sophie. You must be attentive to what she has to tell you. She's doing all she can for you. You must help her transmit her message to you."

Chapter 66: The Jail

The intense blackness that enveloped her was terrifying. Even with her eyes wide open, she could see absolutely nothing. She felt nauseated and lost.

But where was she? What was she doing in such an inhospitable place? She knelt down and waited for everything to stop spinning around her. Seconds passed, long and agonizing, before Sophie began to recover her wits. She knew she still had to be patient for a while before her brain would obey her again. She took the opportunity to try identifying the place where she found herself. The young woman felt at the floor and recognized wood by touch. Parquet, probably. She moved carefully on all fours and reached a wall. She clutched it and stood up gingerly. Her balance was better than she'd feared it would be for a moment. She circled the room until she arrived at a door. Overcome by a sudden burst of hope, she grabbed the handle, pushed it down, and applied all her weight. Nothing moved: locked in! So she was a prisoner! But why?

She had to reactivate her brain, to understand. She concentrated intensely on the previous hours in her day. What had she done?

Suddenly, the veil lifted and all her memories flooded back in a rush!

Lunch with her father, Professor Boisregard's call, the drive up to Uriage. She was in such a hurry to hear the historian's revelations that she'd nearly gone off the road during a turn. Seventy miles per hour in the valley, it was undoubtedly too fast for the road. A skillful turn of the wheel had put her back on the right path and calmed her enthusiasm for driving. She'd then stationed the car alongside the park and found her contact near the children's carousel.

Boisregard was very excited. She'd had to calm him down, his statements were so incoherent. He seemed to be under the effect of an extreme psychotic episode. So they'd walked and headed toward a little wood apart from the main path. Sophie had not noticed, convinced a little activity would allow the curator to get his head on straight. The images were now coming back clearly to her mind . . .

She'd followed Boisregard, who was explaining his train of thought to her. He'd arrived at the name of the person he suspected. His last sentence had rooted Sophie to the spot! She'd turned toward the historian. Within a few seconds, the timid, panicked curator had given way to a man whose self-possession had rendered her speechless. His features had radically altered—they were hard, and the only smile that lit his face was cold and sardonic.

"Oh, yes, my dear Mademoiselle Dupas. My deduction leads me to believe that the man who lent his support to the butcher of Grenoble is me! I couldn't announce it directly to the police, now could I?"

Sophie had remained speechless. Her brain was idling. Boisregard had to be the victim of an attack of dementia. But the cracking of branches had alerted her. She'd turned around abruptly.

That face! She'd seen it recently. But where? No! Him! Sartenas was standing before her. A surge of adrenaline infused Sophie. She'd succeeded in escaping Sartenas's arms when he tried to grab her. *Get out of the woods, get out of the woods, and go back to the protection of the eyes of the* badauds *strolling around the park!* But Boisregard had stuck out his leg, catching her ankle like a scythe. She'd skidded, but managed not to fall. She was athletic! That second of imbalance, however, had doomed her. Sartenas, mad with rage, had caught her by the shoulders. Boisregard had put his hand in his pocket. He'd pulled out a syringe. The needle had approached the young woman's neck. She'd wanted to scream, but she couldn't tell whether a sound had come out of her throat. A sudden prick, then a black hole.

Panic instantly swept over Sophie Dupas. She was alone, doubtless far from all habitation, at Sartenas's mercy. And she no longer had one psychopath to deal with, but two. One, or two—would that change anything about her fate? Chronicle of a death foretold . . . She trembled and retreated to a corner of the room. She didn't want to die. She especially didn't want to die this death. The idea of Sartenas's hand entering her chest to seize her heart repulsed her. No, not that! She sank to her knees and vomited repeatedly, in long streams. Her tears flowed without her trying to restrain them. The shock was too violent. She knew what was waiting for her. She was completely overwhelmed for long minutes, then gradually calmed. She had to survive. She couldn't die like the others, not her! A man was waiting for her out there, and they had more than fifty years to live together.

Sophie looked for a few reasons to hope. Julien had undoubtedly foreseen her disappearance, and the police must now be looking for her. They'd find her and save her life. She decided not to dig deeper into her reasoning. She'd doubtless find multiple arguments that would damage this kernel of optimism. And she didn't want to appear as a willing victim.

She thought back on Sartenas's career. She would not take part in his kill count.

Her phone! She crawled on all fours, scouring the dark room for her handbag. After two minutes of frenetic agitation, she stopped. *Obviously, my poor Sophie, they would have left you your bag, the keys, and a plan for escaping this prison! Now, calm down.* She sat down on the floor and patted the waist of her skirt: she felt a slight protuberance. A smile came over her in spite of herself. She ran her fingers over it and pulled sharply on a thread sticking out: she felt a little packet fall into her hand. Three safety matches wrapped in plastic film and a one and one-quarter inch razor blade protected by a piece of paper. A habit she'd picked up in her younger days during hikes with her father.

If you have enough to make fire, a piece of string, and a knife, you'll be able to get yourself out of almost any situation, the man who'd been her hero at the time told her. As a child and teenager, she'd had those things in all the pockets of her clothing and bags. Then, she'd sewn them into the linings of her clothes. It had been several years since she'd indulged in that kind of mania, but that morning she'd grabbed the first skirt she touched in her wardrobe. And to think she'd wanted to give it to charity the previous week! She took this discovery as a sign of encouragement from fate. She took the matches out of their plastic pouch. She moved up next to the wall and struck one on the stone.

The light given off by the flame lit up the room just enough. Sophie memorized it with her eyes. The red brick walls were about twenty feet wide. Several paintings she couldn't make out the details of were hung there. The ceiling, supported by two thick, barely hewn beams, was low. The ground was covered in a rough wood floor. Against the wall facing the door, a massive stone table—a substantial slate slab comprised the wide tabletop. Behind the table, as if glued to the wall, a wheel, sculpted from a piece of rock. As Sophie approached to look at it more closely, the flame went out, burning the tips of her fingers. She struck a second match and observed the sculpture. She immediately recognized a Mayan solar calendar, later taken up by the Aztecs. If she'd still had the slightest doubt, now it was no longer allowed. She shivered; it was taking tremendous effort to maintain her cool. Letting herself wallow in despair wouldn't help. She suddenly remembered a saying from Cicero, one of her only memories from the Latin proverbs her father tried to teach her when she'd been twelve: "*Dum anima est, spes esse dicitur*. As long as there is life, there is hope." Another sign—there would be no other reason for her to remember that phrase, which she hadn't recalled in forever, at such a dramatic moment. *Hold on, girl, they're looking for you, and you have to give them time.*

Chapter 67: *The Book of the Sun*

6:00 p.m. Pierre-Marie de Morot once more consulted the sheets on the table. Commissioner Mazure, Stéphane Rivera, Nadia Barka, and Antoine Dupas were awaiting his verdict. By calling Father de Valjoney, Mazure had managed to get Morot's private contact information. As luck would have it the historian was stopped at a red light a few hundred yards away from the police station when his phone had rung.

Antoine Dupas had started to study the document. However, he'd quickly proposed seeking out Pierre-Marie de Morot, distinguished Latinist and French specialist in monastic history from fifteenth- and sixteenth-century Europe.

Morot had been studying the document for more than twenty minutes, almost without commentary. When Rivera had asked him for his initial feelings after only ten minutes of reading, the historian had made it quite clear that the request was too soon.

Pierre-Marie de Morot smiled faintly, straightened up, and looked at everyone with a learned air.

"As I told you over the telephone, I'm not a specialist in Aztec culture. Furthermore, it would require days to study this book in detail. But I think I have a rather good mastery of the Latin language and that period in history. The name Fra Bartolomeo is unheard of. I do not pretend to know everything, but I've never seen that patronymic appear in the collections of the time. But that doesn't at all prove he didn't exist."

"Can you tell us about the contents?" asked Mazure.

"I'm getting there. *The Book of the Sun* deals with death. Death and how it can lead to renewed life."

"A sort of resurrection?" asked Rivera.

"Yes and no. Well, more like no. If you take resurrection in the biblical sense, it's based on the voluntary sacrifice of the Son of God who gives his life to save others. In the context of this collection, the Aztecs stole life from their victims in order to save or prolong their own. It would seem Fra Bartolomeo has done a sort of exegesis on these murderous rituals. From what little I've read, he's promoting a pseudoreligion based on purification by the blood of the innocent."

Silence answered Pierre-Marie de Morot's last words. The same connection occurred in the minds of the others in the room. Antoine Dupas was the one who said it out loud.

"Sartenas wants to save himself from his demons. He finds Boisregard, one of his old friends. And Boisregard, blinded by *The Book of the Sun* he discovered who knows where, encourages him, even pushes him to find his salvation in the blood of young women chosen at random."

"That could explain the deaths of Monica Revasti and Camille Saint-Forge, but in the case of Laure Déramaux, why take it that far?" continued Nadia Barka.

"Could it be that reading this document transformed Boisregard into a killer?" Dupas burst out, appalled. "Is it because he found this antiquity one day that my daughter's life is in danger right now?"

"I'm convinced it wasn't the discovery of *The Book of the Sun* that plunged Arsène Boisregard into this morbid mysticism!" interjected Morot.

"And what leads you to believe that?" asked Mazure, surprised by the historian's confidence.

Pierre-Marie de Morot took a deep breath and started in, "As I began to read these pages, I got a strange impression. Not because of their content—though certainly edifying, I can't judge the reliability. No, because of the writing itself. Then I discovered a detail that convinced me I'd been right. Monsieur Dupas, you read Latin, don't you?"

"Yes, it's a language I enjoy greatly."

"Reread the first lines, and tell me what you think!"

As Antoine Dupas grasped the first page, Rivera, annoyed, cut in, "Couldn't you get right to the point?"

"I'd just like to have confirmation of my reasoning. It will only take a minute."

Rivera sat back down, ultimately willing to sacrifice a minute to the beauty of the demonstration.

"It's very good quality Latin," the professor threw out.

"Exactly. Latin of outstanding classicism! If the text had been written by a monk in the sixteenth century, the Latin used should have been much simpler and marked by several Italian, Spanish, or French turns of phrase. But that is not the case."

"Couldn't we be dealing with a scholar who has perfectly mastered the Latin language?"

"I highly doubt it, but let's give him the benefit of the doubt. A second point then serves to annihilate that theory. Fra Bartolomeo explains at the beginning of the text that he set foot on the American continent on the day of the Feast of Christ the King."

"So?" asked Mazure.

"The Feast of Christ the King, which is a Christian feast, was only instituted in 1925 by Pope Pius XI. So this document is clearly false, written less than eighty years ago. Taking into account the precision of the information on Aztec customs, we can very well imagine Boisregard himself wrote it. So all your theories about Boisregard's influence on Sartenas, as well as our curator's propensity to love violence and blood, would be legitimized by his work."

"Fuck, that would mean we've got a real psychopath," concluded Rivera.

An officer knocked on the door and came into Mazure's office.

"Sorry to bother you, Commissioner, but we've just received some important information."

"Go ahead."

"The gendarmerie just sent us a snapshot. They caught Arsène Boisregard's car doing nearly forty-five miles per hour on the Sassenage exit."

"When?"

"Yesterday, early in the evening."

"Do you have a copy of the photo?"

The policeman handed over a photo. Mazure grabbed it and set it on the table. The participants looked at it avidly.

"That's him all right. And look, next to him—the passenger looks like Sartenas!"

"Our hypotheses are confirmed. They are indeed calling the shots together," announced Rivera. "This information will help us. It'll let us concentrate our search and our forces west of Grenoble. Given where they were photographed, they were definitely going either to Vercors or south of Chartreuse."

"They could also have been going toward Lyon," added Dupas.

"That's a possibility. But you told Captain Barka you'd heard Boisregard refer to a manor. We can assume it's located nearby. Still, we'll call our colleagues in Lyon."

Nadia's phone rang at that exact moment. She left the room to answer it.

"Nadia Barka."

"Good evening, this is Father de Valjoney."

Tension gripped the policewoman. She was expecting the priest's call to accelerate the investigation, hoping he could provide substantial aid.

"Good evening. I'm pleased you've called me back."

"I did promise. The idea that took root during our discussion convinced our bishop."

"And . . ."

"If I understood correctly, you think Boisregard and Sartenas are hidden in the area."

"Yes. And most likely in Vercors or Chartreuse. Boisregard's vehicle was spotted yesterday."

"Perfect. I asked our bishop to activate the church network to find those two individuals."

"Can you be more specific about your idea?"

"Of course. In each village, there's a church and parishioners. There isn't necessarily one priest per village, but the community is organized in such a way to compensate for that lack. Furthermore, those communities are active in the mountains. So I asked for the authorization to send photos of those two men to each hamlet to try and locate them."

"And you think you could get quick results?"

"I can only hope so, but I believe we have a good chance. I called in a little emergency team willing to contact the different local people in charge. If you tell me to focus our searches on Chartreuse and Vercors, we'll save time."

"But how can just a few people do these searches?"

"They'll also rouse their parishioners, who will then contact their neighbors. Sort of a grapevine, so to speak. It's almost six thirty. People are starting to come home. I think we'll be able to get results within two or three hours."

"Godspeed, Father, if you'll permit the expression," replied Nadia with a smile in her voice. "Give me your e-mail address, and I'll send you pictures of Boisregard and Sartenas within the minute."

"We're on the warpath."

"Thank you for your assistance."

"Saving a young woman's life and putting away those two monsters are sufficient arguments for us to participate in this search."

"Contact me as soon as you have information."

"Naturally. Can you also give me the phone number of one of your colleagues? In case your line is busy?"

"I'll give you Commissioner Mazure's. And I'm crossing my fingers your search ends quickly."

Chapter 68: Origins

"Fuck, it's stronger than you are! You couldn't help yourself!"

Dominique Sartenas had been angry for more than ten minutes, ever since he'd seen the black sedan come up the driveway leading to Fontfroide Manor's main entrance. Two men had gotten out and rung the bell. For a moment, Sartenas had panicked—the cops! Quickly, the fear had given way to anger. The two men hadn't come to arrest him but rather to attend that night's ceremony.

Arsène Boisregard welcomed them, then settled them in the sitting room before returning to talk with his old friend.

"But what were you thinking?" Sartenas asked. "That it's a public spectacle? No! I have to regain my peace of mind tonight! I have to chase away thirty years of nightmares that hound me on a regular basis. Don't you think for an instant I'm going to let those two assholes fuck up the moment I've been anticipating for such a long time!"

The curator let the doctor vent his spleen, then stopped him. "Under no circumstances is there a risk to you, be sure of that. I know what this moment means for you. And to be practical about it, I wouldn't risk losing the fifteen million dollars you promised me to satisfy those two men's morbid inclinations. Do you find that argument acceptable?"

Sartenas thought about it for a few seconds, then replied more calmly, "It holds up. So, tell me what they're doing here! They've come to dine at the château?"

"They'll have dinner, but you know perfectly well that isn't why they came. Those two men are fascinated by the works of Fra Bartolomeo. They're two important people in Grenoble's political and financial scene. I've known them for more than three years. So I took the liberty of inviting them to what will be for me the resurgence of Aztec practices. Tonight, the blood of an innocent will regenerate you but will also regenerate those who participate in the ceremony."

"Then there are others yet to arrive?"

"Just one person. But an important one."

"And who is it?"

"I can't tell you yet."

"This business is getting close to showbiz. Then again, you're the high priest. And if you assure me it presents no risk to my cure . . ."

"Not only is there no risk, but the presence of these men will only amplify the energy Quetzalcoatl dispenses to us."

Appeased by the historian's convincing tone, Sartenas recovered his serenity.

Boisregard left the room to join his guests. He'd often wondered about Sartenas's sincerity in believing Fra Bartolomeo's writings. He'd seen him again only recently, but he had known him very well during their shared years of studying medicine and up until he'd disappeared, shortly after Magali's death. Cabrade had always been a man without scruples, admirably hiding his contempt for his fellow man underneath a near-perfect charming exterior. He'd always refused to grant credibility to religious facts. He'd also considered all religious practice to be incurable weakness, but, as always, he didn't mention it to anyone. Boisregard had to be one of his only confidants, if not the only one.

The shock expressed by his friend at Magali's death had truly surprised the historian. He knew Cabrade had killed her, but he also knew the word *remorse* was absent from his vocabulary. Cabrade's overnight disappearance, even though he'd never been suspected, had shaken Boisregard. He'd lost his best friend.

Cabrade had heard about Boisregard and Fra Bartolomeo by sheer coincidence six months earlier from a Frenchman he'd encountered who was stationed in Miami. The doctor wasn't necessarily seeking out the company of his fellow countrymen, but he'd learned of a new arrival from Grenoble, and he'd had an evening to kill. He'd taken the Frenchman on a tour of Miami Beach's strip clubs and bars. After the sixth or seventh whiskey, the confessions had begun. And Boisregard's well-protected secret had spilled out on a mahogany table in a Florida club. Cabrade had quickly found his old companion's contact information. They'd chatted twice on the phone, and Cabrade had decided to return to France.

Before the doctor had called him, Boisregard had nearly forgotten Cabrade existed. At their reunion, Boisregard of course hadn't recognized him. It must have taken an effort of will on Cabrade's part to transform his handsome face into such a banal one. Or had the risk of his past catching up with him been so serious that he hadn't had a choice? After the reunion, the historian had been shaken by his friend's psychological changes. This cynical being was now tortured by inner demons. Cabrade and inner demons! He never would have believed it if he hadn't had the proof right in front of him. And even more surprising, the demon—or rather demoness—was named Magali. Year after year, an incomprehensible remorse had plagued Cabrade's dark soul.

Remorse for having killed his wife? Perhaps, but the doctor's recent confidences about his worldly escapades over the last thirty years had proved to Boisregard that the lives of others still weren't his main concern. Or remorse for not being able to keep the son Magali owed him? Arsène Boisregard had leaned toward that answer, but Cabrade descended into black rage each time he talked to him about it. Or did the memory of Magali stir complex motives buried deep in his unconscious? Boisregard didn't know. And really, he didn't need to know.

Boisregard had quickly understood that Cabrade was looking more for psychotherapy than for a dive into the Aztec underworld, but he knew the doctor was willing to do anything to chase away his terrors. Over the years, Boisregard had become well acquainted with the ways of the human soul. It was obvious to him the apparitions of Magali Dupré were merely the fruit of Cabrade's imagination. But he knew they were so deeply rooted that only a shock treatment could erase them. So he'd accepted the personal challenge, eager to test his power over his old friend's unconscious. Fra Bartolomeo would be his weapon! When Cabrade had spoken of financial compensation, Boisregard had at first declined. But then Cabrade had announced the amount, and he was no longer able to refuse. That had added some real spice to the challenge—his mindset had shifted from merely making a best effort to producing actual results.

As he opened the door to the sitting room, he was convinced of his action's success. And taking care of Sophie Dupas excited him terribly. Fra Bartolomeo had never forbidden mixing the useful with the agreeable—quite the contrary!

Chapter 69: The Revolt

Sophie recovered her composure. Her situation was dire, she knew that. But Monica Revasti's and Camille Saint-Forge's were more so. She knew she had only one thing left to do: buy time for the police force to pick up her trail. Of course it wouldn't be easy. Nadia had briefly recounted Laure Déramaux's ordeal, but those torture sessions had lasted for days and days. She just had to hang on for a few hours, just had to push back the moment when Sartenas would prepare to kill her.

She'd managed to shove that eventuality deep down inside her, so as not to be paralyzed with fear. She didn't know how long she could maintain control of herself—as long as possible, she hoped!

Sophie had kept the last match and slipped the razor blade inside a little pocket sewn into her skirt. She'd then climbed up on the table and settled there, cross-legged, facing the door—a position that would allow her to relax. She also hoped sitting this way would confuse her executioners when they came back for her.

Sophie no longer had any sense of the time. Her abductors had left her watch, but the room was still completely dark. She didn't want to use the last match she had to look at how much was left before the fateful moment. She knew the two previous victims had been killed around three o'clock in the morning. But would it be the same for her? She breathed deeply and forced herself to think of Julien. She now regretted not having called him back in the morning; she was convinced he was searching desperately for her. Underneath her athletic, mountaineer exterior, she was very romantic. She even sometimes read sentimental novels she bought at used bookstores. She wasn't proud of it, but from time to time she loved poring over those uncomplicated stories. At the end of those novels, the young woman in love found her Prince Charming. She forced herself to remain in that world of hope so as not to succumb to the horror of the moment.

An abrupt sound woke her from her fantasy—the noise of a key someone was sliding into the lock on the door of her jail. She sat up straight and laid her hands flat on her knees. Her eyes scrutinized the movement in the darkness. The door opened slowly, letting conversation filter in. A bright light flooded the room. By reflex, Sophie closed her eyes. She heard the visitors enter, then noticed their sudden silence. Sophie realized her position had surprised the new arrivals. She half opened her eyes, careful not to let herself be blinded. Four men walked into the room. She immediately recognized Boisregard and Sartenas. Then she observed the other two individuals. The first, short and bald, was a total stranger. The second, however, was familiar. Tall and solid, even portly, that man was looking at her insistently. Sophie's vision was adapting to the ambient light. She recognized him from the birthmark on his neck—Jacques Lèguezeaux. She'd met him at the party her father had thrown for his Palmes Académiques. Had Boisregard assembled a network, then? These men weren't hesitating to show themselves to her—of course, since she wasn't supposed to survive the night.

"So this is the one we'll use to make contact with Quetzalcoatl!" commented Gilles Ballat, the short bald man. "Pretty slip of a girl, young and athletic. Her blood undoubtedly contains the vigor of her youth."

"You're quite right, Gilles!" replied Boisregard. "Her heart will save Dominique from his demons, and her blood will give us the energy we sometimes cruelly lack. Youth should indeed serve the old! I believe that's in the Civil Code, isn't it?"

Hearty laughs answered his monologue. Sophie remained motionless.

Gilles Ballat approached the young woman. "Your blood will serve the representatives of France. And a lovely liquid surely flows through your body," he added, laying a hand on Sophie's bare thigh.

The slap that slammed into him took his breath away. He staggered, taken aback by their prisoner's reaction. "If my blood ever runs because of you, it'll be your curse."

Sophie was aware of the grandiloquence of her phrasing as she said it. But she got carried away by the anger boiling inside her.

"Who do you think you are? Descendants of the great Inca? Servants of the Feathered Serpent? You're nothing but perverted, sex-starved sickos who abuse girls you've abducted. So maybe you're going to rape me, torture me, and kill me? Be sure of one thing: neither my blood nor my heart will ever bring you the slightest comfort! I will be avenged by those who love me."

Sophie's discourse surprised the four men. Even Boisregard was caught off guard. He turned toward his guests and immediately noticed the effect of Sophie Dupas's words on the two men. The short man, outraged at having been humiliated, threw himself at the young woman. Anger made him misjudge his strength. Sophie dodged his fist, grabbed his arm, and pulled him toward her. Off balance, Ballat collapsed on top of her. In one second, she seized the razor blade in her skirt pocket and pressed it against her prisoner's throat. A thread of blood trickled from the man's throat as he screamed in terror.

"She's crazy, save me!"

"Let me leave, or I kill him!"

Boisregard had lost control of the situation. He looked at Sophie Dupas and read such determination in her eyes that he knew she wasn't bluffing. For the first time in years, he was no longer in charge of events.

"Listen to her, do as she says!" begged the financier.

Sophie had tightened her grip on the man, who was starting to have difficulty breathing. She dug the blade into the soft flesh of his neck.

"Let me go, now!"

Boisregard didn't know what to do. He couldn't let her leave—that would sign their death warrant. Neither could he let Ballat get his throat cut, because she would do it, he was certain. He had to buy some time.

"We're going to step aside and let you leave the room," he said calmly to Sophie. "Then we'll be able to talk calmly."

"There will be no discussion!" Sartenas cut in.

Everyone's gaze turned toward him. "The situation is clear, Arsène. These two assholes are not going to compromise my cure. So if she wants to kill him, let her kill him. But she's not getting out of here!"

Sartenas's gaze fell on Sophie's unblinking one. She'd instantly sized up the doctor's resolve. With him alive, she wouldn't leave this room. Gilles Ballat had begun to sob. She felt in her own body the convulsions of her human shield. No one was moving anymore. A tragic act was playing out, an act whose end was known. Boisregard broke the silence.

"The ways of Quetzalcoatl are sometimes mysterious. But perhaps he wants more blood than we imagined? Gilles, your sacrifice will please the Feathered Serpent."

"No, you can't do this to me!"

"I am not in control of events, Gilles. I'm just the toy of powers from the great beyond, like you."

Then he addressed Sophie. "Mademoiselle, he's yours. You're already on the sacrificial table. You have only to plunge your blade into his carotid artery."

Sophie looked at them, one after the other. Sartenas wasn't moving. He was in front of the exit and blocking it. The young woman noticed the scalpel he was holding in his hand. Boisregard had turned the tables—he'd unhesitatingly condemned one of his guests. As for Lèguezeaux, he seemed to find the scene amusing. Discouragement crept over her. She had to think, and quickly. With simple pressure, she could kill the man she was holding against her. And then? The element of surprise had vanished, and her weapon was paltry. In close combat, she could just claw her adversaries.

The three men were starting to move. They were backing up slowly toward the door: she immediately realized their strategy. They were going to leave her alone in the dark with Ballat. They were letting her decide the financier's fate. For them, he was already dead!

Useless! He was useless to her now. For a moment, she'd believed she'd get out. But nothing was negotiable. She was seized by a furious desire to bleed out the swine she held prisoner. She could still see his lecherous gaze when he'd put his hand on the top of her thigh. Her right hand, which was holding the razor blade, trembled, again pressing on the carotid artery. The man screamed and fainted from fear.

Sophie pushed the inert body into the middle of the room. She might have killed him if it would have saved her life. But at that moment, the death of this man brought her nothing. She wasn't like them. She wasn't going to kill to satisfy her urges.

Boisregard had left the room. He came back, weapon in hand.

"We're going to take our friend back. I'd privately wagered you would kill Gilles in the heat of anger. In the end, only your blood will save us tonight, my dear Sophie."

Sartenas pulled Ballat's still-unconscious body toward the exit. "We'll leave you to think about your actions. We'll come back in a few hours. You'll be the heroine of the evening."

Chapter 70: Nothing to Report

8:30 p.m. The tension was at its peak in the briefing room. All the information that came in was checked with the utmost speed. Sartenas had been seen by witnesses throughout the département, and even as far away as Gex and Alpes-de-Haute-Provence. The calls they received led nowhere, but the policemen continued their systematic verification. They knew the passing hours were bringing Sophie Dupas closer to death, and they couldn't neglect any clue.

Father de Valjoney still didn't have reliable information to give them. All the testimony he'd received had already passed through two filters: the individual parishes and the diocese. He didn't want to give useless leads to the policemen.

Antoine and Madeleine Dupas had stayed on site. Their defeated expressions fed the growing anxiety that gnawed at Julien. He was convinced they'd find her trail, but when? The passing time was distilling the poison of failure within him. A few lines of Baudelaire he'd learned in high school came to mind, a gloomy premonition:

> Three thousand six hundred times an hour, Second
> Whispers: Remember! — *Immediately*
> With his insect voice, Now says: I am the Past,

And I have sucked out your life with my filthy trunk!

His phone rang. He answered it in an instant, full of hope. It was Denise Lombard, his adoptive mother . . . no, not his adoptive mother, his real mother, the one who had always been at his side from the first hours of his life. He'd neglected his parents these last few days. Julien decided to accept his mother's invitation to dinner. The wait was stressing him out, and seeing his parents might allow him to recover some minimal calm. They'd probably know how to instill in him the courage he was starting to lack. And Captain Barka had promised to call him if something happened.

He pulled himself together, said good-bye to Sophie's parents and the policemen, then left the premises. Nadia caught him before he could exit the building.

"Stay hopeful, Julien. I know from experience anything is still possible. I'll contact you as soon as we get a lead on Sophie. I'm just asking you to do the same."

"What do you want me to bring you?"

"I'm sure Magali Dupré hasn't had her last word."

"I thought so, too. But not a single sign."

"We still have a little time. She'll know what to do. Just be available. Sophie needs you!"

Nadia Barka took his hand and squeezed it. The warmth of the handshake transmitted the extra energy he needed.

"Thanks, Nadia. You can count on me."

Nadia watched Julien leave. She understood his distress. Nothing was worse than being condemned to inaction. She consulted her phone's messages. She still hadn't gotten the confirmation she'd been waiting for since her discussion with Aurélien Costel. She called again but heard only rings, then voice mail. She left another message, hoping he had the information she was looking for and could call her back that evening. It was a whole lot of *if,* but she needed to check on what the restaurant owner had told her.

10:30 p.m. Silence reigned in the room, just barely disturbed by the clinking of the dessert plates Emmanuel Lombard placed on the table.

"I made Far Breton, Julien," murmured his mother. "It's what you wanted me to make when you were sad. Eating it always helped lift your spirits."

Julien smiled weakly at this evocation. As a small child, he'd always considered Far with prunes to be a magic potion. He didn't really want any, but took some to please his mother. They'd had a long talk during the meal, but Julien hadn't been able to tear his eyes away from the wall clock. He'd called Nadia four times: no new leads. The police and the gendarmes had teamed up to launch neighborhood inquiries, but the territory to cover was so vast!

"I'm convinced we'll be able to decipher Magali Dupré's message," his father said again.

"But I've already pondered it, Papa. I didn't find anything."

"So start again. Magali isn't contacting you so that you can count the corpses. You may not know what to do, but she will. Put yourself at her disposal."

"That's what Father de Valjoney and Nadia told me."

"Nadia?"

"Captain Barka, who's in charge of the search. You're probably right. But I don't believe in it enough anymore."

"Listen, you told us the other girls were killed around three in the morning. If you count one hour for the police to get there, that still leaves us more than three hours to locate Sophie."

"That's true. Will you lend me your armchair?"

"It's yours," replied his father, tenderly mussing his hair.

Julien settled into an old worn leather lounge chair. When he was younger, he'd only been allowed to sit there while watching soccer matches or James Bond movies with his father. He no longer knew where that tradition had come from, but he loved this chair, where his father often sat in the evening to read detective novels, which he then recounted for his family.

His parents surrounded him, providing the calm he needed. Julien closed his eyes, delving into the depths of his memories, determined to find the clues Magali Dupré had undoubtedly planted.

Chapter 71: René Pelloux

Midnight. A man whose features were marked by life in the great outdoors knocked several times on the heavy wooden door. He looked at the old woman standing by his side. She had a black scarf over her hair despite the mildness on this first night of summer.

Typically at that late hour, these two visitors would already have been in bed a long time. But this evening was unusual. The man knocked again. He heard steps inside the house, then light appeared when the occupant opened up. The full moon cast a soft glow on the village and the mountains, creating a crispness to the landscape.

"Is the priest in?" asked the man standing on the doorstep.

"No, he's not here right now. But I can reach him at any time," replied Pierre Mollard, looking at the couple before him. "Come in, please."

The man hesitated a moment, but the woman pushed him into the parish house.

"Ah, hello, Monsieur Pelloux, I hadn't recognized you in the dark. And you have your mother with you. Please come sit down and have something to drink."

The man no longer hesitated and headed toward the table covered in oilcloth. He took a wooden chair and sat down heavily. The old woman remained standing beside her son.

"I can make herbal tea, and there's a bottle of genepy. Please sit down, Madame Pelloux."

The woman refused with a movement of her chin. Pierre Mollard took out three glasses. He filled them with liqueur and served his guests. No words were exchanged before the drinks had been smelled, tasted, and savored.

"It's good!" concluded René Pelloux.

Pierre Mollard, member of the Villard-de-Lans parish and active support to the priest who officiated on the plateau, waited for his guest to speak first. He'd known René Pelloux for twenty years. He appreciated the man, even if their personal convictions diverged. He knew why he was there that night with his mother instead of resting in his bed. He also knew he had to let Pelloux broach the subject.

"Are you the one making it?" asked the farmer.

"No, the priest," replied the retiree, still holding the bottle in his hand. "Another little drop?"

"I wouldn't say no!" accepted Pelloux, holding out his glass. "Your priest knows how to do good things!"

"He was born here, like you. He knows our mountain plants," concluded Pierre Mollard as he filled the glass anew.

A minute ticked by. Each swallow of liqueur was calibrated, then appreciated. The farmer clicked his tongue, then put his glass down on the table. He looked at his mother, who nodded her head to encourage him to speak.

"Look, I wanted to see the priest about the photos going around the village tonight."

"The priest charged me with gathering all the witness statements in his absence. I'm very interested to hear what you have to say."

"Fine. I was in the middle of finishing dinner and watching TV with Mother. It's not that I have too much time to watch, but we like the game show that comes on in the evening," he commented, a bit embarrassed.

"I watch it, too, when I have the chance," Mollard encouraged him.

"Ah, very good . . . it was around nine thirty when the Guillaudin girl knocked on the door. Mother went to answer it and brought her into the dining room."

"A good kid! She's Sandrine's daughter," added Mathilde Pelloux, as if to vouch for the veracity of the facts to come.

Pierre Mollard nodded. He knew he had to respect his guests' rhythm. René Pelloux was a fine man—taciturn and rough, but ready to be of service when the need arose. Pelloux inherited from his father an anticlericalism that the years and the decline of the Church in the towns and villages hadn't attenuated. Pierre Mollard imagined how much effort it must have taken the farmer to come to such a place and understood the reason for his mother's presence.

Pelloux continued. "She came with two photos, and she put them on the table and asked us if we knew them. I looked at them for a long time. One of their faces rang a bell. So I thought about it." The farmer fell silent, as if thinking about it all over again. "I looked at it some more. I was sure I'd seen his mug recently, but dammit, where? I asked Mother to turn down the volume on the set so I could think in peace. Sandrine's little girl left me one photo so that I could take my time. And she left after asking us to come see the priest if we had a lead."

"So is this murderer story true?" asked Mathilde Pelloux, already knowing the answer.

"Unfortunately, very much so. One of those two men, or both of them, has already killed two young girls and is holding a third.

Everyone who could help was asked to assist the police in apprehending them before the worst could happen."

Then Mollard refocused the discussion on the farmer's testimony. "So, Monsieur Pelloux, what did your thinking turn up?"

"After a few minutes, I remembered." He took out the photo of Boisregard and put it on the tablecloth. "The brown-haired one, there. I saw him this morning."

Pierre Mollard shifted in his chair, but he forced himself not to interrupt his guest.

"I was taking a little walk with Milou, my dog. And I saw this guy go running by, jogging, as they say. Well, personally, I find life is tiring enough as it is without adding to it. But it's something city boys do, and I'm not one to judge! I was in a good mood this morning. I had a sick cow that had recovered overnight. So I waved at him. Well, believe it or not, he ignored me, as if I didn't exist. I saw his eyes turn toward me, but nothing! Rotten bastard. So I stared at him, and that's how I kept his face in my head. That's him, no doubt!"

"If he had responded to your greeting, you wouldn't have memorized him?"

"Probably not! I've come across impolite people before, but he shouldn't have been."

"His impoliteness might be fatal to him."

"I hope so. Your priest would say it's God's justice. But it's only that I still have good eyes, and no one should disrespect me."

"I don't know if it's God's justice, Monsieur Pelloux, but I know your testimony is truly a benediction. Where did you run across him this morning?"

"I was over by the Marcel woods, you know, the one where they got the huge boar this winter. But I don't know how many miles a jerk like that could cover."

Mathilde Pelloux interjected, "But he didn't want to say anything at first, this stubborn mule!"

"I've never sold anyone out, Mother, least of all to priests!"

The old woman didn't listen to her son's commentary. "It took me two hours to change his mind. When this ass finally understood the poor kidnapped girl could have been his daughter Valérie, he came to his senses. *I* know he's a good boy, my René."

"His testimony can help save a life. From the bottom of my heart, I thank both of you."

"What's going to happen now?" asked Pelloux.

"I'm going to inform the diocese, who will immediately contact the police. All the searches are going to be concentrated on Villard. One last question: have you seen this man before?"

"No, never. But as you know, there are a lot of tourists when summer comes. What if you had to remember everybody!"

"Indeed, you're right."

Pierre Mollard escorted René Pelloux and his mother to the door. Then he rushed to the telephone.

Chapter 72: Contact

It was midnight, but Sophie had no idea what time it might be. She was waiting. She hoped for deliverance, but feared death—a terrible death. Sartenas's determination had terrified her. This wasn't a man before her, but a beast.

The reaction of the one named Ballat, who had tried to take advantage of her, disgusted her, but she understood his thought process. She knew she was rather pretty, and the situation must have excited the pervert within him. But Sartenas's reaction was illogical. He wanted her death; he was willing to sacrifice everything for it. But why? When Nadia had told her about the torment Laure Déramaux had endured, she'd immediately imagined extreme sadistic practices. A group of madmen getting off on seeing a human being suffer, taking pleasure in dominating a woman.

But here? He wanted her heart. He wanted to devour it! A demented travesty of communion. Why? Why her?

Sophie refocused on more positive thoughts, or at least less negative ones. She had set a course of action. No wallowing in dark thoughts that could lead her to abandon all hope, or even succumb to madness.

There was still a chance, however tiny, she could be found in time. She had to hang on to that, never let go. She remembered a hike she'd gone on several years ago in the Alps. She'd headed out at the end of the season with a group of friends. The weather was splendid, but by the next day, they'd been confronted with a snowstorm the weatherman hadn't predicted. A series of events had separated her from her companions, and she'd found herself alone—alone in the snow and the cold. At first she'd walked aimlessly, gripped with fear. Then, conscious that her approach was futile, she'd taken control of the situation. She'd constructed a shelter out of the snow, protecting herself from the wind and cold. Curled up in a ball without moving, conserving the heat that kept her alive, she'd waited more than twelve hours for the snowfall and wind to calm. Then the storm had lifted as suddenly as it had descended, leaving in its place a limpid sky. Then she'd left her makeshift igloo, and the beauty of the immaculate mantle of snow reflecting the rays of the rising sun had awed her. How could death be this beautiful?

The future! Only the future could save her. She shouldn't turn to her past; she shouldn't think about the last few days, her last conversations with Julien. She knew he was the love of her life. Attentive, intelligent, and funny, he made her laugh, and that was priceless. She decided to tell herself about the days and weeks that would follow her liberation. Sophie had always loved fairy tales. She would comfort herself with these now, even if she didn't yet know whether her own Prince Charming would arrive in time.

She stretched out in a corner of the room, and fatigue began to creep over her. Suddenly, it seemed as though someone was calling to her. The voice wasn't coming from outside, but from within her. She sat listening. At first weak and distant, it grew more and more audible. Julien, it was Julien! Was she dreaming? She pinched herself, and the pain confirmed she was awake. *Sophie, hang in there. We're all looking for you. But you're going to have to help us.* Sophie couldn't see anything. She heard only her friend's voice. *Magali is with me. Let yourself go . . . let yourself go . . .* Overcome by a strange lethargy, Sophie lost awareness of the reality around her.

Chapter 73: Action

Captain Barka hung up, immensely excited. She ran back into the briefing room from the hallway, where she'd gone to use the phone quietly.

"Boisregard has been located!" she announced.

The background conversation noise miraculously ceased.

"Villard-de-Lans. He was spotted in Villard-de-Lans this morning. That matches up with the dates and the photo that was taken yesterday on the road to Sassenage."

"How reliable is this information?" inquired Mazure.

"According to de Valjoney, the witness is sure of himself, and the priest gives credence to it," the young woman responded immediately.

The discussions picked up where they left off. Finally, they had a strong clue, which would allow them to significantly advance the investigation.

"Did you get a more precise location for Boisregard?" asked the commissioner.

"Unfortunately, we don't have the exact location. The witness encountered him while Boisregard was out running. He was north of the village. But we don't have more detailed information," Nadia said regretfully.

"We'll make do," concluded the commissioner. "Rivera, wake up the town hall in Villard for me. I want to know the names of all the property owners who could have a manor in that municipality. It's twenty after midnight—I want the information within an hour at the latest. For my part, I'm going to contact the gendarmerie so they can move in on the Vercors plateau."

"The GIPN intervention group can be there very quickly as well," added Rivera. "They've teamed up with the gendarmes. Normally it's not in their jurisdiction, but they have carte blanche."

"So much the better. Just tell them to avoid landing a helicopter in Villard. Sartenas knows he's being tracked, and that would put the Dupas girl's life in immediate danger," advised Mazure.

"Understood, Commissioner. We're also going to start heading up to the Vercors plateau. Fortin, take your usual group with you and get out of here. We'll contact you en route to assign objectives. Delsol, same thing. Mourad, you gather up the response armament. Then you'll take the group assigned to you and form the third patrol with Drancey. I'm staying here with Garancher and the others to continue to refine Boisregard's location."

"Which car did you put me in?" asked Captain Barka.

Commissioner Mazure answered for Rivera, "You are wounded and on sick leave, Captain Barka. You can stay here to lend a hand to the home team."

Stunned, Nadia looked at him. She didn't understand the decision her superior had just made. "It's all right, Commissioner. I'll hold up. The doc gave me everything I need, and I can guarantee you I'll do my job correctly."

"My decision is final, Captain."

"But, Commissioner, you've been working with me for six years. You know you can trust me, don't you?"

"I have every confidence in you, Captain Barka. But I'm afraid you're overestimating your strength. You took a bullet in the shoulder blade five days ago, and you can't be said to have rested. Your mission is to stay here with Rivera and keep Sophie Dupas's family company."

"Bullshit!" shouted the young woman, overwhelmed with irritation. "I'm on sick leave? Then make do without me!" Furious, she left the room without a backward glance. Madeleine Dupas followed her and caught up to her in the hallway.

"Captain Barka, we need you."

"You have a whole team looking for your daughter, Madame Dupas. They're competent and will find every clue there is to find. You don't need me."

"Listen, my daughter talked to me about you. I don't know what you've told each other, because Sophie was always rather secret about her private relationships. But she really admires you."

"And that's why I don't want Captain Barka out there," added Alain Mazure, who had just joined them in the hallway. "For that reason and because of the Déramaux case."

"Go on, then, explain all your thinking," replied Nadia sarcastically.

"There's a strong suspicion Boisregard is Laure Déramaux's killer. You've taken that case very much to heart, and you've always sworn to find the girl's murderer. And there he is, maybe! So I want to avoid all risk of personal vendettas. If Sophie Dupas is close to you as well, that can only reinforce my decision."

The icy glare full of contempt that his colleague shot him worried the commissioner.

"Because you think I'm an amateur, that I'm going to satisfy my thirst for vengeance ahead of my professional duty! You probably imagine that I'm going to compromise the mission just to get Boisregard at the end of my gun! I've been a cop for fifteen years,

Mazure, and I've never screwed up an investigation. I've had some hard times with colleagues or superiors, but I've never been humiliated like this. So you can go fuck yourself!"

She walked with long strides out of the police station. Angry tears blurred her vision.

Chapter 74: Introductions

The sound of an approaching engine caught Boisregard's ear. He went over to the glass door and pulled aside the heavy velvet curtain. A luxury sedan was heading up the driveway that led to the manor entrance. The driver pulled up in front of the stairs, then turned off the engine, returning the thick night to its quietness.

A man, white shirt and jacket hanging carelessly from his shoulders, got out of his Audi A7 Sportback. He pushed back his sunglasses—of doubtful utility at that hour of the night—atop his impeccably coiffed hair. He checked his appearance in the side mirror, grabbed his overnight bag out of the trunk, and climbed the stairs to the residence at a leisurely pace. Boisregard left the sitting room to meet him. He returned with his guest thirty seconds later.

"This is Thomas Simon-Renouard. We're now all present for tonight's ceremony."

Sartenas was surprised by the presence of this journalist who wrote features for magazine celebrity pages. He observed Lèguezeaux and Ballat, who went over to greet Simon-Renouard. They seemed to know each other. The surgeon wondered for a moment what reason Boisregard could have found to bring such a man into his confidence, but he quickly lost interest in the question. It wasn't his problem. He wouldn't see them again after he'd sacrificed Sophie Dupas and eaten his fill of her still warm and beating heart. His thinking had evolved over the course of the evening. Although the presence of the historian's guests had at first irritated him profoundly, he'd changed his mind. In the end, the staging of himself in the role of high priest quite suited him. It reminded him of his younger days, when he'd officiated from the center of a court of admirers. He'd control the situation, which would avoid any potential blunder connected to one of the participants' fantasies. He had a very cold, even surgical view of humanity and its defects. He didn't deny himself his vices, but he knew them and knew how far he could take them. He had no illusions about the rottenness that lurked within him, and that gave him a certain advantage over those who possessed the same vices but couldn't control the effects.

He greeted the journalist in turn when the man extended his hand like a precious gift. Sartenas couldn't stand this type of individual, but he decided to remain courteous.

"You must be the famous Dr. Sartenas Arsène told me about. The butcher of Grenoble! You're making the front page, old boy! I have colleagues who would sell their souls to interview you. Notably Daphné Fergusson, you know, the new bombshell anchor on channel 2. I'm the one who put her there," added the journalist with a wink meant to be conspiratorial.

The surgeon looked him up and down icily. "I don't watch that sort of program, Monsieur Simon-Renouard, and I am totally uninterested in sexy stories about people who pretend to deliver the news. As for your Daphné, had I met her, channel 2 would have gained in notoriety. She doubtless would have joined the last two women I welcomed into my home who are no longer capable of witnessing anything."

His courtesy had its limits! In a few hours, he'd no longer have to rub elbows with the man. He left the four men to their conversation and moved off toward the window. He pushed lightly on a shutter. The moon was just clearing the mountains, dramatically lighting the Vercors plateau and foothills. The surgeon gazed at the heavenly body, fascinated. In thirty years of drifting around the world, he'd never seen the moon lavish such luminosity. He interpreted it as a sign of encouragement from the gods—or demons from hell. What did he care!

Sartenas had spent the evening with Boisregard and his two disciples. First they'd had to get Ballat back on his feet, which had been quick. Then they'd had to convince him there'd been no danger when they'd abandoned him to the girl, a decidedly more complicated task. Sartenas had sincerely admired how Boisregard had managed to persuade Ballat in less than half an hour.

The historian had then done an exegesis of a passage from *The Book of the Sun*, at which point the group had decided on the course of the ceremony. Ballat had become a ball of hate and proposed only painful torments—his sexual arousal had dropped to zero. But Sartenas distrusted the financier. The victim's suffering wasn't an end in itself, just the consequence of the sacrifice he had to carry out. And he'd already met guys like Ballat during his S&M sprees. Their sick excitement could quickly become a handicap for the group.

These discussions about the next steps, however, had had a positive effect on Sartenas's psyche. Magali hadn't managed to penetrate his awareness nor disturb him just hours before his approaching liberation. He hadn't left her a crack to slip through. They had to go on. He moved closer to the four disciples of Fra Bartolomeo so that he could join in the conversation.

"Gentlemen, I suggest a light dinner before carrying out the sacrifice that will give us all the surplus energy we anticipate," Boisregard said. "Let's move to the dining room. A cold buffet is waiting for us."

After the guests were seated around a richly stocked table, Boisregard spoke again. "Tonight we are celebrating the summer solstice. Thus we will invoke two spirits and not just one— Quetzalcoatl as well as Huitzilopochtli, the god of sun and war. We will feed them on a young woman's vigorous blood so that they will then provide us with their regenerative energy. Tonight, Quetzalcoatl will also chase from Dominique's soul a spirit that has tormented him for years. This will be a resurrection for him."

Their eyes turned, questioningly, toward Sartenas, who remained silent.

"Dominique, I think you can offer some explanation to our friends. They'll only better understand the sacrificial ceremony you will be conducting."

Sartenas reflected for a few seconds. The risk he ran in telling his story was limited—he'd already made an appointment at an Italian clinic to have his face modified a second time, then change his identity. So he was going to tell them his truth, the only one that existed for him. In the end, bringing his partners for this night into the secret of his quest would render them only more receptive to the ceremony he was going to lead in less than an hour.

The doctor recounted his adventure, the suffering his wife was inflicting on him, how he'd found his friend Boisregard. He knew how to hold his audience spellbound. The tale of the abductions and murders of his victims greatly impressed the three guests. When he'd finished his story, Simon-Renouard asked him a question.

"Your story is fascinating, Doctor Sartenas. Just one question: Why did you leave the bodies in those places with religious connotations? Why not abandon them in the forest, or some more accessible place?"

The doctor took several seconds before answering. "As you might have guessed, I didn't choose those places randomly. My wife was a believer, and she tried to convert me. It amused me at the beginning, but she had no idea what she'd yoked herself to," he added with a grin.

"So it's a sort of vengeance?" proffered Lèguezeaux.

"Let's call it a provocation. She comes to torture me in my most private spaces. I return to her the fruit of her labor, where her God has taken possession of men's souls. She'd turned into a sort of mystic during the last months of her pregnancy. As if my presence had become unbearable to her!" he added, slamming his fist on the table.

Boisregard stared anxiously at the doctor. Sartenas couldn't have an attack now. But then he calmed down.

"You must know the cathedral's baptistery and the Church of Saint-Laurent are the two most ancient religious places in the city," he continued. "So I wanted to strike at the root of her faith. It also made a big impression on the public."

"And what do you plan to do with Sophie Dupas?" interjected Ballat.

"She'll have a magnificent sepulchre: the Church of Saint-André, built in the thirteenth century. I'll leave her body under the portico, and the circle will be closed. Magali will have left me for good and will have eternity to meditate on the consequences of her betrayal."

Chapter 75: *In Nomine Patris*

Nadia took a fresh cigarette out of her pack and lit it nervously. She was walking along the boulevard to try to calm her anger. But she knew she wouldn't manage to do it. She was one of the best cops in Grenoble, and Mazure's lack of confidence disgusted her. Yes, she dreamed about coming face-to-face with the murderer, but she wouldn't have let personal vengeance take the upper hand. The only things that counted were finding Sophie alive and collaring Boisregard and Sartenas. And here she was on a sidewalk like an idiot!

No, he wouldn't get away from her again! She set off toward the police station once more. She greeted the guard with a smile, then went discreetly to her office. The response teams had already left, and Mazure was in the briefing room. She gathered up her sidearm and ammunition and vacated the premises. Her vehicle was three blocks away. She was going to head up to Villard-de-Lans, too.

Her phone rang as she was opening her car door. She looked at the number but couldn't remember seeing it before.

"Nadia Barka here."

"Nadia, this is Julien Lombard!" answered a voice she could hear quavering with agitation.

"Julien, what's going on?"

"Magali came to me!"

The police officer felt agitation come over her as well. Fate was putting her back on track. All was not lost, then.

"What did she tell you?"

"She didn't speak to me, but I saw Sophie! She's still alive. And she showed me where she was."

"Perfect, I'm coming to get you."

"There's still a sizable problem," replied Julien.

"What?"

"I've seen what the building where she's being held looks like, but I don't know what village it's in."

"Villard-de-Lans."

"Pardon?"

"It's in Villard-de-Lans, we just got the intel. You'll know how to find the house?"

"Yes. Don't ask me how, but I know she'll guide me to her!" Julien exulted.

"Give me your address, and I'll be right there."

Denise and Emmanuel Lombard gazed at their son with the same question. They'd understood from the tone of the conversation that the search had progressed in the course of the last hour.

"She's in Villard. Nadia's coming to get me, and we're going up there."

His mother was torn between two feelings—the fear of seeing her son confronted with killers, and the hope of seeing Sophie rescued. She'd realized during the evening Sophie's importance for Julien. She understood all the risks he was going to run, even if she feared them. She reasoned with herself, saying he'd be accompanied by experienced police forces. He'd guide them to where Sophie was being held, then the professionals would intervene. She was worrying over nothing.

Julien went into his old room. She heard him rummaging in his closet. He came back with a large-bladed knife in his hand.

"What is that?" asked his mother.

"Your father's hunting knife. He gave it to me for my eighteenth birthday, told me it would be of use one day. I doubted it at the time, but he was right."

Denise Lombard stared at her son. She saw a determination in his face that she'd never seen before. Julien was an even-tempered boy with a charming sense of humor. He was always willing to be of service, even if it meant sacrificing some of his own interest. She immediately knew that wouldn't be the case tonight. He put on a pair of jeans that had been lying in his closet for years and a pair of sneakers, and attached the knife to his belt. Emmanuel Lombard pulled his son to him and gave him an emotional hug.

A horn sounded.

"I have to go. Nadia's waiting for me."

"Good luck, my son," murmured his father.

He knew Julien might run into his biological father. And even if he hated him for what he was subjecting Sophie to, Emmanuel suspected his son would not emerge unscathed from such a confrontation—if he emerged. That thought crushed his heart like a vise.

"See you tomorrow," replied Julien to compel fate. Then he looked at his parents, smiled, and left the room.

The car flew through the Grenoble suburbs. Nadia Barka was concentrating on her driving. She passed Sassenage City Hall at nearly seventy miles per hour, then headed up to Vercors with the mastery of a champion racer. Julien hadn't understood why they were going up there alone, but faced with the driver's silence he hadn't tried to find out. Besides, he didn't really care. He was aware that tonight he had the most determined of allies.

While skirting the village of Lans-en-Vercors, Nadia reopened the conversation.

"We'll be there in ten minutes. I haven't been very talkative, but I had to concentrate on the road."

"Have you ever done rally car racing?"

"Yes, just after entering the police force. Happy that was useful to us tonight! Look, here's the deal. The gendarmerie and the police are already on the scene, but they don't know where Boisregard and Sartenas are hiding in the village. So your presence is indispensable."

"Where are they?"

"Who?"

"Your colleagues!"

"We're not meeting up. You and I are looking for the house, and when we find it, we'll tell them."

Julien looked at the policewoman in surprise. "Is all that in the rules?"

"It's in mine."

"Okay, suits me."

Nadia turned toward the man at her side. She could no longer see the worried young man she'd met the first day. She sensed he was determined and without qualms. Perhaps she would have to curb his enthusiasm. Mazure would see that his own decision had not only been bad but also counterproductive if she had followed it.

The police officer's phone rang. Nadia took it out of her interior jacket pocket and looked at the number on the screen. She swerved but quickly righted the trajectory.

"I don't know who's calling me at this hour. Answer for me."

He picked up and listened.

"An Urbain Biddère wants to talk to you."

She braked suddenly and parked the car on the side of the road. She held out her hand, then listened more than she talked. She spent two minutes on the phone. Julien watched the seconds tick by on the lighted dashboard. When the numbers flashed two o'clock, he felt his anxiety mount. He'd chased away the fear by leaping into action, but it was coming back. The two previous murders had happened around three o'clock, and they were only sixty short minutes away from the fatal moment.

Lost in his thoughts, he was glued to the seat when Nadia pulled out onto the road again. He turned toward her. She looked at him, satisfied and reassuring.

"What was worth losing those precious minutes?" Julien asked, annoyed.

The young woman didn't lose her smile.

"I think we have some good news. It's not one hundred percent certain, but it would be very good news."

Julien looked at her, astonished. What good news could this Biddère have given her at two o'clock in the morning? "Well, tell me!"

"There's a very good chance Dominique Cabrade—or Sartenas, whichever you prefer—is not your father!"

Julien's mouth gaped; he was overcome by this news. It took him several seconds to realize the consequences of the information the police officer had just given him. He was suddenly relieved of a great weight. He had no connection to that psychopath! He wasn't the son of a pervert, a killer! He wouldn't have his father before him, but a wretched killer, a killer who had murdered his mother.

"And who is my father?"

"As I told you, I have only strong suspicions and . . ."

"Cut it short, Nadia! Every second counts! Who is my biological father?"

"Aurélien Costel."

After a few seconds of reflection, he remembered that name. "My mother's childhood friend?"

"The same."

"And where did you get that?"

"I met him today at his restaurant. When he arrived, his face seemed familiar to me, but I didn't realize right away it was you he resembled. We had a long conversation. He told me he'd slept with Magali nine months before her disappearance."

"But are you sure he's my father?"

"Scientifically speaking, no! But Aurélien Costel sent me a photo of himself at thirty. I forwarded your picture, Cabrade's, and Costel's to Urbain. Urbain is a physiognomist in a big casino: he's a wiz. For him, there's no doubt."

The young woman noticed her companion's bewilderment. She decided to provide him with a few more clarifications. "According to Costel, Magali wasn't happy with her husband. One night, she came to confide in him. One thing led to another, they rediscovered their bond, and ended the evening in each other's arms."

"But why did she go back to Cabrade? Why didn't she ask for a divorce?"

"It appears she wanted to try to save her marriage in spite of everything. She met with Aurélien once more, then she was held hostage by her husband. Aurélien never managed to see her again before her death. But the most important part of this story is that bastard who killed your mother and kidnapped Sophie has no blood relationship to you. That's what's important for us tonight.

Focus on that. We have to save your future wife—it's been a long time since I was invited to a wedding I really wanted to attend."

Julien's eyes widened. Nadia burst out laughing. It was the first time he'd seen her so relaxed, only a few minutes away from the action. That calmed him down and restored all his confidence. He forced himself not to think about what Sophie might endure so that he could concentrate on action.

Chapter 76: Let the Games Begin

Sophie struck her last match and looked at her watch in the flickering flame. It was two o'clock. She knew it wouldn't be long now. She remembered perfectly the dreams Julien had told her about. The crimes had always taken place between three and four o'clock in the morning. But contrary to the previous victims, she had two extra pieces of information. First, she knew the fate awaiting her. Second, she'd just set on her trail a team of men and women who would know how to do battle with her captors.

So she had only one thing left to do: stall for time! Every second she could wrench from her executioners would be a step closer to her survival. She just hoped to gain enough. Only that perspective kept her from losing her footing. She still held a tiny part of her destiny in her hands.

She'd studied the question from every angle. Ballat's flushed and lustful face had imposed on her the only option she still had. Abandoning her body to that man, or to the others, would help time play out in her favor. She'd even decided to provoke them, to do anything to postpone the moment when Sartenas would want to tear her heart out. Like a drunken metronome, she teetered between excitement and panic. Excitement at the thought she might get out of this cellar alive, and panic when imagining what she was going to have to do . . . or try to do, because nothing assured her they would want her proffered body. Sophie was now reduced to hoping her abductors would be excited enough to want to take advantage of her! What an unbelievable situation! But she was willing to pay any price for several minutes of life. Shivering with disgust, she'd spread her blouse wide open.

Sophie tried to take a step back from events as she'd envisioned them. She forced herself to empty her mind. Inaction gave free rein to her anxieties. She stood up, then started doing some stretches. An image straight out of her childhood suddenly imposed itself on her. She saw herself reading *Prisoners of the Sun* on her father's lap, admiring Tintin for doing calisthenics mere hours before his sacrifice by the Incas. She just hoped the story would end the same way. She laughed nervously. She was in between laughter and tears— closer to tears, really. No, she wouldn't get away. Julien, Nadia, and the others would arrive, but too late.

The sound of the key turning in the lock brought her immediately back to reality. *Be brave, Sophie, you don't have to show them you're afraid. Your future depends on you.*

Boisregard turned on the light as he pushed open the door. Sophie Dupas was sitting in a corner of the room, blinded, hands over her eyes. He put his sidearm back in his jacket pocket and hurried over to her with Simon-Renouard. He didn't want to find himself in a situation like the one they'd experienced a few hours earlier. They searched her completely: no blade, however small, could have escaped them. The young woman kindled shocks of violent emotion in Boisregard, but he was Fra Bartolomeo's trustee. His primary role was to give life to *The Book of the Sun* and not to let loose his sexual arousal. Thomas Simon-Renouard didn't have the same preoccupations. His hands caressed Sophie Dupas's body, lingering over her most intimate parts. The young woman hadn't reacted. It had even seemed to Boisregard that she'd imperceptibly accompanied the journalist's palpation with slight movements. Accelerated Stockholm syndrome, an attempt to buy back her life, or simply fear stripping her of any notion of reality? Irrelevant; she was now harmless, and that was the main thing.

"You can all come in. We're going to set up for the ceremony."

The five men assembled, encircling Sophie lying prostrate in one of the corners of the sacrificial chamber. Simon-Renouard and Lèguezeaux couldn't take their eyes off the young woman. Their gaze went from her chest, generously offered up by the wide-open blouse, to her tanned, muscular thighs, accentuated by the skirt hiked up to her waist. The taste of blood was exacerbating all their impulses, and this available female was driving them crazy. Their animal instincts were mounting by the second. By mutual agreement, they took Boisregard aside.

"Arsène, you hadn't told me you'd found such a hot babe!" Simon-Renouard began. "I have to admit it's rare for a woman to get me this hard. So I'd like to propose a little modification to the ceremony. Before we revitalize ourselves with her blood, we'll start by doing it with her body."

When Boisregard seemed not to react, Lèguezeaux continued.

"Simply and vulgarly put, we want to fuck her first. That girl is made for sex . . . at least for us, that is," he added with a sardonic smile. "And it could only give more shine to the sacrifice we'll make to Quetzalcoatl. We'll have benefited from the girl's blood both inside and outside of her. It'll add a little spice to what we were able to do with Laure Déramaux—that one was no gift!"

"And you know what I can give you," added the journalist. "I promise if you let us enjoy this chick, you'll be well compensated in return."

The historian didn't know how to respond. He should have refused outright. He wasn't there to organize a gang bang. But he knew humanity well enough to know he could doubtless profit from this rape, the idea of which tantalized his companions so much.

They went back to the center of the room where Ballat and Sartenas were waiting for them. Boisregard gestured toward the young woman.

"Jacques and Thomas find that it would be a pity not to honor what nature offers to us tonight. They propose adding a prologue to our evening, to verify the vitality of our guest."

Dominique Sartenas looked at them coldly. "You want to bang her, is that it?"

"We're willing to let you participate! I'm sure Sophie would have nothing against it," added the journalist, turning toward the young woman.

Sophie didn't respond to the commentary. She was swinging between anguish and satisfaction. In a gesture of feigned submission, she positioned herself to highlight the curves that were unleashing the night's morbid passions.

The doctor began again in an even voice, turning to his friend. "Arsène, would you happen to have any porno to give these men to calm them down? I believe they haven't understood they're not on the set of a snuff film. Tonight, we're sacrificing this victim to satisfy the spirits of the underworld and deliver us of our burdens."

Simon-Renouard reacted like clockwork. "Who do you think you are, Monsieur Mental Patient? Everyone's goal here is to elevate their vitality, not to get some two-bit pseudopsychotherapy. So keep your comments to yourself!"

Sartenas paled at the insult. He gripped his scalpel, knuckles whitening at the effort. He walked deliberately toward the journalist, ready to do battle. He'd confronted the worst kind of men, and this uppity jackass wasn't going to . . .

"Now that's enough!" Boisregard said loudly.

His intervention stopped the mounting aggression in the room, now palpable. The four participants turned toward him. They were awaiting his decision. Boisregard gave a discreet sigh of relief. He was taking the situation back in his hands.

"The sacrifice is our priority tonight. It is essential for Dominique, and his power will rebound to us, be sure of that."

He looked at Sophie once more. "This woman is indeed tempting, but let's not be guided by our base impulses. She's going to bring us much more than an orgasm."

Simon-Renouard and Lèguezeaux silently accepted their companion's decision. The historian appreciated the gesture.

"Jacques and Thomas, you'll prepare the victim. You will respect the ritual and bind her, naked, on the sacrificial table."

The words entered Sophie's brain as though cushioned by a layer of cotton. When she became conscious of her abductors' decision, she screamed.

Chapter 77: End in Sight

The vehicle had been driving around and around for more than twenty minutes in Villard-de-Lans. The village was constructed around an old market town, but extended out over a large area. They'd already encountered three gendarmerie cars, but Nadia had managed not to be stopped. She was supposed to be in Grenoble. She knew it would go badly if they stopped her, and she'd explode. All her energy had to be concentrated on a single goal: finding Sophie and neutralizing her captors. In one hour, the order of her objectives had reversed. Saving her friend had become more important than slaking her hatred for Boisregard and those of his ilk. But she still wondered how she would react when she had the guy on the other end of her gun.

Julien had opened the window and was concentrating on the residences they were slowly driving past. The moon, now high in the sky, silhouetted the houses starkly against the landscape.

"So, you don't see anything that could resemble where she's being held?"

"No. Head north, and we'll keep at it. We're going to come across it, I know it."

"But how can you be so sure?"

"I know it, that's all."

It was now Nadia who was feeling the anxiety of the passing minutes. She furtively glanced at the car clock, as if trying not to startle it into accelerating the flow of time. It was 2:30 a.m. She spied headlights on a road in the distance. She recognized Drancey's vehicle—her colleagues hadn't found anything yet, either. She decided to turn out her lights. They would eventually attract attention. Julien didn't say a word. And the moon's radiance was sufficient for driving slowly through the sleeping village.

"Stop!" ordered Julien.

Nadia stamped on the brake pedal. The car stopped instantly.

"On the right. Look. The big building with the round turret. The pines around it. And the dovecote up on the roof. She's there."

Tingles of excitement ran up the policewoman's fingers. "Are you sure?"

"Certain!"

"Okay. We'll leave the car on the road. We'll go on foot up the driveway, it'll be much more unobtrusive. We should find Boisregard's BMW. As soon as we're sure they're there, I'll call my colleagues. Come on, we're wasting time. From now on, you shadow my movements and follow my orders."

Impressed by the authority emanating from the young woman, he agreed and followed her as she strode smoothly toward the entrance to the house.

Chapter 78: Revelations

Sophie wasn't trembling anymore. She'd gone beyond that stage. She was firmly tied, limbs in a cross, to the stone table enthroned in the room. Nothing could save her now except the miraculous arrival of her friends. But she couldn't believe in the miracle anymore. She watched the blood running down her thighs. She barely felt the pain.

On Boisregard's order, Lèguezeaux and Simon-Renouard had tried to seize her. She'd fought and practically put Lèguezeaux out of action. Boisregard had had to join in to overpower her. He'd struck her violently in the back of the head. She'd then lost all capacity to defend herself. She'd experienced the scene that followed as if in a dream—or a nightmare. She'd felt them tear off her clothes, then something cold on her skin. The journalist had rubbed her body with a heady-smelling unguent. He'd taken full advantage of her skin, lingering over her breasts and buttocks. But she didn't care. She was going to die, and he must be in a state of arousal close to insanity. She had a strange laugh while imagining the journalist's frustration. But she didn't care about that, either. Now she wanted it to be over, to get out of this bad Z movie.

Then Sartenas approached her. He watched her with his demented eyes. And the fear that swept over her reawakened her survival instinct. He started to slash her left thigh. She didn't feel much but had quickly realized the bright red liquid running down her leg was her blood. She screamed again, to Ballat's great joy. The young woman's suffering was revenge for his humiliation.

Sartenas stood at her side. The four men closed in on the sacrificial table. Boisregard spoke.

"Spirits of the shadows, accept the heart and blood of this woman. As Fra Bartolomeo has taught us, may they bring you new life, and may you see fit to shower your overabundance of life upon us."

Sophie forced herself to remain lucid. The eyes of the five participants were hallucinatory. There was no longer any trace of lustfulness in them, just pure madness. Only her blood interested them now. The young woman made a superhuman effort to keep her brain from cutting out. There were still a few seconds left, and she had to gain more.

"Dominique, all yours!"

Dominique grasped his scalpel firmly. "Magali, this blood will push you back into the depths of oblivion once and for all. Die again for your betrayal and the son you stole from me!"

All at once it hit her; it was so obvious. Sartenas raised his arm, lengthened by his instrument of torture.

"Your son isn't dead!" the young woman flung out in a last survival reflex.

The doctor ceased his movement. With a calmness she didn't think she possessed ten seconds earlier, Sophie analyzed the situation. She'd thrown a grain of sand in the works. She had to keep going and make him doubt.

"Magali Dupré didn't kill your son. She abandoned him, and he was picked up. He's alive. Your son lives in Grenoble."

Sartenas was thunderstruck. He wasn't moving anymore, incapable of absorbing what this girl was telling him.

"You lie! She's speaking through you! You're just the channel by which she continues to torture me. But you're going to die, and her, too!"

Sophie had to keep talking, sowing doubt.

"I know your son. He's thirty years old, and his name is Julien."

"Julien," whispered Sartenas. "Julien."

"He's tall, intelligent, and charming. He's an engineer, and his vitality delights his friends." She had to talk, to tell a story. She noticed her discourse was starting to have an effect. "If you want to meet him, I can introduce you," she offered.

"What's his last name?"

"If you want to meet your son, the son you've never known, you'll have to go through me."

"But who are you to say that?" said the doctor, getting worked up.

"A woman who loves your son. We're supposed to get married. You're not going to give your son the corpse of his future wife. I could introduce you to Julien as early as tomorrow if you want."

Sartenas put down his scalpel. The emotion was too sharp. He'd just discovered the son he'd missed so much was alive! If he'd known sooner, his life would have been different. He was certain the girl was telling the truth. She knew the name of his wife, how old his son would be. And she loved him. Sartenas had always been a dissembler, but he was convinced of the sincerity of the sacrificial woman's voice.

"Well, Sartenas, what's happening to you?" asked Ballat.

The financier's shrill voice brought the doctor back to reality. What was happening to him? Simply that he could no longer kill this woman before being reunited with his son.

"My son," he answered simply, "my son, Julien."

"Well, now we're in a family psychodrama. Arsène, would you happen to have a sentimental novel for our friend?" Thomas Simon-Renouard tossed out sarcastically. "I think he needs to recover from his emotions."

Sartenas didn't react, as if he hadn't heard the journalist's comments. Boisregard made a soothing gesture with his hand.

"Dominique, as important as this news is, I think permanently getting rid of Magali is the priority. If you wish, I can take your place and give you the heart. You'll be cured."

"No. I'm asking only that you give me a few minutes to think."

The group looked at one another. They nodded one after the other.

"We'll give you five minutes, Dominique. But in five minutes, we'll have made a decision."

Five minutes. Sophie had snatched five more minutes of life.

Chapter 79: On the Scene

The black X6 reflected the moonlight. The two other cars parked next to it displeased the police officer.

"There's at least four of them. We can't take any chances."

She grabbed her phone and speed-dialed a number.

"Fortin here, is that you, Nadia?"

"This is Captain Barka."

"We're up shit creek, Nadia! We're going around and around Villard-de-Lans. We haven't found anything. The whole village council is awake and going through the files, but we've got zilch. It's starting to . . ."

"I'm in front of the entrance to Boisregard's house."

"Good God, what the fuck are you doing there? And how did you find it?"

"I'll answer questions later. First get down the GPS coordinates."

She looked at the coordinates on her phone and dictated them to him.

"You'll recognize the building. It has a round turret, and it's located at the end of a private wooded driveway."

"Fuck, wait for us. We'll be there in three minutes. We're coming in, balls out!"

"Definitely not balls out. We can't alarm them. This is Sophie Dupas's life. We're going in!"

"We?"

"Julien Lombard and me."

"Julien L . . ."

"I'm hanging up. Come quickly. There are three cars out front."

Nadia didn't give her colleague time to respond. She took out her sidearm and moved toward the entrance.

"We'll just have to hope the house doesn't have a security alarm!"

The policewoman turned the knob on the glass door. It was locked. She grabbed her gun by the barrel and broke the glass. They flinched, afraid an alarm would go off. Nothing happened. Only the tinkling of breaking glass had briefly shattered the silence of the night.

"All right, come on!"

Nadia put her hand through the broken window and turned the key in the lock.

"I imagine this nut job built a cellar or some secret place so he could work in peace. We have to find it," she whispered in her companion's ear. "Let me go first."

They moved quietly from room to room, listening for the slightest noise. But nothing. They would have figured the house was uninhabited if they hadn't seen the cars and the remains of a meal on the dining room table. They went through the rooms again, opening every cupboard. Not the slightest trace of a staircase. Panic started to overtake them. They weren't going to fail so close to the goal. They suddenly heard a sound in the entrance and threw themselves behind a sofa. Men were coming in on tiptoe. Nadia recognized Lieutenant Fortin.

"Étienne, we're here. The house is empty."

Four gendarmes and two policemen were accompanying Lieutenant Fortin.

"Are you sure this is the right place?" asked the policeman.

"Didn't you recognize Boisregard's car outside?"

"Yes, I did."

"So we search everything! Don't leave a single square inch unchecked. And hurry, Sophie Dupas's life may have only a few more seconds."

Without asking questions about the woman's rank and her role in the operation, the gendarmes and policemen followed her instructions immediately, parceling out the rooms. Julien went out on the porch, stomach twisted with fear of losing Sophie. She was there, a few yards away, waiting for him! But where, dammit?

He walked into the garden. The cool of the night only intensified the fire burning inside him. Where? Where had those bastards taken her? The hoot of an owl made him instinctively turn his head. His gaze was attracted by something shining. A metallic object was reflecting the light of the moon. It was sitting on a dark mass they hadn't noticed on arrival. A sort of little sheepfold. Julien ran up to it. A heavy door guarded the access. It was half open and led to a stairwell.

"Nadia, I found it! I'm going in!"

Julien threw himself into the darkness of the sheepfold. Nadia and Étienne Fortin came out when they heard him. They had just enough time to see him engulfed by the hut and ran to lend a helping hand.

Chapter 80: Sacrifices

Boisregard had taken up the scalpel. He still knew how to wield it. He obviously had less dexterity than Sartenas, but he'd give him the heart of the woman he was going to slice open.

The decision had been unanimous, and Sartenas had accepted it. Sophie had given them enough clues. With a little patience and active networking, they'd be able to find a thirty-year-old engineer named Julien in Grenoble. Boisregard had convinced the doctor his contacts in the upper tiers of government would quickly provide him with his rediscovered son's name.

Now they could deal with their sacrifice without qualms. Nothing opposed them any longer. Boisregard had considered his friend too shocked to carry out the offering to Quetzalcoatl. He was going to operate without anesthesia. He didn't feel like sparing this woman who had nearly made him lose face.

Sophie was going to die. She knew it. She'd done all in her power to give her friends time. But they still weren't there. She knew she was going to suffer horribly for a few dozen seconds, but then she'd be at peace. She'd no longer see the vile beings surrounding her, feasting on her pain and fear. She heard Boisregard pronouncing words in a language she didn't know. She glanced around for the last time. She saw only her legs, where the blood had stopped flowing. It would soon spurt from her pierced abdomen. But even at that moment, she regretted not having time to live with the love of her life. *What a waste*, she thought, preparing to feel death enter her.

The prayer was finished. The stab and the pain were going to strike. She squeezed her eyes shut, as if that could allow her to deflect the blade of the scalpel. But nothing came. No! A sound. And a cry! And that cry was . . . her name! Sophie opened her eyes. She no longer knew whether she was floating in a dream or if what she was seeing was real. Julien charged Boisregard, a knife in his hand. She watched, a bystander, like the other participants hypnotized by the scene playing out before their eyes. Julien's attention scattered for a second at the young woman's tortured body. Taking advantage of that moment, Boisregard dodged the blow and drove the scalpel twice into Julien's stomach. The young man crumpled. An inhuman scream tore from Sophie's throat, barely drowned out by the double shot of Nadia's Sig Sauer. The historian was flung backward and collapsed at the foot of the sacrificial altar. His white shirt was decorated with two red stains that blossomed in a few seconds, like two venomous flowers.

Hidden by his two dazed companions, Simon-Renouard moved discreetly to grab the sidearm Boisregard had placed on the ground before taking Sartenas's place. There was only one cop, and he had no desire to be mixed up in this business. The woman didn't see him. He popped up and took aim. Nadia spotted him, but it was too late to react. She saw only the maw of the gun that was going to send her to the great beyond.

A violent blow to her shoulder threw her against the wall. She collapsed as she heard two simultaneous shots. When she regained her balance, she saw her attacker on his knees, his arm dislocated. She turned her head. Fortin had the rest of the petrified group covered.

"Thank you," she said simply.

Three gendarmes appeared next in the room, contemplating the bodies littering the floor. The highest-ranking one grabbed the radio, then went outside to call for help and a helicopter.

Nadia approached Sophie, who was in tears. She'd resisted for the last few hours, but all the fear of this nightmarish day gushed out, even more violently. And the fear of losing Julien was close to driving her completely around the bend.

"How are you, Sophie?"

"Okay," she replied quickly. "But what about Julien? Tell me he's not dead!"

Nadia leaned over her companion and took his pulse. She felt a weak throb. A gendarme freed Sophie. She hurried off the table, crumpled when she tried to stand up, but crawled to her friend. She took him in her arms.

"Julien, don't die. It's thanks to you and for you I survived, so don't die now," she whispered in his ear, flooding him with tears.

Sartenas tried to come closer. The name Julien, spoken several times by the young woman, had just shocked him. Fortin held him back firmly. The doctor fought.

"You undoubtedly think I'm scum, but I'm also an excellent doctor, and that's my son! So let me take care of him before emergency services gets here. If I do nothing, it's obvious he won't survive his wounds."

Nadia didn't have the heart to disabuse him. It might be the only hope of saving the young man, who was losing blood at an alarming rate. She hesitated for an instant.

"Let him do it," asked Sophie.

Surprised, Nadia looked at the young woman, bathed in her own blood and that of her friend. Then she observed Sartenas. She thought she detected an ounce of humanity in the look he was giving Julien.

"It's okay," said Nadia.

"I need medical supplies. I know where Arsène keeps them. Take me into the house so I can get them. During that time, put him gently on the table."

Three policemen who'd just arrived followed the surgeon. Étienne Fortin and Rodolphe Drancey cautiously placed Julien on the stone altar. Sophie, now dressed in Étienne Fortin's T-shirt, didn't let go of her friend's hand, an invisible prayer on her lips.

"Mademoiselle, you'll have to come with me," said a gendarme. "We have to get you some treatment."

"No, not right away," begged Sophie. "I want to stay with him!"

Nadia addressed the gendarme.

"You must have a nurse in your company?"

"Yes, there's Guerinov. He must be in the house."

"Will you please ask him to come down here and give first aid to Sophie Dupas?"

"I'll go look for him, Captain."

"Thank you, Major."

Chapter 81: Funeral

The coolness delivered by the storm that had just broken over the mountain cemetery was starting to dissipate. The two coffins sparkled in the sunlight reflecting off the raindrops that clung to the pale wood. They mesmerized the silent assembly. Only the murmur of the wind whispering in the branches of the fir trees accompanied Father de Valjoney's words of hope.

The priest pronounced a final benediction. The funeral staff manipulated the caskets with extreme caution so as not to disturb their occupants' rest. The deceased were lowered into the grave of the modest family vault. One after the other, the mourners came forward and dropped a flower on their final resting place.

Sophie Dupas, overwhelmed, couldn't hold back her tears. She offered two lilies she'd picked from the surrounding fields. Denise and Emmanuel Lombard, who followed her, meditated a long time before the open pit: the memory of that June day in 1983 would never leave them. Denise was leaning on her husband's shoulder, submerged in a wave of emotion that seemed to drown her. Aurélien Costel's heart was being squeezed by a vise. How different his life could have been! He started to hate Cabrade as he'd never done before, gazing at the two coffins resting at the bottom of the grave. A whole part of his life was down there!

Nadia Barka stood slightly off to the side. It was the first time in more than fifteen years that she was attending a funeral in a professional capacity. She'd even abstained from participating in the burial of Laure Déramaux. Today, the conditions were different. She felt something had changed inside her. Those heinous murders and their perpetrators had forced her to plunge into the depths of her soul. She hadn't dared to do that since that night in the Parisian Métro. She observed the gathered congregation and felt in harmony with it. That empathy, so suddenly recovered, almost frightened her. Étienne Fortin, present at her side, seemed lost in his thoughts.

Sophie stepped forward, pushing ahead of her a man seated in a wheelchair. The mourners parted slightly, as if to give the invalid a moment of intimacy with the deceased. Motionless on his seat, he watched the scene unfolding around him, as if an outsider to the world. His features were drawn, and suffering marked his face. With a grimace of pain, he made an effort to straighten his torso. He wanted to offer the departed a posture worthy of their courage.

Aline Bergson, director of the nursing home, whispered in Nadia's ear.

"Pierre Dupré died happy, Captain. And that's partly thanks to you."

The police officer looked at her in surprise. "I had nothing to do with it," replied the young woman.

"Oh, yes, you did, you had a lot to do with it. Pierre kept me informed of events. You brought him his grandson. It's also thanks to you he can now go to his eternal rest beside his beloved wife and daughter. He was very sick and suffering terribly, but he waited until Julien was out of the woods to let himself die."

Nadia was more moved by Aline Bergson's words than she would have imagined. She'd seen the old man twice. The first time, in June with Julien, and the second time a week ago to tell him the police had found his daughter Magali's body. Without a word, the man had hugged her with his dying arms, and she'd received more love from that embrace than she had in the course of the last fifteen years—aside from the moments she'd just spent with Étienne. She smiled inwardly.

"I'm happy he could die unburdened."

Nadia left the director and went over to the tomb. The man seated in the wheelchair had emerged from his meditation. He was worn out, but his stooped shape nevertheless radiated a spark of energy that reassured her. Denise and Emmanuel Lombard, accompanied by Sophie, came over to the young man in turn. He looked at them gravely.

"It was very nearly me getting buried next to Pierre. Life is strange."

"In this case, it was strangely kind to us," replied Sophie.

He smiled at her, then grimaced as he tried to move his wheelchair. The young woman stopped him and scolded him gently.

"Julien, you got a special discharge from the hospital. Don't strain yourself unnecessarily. You have to take the time to heal."

"Especially," added Emmanuel Lombard, "since you have an extraordinary nurse to take care of you."

Fortin, who'd just joined them, marveled.

"You managed to get a full-time nurse? What's your secret?"

"It's me!" answered Sophie with a smile. "I thought about it a lot over the last few days. I had quite a bit of time, since a night didn't go by without me being woken up by horrible nightmares. I've decided to go back to studying medicine."

Surprise showed on the faces around her. Madeleine and Antoine Dupas, who had joined them, were the only ones not looking surprised.

"Can you enlighten us about your decision?" asked Nadia.

"I studied medicine for three years, and . . ."

"Three quite brilliant years, for that matter," commented Antoine Dupas.

"Thank you, Papa, but let me finish. At the end of the third year, I had a bad breakup with a young doctor, and I decided to stop. I changed direction."

"And what's leading you to go back?" questioned Étienne.

"What I endured during that night of the solstice upset a lot of things inside me. I told myself I wanted to turn my life toward others. And I was touched by the care Sartenas lavished on Julien. I hate that man. He wanted to kill me—and in such a way! He's haunted my nights since that horrible moment I wouldn't wish on even my worst enemy. But I was fascinated by his precise movements, which returned life to the man I love. When I saw him giving first aid to Julien . . . I almost admired him in spite of myself."

"That man is scum!" Julien interjected violently. "He didn't want to save *me*, but a son he'd fantasized about all his life."

"Without a shadow of a doubt, Julien, and it doesn't excuse in the slightest all the harm he could do. That doesn't change the fact it was his hands that kept you alive until help came."

"I know that all too well. But I can't find extenuating circumstances for him. He killed Magali, made her parents suffer for thirty long years, was mixed up in the worst business, killed I don't know how many innocent victims! Certainly, he saved me, but I feel no gratitude inside. And his last gestures will change nothing!"

The injured man's last cryptic words piqued Antoine Dupas's curiosity. He hesitated, then his need to understand overruled his discretion.

"I know I lack tact, but may I know what those last gestures you're talking about are?"

Julien remained silent, wanting to sever all ties with that murderer he'd believed to be his father. Nadia decided to answer the historian.

"For the first three weeks after his arrest, Sartenas said nothing. He just acknowledged the two previous murders but gave no explanation. Total silence. Last Monday, he finally decided to tell us where he'd buried his wife's body. Then yesterday, he decided to give his entire fortune to Julien."

"We talked about it last night," Julien broke in bluntly. "There's no question of touching a single cent of that money!"

"How much is it?" Antoine Dupas dared.

"According to Sartenas," Nadia said, "not far off thirty million dollars, distributed across various accounts in offshore tax havens."

"It'll be given to charitable organizations," explained Julien. "That money is undoubtedly blood money, but it'll serve to alleviate suffering."

"You didn't tell him Julien wasn't his son?" questioned the historian.

"We left that decision up to Julien," replied Nadia.

"I wanted to tell him," the young man sighed. "I wanted to see him suffer as he might have made those around him suffer for years. But Sophie asked me not to do it. Not out of some gesture of pity or mercy, but to thank him for having saved my life and given both of us the chance to be able to live together."

"And . . . ?"

"And I didn't regret it. His remorse, or his desire to give me something, pushed him to reveal Magali's resting place. In spite of himself, he made Pierre Dupré happy that way."

"And why did he give you his fortune?" asked Denise Lombard.

"I don't know. Out of remorse as well?"

Nadia's phone rang. She stepped away and came back a minute later. Her attitude shouted to the waiting group.

"I think we have the answer to our questions." She continued, responding to Julien's silent interrogation, "It was probably his will. Dominique Sartenas just hanged himself in his cell."

Epilogue

August. Julien got up from his chair, grabbed his crutch, and headed for the barbecue.

"Stay seated, Juju, I'll do it!" Sophie stopped him, catching him by the arm.

"Juju?" repeated Emmanuel Lombard, laughing. "What does that mean?"

Julien looked at him, a smile on his lips. He'd started to recuperate and could manage to get around by himself, even though the pain was still present.

"It means Sophie has been allowing herself to take liberties in public for three days. It also means I've recovered enough energy to go down on one knee before Antoine here to ask him officially for his daughter's hand."

"Lovely!" exclaimed Nadia, clapping her hands in parody of a teenager from an American TV show. "But I didn't think you were so old school!"

Madeleine Dupas intervened in the conversation. "Julien isn't old school, but my husband is. And his dream was to see his daughter's suitor ask for her hand in the old way. I mentioned it to Julien, who found the idea amusing."

"I find there's some good in traditions," commented the historian, satisfied with himself.

"I implored Julien not to do it, but he didn't listen to me!" concluded Sophie, arriving with a tray of smoking kebabs. "In any case, you will of course be the guests of honor at this wedding. Nadia, will you be my maid of honor? I'll get your dress for you."

Nadia jumped, then replied.

"Sophie, you're an excellent friend, but you still shouldn't ask too much of me. Being dressed in pink meringue, even for you, I just can't."

"I was joking," Sophie reassured her.

"That's better!" Then she added, "Could I ask you a favor?"

"No point. Étienne is quite obviously invited. He hasn't arrived yet, either?"

"No, he had paperwork to collect. But he shouldn't be long."

Emmanuel Lombard changed the conversation. "Have you been part of the investigation into the cult Boisregard created?" he asked the policewoman.

"Sort of. Commissioner Mazure didn't want me to be too involved in that case. He thought I'd been tested enough by Boisregard's actions. He preferred to keep me away from the investigation so as not to throw me into the middle of that media circus."

"And what were the findings?"

"What you could read in the newspapers. The three participants in what the press is now calling 'The Night of the Solstice' might get the maximum penalty. Boisregard's apartment was searched, and the police found references to well-stocked foreign accounts. I also understand they found a certain number of compromising photos. But it would appear someone in high places wanted to hush up the scandal. Furthermore, the files on the murders committed when he was in Bordeaux have been reopened. They're going to be restudied in light of Professor Boisregard's new personality."

"Do you think he killed those young women?" asked Antoine Dupas.

"I don't have the documents on hand, but you must admit the hypothesis merits a serious look."

"And Sartenas?" asked Julien's father.

"We've started tracing his past. But aside from the Grenoble murders, all the other crimes he might have committed were perpetrated outside of French territory. So we've passed our information on to several countries interested in his criminal acts. His suicide put an end to our investigations into his activities."

"His suicide also helped me to recover some semblance of normal nights," added Sophie. "I think it's the best thing he could have done."

The conversation was halted by the crunching tires of a car stopping in front of the gate. A few seconds later, Étienne Fortin appeared on the lawn. Sophie went to greet him affectionately, but his concerned look troubled her. Nadia noticed it at the same time.

"What's going on?" asked the alert policewoman.

The policeman laid a brown paper envelope on the table. He pushed it toward Julien. "I'll let you open it. You should be the one to find out what's inside."

Anxious, Julien hurried to unseal it. In silence, he read the letter that accompanied a sheaf of papers. His face suddenly lit up.

"Oh, how clever! You're so pleased with your joke!" he shot at him, half angry and half laughing.

"Could you tell us what's going on, perhaps?"

"Julien has just received proof that he has no blood relationship with Dominique Cabrade. The DNA analyses are official."

"And you just had to tell him like that?" commented Nadia, appalled. "What am I doing with a guy like you?"

Julien Lombard didn't give the policeman time to respond. "Aurélien Costel is my father, or rather my progenitor," he corrected himself, looking at his father. "Although I highly doubted it, I must confess this official confirmation is a relief. Cabrade's line is extinct!"

Afterword

I've always taken pleasure in reading or telling stories: scary stories when, as teenagers, we took walks with friends in the moors of Brittany; stories about valiant heroes and princesses, later, for my children; and stories of fantasy and suspense today.

Trained as an engineer, I've had cause to travel around the world, experiencing transatlantic flights, interminable connections in airports, even a few strikes now and then! Which might give rise to another novel a bit later . . .

Writing has become a means of transforming those long hours of waiting into enthralling moments. Setting up suspenseful situations, diving to the edge of the fantastic, giving life to characters who accompany me for weeks or months and then take you to the heart of their stories.

When I start writing a novel or a story, I know only the frame very vaguely at first. It seems certain writers have perfect command over the map of their manuscripts before beginning: I must admit I am not one of them. I discover the story as I write it, and I want it to hold me spellbound as much as it will the reader who discovers the book.

Furthermore, if you want to be informed about my future books or promotions, send an e-mail to vandroux.jacques@gmail .com, simply specifying "e-mail list" in the subject line. Your e-mail address will not be shared with any third party and will not be used for other purposes. If you'd like to write me a little note as well, don't be shy! I'll respond to you personally!

My blog for everything about my novels, and especially for photos of the various locations: jacquesvandroux.blogspot.fr

My Facebook page: facebook.com/vandroux

My Facebook account: facebook.com/jacques.vandrouxauteur

About the Author

© 2011 Simone Vandroux

Jacques Vandroux has spent most of his life in Paris and the French Alps. As an engineer, he used his time traveling the world to write books and short stories. His first two novels, *Les Pierres Couchées* and *Multiplication*, were bestsellers in France. *Heart Collector* is the new English translation of *Au Cœur du Solstice*, which was published to great acclaim in Vandroux's home country.

About the Translator

Wendeline A. Hardenberg first became curious about translation as an undergrad at Smith College, where she ultimately translated part of a novel from French as a portion of her honors thesis in comparative literature. After receiving a dual master's degree in comparative literature (with a focus on translation) and library science at Indiana University Bloomington, she has gone on to a dual career as a translator and a librarian. Learning new languages and trying to translate from them is one of her favorite hobbies. She lives in New Haven, Connecticut.

M .